14 Days

W9-AYP-608

WITHDRAWN

THE QUEEN FROM PROVENCE

JEAN PLAIDY

The Count of Provence had four daughters. Although they were beautiful and cultured, they were without dowries and it seemed unlikely that they could make the marriages their father wanted for them. The eldest, Marguerite, helped by good luck and the Count's wily minister, married the King of France; and her sister Eleanor was determined to make as grand a match.

Eleanor, the most beautiful of the four, knew exactly what she wanted and aimed to get it. Only a miracle could bring her to the notice of the King of England. Eleanor contrived to bring about that miracle.

England was in an uneasy state. Henry, the King, meant well, but he was weak, and the barons remembered the reign of Henry's wantonly cruel and recklessly foolish father, King John. Magna Carta was the symbol of their triumph over him, and Henry was never allowed to forget it.

When he married the girl from Provence, Henry immediately became her slave. His great joy was to shower gifts on her, and the heavy taxation he levied in order to please his wife and her relations inevitably led to revolt. The man at the head of this was Simon de Montfort, the adventurer who had romantically and secretly married the King's sister.

(Continued on back flap)

The Queen from

Provence

JEAN PLAIDY

G. P. PUTNAM'S SONS   New York

First American Edition 1981

Library of Congress Cataloging in Publication Data

Plaidy, Jean, 1906–
    The Queen from Provence.

    (The Plantagenet saga)
    Sequel: Edward Longshanks.
    Sequel to: The battle of the Queens.
    Originally published: London : Hale.
    Bibliography: p.
    1. Eleanor of Provence, Queen, consort of
Henry III, King of England, 1223 or 4–1291—Fiction.
I. Title. II. Series.
PR6015.I3Q4   1981   823'.914   81-8523
ISBN 0-399-12656-2   AACR2

CONTENTS

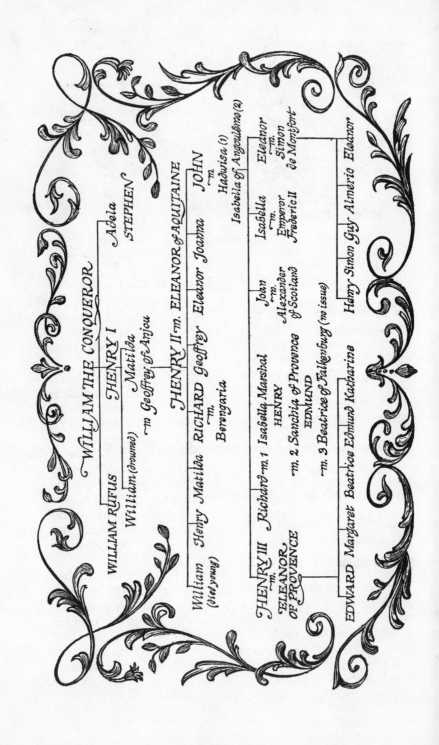

WILLIAM THE CONQUEROR

WILLIAM RUFUS   HENRY I   Adela
William (drowned)   Matilda   STEPHEN
m. Geoffrey of Anjou

HENRY II—m. ELEANOR of AQUITAINE

William   Henry   Matilda   RICHARD   Geoffrey   Eleanor   Joanna   JOHN
(died young)   m.   m.
                          Berengaria   Hadwisa (1)
                                                        Isabella of Angoulême (2)

HENRY III   Richard—m. 1 Isabella Marshal   Joan   Isabella   Eleanor
m.   HENRY   m.   m.   m.
ELEANOR   m. 2 Sanchia of Provence   Alexander   Emperor   Simon
OF PROVENCE   EDMUND   of Scotland Frederic II de Montfort
                m. 3 Beatrice of Falkenburg (no issue)

EDWARD   Margaret   Beatrice   Edmund   Katharine   Henry   Simon   Guy   Almeric   Eleanor

In Search of a Bridegroom

As Raymond Berenger, Count of Provence, and his friend, confidant and chief adviser, Romeo, Lord of Villeneuve, strolled together in the lush green gardens surrounding the castle of Les Baux, they talked of the future.

Raymond Berenger had had a happy life; his beautiful wife was as talented as he was himself. Between them they had made their court one of the most interesting intellectually in the whole of France, and as a result poets, troubadours and artists made their way to Provence, sure of a welcome and appreciation. It was indeed a pleasant life and the Count and Countess wished it might go on for ever. They were not foolish enough to think it could. But no earthly paradise could be completely perfect and though, during their married life, they had prayed fervently for a son who would govern Provence beside his father for many years and afterwards preserve that ambience of gracious ease and luxurious comfort, they had produced only daughters.

Even this they could not entirely regret, for dearly did they love their children and admitted that they would not have changed one of their girls for the son for whom they had petitioned so earnestly. Where in the world, Raymond Berenger asked his Countess, could be found girls who were as beautiful and talented as theirs? And the answer was: Nowhere.

These girls were growing up now and the decisions which would have to be made were the subjects of the conversation between the Count and Romeo de Villeneuve.

Marguerite, the eldest of the family, was nearly thirteen years old. A child, said the Countess, but she knew that outside her family, Marguerite would be considered marriageable. The search for a suitable husband could not be put off much longer; moreover there were the others to consider.

'I confess, Romeo,' the Count was saying, 'these matters give me cause for the greatest concern.'

'I am sure we shall find a solution as we have to so many of our problems,' replied Romeo.

'Many times have I put my trust in you, Romeo,' sighed the Count, 'and never found it misplaced. But how shall we find husbands for the daughters of an impoverished Count when they have little to offer but their grace, charm and beauty?'

'And their talents, my lord. Do not let us forget they possess these in greater abundance than most girls whose fathers are looking for husbands for them.'

'You seek to cheer me. I love my girls. They are beautiful and clever. But gold, silver and rich lands are considered to be more desirable than charm and education.'

'Provence is not so insignificant that the Kings of France and England would not wish to have us as their friend.'

'The Kings of France and England!' cried the Count. 'You must be jesting!'

'Why so, my lord? The Kings of France and England are young men, both seeking brides.'

'You cannot really be suggesting that one of my girls could become the consort of one of these Kings!'

'Nay, my lord, not one but two.'

The Count was aghast. 'It is a wild dream.'

'It would indeed be a great achievement if either of these projects came to pass, and, to start with, I do not see why a marriage between France and Provence should not be considered worthy of consideration in Paris.'

'How so, my dear Romeo?'

'We could bring a certain security to France. Oh, I know we are impoverished. We cannot offer a great dowry, but we have something which Blanche and her son Louis might consider worth having. Beaucaire and Carcassonne have recently come into their possession. On the other side of the Rhône is the Holy Roman Empire and we have lands there which we could bring to France. In view of their strategic position I think they could be called quite valuable, for if they were under the control of the King of France his position would be strengthened against the Holy Roman Empire.'

'That's true enough. But would such a matter impress the French?'

'I am determined that they shall be impressed by it. I have not been idle. I have sent some of our songsters to the Court of France, and what do you think has been the burden of their song?'

'Not the rich dowries of my daughters, I'll swear.'

'Nay. But their beauty and charm—unsurpassed in France.'

'My dear friend, I doubt not your loyalty to this house, but I think your friendship for it has carried you far away into the realms of fancy. The Queen of France will select the wife for her son with the greatest care, and how many do you think are competing for that honour?'

'Queen Blanche is a wise woman. She will consider carefully what she has been told.'

The Count, laughing, shook his head, and said he would go into the castle and tell the Countess what Romeo was suggesting. She would doubtless laugh with her husband while at the same time she would agree with regard to the loyalty and good intentions of the lord of Villeneuve.

*   *   *

It was that hour when the four daughters of the Count and Countess of Provence were together in their schoolrooms. Thirteen-year-old Marguerite, the eldest, stitched at her tapestry. Eleanor, two years younger, sat writing at the table; Eleanor was constantly writing verses which she set to music, and she was now engaged on a long narrative poem, which her tutors said was an astonishing achievement for a girl of her age. Eight-year-old Sanchia was stitching with her eldest sister and Beatrice, the youngest, who was barely six, was looking over Eleanor's shoulder as she wrote.

All the girls had been endowed with their mother's good looks; and because they had been brought up in a fashion unusual with families of their rank, theirs had been a happy childhood. They saw their mother each day and their father also when his commitments allowed him to remain in his home. Because they were girls it had not been necessary for them to go away to be brought up in some nobleman's household where they must learn to face a hard and cruel world. The domestic life of the Count and Countess of Provence had in many ways been simple while at the same time all the girls were given the kind of education which was rarely bestowed on members of their sex. Although they were skilled in feminine arts—such as needlework, singing, dancing—they had been brought up to think, to express themselves lucidly, to have some knowledge of the events of the day and above all to love music and literature. The Countess Beatrice, their mother, the daughter of the Count of Savoy, was a musician and poet and she saw no reason to neglect these skills. She imbued her daughters with an appreciation of the matters nearest her heart and as a result the girls were not only beautiful but accomplished and on the way to becoming very well educated.

The cleverest of the four was undoubtedly Eleanor. Marguerite was skilled at needlework and a good musician, but in everything except needlework Eleanor was superior. It was Eleanor whose poems were put to music and sung throughout the court, and Eleanor whom their tutors praised constantly.

Because of her talents she was inclined to a certain arrogance which her parents noticed and deplored but thought was understandable. 'She will grow out of it,' said the Count in his easy-going way. He liked everything to run smoothly and this attitude was suited to the comfortable tenor of life in Provence where brilliantly coloured flowers and rich green shrubs flourished without much attention and where the people loved to lie in the sun and listen to the strumming of the lute. There was poetry in the air in Provence; and the fact that Eleanor was a poetess already meant that she was a true daughter of her native land.

Marguerite was of a sweeter nature. She was ready to stand aside for her younger sister; no one applauded Eleanor's efforts more than Marguerite; and the result was that Eleanor was a little spoiled by the family. Eleanor looked for praise; she shared her sisters' beauty—and many said surpassed it—but she was the clever one. She had seen the looks of wonder in her parents' faces when she had shown them her poems. They insisted that she read them aloud to the family and when she had finished her parents would lead the applause and in Eleanor's eyes no one was quite as important at the Court of Provence as she was.

Sanchia the next sister followed her in everything, imitating her way of speech, her gestures, trying all the time said Marguerite, to make herself another Eleanor. Eleanor herself merely smiled encouragingly. After all she could quite understand Sanchia's desire to walk in her footsteps.

Beatrice was too young as yet to have much character. As

a six-year-old she had only recently joined them in the schoolroom.

'How goes the poem?' asked Marguerite pausing in her work and making a very charming picture, seated in the window with her work on a frame before her, her pretty hand daintily holding the needle while she lifted her brown eyes to smile across at Eleanor.

'It goes well,' replied Eleanor. 'I shall read it to my lord and lady tomorrow, I doubt not.'

'Let us hear it now,' cried Sanchia.

'Indeed not,' retorted Eleanor.

'It must be launched in a becoming manner,' said Marguerite with a smile.

Eleanor smiled complacently, already savouring the applause, the looks of admiration in her parents' eyes, the wonder as they exchanged glances which betrayed the fact that they thought their daughter a genius.

Marguerite had turned to the window. 'We have visitors,' she said.

Eleanor and Beatrice immediately rose and went to the window. In the distance but making straight for the castle was a party of men. One of them carried a banner.

The girls stood very still. Visitors to the castle always provided some excitement. There would be special feasting in the great hall which the girls would be able to attend; they would join in the singing and music though if the carousing went on into the night they would be sent to their chambers. Visitors were a great event in their lives and one to which they all looked forward.

'They come from the Court of France,' said Eleanor.

'How do you know?' asked little Beatrice admiringly.

'Look at the standard. The golden lilies. That means France.'

'Then they must be important,' added Marguerite.

Eleanor was thinking of what she would wear. She had a gown of silk with a tight-fitting bodice and long trailing skirt; the sleeves were fashionable, tight to the wrists where they widened so much that the trailing cuffs reached to the hem of her skirt. These cuffs were decorated with the silk woven embroidery which she herself had worked with the aid of her sisters. It was a most becoming gown. Her mother had given her a girdle which was decorated with chalcedony, that stone which was said to bring power and health to those who possessed it.

She would wear her thick dark hair in two plaits and would
refuse to cover it with either wimple or barbette which she had
said to Marguerite were for older women or those who had not
the luxuriant hair possessed by the sisters.

'We shall soon hear doubtless,' said Sanchia. 'I wonder why
they come?'

'I trust it is not war,' said little Beatrice, who had already
learned that trouble in the neighbourhood could take their
father away from them and make their mother anxious, and
so disturb the peace of Les Baux.

'We shall soon know,' said Marguerite, putting aside her
needlework.

'Should we not wait in the schoolroom until we are summoned?' asked Sanchia.

'Nay,' retorted Eleanor. 'What if we were summoned to
greet the visitors. I would be ready.'

It was significant that the younger girls looked to Eleanor
rather than Marguerite for directions.

'Come,' said the forceful sister, 'let us prepare.'

*　*　*

The visitors were led by Giles de Flagy who had come
from Queen Blanche on a special mission.

When he heard what that mission was Raymond Berenger
could scarcely believe his ears. It seemed that Romeo de
Villeneuve was indeed a magician. Could it really be that
the Queen of France was seeking a daughter of the Count of
Provence to marry her son?

In the Count's private apartments Giles de Flagy discussed
the matter with the Count, the Countess and Romeo de Villeneuve.

The Queen Mother of France had heard much of the excel-
lence of the Count's daughters. She was well aware of the
Count's financial difficulties, but she had decided that these
were not of major importance. The Count's daughters were
beautiful and had been well educated. These were the qualities she would look for in a Queen of France, and the last was
of particular importance.

Louis IX was twenty years of age. It was time he married
and Blanche had decided that the daughter of the Count of
Provence might suit him very well. Terms of the marriage
could be gone into later, but the Queen was eager that not
too much time should be lost. She understood the Count's

eldest daughter was thirteen years old—young but marriageable. The King of France was a young man of immense ability. He would not want a foolish wife; and the Queen believed that if a girl was to be trained to be a great Queen the training in the royal household could not begin too soon.

Giles de Flagy hoped he would have an opportunity of meeting the Count's daughters during his brief stay at Les Baux.

The Count and Countess, beside themselves with excitement, assured him that he should see the girls.

It was the Countess who sent for the two eldest, and Marguerite and Eleanor, deeply conscious of the air of tension throughout the castle, eagerly obeyed the summons.

'We have a very important visitor,' began the Countess.

'From France,' interrupted Eleanor. 'I saw the lilies on the standard.'

The Countess nodded. 'You girls will be presented to him when we sup tonight. I want you to look your best, and to behave with your best manners.'

Eleanor looked reproachful. 'Of a certainty we shall,' she said reprovingly.

'My dear child,' said her mother firmly, 'I know it well. But this is a very important visitor and perhaps on this night it would be better for you to remain a little subdued. Speak only when spoken to.'

Eleanor lifted her shoulders in a gesture of resignation and the Countess turned from her to her eldest daughter.

'Now Marguerite, be discreet but ready with your answer should the conversation come your way. Be unobtrusive and yet at the same time....'

Eleanor burst out: 'Oh dear lady, what would you have us be ... ourselves or puppets performing in a show?'

'Perhaps I am wrong,' said the Countess. 'I should leave you to be your natural selves. But understnd me. I do want you to make a good impression on the ambassador of the King of France. Now shall we decide what you shall wear?'

'I have already decided on my blue and my girdle with the chalcedony,' said Eleanor.

The Countess nodded. 'A good choice. It becomes you well. And Marguerite?'

'Oh my grey and purple gown with my silver girdle.'

The Countess nodded. 'And I shall give you a diamond ring to wear, Marguerite. It will look well with the grey and purple.'

'A diamond!' cried Eleanor. 'Diamonds are said to protect

people from their enemies. What enemies have you, Marguerite?'

'None that I am aware of.'

The Countess seemed suddenly overcome by emotion as she looked fondly at her eldest daughter. 'I pray you never will have, but if you attain to a high position in the world there would assuredly be those who would not wish you well.'

'Is that why you are giving her a diamond?' asked Eleanor.

'I give it to her because it will become her. She has pretty hands.'

Eleanor looked at her own which were equally pretty. Why should Marguerite be especially selected? Was it because she was the eldest?

Thirteen! It was a great age and she was but eleven. Could it really be that the ambassador from France had come with some proposition for Marguerite?

Later it became clear that this was the case. Although they were both presented to Giles de Flagy it was on Marguerite that his eyes lingered.

Eleanor could not help feeling somewhat piqued, particularly when she was not even asked to read her latest poem.

Giles de Flagy rode away but the object of his visit and its success was soon made clear.

The Count and Countess came to the schoolroom where the girls were working. Eleanor knew what it meant because their expression betrayed their feelings. There was pride, elation, wonder which showed that they scarcely believed what was happening to them and at the same time there was sorrow and regret.

The girls all rose and curtsied.

The Count came forward and took Marguerite by the hand.

'My dearest child,' he said, 'the greatest good fortune has come to you. You are to be the Queen of France.'

'Does it mean Marguerite will go away?' asked Beatrice, her face beginning to pucker.

Her mother drew the child to her and held her against her skirts.

'You will understand what this means in time, my child,' she said.

The Count went on. 'I would never have believed this could happen. King Louis is a young man of great qualities; he is clever, kind and good, determined to rule his country well. And he has decided that he will marry our Marguerite.

My child, you must never cease to thank Heaven for your good fortune.'

Sanchia was watching Eleanor for her cue. Beatrice was clearly miserable at the thought of her sister's leaving them. Eleanor kept her eyes to the ground. This was the greatest honour which could befall them and it had come to Marguerite, not because she was more clever or more beautiful —she was neither—but simply because she was the eldest.

Marguerite herself was bewildered. She knew that she should be grateful. She was aware of the great honour done to her but at the same time it frightened her.

For thirteen years she had lived in the shelter of her parents' love. Now she was to leave that to go to . . . she knew not what. To a great King who would be her husband. She looked at Eleanor, but Eleanor would not meet her gaze lest she betray the envy she was feeling.

It is only because she is older, was the thought which kept going round and round in her head.

'You will be very happy, I know it,' said the Countess. 'Queen Blanche will be a mother to you and you will be under the protection of a great King. Now why are we looking so glum? We should all be rejoicing.'

'I don't want Marguerite to go away,' said Beatrice.

'No, my dear child, nor do any of us. But you see her husband will want her with him and he has first claim.'

'Let him come here,' suggested Beatrice smiling suddenly.

'That could not be, baby. He has a kingdom to govern.'

'We would help him.'

The Countess laughed and ruffled Beatrice's hair. 'We are going to have a great deal to do, Marguerite, I want you to come with me now. We must discuss your clothes and I shall have much to tell you.'

The Count said: 'This is indeed a happy day for us. It is like a miracle. I should never have believed it possible.'

Eleanor raised her eyes and said: 'I have written a poem.'

'That is good,' said her father.

'May I read it to you now?'

'Not now, my dear. Another time. With so much on our minds. . . .'

'Come, Marguerite,' said the Countess.

The door shut on them and the three girls were alone.

Sanchia was watching Eleanor expectantly. Eleanor went to the table and took up the poem she had written and which she had so looked forward to reading to her parents. They were not interested now. All they could think about now was Marguerite's wedding.

'It is only because she is the eldest,' she said. 'If I had been, I should have been the one.'

* * *

Now Les Baux was given over to preparation. There was no other conversation but that of the coming marriage, whether in the great hall or in the rooms of the serving men and women. Les Baux was no longer the mere castle of the Count of Provence; it was the home of the future Queen of France. Marguerite, who had at first been apprehensive, was now radiant with expectation. The news she had of her bridegroom was that he was not only kindly and good but a man determined to do his duty and make France great.

Marguerite was passed from the hands of the dressmakers to her parents that she might be closeted with them and listen to advice that seemed interminable. When she considered what she must do and must not do, she told Eleanor, she got them hopelessly muddled so that it would have been better to have had no instruction at all.

Eleanor listened almost grudgingly. How she wished that all this fuss had been for her! If only she had been the eldest and was going to France, how excited she would be! Instead of which she would stay at Les Baux for several more years and then a husband would be found for her. Who would it be? Some Duke? Some Count? And she would have to pay homage to her sister for the rest of her life!

And had she been born the first she would have been the one.

It was bad enough to lose Marguerite whose company would be sadly missed, but that she should have this honour showered on her and be so much more important than the rest of them was even harder to take for someone of Eleanor's temperament.

At first she remained aloof, but then her curiosity got the better of her and when Marguerite confessed that she was frightened and at times wished the whole thing could be forgotten, she scolded her and pointed out what great honour was being done to the family and that she should be rejoicing in her good fortune.

So the time passed and in due course the ambassadors of the King of France returned to Les Baux. They had come, they said, on the command of the King to take his bride to him without delay. So Marguerite was to leave with them, taking with her a few attendants and one of the minstrels from her father's Court, and on the road she would be joined by the Bishop of Valence who would lead her to Sens where her bridegroom would be waiting for her.

She would be received by the Archbishop of Sens who would perform the ceremony and coronation, for Marguerite was to be crowned Queen of France at that same time as she was married to its King.

What excitement there was throughout Les Baux while the packhorses were laden with all the splendid garments which had been made for Marguerite. In her chamber the Countess was giving the last advice to her daughter, reminding her that she and the Count would be present at the wedding and would shortly be leaving in their daughter's wake. Then a magnificently attired Marguerite, looking like a stranger with that aura of royalty already settling about her, was led out of the castle.

Eleanor forgot her jealousy in that moment as she embraced her sister, and Marguerite clung to her whispering that when she was Queen of France her dear sister who was closer to her than any of the others—even their dearest parents —should come to her Court and be her companion.

It was a comforting thought although Eleanor's good sense told her that there was little likelihood of its coming to pass.

Then Marguerite rode off in the centre of the cavalcade, most carefully guarded for she had become very precious; and her father's knights and those of her husband-to-be were ready to guard her with their lives. The golden lilies of France were fluttering ahead of her.

There was a sombre atmosphere in the castle that night, yet a strange one. The family had risen in prestige through their new connection with the royal house of France, naturally, but how they missed Marguerite!

Then they were caught up in more bustling preparations for now the Count and Countess must leave for Sens to be the proud witnesses of their daughter's wedding and coronation.

* * *

It was galling to have to remain behind, to be considered a child. Yet, thought Eleanor, *I* am the eldest now. The next time suitors come to the castle they will come for me.

But what marriage could there be to compare with that of the King of France!

'When I marry,' she told Sanchia, 'my marriage must be
every bit as grand as that of Marguerite.'

'Then you must have a King, sister,' said Sanchia.

'I know. Nothing less will I take.'

'What King will it be?'

Eleanor was thoughtful. 'There is a King of England,' she
said. 'I suppose he will be the one.'

In due course their parents returned and there was great
rejoicing in the castle that night. Everything was even more
satisfactory than they had dared hope.

They told the children how happy their sister was. Her
bridegroom had fallen in love with her on sight and she with
him.

'And small wonder,' said the Countess. 'The King of
France is the most handsome man in his kingdom. His hair is
so fair that it shines like a golden halo in the sunlight. His
eyes are blue and his skin so delicately coloured that men
marvel at him. But what pleased us most is his obvious goodness. They say France is a happy country to have such a
King.'

'And a Queen,' put in the Count smiling.

'I wish you could have seen her at her coronation,' went
on the Countess.

'I wish it too,' said Eleanor.

'Her mantle was lined with vair, her gown of blue velvet
trimmed with sable and ermine,' continued the Countess. 'I
have never seen Marguerite look as beautiful as she did at her
coronation. The people in the streets cheered and cheered.
The King was so happy and before the crowd he took her hand
and kissed it tenderly to show them all how pleased he was
with his bride and he was of course telling them so they must
be too. Your father will tell you how I could not stop my tears
as I watched them.'

The Count was nodding happily.

'Her golden crown—given her by the King—cost fifty-eight
livres. He has showered gifts on her. Beautiful furs and golden
ornaments. Was not her diadem beautiful?' demanded the
Countess and the Count assured them that it was indeed.

'There was a gold cup made for them and we saw them
drink from it at the banquet. He held it to her first and then
put his lips where hers had been. It was most touching. Oh,
this has been a happy year.'

Eleanor listened.

Oh fortunate Marguerite! She was more determined

than ever that no one less than a king would do for her.

*   *   *

The marriage had changed the family. Marguerite, though absent, was its most important member. She was the subject of constant comment and accounts of her life as the Queen of France became a daily recital.

It was good, Eleanor knew, that they should have become so important. There were more callers at the castle now, and there had been one never-to-be-forgotten time when the King himself had visited them with Marguerite. The King was certainly an ideal bridegroom. All the praises Eleanor had heard of him had not been exaggerated as far as she could see. He was undeniably handsome; he had delicate but beautifully chiselled features; his complexion was so fresh and his skin so clear that had he been a woman it would have seemed he had painted it so, but this was seen to be pure natural freshness. He had blond hair which was abundant and glossy; and he and Marguerite made such a handsome pair that for their looks alone they delighted the people who came out of their houses to cheer them as they passed by. And what delighted the Count and Countess most was the obvious evidence that this love between the royal pair was no myth. Louis, it was said, had become more serious since his marriage; he was determined to be a good husband and a good king. As for Marguerite she was in such a state of bliss that she no longer seemed like their sister. Eleanor was filled with an even greater determination to do as well for herself as her sister had done. But how could she?

The King of France had brothers but Eleanor had no great desire to be the bride of a younger son; if she married one of the King's brothers—and it seemed very likely that in a year or so this proposition might be considered—she would always be subservient to her sister. Not that Marguerite would ever stress the fact that she was the superior. That was unimportant. She would be.

A year had passed and Eleanor was getting nearer and nearer to the day when a husband would be found for her and she was restive.

There was only one King that she knew of who, by marrying her, could give her equal standing with her sister and that was the King of England. He remained unmarried although it seemed unlikely that he would be so for long. He was much

older than Marguerite's husband being twenty-seven years old
—and wives were usually found for kings long before they
reached that age.

She determined to find out all she could about the King
of England and the most likely member of her father's Court
to supply the information would naturally be Romeo de Villeneuve.

She made opportunities to talk to him and he was nothing
loth. He was very proud of having played a part in arranging
Marguerite's marriage; and she knew that he would like to do
equally well for her, so he was a good ally. She had heard him
say that the brilliant marriage of the eldest sister would pave
the way for the others. There were many who would hesitate
to take the daughter of the Count of Provence, but few would
not consider marriage with the sister of the Queen of France
a good one.

Eleanor pinned her hopes on Romeo.

She had learned a great deal about the English King. He
had been on the throne nearly twenty years, for his father
had died when he was nine years old. England had been occupied by the father of the present King of France who had
been invited there because the barons had so loathed Henry's
father King John, that they had thought a foreign ruler would
be better than he was. When John died Henry had been hastily
crowned with his mother's throat collar, the crown jewels
having recently been lost in the Wash when King John's army
was crossing that stretch of water.

So he had been King when he was younger than she was.
He had had good advisers—always essential, said Romeo with
a twinkle in his eye and so calling attention to his own worthi-
ness, which she would be the last to deny. Because of these
advisers, the French had gone back to France and Henry
continued to reign in peace—entirely due to these strong men
whose advice he took.

'What sort of man is the King, Romeo?' she asked. 'Is he
like the King of France?'

'I doubt anyone is like the King of France, but Henry is a
great King and if he is wise could be more powerful than
Louis.'

That made her eyes sparkle. That was what she wanted.
Henry to be more powerful than Louis—that was if she married him.

But what wild dream was this. There had been no emis-
saries from England asking for her hand. How infuriating that

it was the man who must ask for his bride and not the bride
for the groom!

But her questions about England had set Romeo's mind
working. She knew that. And he was thinking, as she was,
what an admirable state of affairs would be brought about
if while one of the Count of Provence's daughters was the
Queen of France, the other was the Queen of England.

She was impatient for action. But what could she do? Romeo
could not send minstrels to the Court of England to sing
of her charms. And she was only twelve years old. If only
she had been the eldest.

She became obsessed by England. She discussed that country
with Romeo. She already knew how it had been conquered by
William of Normandy and that Henry was a descendant of
his. She knew that because of the folly of King John very few
possessions were left to the English Crown.

'They will attempt to regain them,' said Romeo, 'and the
King of France will do all in his power to hold them.'

It was an interesting situation.

She found solace from her impatience in writing and it
was natural that she should write about England. She liked
the ancient legends which had come down over the years and
took one of these on which to base a narrative poem.

This was about a certain Blandin of Cornwall and Guil-
laume of Miremas who fell in love with two sisters, the
Princesses Briende and Irlondë. To win these ladies the two
knights must perform deeds of great daring. Eleanor glowed
with pride and passion as she invented the seemingly impossible tasks. And in her imagination she was the beautiful
Briende.

When the poem was completed her parents summoned
several members of the Court that they might hear their
daughter read it, for in addition to her literary talents she had
a beautiful voice and could sing where singing was required
and then break into impassioned recitation.

It was a superb performance and when it was finished
Eleanor, flushed with triumph, looked up to find the eyes
of Romeo fixed not upon her but staring into space as though
his thoughts were far away.

She was piqued and angry. It was clear that he had not
paid attention to the reading.

Her mother was embracing her.

'It is your greatest achievement,' she said. 'You are indeed
a poet, daughter.'

'Romeo did not appear to think so,' she said curtly.

Romeo was immediately on his feet. 'Indeed, my lady Eleanor,' he declared, 'you are wrong. I thought it a remarkable piece of work. I was thinking what a pity it was that the whole world could not know of your talent.'

'Eleanor is happy to delight her family, I know,' said the Count fondly.

It was later that day when leaving the castle for a walk in the grounds with Sanchia, she met, as though by chance, the Lord of Villeneuve.

She was astute enough to know that this was no chance meeting and when he implied in the most discreet way that he wished to speak to her alone she sent Sanchia into the house to get a wrap for her and bring it to the shrubbery, deciding that whether or not she was in the shrubbery when Sanchia returned depended on the importance of what Romeo had to say and the time it would take.

Romeo came straight to the point. 'Your poem impressed me greatly. You did not think so because I was carried away by a thought which had struck me as to how the poem could be used to good advantage.'

'What is this?' said Eleanor.

'The poem is set in Cornwall. Did you know that the Earl of Cornwall is at this time at Poitou?'

'I did not,' she said, and added though she knew very well, 'Is he not the brother of the King of England?'

'He is indeed. And at this time he is planning to go on a crusade. That is why he is in Poitou. It has occurred to me that as the poem is set in Cornwall, the Earl would be pleased to see it.'

'What do you suggest?'

'That you send it to him with a charming letter in which you modestly say that you have written the poem and hearing he was near and it was set in his dominion, you thought it might interest him.'

'What does my father say?'

'Your father would doubtless consider it an unusual action, as he did when I sent a minstrel to the Court of France to sing of your sister's beauty and talents.'

'And you think because of that....'

'No. But it helped. Young, beautiful, well educated ... those are the qualities which Kings of this day look for in their brides.'

'But Richard....'

'Is the brother of the King, who will shortly be returning to England where the King is thinking of marriage. He must be because it will be his duty to marry and he has left it long.'

'So ... if I send the poem... ?'

Romeo nodded. 'With a charming note ... the sort a young girl might write on impulse. Who knows... ?'

'I will do it,' said Eleanor.

'Without delay,' warned Romeo.

She nodded. He left her then and she sped to the shrubbery where Sanchia was impatiently waiting with her wrap.

*   *   *

All his life Richard, Earl of Cornwall, had been reminded of his uncle after whom he had been named—Coeur de Lion. The greatest soldier of his day who had already become a legend in his country—the fearless fighter whose very name had struck terror into the Saracen. In spite of the military skill and courage of Richard the Lion Heart, he had not succeeded in capturing Jerusalem, although it was said he would eventually have done so if his life had not been cut short by an archer outside the walls of Chaluz castle.

For a young man who, in spite of all his efforts to deny this, was not physically strong, such a heritage could be a handicap. It could be said that Coeur de Lion had been troubled by periodic attacks of the ague, but once they were over he was full of vigour. His nephew's disability was less easy to define and manifested itself in a general lassitude rather than any obvious symptom.

Richard had always known that sooner or later he would have to go on a crusade. It was expected of him; and now seemed a good time. He was, in truth, heartily tired of his marriage. He had been foolish when only twenty-two years of age he had married a woman a good deal older than himself. It was a reckless and impetuous act. He had been warned —even by the lady herself—that it could not be satisfactory and how right they had all been.

Isabella was the daughter of old William Marshal, one of the most important—it could be said the most important— men in England at the time of King John's death, for if William Marshal had not supported Henry he would not have been accepted by the people.

What a fool he had been to marry the widow of Gilbert de Clare who had already borne her husband six children. He must have been mad. Of course Isabella was an exceptionally beautiful woman and at that time he had thought her seniority piquant. He had told himself he wanted no young girl. A mature woman was much more to his taste. So he had married and what had happened? She who had given her previous husband six children had so far given him only one son, and because his visits to her became less frequent she had grown melancholy so that his great desire was to get away from her.

What a situation! Henry would say 'I told you so.' Henry was very good at that. He had not been so fortunate in his matrimonial affairs after all. It was time he married. A King had his duty to the State. But Henry seemed to be unlucky. It really looked as though—King that he was—no one was very eager to marry him. He had already sent feelers out to Brittany, Austria and Bohemia—without result. Then of course he had tried for a Princess of Scotland but as her sister had already married Hubert de Burgh—the King's chief minister after the death of William Marshal—it was considered inadvisable for the King and his minister to marry sisters. It was said that Hubert, being anxious that none of these marriages should take place, had set rumours in motion that the King of England had a squint, was of a lewd and generally unpleasant character being deceitful and a coward; it was even whispered that he was a leper. Of course poor old Hubert was now in decline being hounded by his enemies who were ready to bring any charge against him however ridiculous. Richard did not believe that of old Hubert. No, Hubert was a good man. Of course he had his eyes on the main chance, and wanted to gather as much land and money as he could ... (well, who did not?) but Hubert was honourable ... as men went. And Richard refused to believe the tales of his enemies.

The fact remained that Henry was no longer very young and still had no bride. He was a little humiliated by this and wanted to marry. He did, however, show very little sympathy for Richard's predicament. Richard had behaved like a fool was his judgment, and must take the consequences.

But Richard was not a man to accept his fate. He had already sent feelers to Rome with the usual plea of consanguinity, but the Pope was not sympathetic; so at this stage Richard, being married to a woman who no longer pleased him, could view with interest a crusade to the Holy Land.

Such a project needed a great amount of preparation and it would be some time before he could leave, probably a year or more; in the meantime he could enjoy the preparation.

He was surprised when a messenger arrived from Les Baux

with a package for him and he was amused and somewhat intrigued when he discovered the letter written in a good hand, but obviously by a young person which explained that the narrative poem was a gift to him from the daughter of the Count of Provence. She sent it because she had set her scene in Cornwall, a land which fascinated her and she knew that it belonged to him so it seemed to her that because of this he might consider her work with kindness.

Puzzled he questioned the messenger.

'It was given to you by the Count's daughter?'

'That is so, my lord.'

Richard smiled. 'I believe the Count has several daughters.'

'He has four, my lord.'

'And one, not so long ago became the Queen of France. It was the second eldest who gave you this?'

'The Lady Eleanor, my lord.'

'She is a young girl—'

'Very young, my lord.'

'So must she be for the Queen of France is but a child and the Lady Eleanor is younger.'

'By some two years I believe, my lord.'

Richard nodded and dismissed the man to his servants that he might be refreshed after his journey. Then he read the poem.

It was good. It showed a style which was mature and the adventures of the knights were told with a verve and authenticity which was really amazing coming from a girl who could not be more than thirteen and had never set eyes on the terrain of which she wrote. An unusual girl, one might say a brilliant girl. Richard pictured an ardent little scholar peering at her books.

He must write a gracious note of thanks and compliment her on her skill. Skill! For a girl of that age to write such a poem about a land she could never have seen was little short of genius.

He sent for the messenger and when the man came to him he said: 'Tell me about the Lady Eleanor. Is she handsome?'

'My lord, she is said to be the most handsome of all the sisters and I doubt a more good-looking family could be found in France.'

'Is that so?' mused Richard.

'My lord, it is. The lady is called Eleanor la Belle. Yet her sisters are beautiful girls also.'

'The lady has done me much honour. I should welcome

the chance of thanking her in person. Ride back to Les Baux
and tell the Count of Provence that I shall be passing through
his land and should feel honoured if I might call at the castle.'

'The Count will be overjoyed, my lord, I doubt not.'

'Then when you are refreshed ride off. I doubt not I shall be
close behind.'

*   *   *

Eleanor saw the messenger returning and hurried down
to question him.

'What said the Earl of Cornwall when he saw what the package contained?' she demanded.

'He wishes to come here in person to thank you.'

She was elated. She turned and went without delay to search
for Romeo.

She found him with her father and she felt that there was
no time for delay, so she blurted out what the messenger had
said.

'The Earl of Cornwall,' cried the Count. 'We must give him
a good welcome. But how did this come about?'

Eleanor looked at Romeo who said: 'The lady Eleanor
sent her poem to the Earl. It seemed it would please him since
it was set in his country.'

The Count looked from her to Romeo in disbelief.

'It was on my advice,' said the Lord of Villeneuve quickly.
'I saw no reason why the Earl of Cornwall, being in the neighbourhood, should not be made aware of the lady Eleanor's
talent.'

The Count gave a short laugh. 'My dear Romeo, is this
another of your schemes?'

Romeo opened his eyes wide and said: 'But it seemed
so natural. The poem is set in Cornwall. The Earl of Cornwall
is close at hand. I am sure he was delighted. He will be able
to tell you, my lady, whether your descriptions of his country
were good.'

Eleanor was looking from the minister to her father. The
Count looked vaguely uneasy. Of course she was thinking,
Richard was not Henry, but he was his brother and soon he
would be returning to England. It was a way in. It appealed to
her nature to do something—however wild—rather than to do
nothing at all.

The Count said: 'The Countess must be told without delay.
It will be necessary to make preparations for the brother of
the King of England.'

*   *   *

She was a beautiful child, thought Richard, for child she was in spite of the fact that she was so self-possessed. Eleanor la Belle indeed! And when he considered her poem which he had at first thought he must skim through and then had become excited about, he was astonished. She was not only beautiful but clever.

She made him feel more and more dissatisfied with his marriage. By God's eyes, he thought, were I not already married I would ask for her myself.

There was a banquet in the great hall given especially for him and he expressed himself so enchanted by the Count's daughter that he asked that he might be presented to the others.

Sanchia and Beatrice, with Eleanor, were a charming trio; and if perhaps Eleanor surpassed her sisters in beauty and poise the others were not far behind.

He made himself very agreeable and talked to them of Eleanor's poem about Cornwall which he said amazed him by the manner in which it expressed the atmosphere of the place.

Then he told them about Corfe Castle where he had spent much of his early life and how he had been most strictly brought up under the care of the stern tutors. He spoke of Cornwall—that most westerly part of England which tapered into a bony ridge of land pushing its way far out into the ocean. He told of the moors and the rugged coast so treacherous to ships and the queer brooding mystery of the land where in the past so many strange deeds had taken place. He believed that King Arthur and his knights had roamed those moors.

He turned to Eleanor. 'With your imagination, dear lady, you would find much to write of in my land of Cornwall. You would find many such as the brave knight Blandin. I would I could show it to you.'

'How I long to see it,' cried Eleanor.

'Mayhap you will one day,' replied Richard; and he looked at her so intently that the colour came into her cheeks and she cast down her eyes lest he should read her thoughts.

'I should like to come too,' said Sanchia, who was too young to hide her admiration for their guest.

'Let us hope that in some way this will come to pass,' said Richard. 'Why should I not invite you all?'

'It is so far,' said Sanchia. 'Over the sea.'

'I should like to go on a boat,' put in Beatrice. 'You came on one, my lord.'

' 'Tis true I did and the sea was so unkind to us that more than one of my men wished himself dead.'

'But you did not,' said Sanchia.

'I am a tolerable sailor,' he answered, 'which is a mercy for in my family we used to spend our lives crossing the sea. It may well be that we shall return to the habit.'

Eleanor was the only one who knew that he was referring to the regaining of the lost possessions. She was silent because her whole attention was centred on what he had to tell. She wanted to hear more and more of England; and hearing of England meant hearing of its King.

'My brother, as you know, has been a King for a long time. He is only slightly older than I. Just think. Had I been born fifteen months sooner and he fifteen later it would be the King of England who sat talking to you now.'

'You would not be here then,' Eleanor pointed out.

'Why should I not be? I tell you this. If my brother knew of the talents and beauty of the daughters of the Count of Provence he would be unable to resist a visit.'

'When a King comes travelling to France,' Eleanor pointed out, 'there would be many to suspect his reasons. He could not do so merely to see my father's daughters.'

'I see you are wise indeed. No, the King could not come here without much pomp and noise. There would be suspicions that he was asking the Count's help against the King of France.'

'He is our brother-in-law,' piped up Beatrice.

'So you see, my dear ladies, that there would be consternation if he came. How fortunate I am that I am merely his brother for I may come and go as I please. But rest assured I shall tell my brother of my visit here. I shall make him envy me . . . for once.'

By which he betrays, thought Eleanor, that *he* has envied the King more than once.

Then she begged him to tell her of England and she learned much of the Court and its ceremonies and how the ladies were so eager to show their hair that although they had elaborate head-dresses they often carried them in their hands; the gowns worn by the ladies were of similar fashion to those worn in Provence, for fashions passed from country to country; the nobles wore brocade and velvet, silk and fine linen and the poorer people spun their own cloth from wool flax or goat's hair just as in Provence. The King was very interested in architecture and for this reason buildings were springing up all over the country. The King was a man who greatly enjoyed music and literature.

'I shall show him your poem when I return to England,' said Richard to Eleanor. 'I know he will admire it very much.'

Again Eleanor blushed and lowered her eyes. Triumph indeed. How wise Romeo was! This was the way.

'Perhaps you will show it to his Queen as well as to him,' she said.

'My brother has no Queen.'

'But very soon he will have one I doubt not.'

'He must. It is his duty. Though while he has not I am heir to the throne you know.'

Eleanor was alert. Here was a very ambitious man. Then would it not be to his interests to keep his brother unmarried? Oh no, he could not do that. It would not be permitted. More-over, surely Henry as King would be the one to decide when he would marry.

Richard went on: 'Yes, I think he will eventually marry. In fact that day may come soon.'

'He is affianced?' asked Eleanor.

'Not exactly, but I believe negotiations are going afoot.'

Her heart was beating fast. Too late. It was too late. She saw this prize—the only remaining prize—slipping through her fingers.

She felt a great sympathy with Richard of Cornwall. They had both been born too late.

Richard started to tell them about the Court; the banquets that were given, the games that were played. Questions and commands was one of the favourites and also roy-qui-ne-ment, the King does not lie, in which questions were asked and the answers given must be the truth; chess was played a great deal and without asking he knew that the girls were experienced at the game for to play well was considered a necessary part of the education of well brought up girls and boys; then there was a game called tables in which two people played draughts-men, the moves being determined by throwing a dice; there was vaulting, tumbling, juggling and of course dancing and music.

'And does the King ride through the country in royal pro-gress?'

'Indeed he does. My brother has a love of splendour. And this of course is reflected in his Court. The people like it.'

'It is how a King should be,' said Eleanor.

'Lavish entertainments are arranged for him in the castles

he visits. We have the jongleurs of course who come with songs
and dances. Some of the jongleurs are women; they dance well
and can sing; they are good mimics; they act little plays. I
can tell you there is no lack of gaiety at my brother's Court.
He favours most the musicians though and the poets and
those who perform a certain kind of dance. He was always
more studious than I. I think he loves his books almost as much
as his kingdom.'

'Who is the lady who will share his throne?'

'It is Joanna, the daughter of the Earl of Ponthieu.'

The Earl of Ponthieu! thought Eleanor. She was of no
higher rank than the daughter of the Count of Provence. And
for her a crown! Oh, they should have acted sooner.

'When ... when will the betrothal take place?'

'I doubt there will be any delay. My brother feels he has
waited too long ... and so do his ministers. I believe the proposals may already have gone to my brother. I know he is
eagerly awaiting them.'

Eleanor seemed to have lost heart. It could have worked.
But it was too late.

When Richard rode away the three girls stood with their
parents waving him farewell.

He looked back and thought what a charming group they
made. Certainly the reports of the girls' beauty had not been
exaggerated. Eleanor was very gifted; Sanchia was charming—so young and appealing; and even little Beatrice was
going to be a beauty when she grew up.

He carried with him the poem. It was quite a work of art.

He turned in his saddle and called: 'We shall meet again.
I promise it to myself.'

Then he rode away.

Sanchia clasped her hands and murmured: 'He is the most
beautiful man I ever saw.'

Her parents laughed at her tenderly. Eleanor was silent.
Too late, she was thinking. But a few weeks too late.

A Journey through France

THE King was awaiting the return of the messengers from Ponthieu with some impatience. As he had said to one of his chief ministers, Hubert de Burgh, it was ridiculous that a man of his age—he would be twenty-nine in a year's time—had never married. And he one of the biggest prizes in the matrimonial market!

It was no fault of his that he had so far failed. He had tried hard enough. What mystery was this? Why should a King have to *try* to find a bride? It should be that all the richest and most important men of Europe would bring their marriageable daughters to his notice.

Is there something wrong with me? he had asked himself.

Looking in his mirror he could find nothing that should stand in the way of marriage. He was not exactly handsome and yet by no means ill favoured. He was of medium height and had a good strong body. It was true that one eyelid drooped so that the eye beneath it was hidden and this gave him an odd look which might to some seem a little sinister, but in some ways it suggested an air of distinction. He was no tyrant. He reckoned that he was liberal minded and a benevolent man—except in rare moments when his anger was aroused. He was known as a patron of the arts and a man of cultivated taste. But it was not only these gifts he had to offer a bride. He was the King of England and the woman he married would be a Queen.

It was therefore astounding that he should have remained so long unmarried. Before this he had made three attempts and none of them had come to fruition.

He was growing a little suspicious.

He sent for Hubert de Burgh. Hubert was back in favour but the relationship between them would never be the same as it had been. Once when he was but a boy he had idolized Hubert, for Hubert—with William Marshal—had given him his crown. He had been but a boy of nine, the French in possession of the key towns of England, his mother recently free from the prison in which his father had placed her, when Hubert and William Marshal had set him on the throne, rallied the country and made it possible for him to be a King.

Such a deed should have made Hubert a friend for life, and when William Marshal had died Hubert became his Chief Justiciar and adviser. Henry had listened to Hubert, had believed in Hubert, but as Hubert grew more and more influential he had become richer and had taken advantage of every situation to enhance his own power and that of his family. He had even married the sister of the King of Scotland. Hubert's enemies then began to pour the venom of envy into Henry's ears and he had believed it. After all there must have been some truth in what they suggested. Old Hubert had been hounded from his posts, his life placed in danger, and Henry himself had come near to killing him with his sword on one occasion. Something he regretted later for he was not by nature a violent man. But what he could not bear—and it had been so particularly at that time—was anyone to suggest that he was young, inexperienced and incapable of making decisions. He had had to endure too much of that when he was very young, surrounded as he had been by advisers who fancied themselves so wise.

But now Hubert was taken back into favour. His lands and honours were restored to him; and to show his contrition Henry tried to behave towards him as though that terrible time when he had been hounded from sanctuary and come very near to violent death had never taken place.

Hubert arrived and came straight to the King's apartment.

Poor Hubert, he had aged considerably. He had lost that buoyancy which had been a characteristic of his; his brow had become very furrowed and his skin had lost its freshness. Moreover there was a look of furtiveness in his eyes as though he were watchful and would never trust those about him again.

This was understandable. He might so easily have ended up a prisoner in the Tower of London to emerge only to suffer the traitor's death. It had happened swiftly and suddenly and in Hubert's mind without reason. He would never rid himself of the fear that it could come again.

'Ah, Hubert.' The King held out his hand and smiled warmly.

Hubert took it and bowing low, kissed it. So he was safe for today, he thought with relief. The King was concerned but Hubert was not to be held responsible for what was troubling him. Hubert softened a little. Henry was not to be blamed entirely. He had been led away by malicious men who had been determined to destroy Hubert de Burgh, a man whose possessions and standing with the King they envied. But that was in the past. By great good fortune from Hubert's point of view, Edmund the sainted Archbishop of Canterbury had deplored the influence Hubert's arch enemy, Peter des Roches, Bishop of Winchester, was gaining over the King. He had not been alone in this and backed by powerful barons the Archbishop had threatened the King with excommunication if he did not dismiss the Bishop.

Henry, whose religious instincts were strong, had been impressed by the saintliness of the Archbishop of Canterbury, and in due course dismissed Peter des Roches. Thus the way had been paved for Hubert's return to favour.

But there must be tensions between them which could never be overcome. Hubert could not forget that the King had turned against him and only extreme good luck had prevented his enemies from destroying him; Henry would always remember the rumours he had heard of Hubert. They would never again entirely trust each other.

Peter des Roches had left England taking with him much of his wealth which he had placed at the service of the Pope who was engaged in war with the Romans. But his memory lingered on and the harm he had done to Hubert would never completely be elminated.

All this they both remembered as they faced each other.

'The messengers are long in returning from Ponthieu,' said Henry.

'My lord, there is much for them to settle. When they return the contracts will have been agreed and your bride will be making her preparation to come to England.'

'I trust she is as comely as we have heard, Hubert.'

'She is young and I doubt not that she is also comely.'

'This time,' said Henry, 'I shall make sure that nothing prevents my marriage.'

'I see no reason, my lord, why it should.'

For a moment Henry regarded the Justiciar through half-closed eyes. Was it true or malicious talk that Hubert had been responsible for stopping the negotiations for those other matches? No, he did not believe Hubert would behave so. Moreover, what point would there have been?

'The Count of Ponthieu is eager for the match,' went on Hubert, 'and so I believe is his daughter. In fact, my lord, I have it on the best authority that they cannot believe their good fortune.'

'This does not surprise me,' answered Henry complacently. 'Ponthieu is of no great moment when compared with England. It will be a grand match for the girl.'

He smiled. He would enjoy being kind to his bride, showing her what a fine match she had made, letting her know that in every way he was her superior. How she would love him for showering such benefits upon her!

'Hubert,' he said, 'I want you to press ahead with this marriage. There has been too much delay.'

'It was my intention to do so, my lord,' replied Hubert. 'Rest assured that within a few weeks your bride will be here.'

*   *   *

When Richard had returned to England his first duty was to present himself to his brother. Even as they had greeted each other they were both aware of the caution which had crept into their relationship. They had lost the trust they had once had. Since that day when Henry had quarrelled with Richard and had even thought of making him a prisoner, and Richard had gathered together some of the chief barons to side with him, Henry had been wary of his brother. From the very day he had ascended the throne in the manner of every baron about him had been the implication that he must remember what had happened to his father. Runnymead! The very word held a grim warning. It happened to King John; it could happen to you. The barons would never again let any King of England forget what a power they were. And when a King had an ambitious brother who had already shown himself capable of standing against him, he must indeed be cautious.

Richard would never forget that, urged on by the Justiciar, Henry had once been on the point of arresting him and but for the loyalty of some of his servants and his own prompt action he might have found himself the King's prisoner. He had been forced to arouse those barons who were watchful of the King and ready to side with him before he was able to feel free again. And although he and the King had become friends afterwards, such incidents left their mark.

Richard was intensely aware of the rivalry between them. He himself could never forget that it was only the timing of their birth which had placed Henry in the superior position and he naturally thought that he would have made the better King. Henry was aware of his feelings and this did not endear him to his brother.

Still, because of their close relationship they both knew that outright animosity between them would be uncomfortable for both of them.

Henry was irritated because his matrimonial adventures had failed but at the same time pleased because Richard's adventure in that direction, although positive, was far from satisfactory.

'So, how did you fare?' the King asked.

'Well enough.'

'And you make progress with your preparation? When shall you be leaving for the Holy Land?'

'There is much yet to be done. It could be two years at least.'

'So long! Well, you will have a little time with your wife before you go.' The faint smile, the glance from under the drooping lid irritated Richard. There was no need for Henry to gloat. Richard knew he had made a mistake. But at least he had married and had a son to show for it.

'The boy flourishes,' he said with a hint of malice. Henry flinched. How he would have loved to have a son. 'You must see him, Henry. After all he is named for you.'

'I am happy to know all is well with him. I trust that ere long he will have a boy cousin.'

'Ah, so the marriage plans are going ahead.'

'We are still waiting for the return of the embassy. When they arrive I shall lose no time.'

'I understand well. You have waited over long.'

'Did you see Joanna when you were in Ponthieu?'

'I did.'

'And you thought her beautiful?'

Richard hesitated and he saw the anxiety dawn in Henry's face.

'Oh fair enough,' he said.

'Fair enough,' cried Henry. 'Fair enough for whom ... for what?'

'One cannot ask too much of a bride in a state marriage, can one? If she was born in the right bed and the marriage brings the desired terms, what matters it whether the lady be fair?'

There was a silence, while Henry's looks grew darker. Then Richard laughed. 'Oh, brother, I but tease. She is comely . . .'

'Enough?' added Henry.

'To tell the truth I compared her with one other whom I met rather by chance.'

'Oh have you fallen in love again then?'

'I could well be on the way to it. She is the daughter of the Count of Provence. I believe I have never seen a more beautiful girl. She is clever too. A poet . . . a musician . . . a girl who has been unusually well educated. This is obvious in her manner . . . her speech . . . and of course her poetry.'

'You are not speaking of the Queen of France?'

'Nay. I did not meet her. 'Twas hardly likely that I should have been received with much friendship at the Court of France. The girl who so impressed me was her sister, Eleanor. You would enjoy the Court of Provence, brother. They set great store by music. The conversation sparkles with wit. Troubadours come from all over France sure of appreciation. I can tell you it is a paradise. The Count has four beautiful daughters. One you know became the Queen of France. That left Eleanor, Sanchia and Beatrice.'

'And the one who enchanted you?'

'They all did, but Eleanor is thirteen years old. It's a delightful age—particularly in one as talented as Eleanor.'

'And how does she compare with Joanna of Ponthieu?'

Richard shrugged his shoulders and lowered his eyes.

'Come,' said the King sharply, 'I would know.'

'Joanna is a comely girl . . . a pleasant creature. . . .'

'But Eleanor surpasses her?'

'The comparison is unfair. There is none who could compare with Eleanor. When I read her poem I did not believe one so young could have written it. I determined to see her, then. . . .'

'What poem is this?'

'I will show you. She wrote a long poem set in Cornwall and since I was nearby she most graciously sent it to me. Once I had read it, I must see its author and that was how I came to spend those delightful days at the Court of Provence.'

'Let me see this poem,' said Henry.

'I have brought it for you. Read it at your leisure. I am

sure with your own poetic gifts you will realize the talent of this girl.'

'Your voice grows soft at the mention of her name. I do believe you are enamoured of her.'

Richard looked sadly ahead of him. 'You know the situation in which I find myself.'

'In which you placed yourself,' Henry corrected. 'It was your reckless nature that put you where you are today ... married to an old woman. I could have told you you would regret it. And the Pope refusing a divorce.'

'It may be that I shall persuade the Pope one day.'

Henry looked impatient. 'Tell me more of Provence.'

'The Count is proud of his daughters. Who would not be? Having secured the King of France for one of them he will look high for the others.'

'And how does Eleanor compare with Marguerite?'

'I heard it said in the castle that she was even more beautiful. In truth because of this she was always called Eleanor la Belle.'

'Give me the poem. I will read it.'

'Then I will leave you to it, Henry. I shall be interested to know what you think of it.'

'Rest assured I shall tell you.'

As soon as he was alone the King glanced at the poem. The handwriting was exceptionally good and only slightly childish. It was written in the Provençal dialect and through their mother Henry and his brother and sisters had some knowledge of this so he was able to read it with ease.

It was charming, delightful, fresh ... and full of feeling. It was true, the child was a poet.

Richard admired her. He was regretting his marriage more than ever. Had she been of more lowly birth he would have done his best to make her his mistress. Henry knew Richard. But of course that was something the Count of Provence would never allow.

She was beautiful—golden haired with brown eyes. He pictured her clearly. Soft skin, fine features, her youthful figure perfect in every detail. Richard was a connoisseur of women and he had thought her the most beautiful child he had ever seen. Her sister was already Queen of France. That was an interesting situation.

Why had he not heard of Eleanor before he had gone into negotiations with Ponthieu?

Still, he was not yet bound to Joanna. There was still time.

The idea obsessed him. Eleanor la Belle. The delectable thirteen-year-old child. He wanted a young girl, someone whom he could mould to his ways. He would have been afraid of a mature woman. Most kings of his age would have had several bastards scattered about the country by this time. Not Henry. He was shy with women; he did not want wild amorous adventures. He wanted a wife whom he could love; someone who would look up to him, and he felt this was certain to be a young girl; he wanted children; fine sons. That was necessary to the well-being of the nation. Richard might think that the succession was safe through him but that was not what Henry wanted. His own son must follow him and this beautiful young wife would provide that son.

He was already disliking Joanna and half in love with Eleanor.

But it is not too late, he told himself.

He sent for Hubert.

'I have changed my mind,' he said. 'Have the messengers returned from Ponthieu?'

'Not yet, my lord,' replied Hubert.

'I have decided against the marriage.'

'My lord!' Hubert looked aghast.

'It is unsuitable and I have found the bride I want. She is Eleanor, daughter of the Count of Provence.'

Hubert found refuge in silence. He was thinking of the negotiations which had been going on with Ponthieu and the difficulty of breaking them; but he said nothing; the memory of the occasion when he had attempted to warn the King for his own good was too vivid. He would never fall into that trap again.

'She is cultivated, and beautiful. Her sister is the Queen of France. You will see, Hubert, that that fact alone makes the marriage desirable.'

'It makes an interesting situation, my lord.'

'And a politically strong one.'

'It could be of great service in our dealing with France, my lord.'

'So thought I. I want a message to be sent to the Count of Provence without delay.'

Hubert nodded. 'And the embassy to Ponthieu, my lord?'

'We will deal with that in due course. In the meantime let us consider the Count of Provence.'

'We shall tell him of your desire and ask what his daughter's dowry will be.'

'That will take time.'

'Such matters always do.'

'There is no need to tell me that. I am well aware of the delays in other negotiations.'

'Which, my lord, you will now be glad did not come to fruition.'

Henry laughed, friendly again. 'You are right, Hubert. I hear that Eleanor of Provence is ... incomparable. Now, we will make ready, with as much speed as possible. You understand me.'

'Perfectly, my lord,' said Hubert.

Before the day was out courtiers were on their way to Provence. Henry waited in an agony of impatience.

This must not go wrong as all his projects had before.

He must have Eleanor. He pictured her—the perfect wife —beautiful, talented, enchanting. All would envy him his bride and none more than his brother Richard.

There were many qualities which made the prospect enticing and not the least of Eleanor's attractions was Richard's clear appreciation of her charms.

*   *   *

No one could deny that a marriage between the King of England and the sister of the Queen of France was a good proposition, so Henry had no difficulty in persuading his ministers that in changing brides he was scoring a political advantage. It was true that not only had he made overtures to the Count of Ponthieu but he was also in process of getting a dispensation from the Pope as in royal marriages there was always the question of consanguinity to be reckoned with. However, he was determined. So he sent messengers to Ponthieu and to Rome to cancel those negotiations and summoning the Bishops of Ely and Lincoln to him he told them that he wished them to leave at once for Provence with the Master of the Temple and the Prior of Hurle and there lay his proposals before the Count of Provence.

The Bishops, aware of the political significance of the proposed match were eager to set out at once; but when they heard that Henry would want a large dowry with his bride they were dubious as to his obtaining this.

'The Count of Provence is greatly impoverished, my lord. It will not be possible for him to raise the dowry for which you ask.'

'It is surprising what a father can do for his daughter when the marriage is as grand as this will be.'

'If he has not the means ... my lord....'

'Doubtless he will find a way. I should enjoy being there to see his delight when he knows your mission.'

'It will be great, but when he hears what you ask it may well be that he will have to refuse your proposal on his daughter's behalf.'

'I am eager to have Eleanor as my bride, but I see no reason why I should allow her father to elude his obligations.'

'We will put your proposals to him, my lord.'

'When can you leave?'

'This day.'

'I am glad of that. I eagerly await the outcome. I want it known throughout the land that I am to be married. There will be great rejoicing.'

He watched the embassy depart and prayed for a good wind that there might be no delay crossing the sea.

His brother Richard came to him smiling secretly.

He had arranged this, he told himself. Young Eleanor, if she was crowned Queen of England, would owe her crown to him.

*   *   *

There was great excitement in Les Baux when the embassy from England arrived.

Eleanor watching them could scarcely wait until her parents summoned her. She had recognized the visitors as coming from England but having heard that arrangements between the King of England and the Count of Ponthieu were progressing, she could not believe that the visit concerned her.

When she was summoned to her parents' chamber her heart was beating wildly. It could not be. Perhaps she had been mistaken. Perhaps the visitors had not come from England after all. They were not from the Court of France—that much she did know.

Her mother took her into her arms and embraced her, while her father watched with tears in his eyes.

'My dear daughter,' he said, 'this is a great day for us.'

She looked eagerly from one to another.

'Is it something that concerns me?' she asked.

'It is,' said her father. 'An offer of marriage.'

'We never thought there could be anything to compare with Marguerite's ... but it seems there is.'

'England?' she whispered.

Her mother nodded. 'The King of England is asking for your hand in marriage.'

Her head was whirling. It had worked then. Richard of
Cornwall and the poem! It was incredible.

Romeo had come into the room. He was smiling complacently. No wonder. Once again they would owe their good
fortune to him.

She could not entirely believe it. It was like a dream coming true. It was too neat. Marguerite Queen of France. Herself Queen of England. And largely because of the clever
juggling of Romeo de Villeneuve. If she had not written that
poem ... if she had not—on Romeo's advice—sent it to the
Duke of Cornwall. ... No, it was too much to believe. It was
what she had wanted more than anything. Marriage with
England was the only one which could possibly compare with
Marguerite's. And it had come to pass.

'You may well be bewildered,' said the Count. 'I confess I
feel the same.'

'But,' she stammered, 'I had heard he was betrothed to
Joanna of Ponthieu.'

'A marriage is no marriage until it has been solemnized.
Everything is over between England and Ponthieu. Negotiations have ceased, the offer has been withdrawn. The King's
messengers, and they are men of great standing, tell me that he
is so eager for this match that he wishes there to be no delay.'

'What does it mean?' said Eleanor. 'That I shall leave at
once? Should I prepare?'

'My dearest, are you so eager to leave us?' asked her mother
almost reproachfully.

'Oh no, dear Mother. But I would know what is expected
of me.'

'You are not afraid. ...'

'Afraid? Ever since Marguerite went I knew that I should.
I doubt she was ever so happy before her marriage as she was
after—although no one could have had a better home.'

'It's true,' agreed the Count. 'And that is how I would have
it. If you find the happiness at the Court of England that
Marguerite has at the Court of France, I shall be content.'

'I shall. I know I shall.'

'Well, my dear,' said the Count, 'we came to prepare you.
We now have to talk of the terms which are a necessary part
of contracts like this. But we wanted you to know at once
what this mission is about, so that you can prepare yourself
for a new life.'

Her mother took her into her arms and kissed her tenderly.

'I am proud of my girls,' she said.

When she had left her parents she went straight to the schoolroom where her sisters were awaiting her.

They looked at her expectantly as she entered. That something very important had happened was obvious and Sanchia who remembered Marguerite's departure was very apprehensive.

'What is it?' she cried, as soon as her sister came in.

'It is an embassy from England. The King of that country is asking for my hand in marriage.'

'Eleanor!'

Her sisters stared at her with wondering eyes and she was silent for a moment savouring their admiration.

'It's true,' she said. 'I think he must have heard of me through his brother.'

'Richard, Earl of Cornwall, the most handsome man I have ever seen,' sighed Sanchia. 'Wouldn't you rather marry him, Eleanor?'

'He is not a King.'

'He would be if his brother died.'

'Oh Sanchia, don't be so ... young. The King of England is not going to die. I am going to marry him and be the Queen. It is every bit as good to be the Queen of England as it is to be the Queen of France.'

'It's better really,' said Sanchia, 'because Richard will be your brother.'

Eleanor laughed with happiness and excitement.

'I shall have such a grand wedding.... There has never been a wedding as grand as the one I shall have. I shall be a Queen. You have seen Marguerite in her crown; mine will be bigger, more glittering ... full of stones that are far more precious.'

'How do you know?' demanded Beatrice.

'Because I do. I wanted to marry the King of England and although he was almost married to someone else ... all that changed and I am to be his Queen. It's like magic. It *is* magic. And yet *I* planned it....'

They were looking at her expectantly and she took their hands and led them to the window seat.

Her eyes were brilliant. She started to describe the English Court to them just as though she were writing a poem. She told them of her husband. He was rather like Blandin the Cornish knight. He was ready to do all sorts of impossible tasks to gain her hand.

'What sort of tasks?' demanded Beatrice.

So she sat there in the window seat and talked of some of the tasks Blandin had had to perform to win the hand of the fair Princess Briende. Only in this case instead of being Blandin and Briende it was Henry and Eleanor.

While she was weaving her stories, there were more arrivals at the castle.

From the window Eleanor saw three of their uncles riding into the courtyard in great haste. They had clearly heard the news. They were Uncle Peter and Boniface and William who was Bishop Elect of Valence. These were her mother's brothers. She had had eight and all of them were ambitious, adventurous and their mission in life was to advance the fortunes of the House of Savoy. The importance of the present occasion was implied by their immediate arrival.

The girls watched their parents greet their uncles and Eleanor eagerly awaited a summons to appear when she expected to be congratulated; they would be delighted with her for being the means of bringing so much honour to the family.

But the summons did not come. There was a sombre air about the castle—almost a desperation—and it began to dawn on Eleanor that something had gone wrong.

All through the day the uncles were with her parents. There was no feasting in the great hall as there should have been on such an occasion; early next morning the Countess sent for Eleanor. Her expression was gloomy and she was clearly very depressed.

'My dear child,' she said, 'you must not just yet think too much about this English marriage.'

'What has happened? Oh pray tell me quickly,' begged Eleanor.

'The King of England asks for such a dowry as your father cannot possibly provide.'

'You mean he wants to be *paid* to take me.'

'It is customary for brides to bring a dowry to their husbands, my dear.'

'Do you mean that we cannot *afford* this marriage?'

'That is what we fear, Eleanor. You see it is a great marriage ... as important as that of Marguerite.'

'The King of France did not ask for a dowry.'

'No. He was content with your sister and knew full well that it was not in your father's power to provide it.'

Eleanor stared blankly at her mother. She saw her beautiful dream evaporating.

Wild thoughts came into her mind. 'Perhaps I could go to

England. If I could see the King, speak with him ... let him see me, know me....'

'My dear child,' said her mother quickly, 'that is out of the question. Do not despair. It may well be that you would be happier in another marriage.'

'I shall not,' she cried. 'If this fails I can never be happy again.'

'You talk like the child you are,' said her mother. 'If there is no marriage I shall not be sorry. It will give you time to grow up ... to learn something of the world ... what marriage means....'

Eleanor was not listening.

Of course, she was telling herself, it had been too good to be true. It was like one of her epic poems. Real life was rarely like that.

* * *

Her uncles were not men to relinquish such a prize without a fight. Messengers went back and forth to England. The Count of Provence found it quite impossible to meet the demands of the King of England while the King of England felt that what he asked was small indeed compared with the honour which he was bestowing.

'This King of England would seem to be a most mercenary man,' said the Count.

The Countess agreed. 'Perhaps after all it would not be such a good marriage. It would be asking too much to expect another bridegroom like Louis.'

'Louis is not only a king but a great man,' replied the Count. 'His goodness shines from his face. I would reckon Marguerite lucky to have such a husband if he were the humblest count.'

'It is clear that Henry of England is of a different nature. It is to be expected. Remember his father.'

The Count smiled at her affectionately. She was telling him not to be depressed because this marriage would not take place. So she had made up her mind that it would not. Henry had entered into several negotiations and it was significant that none of them had ever come to fruition.

'It might well be,' said the Count, 'that Henry is a man who likes to contemplate marriage but when the time approaches for it to take place he shrinks from it.'

'Do you really think this?'

'It would seem so. There have been so many plans. He is no longer young. In fact I feel he is a little old for Eleanor.'

Oh yes, they were comforting themselves.

But the uncles were reluctant to give up in view of what was involved, and negotiations went on. A gleam of hope came when Henry reduced the amount for which he was asking.

'It is still too much,' said the Count. 'Even what he asks now is far beyond my means.'

'He will come down further,' Uncle Boniface assured him.

'And I,' replied the Count with dignity, 'do not care for this bargaining over my daughter. She is a princess, not a piece of land to be bartered for. I tell you this, Boniface, grand as I am well aware this marriage is, I am beginning to have had enough of it.'

As far as he was concerned he would have put an end to the haggling, but the uncles were determined to continue with it.

* * *

Richard was amused by the prolonged arguments. Because he felt himself to have been the cause of the proposed marriage, he was eager to see it carried through. Eleanor was an unusual princess; he knew that his brother would be delighted with her; moreover she would be grateful to him and since he was often in disagreement with the King it could be good to have an ally in the Queen.

'So the marriage plans hang fire,' said Richard when he and his brother were alone together.

'These matters always do.'

'Not always. I believe the marriage between Eleanor's sister and Louis suffered no such hindrance.'

'It is my opinion that she should receive a reasonable dowry.'

'You ask too much, Henry. The most beautiful girl in the world and her weight in gold!'

The most beautiful girl in the world! That had shaken him. The bride of the King of England *should* be the most beautiful girl in the world, of course—but also she should bring a dowry worthy of her bridegroom.

'I think they will give me what I want,' said Henry.

'My dear brother, you do not know the poverty of Provence.'

'You have always spoken in such glowing terms of the Court there.'

'It is a matter of culture, not extravagance. *You* should understand that, Henry.'

'I do. I respect the Count for his devotion to music and literature. But I cannot believe in this plea of poverty and I think that possibly having three daughters to place in the world he does not want to give the eldest her share but to save it to buy good marriages for the others. I want him to realize that what his daughter is being offered is no ordinary alliance.'

'He will value the alliance for what it is worth. But he is not a worldly man.'

'What do you mean by that?'

'He would consider his daughter's happiness before her advancement. What I mean is, brother, that he would rather see her a happy countess than an unhappy queen.'

'There is no reason why she should not be a happy queen.'

'He might think there is. You see, in these negotiations you have revealed yourself as a somewhat mercenary man. You have the opportunity of marrying this unusual girl and you barter. Messengers go back and forth and there is no satisfaction. Remember I have met this Count. I have seen him in his own home. He will resent this insult to his daughter.'

'But I mean no insult. How could I insult my own Queen!'

'Yet you do, Henry, by weighing up what she will bring to you. Romantic Louis said of her sister: I want her. She will suffice.'

Richard could see that his strategy was working. 'What did the Count say to you in his last message?' he went on.

'That he could not afford what I asked even though I had reduced it.'

'I mean in what manner did he say it? That is important.'

'I will show you his last communication.'

Richard read what the Count had written and nodded slowly.

'I understand well. He is a very proud man. His pride is wounded. He shows here quite clearly that he will soon put an end to this haggling. How go the negotiations with Ponthieu? Methinks if you have not stopped them....'

'You know full well they have stopped.'

'Open them again. Joanna's father may be able to provide the dowry you want.'

'I have no intention of taking Joanna. It is Eleanor I want.'

'Do you, brother? Not enough it seems. Soon people will be saying, "Another of the King's proposed marriages gone astray!"'

'They will say no such thing, because this is not going astray. I shall marry Eleanor of Provence. I am determined on it.'

'But what of the dowry?'

'I have made up my mind. I shall ask for no dowry ... only
Eleanor. I shall summon Hubert and tell him this. I want
Eleanor sent to me without delay.'

Richard smiled.

'You won't regret this,' he said. 'I promise you.'

*   *   *

What excitement at Les Baux when the messengers arrived
from England.

The King was weary of correspondence. He wanted his
bride. As for the dowry that was a matter which need not
delay them. What he was eager for was the wedding.

Sanchia said it was like being on a see-saw. Up one moment,
down the next.

'Nay,' cried Eleanor. 'This time I am going to stay up.'

It seemed she was right. Messengers from England told of
the King's impatience. Just as a short while before he was
insisting on the dowry, now he demanded the immediate departure of his bride.

'We must leave without delay,' said Uncle William Bishop
Elect of Valence; and to the delight of the Count and Countess
he declared his intention of accompanying Eleanor to England.

The Count decided that he and the Countess with their two
daughters should go with Eleanor to Paris which would
give them an opportunity of seeing Marguerite. It was a gay
cavalcade which set out on that autumn day. The sun was still
warm though there was a certain chill in the morning. The
leaves were still thick on the limes and birches but a few of
the fallen ones made a carpet on the grass as a warning that
summer was fading. Eleanor was aware of the lush green
countryside which she might be seeing for the last time, for
although her family assured her that she would come back, the
sea would separate her from her childhood home and the new
country over which she was to reign as Queen.

Surrounded by her family, she felt almost gay although it
would be sad leaving them. Sanchia was ready to burst into
tears at the thought and Beatrice would do the same.

Sanchia said it seemed so much more important than Marguerite's marriage had been, perhaps because of all the fuss
there had been about it.

'Or perhaps we were younger then,' she added sagely.

Eleanor told them that when she was Queen of England she
would insist that they come to stay with her.

'What if the King does not want us?' asked Sanchia.

'I shall tell him it is my wish,' was the reply.

Perhaps she would do even that, thought Sanchia. Eleanor had always been the one to get her way.

As they came to the borders of Champagne they were met by its Count who was notorious throughout France as the Troubadour King. Some said he was the greatest poet of the age.

He offered them lavish hospitality and rode to his castle with them between the Count and Countess of Provence, at the head of their cavalcade.

There was something attractive about Thibaud de Champagne, which was scarcely due to his appearance. He was so fat as to be almost unwieldy. But he had a merry good nature and when he spoke it was said his voice was silver and when he sang it was golden.

Even as he rode along he could not refrain from breaking into song and all listened with admiration.

Moreover the songs he sang were of his own creation; he excelled with both words and music.

He was enchanted by Eleanor. He whispered to her that her husband would love and cherish her. He had read one of the poems she had written and thought she had a fine talent.

'I am a poet and of some merit they tell me. But as you see, my looks do not match the beauty of my words. How different it is with you. You have been doubly endowed, my lady Eleanor, and your husband will love you so dearly that he will not be able to deny your smallest wish.'

Such talk delighted Eleanor; she felt that she was living in a haze of glory.

To Thibaud's castle they went, there to rest awhile and give him an opportunity to entertain them.

This he did in a royal fashion for he was eager for all to remember that he was the great grandson of Louis VII and if his grandmother had been a boy instead of a girl he could have been King of France.

The men-at-arms stationed at the keep made a feint of challenging the party as it arrived, but this of course was merely a formality. Everyone in the castle was ready to receive them for the watch whose task it was to sit at the top of the tower and scan the horizon for the sign of any rider, had long since seen them, recognized his master and knew that he brought with him the Count of Provence and his family who were to be royally entertained.

Spectacles had been arranged for them.

Young Beatrice was wildly excited but Sanchia could not forget the imminent parting with her sister. It was not only that she would miss Eleanor but she would then step into place as the eldest daughter at home and very soon her turn would come to say good-bye to the parental home.

The castle was built after the style familiar to all, the great staircase being one of its most important features, for on it the guests liked to take their fresh air when the weather was warm. At the top of this staircase was a platform which was used by the lord of the castle as a kind of court where he met his vassals and meted out justice when it was required. When the lord of the castle was entertaining he and his guests sat on chairs on this platform to watch the jousting and games which took place at the foot of the staircase; and the steps were used as seats by those who watched the joust.

The family of Provence, of course, had their places of honour on the platform beside the Count of Champagne and many people came from the neighbouring villages to watch the performances but chiefly to see the Princess who had been chosen by the King of England to be his bride.

Inside the castle opening from the top of the staircase was the great hall, and if the nights were chilly a fire would be lighted in the centre and round it the guests would cluster and listen to the minstrels and either watch or take part in the dancing.

The hall was vast—at one end was the dais and on this was the high table which overlooked the low table and it was at this high table that Eleanor and her family sat with the Count of Champagne as his guests of honour.

Each day the stone-flagged floor was strewn with fresh rushes and, again in honour of the guests, sweet-smelling herbs and flowers.

It was a wonderful experience and best of all was the night when darkness fell and the tables on their trestles were removed from the hall, and the Count sang his love songs to them.

He was a romantic figure in spite of his size for many of his songs were of unrequited love; and there was one lady of whom he sang continually. Eleanor wondered who she was.

They stayed for five days and nights at the castle and during that time she found an opportunity of asking him.

It was growing late; the logs burning in the centre of the great hall glowed red; many of the guests were nodding drowsily, sitting on stone seats which here and there formed part of the wall, or on the oak chests which contained some of the Count's treasures but which served as seats on occasions such as this.

Eleanor said to the Count: 'You sing of one lady always do you not? Or perhaps there are several. But you sing always of her fair looks and her purity and remoteness. Is there just one, or do you sing to an ideal?'

'To one and to an ideal,' he answered.

'So she does indeed exist.'

'Yes she does.'

'And she does not love you?'

'She does not love me.'

'Perhaps one day she will.'

'She will never glance my way. She is a great lady. She is far from me ... and always will be.'

'Who is she? Is it a secret?'

He looked at her quizzically. 'You believe that you could lure a man to betray himself, do you not?'

'I had not thought of it,' she denied.

'Ah, you have charm enough, my lady. Look at me. I am not a romantic figure, am I? Do you know what one poet wrote of me? I'll tell you. You see I was sighing for my love, yearning to clasp her in my arms and this is the song that was written:

> "Sir you have done well,
> To gaze on your beloved;
> Your fat and puffy belly
> Would prevent your reaching her." '

Eleanor began to laugh.

'There, you see,' he murmured. 'You, too, mock me.'

'Nay,' she cried. 'That is not so. I think your lady might love you for the words you write of her. You give her immortal life for she will be known for ever through your songs.'

'She is one who does not need my songs for that. She will live through her deeds.'

'So she is a lady of high rank.'

'The highest.'

'You mean the Queen.'

'God help me, yes. The Queen.'

Eleanor blushed scarlet. Marguerite! she thought.

He read her thoughts at once and cried: 'No. No. It is not the young Queen. She is but a child. It is Blanche ... the in-

comparable Blanche ... the White Queen with her gleaming
fair hair and her white skin and her purity.'

'She must be very old. She is the mother of the King of
France.'

'Beauty such as hers is ageless,' murmured the Count.

Then he strummed on his lute and once again began to
sing softly of his lady.

* * *

Eager as she was for her marriage, Eleanor was sorry to leave
Champagne. Thibaud insisted on joining the party and accompanying it to the French frontier. So with much pomp
and extravagance they set out. The people from the villages
came out of their cottages to gape at the magnificence which
they would remember ever after. In due course they were at
the French frontier and there Thibaud took his leave of them.

Eleanor regretted his going but the excitement of meeting
her sister made her soon forget him. For there was Marguerite
—changed since her childhood in Provence, the Queen of
France and beside her King Louis.

The Count and Countess were overcome with emotion at
the sight of their beautiful daughter and her husband. They
were indeed a handsome pair. Marguerite, no longer the very
young girl who had left her home, had grown into a queen.
There was an air of regality about her which deeply touched
her parents and made them very proud.

Eleanor noticed it and rejoiced that life was giving her a
role as exalted as her sister's.

As all must be she was deeply impressed by Louis and could
not help wondering if Henry would be like him. He towered
above his companions and as he was also very slender he appeared to be even taller than he actually was. His very fair
hair made him conspicuous; and although he did not dress as
magnificently as Thibaud had done, he yet seemed to be every
inch the King.

The Count thanked him for all the happiness he had given
his daughter to which Louis replied in most gracious terms
that his thanks were due to the Count for having given him
Marguerite.

It was thrilling to ride alone with the King and Queen of
France—the golden lilies carried before them.

Louis quickly realized that Eleanor had a bright alert mind
as her sister had, and he enjoyed talking to her. He talked
about England, admitting that he had never been there, but

his father had, and he had on one or two occasions talked to him of that country.

'So often,' said Louis, 'our countries have been at war, but with two sisters as their Queens that should make us friends.'

Eleanor said she could never be an enemy of her dear brother and sister, to which Louis answered gravely: 'We will remember it.'

Eleanor was inclined to think that Louis was rather solemn. She intended to find out whether Marguerite thought this and if she would have preferred someone more fond of the gaiety of life.

On their way to Paris they were entertained in a similar manner to that they had enjoyed with the Count of Champagne. Marguerite hinted that she was a little tired of all the jousting and tilting which was put before them. Eleanor, however, had had less of it and as it was done in honour of her, it had a special appeal.

As they approached the capital they were met by a cavalcade at the head of which rode the Queen Mother of France. This, thought Eleanor, was the heroine of all those songs the fat troubadour had sung.

She was indeed beautiful—like an exquisitely carved statue, Eleanor thought her. Her features were perfectly chiselled; she looked too young and slender to be the mother of the King —and several others also. Her hair, which Eleanor later discovered was abundant and very fair, was hidden by her silken wimple. It was clear that she was a very forceful woman and owing to the devotion she had inspired in Thibaud, Eleanor was particularly interested in her. Then she realized that her coming brought about a subtle change in the manners of the young King and Queen. Louis paid a great deal of attention to his mother—which she clearly demanded—and less to his Queen.

Eleanor thought indignantly: If I were in Marguerite's place, I would never allow that.

Everyone deferred to the Queen Mother. The ice-blue eyes surveyed Eleanor with approval. She was glad that her daughter-in-law's sister was going to marry the King of England because, as Marguerite had mentioned, in France it was considered the marriages of the two sisters would be helpful in maintaining peace between the two countries.

So they rode into Paris where they admired the improvements which had been set in motion by the young King's grandfather Philip Augustus. It no longer deserved the epithet 'Mud Town' which the Romans had bestowed on it, for Philip Augustus had supplied it with hard, solid stone which was washed by the rain and, if that failed, by the people who were proud of their city.

They admired Les Halles, the shut-in market place which he had built, the great Cathedral of Notre Dame and the improvements to the old palace of the Louvre.

And so they came to Paris on the last stage of their journey through France. There they would rest awhile before continuing their journey to the coast.

* * *

Marguerite was anxious to be as much with her family as possible and she prevailed on them to spend a few days with her at Pontoise which, she confessed to Eleanor, she and Louis liked better than any other of their residences.

So the party set out, taking with them the necessary furnishings including tapestries to hang on the walls, for most of the royal castles were almost empty when not inhabited. Serving men and women went on ahead to prepare for their comfort.

The King did not accompany them. His mother had said that it was necessary for him to stay in Paris.

'I am sure Marguerite would enjoy having her sister to herself,' she said.

Eleanor had quickly realized that when the Queen Mother made such statements, they were meant to be a command. It was disconcerting to see the ability she had for cowing Marguerite, and it was clear to Eleanor then that her sister's marriage was not quite the ideal alliance she had been led to believe.

Of course Marguerite was Queen of France and wherever she went she was treated with great respect; homage was paid to her every moment of the day. Louis quite obviously loved her. But he obeyed his mother and if that meant being parted from his wife he accepted it.

In the castle of Pontoise, Eleanor had an opportunity of talking to her sister about her marriage and gradually it seemed she gained the ascendancy which had been hers in Les Baux in spite of Marguerite's status.

She wanted to hear about the wedding and the coronation ceremonies, what Louis expected of her and whether she was truly happier than she had been in her parents' home.

Marguerite was reticent about what happened in the bedchamber. That, she said, with a certain smugness which irritated Eleanor, was what she would have to find out, and what she would accept because it was her duty to do so. Louis it seemed was a paragon of virtue. She could not ask for a kinder, more loving husband, if only....

There. She had betrayed herself. It only what? Eleanor wanted to know.

'If only we could be alone more often. *She* is always there.'

'You mean Queen Blanche?'

'Of course she is his mother, and he thinks that she is wonderful. You see he was only twelve when his father died and she made a King of him, he says. He always listens to her. I know she is very clever and it is right that he should do so. But she tries to separate us. Sometimes I think that she is jealous of me.'

'Of course she is. She wants her beautiful son all to herself. Thank Heaven Henry has not a mother living at the Court.'

'She is far away and from what I hear she leads her new husband a dance. Yes, you should be thankful, Eleanor, that Isabella of Angoulême will not be living at your Court. Though it would please us mightily if she decided to leave Lusignan for England.'

'We shall see that she remains in Lusignan. I would not endure what you do, Marguerite. If I were you and sure that Louis loved me, I would say it was time for his mother to retire into the background.'

'You would not,' said Marguerite, 'if your mother-in-law was Queen Blanche.'

'So your Louis is afraid of her.'

'No, no. But he is so kind, he would never hurt her. He listens to her but if he does not agree with her he goes his own way. He is greatly respected, Eleanor. He is so eager to govern well. He will be a better king than even Philip Augustus. He cares about the people. He gives much to the poor. Sometimes, after Mass, he goes into the woods and there sits on the grass and asks any, however humble, to talk to him and tell him what they think. He listens to what they have to say. He wants to hear if they consider there are injustices in France. I have seen him do this even in Paris in the gardens of our palace there. He does not greatly care about his dress. I have often seen him in a coat of that stuff I hate ... half wool, half cotton. They call it tyretaine. He goes hatless, too. He says that he wanted to make the people see him as a man ... not a king.'

'That is not the way to win the people's respect.'

'He thinks it is and they do respect him. What do you think he said to me when I complained that he did not look like a king?'

'He said he would dress richly to please you, I doubt not.'

'He said something of the sort ... but with a difference. Everything Louis does is not what is expected. "To please you, Marguerite," he said, "I will dress in extravagant garments. But if I dress to please you you must dress to please me. That means that you will wear simple garments and give up your splendour.'

'And that I see you declined to do.'

'"Tis clear is it not?'

'At least he does not command you to cast off your silks and jewels.'

'Louis would never command that. He likes people to have freedom. I tell you, Eleanor, there is no man like him in the whole world. France is fortunate to be ruled by such a King.'

'Who is ruled by his mother.'

'That is not true. But she is clever ... and she would be beside him.'

'In your place?'

Marguerite was silent.

'When I reach England,' said Eleanor, 'I shall govern with my husband.'

'If he will allow you to do so.'

'I shall make sure that he does,' vowed Eleanor.

Marguerite looked at her steadily. Knowing Eleanor she believed that she would.

The Queen of England

THE crossing was stormy but Eleanor discovered with relief that she was not a bad sailor. It would have been undignified to have arrived in her new country wracked by the seasickness which had affected some of the company. Her uncle was beside her as they stood on the deck watching as the ship approached England. The cliffs rose white and stark out of that frothy grey sea and there could not have been a land more different from Provence. Uncle William put his hand over hers as though to reassure her, but she did not need his comfort. She was excited. Grey seas and cool winds were unimportant. So long she had wanted this marriage; ever since Marguerite had left them to be the bride of the King of France she had wanted the crown of England as the only one to compare with that of Marguerite, and having seen Marguerite, dominated by her mother-in-law, she no longer envied her. That was why she could stand beside her uncle at the approach to England with the utmost confidence in her future.

Now they had come so close to land that she could see the bold grey towers of that castle perched high on the hill, menacing, formidable, defiant. It had been graphically called the Key to England, and she thought the name apt. That key was being given to her; and she would employ soft words and subtle manners until this land was hers to command. Everything depended on her husband, and she would shortly discover what manner of man he was and whether her task would be easy.

'You are on the threshold of a new life, my child,' said Uncle

William. 'So much will depend on you. I trust you realize what this means.'

'I do,' replied Eleanor.

'You will have me to guide you.'

She nodded.

'I shall do that whatever the opposition,' he went on.

'You expect opposition?'

'There is always opposition in Courts. So much depends on the King.'

Now the castle was taking on definite shape. The great keep which had been built by the bridegroom's grandfather dominating the great pile of stones. It was impossible not to be impressed by all that magnificence of Kentish rag mingled with that Caen stone which had been brought from Normandy by the same Henry II. As she gazed at those great buttresses rising into turrets, Eleanor could not help but be moved, for they symbolized the might of England.

They had arrived.

* * *

Henry had decided that he would greet his bride at Canterbury where the Archbishop would be waiting to perform the marriage ceremony. He was beside himself with excitement at the prospect of at last having her with him. So much had gone wrong with his previous attempts that he had begun to believe fate had decided against his marrying; but on this occasion his bride was actually in England and in a short time would be with him.

Everyone was delighted. It had been a source of some dismay that he having reached the age of twenty-eight should not have married so far. He should have had a nursery full of sons by now. Never mind. It was going to happen at last. His bride was very young, only fourteen years of age; but that was not too young for a royal bride. It was a great pleasure—and a change to do something that gratified both himself and the people at the same time.

Yes, it was indeed true that everyone was delighted that he was to marry. Hubert de Burgh thought it time and that since the eldest daughter of the Count of Provence was the wife of the King of France it was no bad thing that his second daughter should be Queen of England. Even old Edmund, Archbishop of Canterbury, believed that the marriage was necessary for state reasons. As for Henry's brother Richard, he regarded himself as the one who had brought it about (which indeed he had been) so therefore he, seeing himself as a policy maker, was all in favour of it.

There was no dissenting factor in whichever direction he looked and with a light heart Henry set out to greet his bride.

She rode on a white palfrey and her hair fell about her shoulders; on her head was a diadem to proclaim her royalty. She was dressed in blue with touches of gold thread, and her long semi-circular cloak was fastened by jewelled buckles held together by a golden chain. Henry looked at her and his heart leaped with exultation. Eleanor la Belle was aptly named.

He thought: She is indeed the most beautiful girl in the world—and she is my Queen.

In that moment he knew that well worth while were the long wait, the disappointments and frustrations during that time when he had thought that Fate had decided he should never have a bride.

He took her hands in his and kissed them.

'Welcome,' he said. 'My heart swells with delight at the sight of you.'

No words could have made her happier or more sure of herself.

She said: 'I am happy to come.'

She studied her husband-to-be. He was not tall, but neither was he short. He did not look in the least delicate; in fact he was more robust than his brother Richard and bore some resemblance to him. She noticed that distinguishing feature which she had never seen in any other: his eyelid falling over one eye so as to conceal the pupil might have given him a look which could have been sinister if he were angry. But at this time, when it was clear that he was filled with delight, it was merely interesting. By her standards he was quite old; this did not displease her, because his maturity but called attention to her charming youth.

Riding between the King and Uncle William she rode into Canterbury. It was one of those occasions when it seemed to be the most delightful prospect in the world to be a King and Queen. In the streets banners fluttered; the people had gathered everywhere to see them pass. They called loyal greetings; they smiled and cheered.

Eleanor could not quite understand them but Henry told her: 'They are amazed by your beauty.'

Richard was there to greet her warmly as an old friend.

'What a good day for England when you decided to write a poem about my country,' he whispered.

'You think that but for that it would never have happened?'

'I am sure of it,' he answered, determined that she should remember and be grateful to him.

He looked at her longingly. How enchanting with the dew of youth on her; with that perfection of feature and those serene eyes where intelligence was as clear to see as all their beauty.

Richard was envious. This fair young girl for Henry and for him an ageing wife. He did not grow to love his Isabella more as the years passed; and the Pope would not allow him to put her from him. Life was unfair. He reminded himself that he had his adorable son, Henry after his royal uncle, and Isabella was his mother. Yes, he had Henry, but that did not prevent his grudging Henry this lovely girl.

The King was much aware of his envy; it delighted him. As for Eleanor he could not take his eyes from her. He had already given her jewels of such magnificence as she had never seen in Provence and even Marguerite's could not compare with these.

She was going to be happy here. She was ready to love this man with those strange-looking eyes who was already doting on her when so far she had done nothing but look beautiful which was the easiest thing in the world to do.

She had brought several of the women from Provence with her, though her father had warned her that often when brides married into foreign lands their husbands dismissed their attendants and supplied others of his choice.

She would keep hers with her, she promised herself. She was not going to speak English all the time, though she had a fair knowledge of it and because she could pick up languages easily she would quickly learn. Sometimes, though, she would want to speak her native Provençal and recall memories of her childhood with those who had shared them. Perhaps that would be the first battle between her and Henry. She would welcome it because it would give her an insight into how much she would be able to lead him.

The marriage was to take place immediately in Canterbury and the ceremony would be conducted by the Archbishop of Canterbury; afterwards she and her husband would ride to London for the festivities.

In her apartment in the Archbishop's palace her Uncle William came to see her. She could see by the brilliance of his eyes and colour in his face that he was excited.

He took her into his arms and held her against him for

some seconds before he said with emotion: 'I am proud of you.'

'Why, Uncle, what have I done?'

'You have enchanted the King. I see that.'

'Is that not what is to be expected?' she asked.

'It is to be hoped for—and rarely does it happen as it has this day. I can see that he loves you already. Oh, my child, this is a good day for the House of Savoy.'

'And for England I hope,' said Eleanor.

'Aye, for England. Tomorrow you will be a Queen—and after this ceremony here in the great Cathedral, you will go to Westminster for your crowning. My child. I never thought this could be possible. We rejoiced at Marguerite's good fortune . . . and now you. Two Queens. . . .'

'Romeo de Villeneuve told Father that he would make each of his daughters a queen.'

'Let us be thankful that his prophecy has come true for two of them.'

'Poor Sanchia and Beatrice! I'll warrant they are envying me. My parents will be telling them now of our stay in Champagne and at the Court of France. I can picture it.'

'Let us concern ourselves with your future, my dear.'

'That is a matter in which I have great interest.'

'I believe the King will be guided by you . . . if you are clever.'

'I am clever, Uncle. It is my cleverness which brought me here.'

'Oh, I know the story of the poem, and I know well your skill with words and music. But I was thinking of other skills. We have yet to discover whether you possess those.'

'If I do not now, I soon will, Uncle.'

'Like the King, I rejoice in you. Moreover I have taken a liking to this land, Eleanor.'

'That pleases me since it is to be mine.'

'You realize, do you not, that your husband can play a very big part in the history of Europe. I want it to be a part which brings good to England . . . to Provence and to Savoy. For that reason I should like to be here to guide you . . . both.'

'You mean you do not wish to go home.'

He looked at her steadily. 'I want to stay here, Eleanor. You will need me. I want to look after you. You are a clever girl. Oh, I know that well, but you are so young and cleverness is often no good substitute for experience. No more of this now. It may be that you will have some influence with your husband, and if you do. . . .'

'I have formed the opinion that my husband will wish to please me,' she said.

William Bishop Elect of Valence smiled. He felt that was enough for the moment.

* * *

On the evening before her wedding Eleanor had sat beside Henry at table in the palace and he had talked to her of his country and his interests and they were delighted to find hers were similar. He was a great admirer of the poets and he told her that he had read again and again the magnificent epic she had written and sent to his brother of Cornwall. He would never forget that it had, in some measure, brought her to him.

He could not take his eyes from her. He told her that he had not lived until he saw her, that he rejoiced that he had waited for marriage until now—although he had been tempted to undertake it before. The fates had saved him for this, because he had known as soon as he had set eyes on Eleanor, no one else would suit him.

All this was intoxicating, as was the admiration of his courtiers, and her contentment added to her beauty. She could talk freely with Henry for he spoke her native Provençal. Then she tried her English which he declared was enchanting and he wanted to issue a law that all the English should speak their tongue as she did.

There was only one who was not susceptible to her charm and that was the old Archbishop of Canterbury. Much did she care. Poor old man. He was supposed to be a saint and all knew how dull they were. It was said that he ordered monks to beat him with horsehair thongs; that knotted rope cloth was tied about his body where best it could torment it; that he never went to bed but spent nights sitting in meditation or on his knees.

A most uncomfortable man and one she hoped she would see little of.

But he was the Archbishop of Canterbury and it was he who married them in the great Cathedral—Henry told her that this most impressive edifice and Westminster Abbey were the first two churches to be built by the Normans in England. How solemn was the ceremony. Eleanor was deeply conscious of her uncle William and remembering what he had said to her, was overwhelmed by the importance of what was happening and when they went to the palace for the wedding banquet she was somewhat grave. So was Henry, but none the less loving.

She sat beside him and he fed her the best pieces of the food which had been put on his platter. He was very tender and assured her that his greatest wish was that she should be happy.

She told him that as soon as she had heard he had chosen her for his bride she had felt exalted, and then a little fearful that she might not please him. Now that he had shown her that she did, she could experience only happiness.

The next day they were to leave for London where the real celebrations would begin.

'The people of London are jealous of their privileges,' he explained. 'The marriage of course should take place in Canterbury and be celebrated by our premier churchman. But it is London which will decide whether it is going to love you or not.'

'What do I have to do to make it?' she asked.

'All you need to do, my queen, is to sit on your white horse and smile at them.'

'They are easily pleased,' she replied.

'Nay, they are the most difficult people to please in my country. And woebetide the ruler who does not please them. They have memories as long as their river Thames and no compunction in showing their displeasure.'

'Then I must indeed put forth my best smile. But you are a King and would not allow them to dislike me, I know.'

'I can see you already have a good opinion of your husband.'

And so they talked while his fond eyes never left her.

When they were alone in the chamber prepared for them he was a little uneasy.

He said: 'You are very young. I would not displease you for the world.'

'You please me greatly, my lord,' she answered.

'I fear that your opinion might change.'

'I do not fear,' she answered, 'so why should you?'

'You are but fourteen years of age. It is very young,' he said.

'Princesses are ripe early, my lord. I understand full well. As your wife, the Queen, I am expected to give you an heir to the nation. I am ready.'

'You can know nothing of these matters, child that you are.'

She put up her hands and taking his face in them kissed it.

'When I was very young I read the works of our poets. They always seemed to write of love. Unrequited love; fulfilled love. I observed much, my lord. I know there is even more that I do not know, but you will teach me. That is a husband's duty, is it not? I can only say, Henry, my King and husband, that I am ready.'

Then he held her tightly in his arms and said that he had never dared dream of such delight.

And she knew that from henceforth he would be her slave.

* * *

Side by side they rode to London.

As they passed through the country men, women and children ran from their cottages. The weather was cold for it was January, but wrapped in her cloak lined with vair and edged with miniver Eleanor did not notice this. The frosty air put a pinkness into her cheeks and a sparkle into her eyes. It seemed to Henry that she grew more beautiful every day.

As they approached the city of London the crowds intensified.

'Long live the King! Long live the Queen!' The loyal cries of the people were something she would remember throughout her life, particularly on less happy occasions.

And so they came into the capital city.

Across the streets banners had been fixed; silk hangings fell from the windows. There were gleaming lamps and tapers; everywhere were displayed the two crowns—those of the King and the Queen. Most marvellous of all the citizens, proud of their city, had swept away all the dirt and refuse which usually marred it; many of them had scrubbed the cobbles clean and what was most startling to those who knew it well was the sweet cleanliness everywhere.

All the dignitaries of the City were present and they were determined to impress the new Queen with their splendour. They followed the procession from the City to Westminster where, the King told the Queen, they would act as butlers.

'It is a custom for the leading citizens to do this on a coronation,' he added. 'They are very jealous of their traditions and determined to cling to them.'

'This seems a good one,' said the Queen.

They certainly presented a colourful sight in their silk garments and gold-woven mantles. Their horses had been newly caparisoned and between them they carried three hundred and sixty gold and silver cups; and the King's trumpeters rode before them sounding their trumpets while the people cheered.

And with all the pomp and ceremony of a royal coronation Eleanor of Provence was crowned Queen of England.

* * *

After the ceremony, the feast. Eleanor had never seen such splendour. She wondered whether Marguerite's coronation had been as splendid. She doubted it. Louis would not have cared for so much extravagance—as for Blanche she would have wanted to play the central part and as she could scarcely do that at Marguerite's coronation she would want as little display as possible.

How different was Henry! Henry could not do enough for his Queen. He loved the spectacle because it was for her.

How thrilling it was to walk beside the King, wearing her newly acquired crown while over her head was a silk canopy held up with four silver lances carried by four knights—two on either side of her. Over the King was held a similar canopy, his supported by barons of the Cinque ports.

There she sat beside the King at the high table and on their right were the archbishops, bishops and abbots and on their left the earls and highest nobles of the land.

Eleanor particularly noticed the Seneschal because of his air of distinction. He was a man who would stand out in any company.

'Who is he?' Eleanor asked the King.

'Oh ... the Seneschal. He is Simon de Montfort—an ambitious young man.'

'I have heard his name.'

'It would be doubtless his father of whom you heard. He was Simon de Montfort l'Amaury, Captain General of the French forces in the war against the Albigensians. A man of much military skill and cruelty.'

'And is the son like the father?'

'Nay, but he is a man of good sense, I believe. He will climb through a shrewd mind rather than a sword. There is a battle of sorts going on now between him and Norfolk. This office of Seneschal which he now fulfils he insists belongs to the Earls of Leicester. He, through his grandfather's marriage into the Leicester family, has claimed the title. The Earl of Norfolk declares the office belongs to him.'

'So they have fought over the honour to serve us?'

'That is so.'

'And Simon de Montfort won. That does not surprise me.'

It had occurred to her that he was a man to watch so she would learn all she could of him. At this moment the King was a little restive to see her interest in another man so she dismissed the subject of de Montfort and asked Henry to explain the formalities of the banquet. This he was happy to do.

He told her that Walter de Beauchamp who had laid the salt cellar and the knives would claim them, after the banquet, as his fee. The Lord Mayor, Andrew Benkerel, was officiating in the butlery with the three hundred and sixty gold and silver cups which had been brought so ceremoniously through the streets.

All those who served would take away some item from the table—it might be a gold or silver knife, one of the Seneschal's robes, or the cup from which the King and Queen had drunk ... whatever it was, they fought for what they considered their rights and Eleanor commented that perhaps it was out of the desire for gain rather than loyalty which made them so eager to serve the King.

But it was a merry banquet and the new Queen was very conscious of her uncle's eyes upon her. It delighted her to be so admired. She was not only beautiful but she was wise. Uncle William had suggested that she could do much to help her country—and Savoy in which he was naturally mainly interested.

The future seemed very bright to her. She had wanted to vie with Marguerite. But she had done more than that.

It was true that many would say Louis was the more handsome husband of the two. He was nearer Marguerite's age and Henry was double Eleanor's. Never mind. What cared she? There was no dominating mother-in-law to be grappled with here. It seemed to Eleanor that in England she had a clear field.

After the banquet the tables were cleared away and the company sat about the hall—some on the stone seats cut out of the wall; others on chests which contained some of the King's gold and silver; some sat on stools. The King and Queen were close to the fire in their chairs of state; and the minstrels and jongleurs were brought in to amuse the company while the squires served sweetmeats and hot spiced wine.

On a stool close to the Queen sat the Princess Eleanor, the King's sister, a young woman of about twenty-one, and she was joined by her brother Richard who never lost an opportunity of being near the young Queen.

Richard asked Eleanor what she thought of English hospitality to which she replied that it was the most lavish she had ever encountered.

'A Queen is not crowned every day,' Richard reminded her.

'A mercy,' retorted Eleanor. 'A country needs only one Queen and once she and her husband are crowned there is an end to coronations for many years to come.'

'Amen,' murmured Richard.

The Princess Eleanor looked at her brother with some amusement, the Queen noticed.

She studied Eleanor—her namesake. In nothing else did they resemble each other.

The Queen asked her sister-in-law if she would remain at Court for she believed she had recently come from the country.

The Princess replied that the Queen was right. She had been staying at the house of her sister-in-law. She looked at Richard. The Queen had heard that Richard was married to an ageing wife of whom he was tired. News travelled swiftly round courts and Uncle William had already discovered this. He had said that it was well that she should be kept informed of all matters concerning the country and her new family. It made her feel like a conspirator.

'That must have been pleasant,' said the Queen and there was a question in her voice.

The Princess hesitated. 'The Countess of Cornwall is very sick, my lady. She is often downcast because of this ...' another look at Richard ... 'and other matters.' The Princess was of a rebellious nature. She was clearly fond of the sister-in-law and deplored her brother's attitude; nor did she hesitate to show it. Interesting! thought the Queen. She threw a slightly coquettish glance at Richard for she knew he admired her, and she guessed that he would have delighted to have her as his bride in place of this ageing woman he had married.

The Princess Eleanor went on: 'But she has a most beautiful boy. That's true is it not, brother?'

Now there was animation in his face. He doted on the boy at least. 'He is a fine little fellow,' said Richard. 'Advanced for his age. Is that not so, sister?'

'I thank God for him for Isabella's sake,' said Eleanor, and that was a reproach again.

That the Princess Eleanor was an outspoken and forthright young woman was becoming clear and being about seven years older than the Queen she was inclined to regard her as a child.

No matter, thought the Queen. As yet that would be well enough. She glanced about the room and saw coming towards the royal party, the Seneschal of the banquet, the man who had been pointed out to her as Simon de Montfort.

He made his obeisance to the King first, then to the Queen.

Henry said: 'Have you settled your differences with Norfolk, Simon?'

'My lord, I had right on my side. He could not dispute that.'

'I knew you would be the victor, Simon,' said the King.

Clearly, thought Eleanor, her husband had a feeling of friendship for this man.

Richard, who had noticeably been a little depressed by his sister's reference to his marriage, began to talk to Simon de Montfort and as the King turned to one of the barons on his right—the Queen and Princess Eleanor with Simon and Richard formed a small group.

They talked of the banquet and the richness of it and how the various servers would demand their reward in the gifts they would carry off from the King's table. Richard had seated himself at the Queen's feet and discussed with her the crusade on which he intended soon to embark. Simon was talking to the Princess.

Richard asked if the Queen had heard from Provence and said he would never forget sitting in the great hall there and listening to the minstrels and the content he had found in the home of the Count and Countess, and their three beautiful daughters.

'Each one worthy to be a Queen,' he said. 'The Queen of France ... the Queen of England.... What awaits the lovely Sanchia, think you, my lady?'

'I can only hope that she is as fortunate as her two elder sisters.'

'The Queen of France ... do you think she is as content with her lot as the Queen of England with hers?'

'I do not think that would be possible. Besides, she has a very domineering mother-in-law. I fortunately have escaped that.'

'By the skin of your teeth. It would have been a different story if my mother had not decided to marry out of the country.'

'Ah, but she did. So we need not consider her.'

'She is a woman one would always have to consider while she lived.'

'But at least she is not here to order me ... as Mar ...'

She paused. Uncle William had said that she must be diplomatic and never forget that she was no longer merely a child in a nursery. She was a queen . . . and so was Marguerite.

'Madam,' said Richard smiling into her eyes, 'methinks you would never be one to be so ordered.'

'I think you may be right.'

'You know I am right.'

The Princess Eleanor had undergone a change; her eyes sparkled, her cheeks were flushed and she looked very pretty. Simon de Montfort had had his effect on her.

There is so much to learn, thought the Queen, and although I am clever, I am very young and inexperienced. Fortunately she had Uncle William at hand to help her.

She kept thinking of Richard's words. 'Methinks you would never be one to be so ordered.' Admiration was there, but speculation too. Yes, Uncle William was right. She had a great deal to learn; she must curb the impulse to say what pleased her. She must be watchful of everyone around her.

The coronation and the state banquet had been a revelation and the importance of her position had been brought home to her. It was due to all those fierce-looking barons assembled to do their homage to her and the King; but she knew something of the history of England and it was many of these very barons who had turned against Henry's father, King John, and forced him to sign Magna Carta and then because he failed to keep his word, brought in the French to take the throne.

Uncle William was right. She needed him.

How much did Henry wish to please her? she wondered. In the intimacy of their domestic life it appeared that there was nothing he would not do. But she was wise enough to know that a King's private life and his public one were two very different matters.

During the last few days she had been presented with girls of her own age whose fathers performed some service at the Court and she knew that these girls wished to take service in her household. It was the custom when a royal bride came from a foreign country to send back those attendants whom she had brought with her and to select others from her new country, to make the newcomer realize that she now belonged to her new land.

Every Princess protested at this and of course she would. How could she be expected to say good-bye to old friends and welcome strangers? But it was the custom, and she would be expected to submit to it.

It would be a test. If she succeeded she would know that there would be no difficulty. It would be an indication of whether she was as skilled as she believed herself to be.

They were at last alone and in their chamber.

He turned to her and taking her hands drew her towards him.

'Well, little bride,' he said, 'what think you of your King and his country?'

'I think I am the luckiest Princess in the world.'

'Then I am happy.'

'I have a King,' she said, 'who shows his love for me by his indulgence. What more could I ask than that?'

'You are right, my little love. There is nothing I would not give you.'

Now was the moment. Her heart was beating fast. Dare she? Was it too soon? Perhaps she should have asked Uncle William first.

'You must not make rash promises, Henry, which you might not be able to keep.'

'I ... not be able to keep my promises! Why, my dearest, have you forgotten that I am the King?'

She understood him. He was very anxious that everyone should remember that. He was one to assert his royalty which must mean that within him he sensed some weakness. Henry was no fool. He was clever, but sometimes such cleverness as his was a hindrance rather than a help. In his heart he would know of his inadequacies and would do his best to hide them or deceive people into believing they did not exist. Hence his desire that all should recognize his royalty; hence his sudden quick temper when he thought himself slighted, his affability when he thought he needed a man's friendship.

'No, I do not forget,' she answered. 'But your barons are formidable men.'

'Did you think so?'

'Yes, I did.'

'Were any disrespectful to you?'

'None. They accept me as their Queen, I know well. I shall be happy here when I am used to it. I am thankful that I have some friends about me.'

'They will soon be longing for the blue skies of Provence.'

'They would never wish to leave me ... *never.*'

'My dearest!'

She put her arms about his neck. 'Henry, will you do one thing for me?'

'Anything ... but do not make it little.'

'Perhaps it is not little. My women are a little afraid, Henry. They have heard rumours.'

'Rumours? What rumours?'

'That they may be sent away.'

'Oh ... in due course. When they go you shall select those you would like to replace them.'

'Yes ... that is what they feared. I reassured them, Henry. I told them that you were so good and kind to me, and that was why I loved you so dearly. I said you would never make me unhappy by sending them away.'

Silence. Her head against his chest so that she could not see his face. She waited with trepidation. This was more than sending away a few attendants.

At last he spoke, stroking her hair as he did so.

'My dearest, it is the custom you know. The people do not like foreigners at Court. Oh, I know they are not foreigners to us, but they consider them so.'

'You mean ... you would send them away!'

She broke free from his arms and sat down on the bed, and covered her face with her hands.

He was beside her, his arm about her.

'Eleanor, understand this....'

'No,' she said. 'There is no need to say more. I was wrong. It is not as I thought. I must tell them that I was mistaken....'

'Mistaken? What do you mean?'

'I told them that I could never be really happy if they went and that when I told you, you would let them stay.'

'Oh, my dearest child....'

Henry's expression was wretched. He could hear Hubert's voice. 'It is time the foreigners left. The people do not like to see them in the country. There are many who look for the posts....'

But *she* wanted it. It was necessary to her happiness.

'Come,' said Henry, 'it is a matter which we need not decide yet.'

She shook her head. 'You cannot deceive me, Henry, I know. It is already decided. I will have to tell them tomorrow that I have spoken to you ... and you are against us.'

'No ... no ... you do not understand.'

'Alas, I do.'

She stood up sadly. He was beside her.

'Eleanor, you want this very much, do you?'

'I want it more than anything. It was all so wonderful ... to be here with you ... happy ... your Queen. Well, now it is not so.... That is all.'

'Nay,' cried Henry, 'they shall stay. I promise you. My love, you shall keep them as long as you wish.'

Her face was illumined with joy as she flung her arms about his neck.

'Careful,' said Henry. 'Would you strangle the King of England?'

'Nay. I would comfort him, cherish him and love him for ever.'

It was the first victory for the Queen of England.

Married Bliss

When Eleanor told her Uncle William that the King had promised her she should keep her Provençal attendants as long as she wished to, he was amazed and delighted.

'You surprise me,' he cried. 'This is unheard of.'

She laughed at him. 'Henry is anxious to please me. He says there is nothing he can deny me.'

'My dear child, you have great power in your hands. We must make sure that you use it in a proper manner.'

'Have I not done so?'

'Perfectly. Perfectly. There will be a great test ... soon.'

'Yes, Uncle?'

'I wish to stay here. You need me. There is much good we can do ... to Provence and Savoy. Our family are going to bless you, Eleanor.'

'I shall do everything I can.'

'Imagine their pride in you at your father's Court. I believe this could mean the end of poverty for him. I am sure Henry would be eager to help him. Look how he gave up the dowry he was asking for. He does not regret it, I know. There are so many of us there who could do well in England. Your Uncle Boniface might come. Who knows.... Here there are innumerable opportunities for those who know how to take them. We must take them, Eleanor.'

'Naturally I wish to do everything I can to help.'

'You have not done badly so far, dear child. But it is a

beginning. If I could stay here ... perhaps there would be some appointment ... some high office in the Church.'

'That would be wonderful, Uncle.'

'Well, let us see what we can do. Do not mention my staying here just yet to Henry. There will be opposition, you can depend upon that. But you and I together will overcome that. Do you not agree?'

She was flushed with success. It had been so easy to get Henry to agree to her attendants' remaining. Of course a high post for her uncle would be a more delicate matter ... but it was a challenge she would enjoy.

It was amusing, exhilarating and gratifying to show everyone what influence she already had over her husband and it would be her aim to gain more and more.

*   *   *

When Henry saw her delight in the company of her uncle he determined to share it. He was so happy in his marriage that he wanted everyone to know how he appreciated his Queen. Not only was she very beautiful but her love of literature, her ability to write, to sing and understand music accorded so well with his own nature that he assured himself that he had found the perfect wife.

Like him, she wanted children and he was certain that before long such a union as theirs would be fruitful. In those first months he was in a state of such euphoria regarding his marriage that he was completely happy. He wanted to give her everything she asked.

Eleanor, basking in the approval of her husband and the uncle whom she had been brought up to respect, was very pleased with her lot; and when she thought how it had been brought about by the cleverness of Romeo de Villeneuve—and herself of course—she never failed to marvel. There were frequent communications with her family and Romeo wrote to her too. She and Uncle William read these despatches and what she wanted more than anything was to bring good to her family which meant not only Provence but Savoy, the home of her ambitious uncles.

Between the doting of her husband and her uncle Eleanor felt herself to be a very cherished person indeed. It often happened that when Eleanor and Henry were alone together Uncle William would join them. Then they would discuss state matters, so close to Uncle William's heart, and he would put forth his point of view to which Henry listened with something like reverence.

Within a few months of her arrival in England friends began to come from Provence and Savoy. Eleanor was so delighted to receive them that Henry had to be too; and when she suggested that they should be given posts, how could he disappoint her by refusing?

It seemed at that time that there was only one shadow on their happiness: Eleanor's inability to become pregnant.

Henry soothed her. 'You are but a child my love,' he told her. 'We are apt to forget your youth because of your wisdom, but it is true. Don't fret. We shall succeed in time. Then I'll swear you will have the finest sons and daughters. They must be so ... if they resemble you.'

Such devotion seemed somewhat fatuous to the Court. Some sought to take advantage of it and one of these was Simon de Montfort, Earl of Leicester. Simon had decided to try his fortunes in England which, because of the lands which his father had held, and which the King had allowed him to retain, and because of the title of Earl of Leicester which had come to him, he felt might be more profitable than France. Twice he had sought advantageous marriages—and both with wealthy middle-aged widows, the Countesses of Boulogne and Flanders. On both occasions the King of France had frustrated his hopes. So it was understandable that he had turned his back on France. Henry had been kind to him; under the influence of the Queen Henry was becoming more and more inclined to smile on foreigners, especially those who could ingratiate themselves with the Queen. Simon was considered a foreigner by those Englishmen who were eager not to have strangers poaching on their land. Recently he had started to have very high hopes. His rather prominent dark eyes glistened at the thought. Of course it would be frowned on. It would not be easy; but the King's sister Eleanor was a very determined young woman and once she had made up her mind it would be hard to divert her. It was a wild dream perhaps ... but who could say that it might not come true. In the meantime he must join William de Valence and show that he would be a good supporter—because if he were to advance it would more likely be through the foreign influence than that of the English.

William de Valence had already a following in the country but his ambitions were growing rather too big for him to control. It was not possible for this state of affairs to pass unnoticed. There were whispers. 'What is happening at Court?' 'Is it true that there are secret meetings between William de Valence and his friends?' 'Can it be that these foreigners are trying to rule our country? This is due to the Queen. The foreigners came with her. The King receives them to please her and they are making a puppet of him.'

When the Queen rode out in the streets sullen looks came her way. Someone daringly shouted at her: 'Go home. We don't want foreigners here.'

It was shattering to her. She had believed that everyone must be charmed by her good looks.

The King had not been with her when it had happened and she had gone at once to him, almost in tears.

He had soothed her. 'It must have been a madman,' he said. 'People of good sense must love you.'

'It was not only what was shouted. It was the way they looked at me . . . as though they hated me.'

'Oh, the people are fickle. Hosanna one day . . . crucify Him the next.'

'I don't want them to crucify me. I want them to love me.'

'I shall command them to,' declared the uxorious husband.

But it was not as easy as that.

Richard called on his brother. He said that he wished to speak to him entirely alone.

'You do not realize it, Henry,' he said, 'but there is growing unrest throughout the country. I have had it from several of the barons. They don't like what's happening.'

'I fail to understand,' said Henry coldly.

'That is why those who wish you well must enlighten you. If you do not stop this pampering of foreigners the barons will be in revolt. It will be our father's troubles all over again.'

'I will not have it.'

'Alas, it is a matter in which one has no choice. The barons are meeting . . . as they have done before. They are talking about Magna Carta and you know what that means. It is even said that William de Valence is gathering together a council of foreigners in secret and that they are your advisers.'

Henry turned pale. It was true that he did discuss matters of state with William and some of those friends of whom he was growing fond. He scarcely saw Hubert de Burgh now, nor the leading earls and barons. He knew that Edmund of Canterbury was displeased with him, and he was always afraid of antagonizing the Church. He could picture Richard's placing himself at the head of his critics; and he knew from what had happened in his father's case that they were capable of desperate acts to get rid of a King who displeased them. And there was Richard—the baron's friend, ready to serve them if they should decide to take the crown from one brother and place it on the head of the other.

He had been rather foolish. He had been so happy with his fair Eleanor; he had welcomed her friends and her relations and they were more interesting to him than many of the English barons. They liked poetry and music; they liked discussion and subtle conversation; and could it really be that while they charmed him with these, they wrung concessions from him which were the cause of dissatisfaction?

Richard said: 'There is much to occupy you, brother, and the English will never be ruled by others than themselves.'

'That was not so when our father was on the throne. Didn't they invite the French to come over and rule them?'

'Henry, let us look the truth in the face. There was never a King such as our father. He committed every known folly. They were determined to be rid of him. But when you came to the throne how long did it take England to rid herself of foreigners?'

'They went willingly.'

'Because they knew they must. The English will not have foreigners on this soil, Henry. If you permit it, they will find some means of ridding themselves of you as they did our father.'

'I wish people would not talk constantly of our father.'

'He is a lesson to any King ... how not to behave. Henry, I stand with you, and I am warning you. Trouble could rise ... quickly. Moreover it is about to rise.'

'Then what must I do?'

'Get rid of William de Valence.'

'But he is the Queen's uncle. She loves him dearly!'

'I hope she loves you more dearly. The price of keeping William de Valence here could well be your crown.'

'You talk rashly, Richard.'

'I talk for your good, brother.' Richard shrugged his shoulders. 'You will not heed me. Very well. I have done my duty. You will see what happens. Within a few weeks....'

'I simply don't believe it.'

'No, I am sure you do not. You haven't noticed the sullen looks of the people ... the murmuring.... And the barons, I warn you, Henry, are making ready.'

Richard turned and was about to leave when Henry called him back.

The brothers looked at each other steadily and Richard said slowly: 'Get rid of William de Valence ... or there will be war as there was with our father ... war between the crown and barons. I have no more to say.'

*　*　*

Henry paced up and down. What could he do? In his heart he knew that Richard was right. He had been aware of the discontent. He had been warned by others. Hubert had hinted but Hubert never said much now. After his persecution he no longer trusted the King. He could imagine what they were saying, what they were doing.

Yet how could he tell Eleanor that her uncle must go? She would weep and entreat and he could not stand out against her tears.

He was saved from this by the appearance of William de Valence himself.

He was alarmed. He had heard rumours. He believed that some of the barons might take him prisoner.

'I should never allow that,' cried Henry.

'No, but they might attempt it all the same.'

'What will you do?'

'I shall go back to Savoy. My dear nephew, do not try to persuade me. I can see this is what I must do.'

'Eleanor will be distressed.'

'Dear child! Come with me to her apartment. I would speak to you both.'

They went to Eleanor who, when she heard of her uncle's decision, threw herself into his arms.

'My dearest child,' said William, 'do not grieve. I can see that I am in danger and no good could be served by my staying here. I will go immediately.... I shall leave with stealth ... disguised perhaps. But I tell you this: ere long I shall be back.'

'Oh, Henry,' cried Eleanor, 'what shall we do without my dearest uncle?'

'We have each other,' replied Henry.

'Ah, my dear children, I rejoice in that. I shall go now ... and come back. Then perhaps Henry will have some office in the Church to give me which would be a good reason for my living here. I am determined to come back. This is but a temporary farewell.'

He embraced them both and with some speed left them for his residence.

In a few days many people were delighted to learn that William de Valence had left the country. They were less pleased when it was revealed that he had taken with him all the treasure he had accumulated since he had come to England.

*   *   *

It was a warning. Neither Eleanor nor Henry talked much of it, but it was in their minds. His leniency with her friends and relations, although it pleased her, had the opposite effect on his people, and she had learned enough to know that they must not be too blatantly offended.

It was therefore comforting to turn to more domestic matters.

Henry confided in her that Eleanor his sister wanted to marry Simon de Montfort. 'I never heard such nonsense,' he said. 'He has a high opinion of himself ... imagining he can marry into the royal family! I am deeply disturbed, my love.'

Eleanor was thoughtful. She tried to put herself in the place of her sister-in-law. It was difficult. The marriage of the sister of the King of England with a mere Earl of Leicester could not be considered a very brilliant one and she could not imagine herself wanting to make it; but suppose she did, well then, undoubtedly she would bring it about and she fancied that the Princess was as strong-minded as she was herself.

'You are thoughtful, my dearest,' said Henry.

'I believe she will marry him whatever you say.'

'She dare not.'

'She is a woman who would dare a great deal. She was married once for state reasons when she was but a child. I have a fancy that now she will marry to please herself and it is only necessary to see them together to realize that Simon de Montfort is her choice.'

'You have a high opinion of my sister.'

'I recognize her nature.'

'She has grown into a determined woman during her widowhood, it is true. So my little Queen noticed that.'

'Yes, your little Queen did and she thinks that it might be interesting for you to agree to the marriage of these two.'

'Eleanor. My dear!'

'Simon de Montfort is a man of strength. You see that at once. Remember how he got the better of Norfolk at the coronation. He is a man, I believe, whom you should have on your side.'

'What are you suggesting? That I should give my consent to this marriage?'

She nodded. 'Something tells me that they will marry even if you do not.'

'But they dare not!'

'I have said she would dare a good deal, and so would he. We have too many enemies. Would it not be well, my lord, to have them on our side?'

'My love, there would be great opposition to a marriage like that. De Montfort is disliked for being a foreigner. The English are an insular race. They think there is something divine in being born an Englishman. If a man they called a foreigner was married to my sister there would be trouble, I do assure you.'

'And there will be trouble if they do not marry.'

'You see,' said Henry fondly, 'there are many trials in being a King.'

She put her arms about his neck. 'But you will always over-come them, Henry . . . with me to help you.'

He kissed her fondly. How he dotes on me! she thought. It had been every bit as easy as she had always believed it to be to charm him, to rule him. He was a man who had been deprived of affection, and a little display of it moved him deeply, particularly from her.

'I have a plan, Henry,' she said. 'Send for your sister and tell her she may marry.'

'There would be some angry barons in England if I did. I do not think my brother Richard would be very pleased for one.'

'You are the King. Let it be secret. Then Simon de Montfort will be your friend for ever more.'

'What a wise little creature you are.'

'You are teasing me.'

'Nay. I mean it.'

'Then show it by taking my advice on this.'

'By the saints, I will.'

'I know they will be on your side for ever if you do, and I fancy Simon de Montfort will be a man to reckon with.'

He slipped his arm through hers and they walked to the window and stood there together. 'Can you guess,' he asked, 'what it means to me to have you beside me? Never was a king so contented in his marriage as this one.'

'There is one thing we lack ... a son.'

'He will make his appearance ... in time. You will see.'

'I trust so,' she answered fervently.

*   *   *

It was a cold January day when Simon de Montfort was married to the King's sister in the royal chapel at Westminster, and, although the ceremony took place with the utmost secrecy, Henry himself gave the bride away. As soon as it was over his misgivings were great. The bride and groom however were delighted and as the Queen had prophesied showered him with thanks and protestations of loyalty.

When Henry and the Queen were alone she took his hands and kissed them. Had it not been wonderful to see the happiness of those two? How could they who were so happy themselves fail to delight in it? The Princess Eleanor and Simon her husband would thank them for ever.

'Unless,' said Henry, 'they come to regret the marriage.'

'People in love as they are do not regret their marriages,' replied the Queen sternly.

She enchanted him. He had never believed married bliss could be like this. He often thought of poor Richard tied to his ageing wife whom he visited as infrequently as he could. Since this enchanting little Queen of his had come to England he had ceased to envy Richard. As for Richard he not only coveted his brother's crown but his wife as well.

It was a very satisfactory state of affairs, thought Henry. So did his Queen, for it was becoming more and more clear that she had only to ask for what she wanted and the King could not resist giving it to her.

*   *   *

Two months after the secret marriage the Queen was seated in the solarium surrounded by some of her Provençal attendants when a serving man came to her to announce that there was a visitor to see her.

'Who is it?' she demanded.

'He asked that no name should be given, my lady.'

The Queen was puzzled.

'Where is he?'

'He waits in the guardroom, my lady. He said to tell you first before the King.'

'Where is the King?'

'He is in the state chamber with the Earl of Cornwall and the Earl of Chester, my lady.'

Eleanor nodded and said she would go at once to solve the mystery.

In the guardroom a cloaked figure came towards her and took her into his arms.

'Uncle ... William!' she cried.

'Yes, you see me returned.'

'It is wonderful to see you. When did you arrive?'

'But a day or so ago. I came straight here.'

'Without warning. We should have known.'

'I thought I would test the climate first. Remember I was all but driven away.'

'The barons are stupid ... jealous ... always afraid that someone who in any case is cleverer than they are, will take something from them. This time, dearest uncle, you must not go away.'

'Perhaps it was well that I went when I did,' said the Bishop Elect of Valence; and he smiled secretly. It had been a profitable retreat. He had now in safe keeping all the treasure he had taken with him; and if he could garner so much in one short year, it showed what a treasure there was in this land waiting to be taken.

'Now you are here, dear uncle, you will see that there is no lack of welcome from me or from Henry.'

'You think Henry will be pleased to see me?'

'If I am, he will be.'

'Oh, so it is still thus, is it?'

'It is thus now and shall always be so.'

'My clever little niece!'

'I hope, dear Uncle, that you will not be forced to run away again.'

'I shall do my best to consolidate my postition and the best way of achieving that is for me to have some high post in the kingdom ... the Church of course since I am trained for it.'

Eleanor was silent. She knew that she could persuade Henry, but her uncle had been forced to fly the country because of the animosity of the barons.

'I will explain why I have returned now. I have heard that Peter des Roches, the Bishop of Winchester, since his return to England has become so enfeebled that he is not expected to live much longer. The See will soon be vacant. I want Henry to be persuaded to give it to me.'

'The See of Winchester! It is one of the most important in the country. Why it vies with Canterbury.'

'I know, my dear. That is why I want it.'

'You are asking a great deal, Uncle.'

'But I have the utmost confidence in your help. I know you will get it for me. You see, my dear, your marriage has been so good for us at home, as you know. There is no reason why it should not be better still. When I have the See of Winchester your Uncle Thomas must come over. I am sure we could do something for him, eh?'

'We will,' said Eleanor firmly. It was most gratifying to be considered of such importance.

Henry was delighted that William de Valence had returned to England.

'The fact that I do not want to blazon your presence throughout the country does not mean that you are not welcome,' he told him. 'I should be most distressed if you were shown that inhospitality once more from which you suffered such a short time ago.'

Uncle William said he had the best niece and nephew in the world and he was sure that the unkindness shown to him had hurt them more than it had hurt him.

He did realize the wisdom of keeping his return as quiet as possible and it was not until the month of June when Peter des Roches died, that he emerged from hiding.

Then Henry, prompted by Eleanor, announced that he had the very man to take over the See of Winchester. A man of wide experience, of saintly habits, and one who had the good of the Church at heart; his wife's uncle William de Valence.

The response was immediate.

Richard came to see him. 'Henry, do you know what people are saying? Do you want a return of the old days?'

'I beg of you,' said Henry coldly, 'do not once more remind me of Magna Carta. I know it exists and I know I have to keep a wary eye on the barons. But I am *not* our father. We have left those evil times behind us. I am a King who will rule.'

'I tell you this,' cried Richard angrily, 'if you continue to favour these foreigners you will find your subjects rising in protest all over the country.'

'Please remember that they are my subjects ... and so are you.'

Richard bowed his head. He was beginning to wonder whether the royal marriage was as beneficial as he had thought it would be. True Eleanor was a lovely girl, but she was exercising too much power over the King and her family was becoming a nuisance. The fact was, she was too strong-minded and the King was too besotted. Trust Henry to become uxorious to the brink of folly.

Richard said: 'I have heard another rumour which makes me very uneasy. I do not believe it ... and yet there must be some attachment for it to be talked of. It is said that Simon de Montfort is hoping to marry our sister.'

'Well?' said Henry sharply.

'It could not be so, of course....'

'Could it not? Why not?'

'It would be too unseemly.'

'Who says so? You, brother? You do not rule this land. If I agree to a marriage between Simon de Montfort and Eleanor a marriage there should be.'

'You would never be so rash.'

Henry felt a familiar tingling in the back of his neck which he had always had when he was afraid.

He cried suddenly: 'Then let me tell you this, brother. They are married and I gave my consent.'

Richard stared at him in horror. 'You have given your consent and they are married! This will never be forgiven. Who is this man ... this foreigner?'

'He is now our brother-in-law.'

'Henry! You are following in the footsteps of our father.'

'What nonsense!'

'What do you think the barons' reaction will be to this?'

'I know not. Nor do I care. I shall tell them that I am the King and who shall marry whom and who be elected to what See is my affair.'

'Nay, brother, that is something to which they will never agree. You forget Magna Carta.'

'If you mention that again to me....'

'Henry for God's sake don't forget it. A king always has his enemies, and you have yours. There will always be those to say that no son of John could ever rule them well. You know that.'

'I know this,' retorted Henry, 'I am the King and will see that it is remembered.'

Richard looked at him sorrowfully and Henry was so stricken with fear that he said: 'The marriage was necessary.'

'Necessary? To whom was it necessary?'

'To our sister,' he blustered. 'He had seduced her. She could not for that reason have been married to anyone else. I agreed because of the necessity to make an honest woman of her.'

'The scoundrel!'

'Ah, you—the seducer of many—are shocked I see.'

'Our sister is a royal princess.'

'And that intensifies the crime?'

'It does indeed, Henry, you will hear more of this. Think not that it is an end of the matter. There is something else. The people will never accept William de Valence as the Bishop of Winchester.'

'If I bestow the See on him, they will accept it.'

Richard said, 'You will excuse me, brother.'

And with that he turned and left the apartment.

*　　*　　*

Henry was uneasy. Richard's warnings kept ringing in his ears. He despised himself too for the calumny he had uttered about Simon de Montfort. It certainly was not true, but it had seemed a way out, an excuse for acting as he did. It was better than saying: My wife wanted it and I could not refuse her.

Hating himself he began to hate Simon de Montfort. This was a trait of his. He wanted to be good, to do right; but when he was caught he would make excuses for himself no matter how he falsely accused others in doing so; he despised himself and soothed his vanity by hating the people who made him dislike himself.

He tried to forget the unfortunate matter of the See of Winchester, which in spite of his efforts, he feared he might not be able to give to Uncle William, in disliking Simon de Montfort and assuring himself that Simon was in truth the seducer of his sister.

He waited in some trepidation for consequences. They were not long in coming. The barons were loudly expressing their disapproval, and Richard had placed himself at the head of them.

Henry fumed with rage. 'What is he doing now?' he demanded. 'Why does he not go on his pilgrimage?'

The answer was that he had domestic difficulties at this time. His wife was ailing.

'Much he cares for her,' sneered Henry. 'If he stays it is only because he hopes she will die and leave him free to marry elsewhere.'

Then he laughed with pleasure, for he knew that Richard would have liked to marry Henry's Eleanor. He could not, however, have all his own way.

So while the barons were in revolt against what they called the King's folly in allowing the marriage of a foreign outsider to his sister and granting too many favours to his wife's family, Henry doted more and more on his wife, finding great joy in her, and granted her every wish so that the whole world should know how he esteemed her.

The Mad Priest of Woodstock

THE barons were in revolt, and at their head was Richard.
They were implying that the King was not giving his people
the satisfaction they demanded. If we deposed him we might
set his brother Richard on the throne was the theme of their
discourse. There was a real danger of this happening, and
Eleanor was dismayed.

'It could never come to that,' Henry soothed her. 'You do
not know my brother Richard.'

He sent for Simon de Montfort and commanded him to
make his peace with Richard.

'Offer him gifts,' said Henry. 'He will not be able to resist
taking them. He never could.'

And how right he proved to be, for Richard did allow himself to be persuaded that Simon would be his good friend
if only he would stop persecuting him. The marriage had
taken place, had been consummated, and nothing could
change that now. Was it not in the best interests of all to accept
it?

Richard saw this, and characteristically accepted Simon's ex-
planation, along with his gifts, and declared himself his friend.
He then shrugged off the matter of the See of Winchester.
Henry would simply not be allowed to give it to William de
Valence and there was an end of it.

Henry laughed. Was this not typical of his brother? His
enthusiasms had always been short lived. Richard had ever
tired of an enterprise before he had completed it.

The monks would not allow Winchester to pass into Uncle

William's hand. Very well, he would wait. In the meantime he would go to one of his favourite palaces, Woodstock, with his sweet Eleanor. Perhaps there his dearest wish—that he should have a son would be granted.

* * *

Woodstock, this beautiful palace in the heart of Oxford-shire, had always fascinated Henry. It was as though his mighty ancestors had left something of themselves behind in this place, and when he was there a little of their grandeur seemed to fall on him.

The forests surrounding it provided good hunting ground; and there was the deer-fold put there by his great great grand-father Henry I which he had filled with strange beasts from foreign lands. There lived lion, leopard, lynx and what had been a wonder at the time and still was, a porcupine. The deer-fold was protected by a high stone wall to prevent the animals escaping. These animals had given great delight to that wily ancestor of his; and it was comforting to hear that he often indulged in his pleasures, mostly hunting—animals but chiefly women—and in spite of this he had been known as the Lion of Justice because of the good laws he had intro-duced into the country. Then there was his grandfather Henry II whose name was often mentioned in connection with Woodstock. Here he had kept his mistress Rosamund Clifford, about whom many ballads had been made. Henry liked to consider the troubles in the lives of those men who were always held up as an example for him to follow. His grandfather had kept Rosamund in a bower close to the palace which was approached through a maze of trees. That maze was still here; so was the little dwelling known as Rosamund's Bower. Henry II was a notorious lecher. His wife, the forceful Eleanor of Aquitaine, had hated him for it. She had discovered the exis-tence of Rosamund in her bower because she had seen attached to the King's spur the end of a ball of floss silk. She took the ball and holding it loosely she was able to track him through the maze and thus she learned the way to his mistress's abode. When the King left Woodstock she remained behind and Queen Eleanor having discovered the way through the maze visited Rosamund on whom she was determined to be re-venged.

He walked with his own Eleanor through the maze and showed her Rosamund's Bower. How charming it was, yet full of shadows and if the legend was true what terror the beautiful young woman must have suffered within those walls.

Henry shivered as he put his arm around his wife.

'Here my grandfather kept his mistress and here his wife discovered her. According to some her revenge was terrible.'

'She was a very jealous woman doubtless.'

'Indeed she was. She did not love the King herself but resented any other woman doing so.'

'It is understandable that a wife should resent her husband's mistress.'

'Yes, but to take such a revenge as some said she did! I often wonder how true these stories are. One was that the Queen came to her with a dagger and a bowl of poison. "You may take your choice," she said.'

'And which did she choose?'

'It is not known. Indeed I do not think she was ever presented with such an alternative. There is an even more gruesome story of how the Queen stripped her naked, tied her hands and feet and had her beaten until the blood ran; then two toads were set at her breasts to suck her blood; and when she died the Queen had her thrown into a filthy ditch with the toads. This is completely false I am sure.'

'Poor Rosamund, she should never have become the King's mistress.'

'It was said that she truly loved him. Should she not have some mercy for that?'

Eleanor was silent, asking herself what she would do if she discovered she had a rival for the King's affections. Perhaps she would be as ruthless as her namesake.

Henry was still brooding on the love of his great ancestor for the Fair Rosamund.

'One poet says that she was not buried in a ditch but put into a chest and taken to Godstow where the Queen said she should be buried but on the road the cortège was met by the King who demanded to see what was inside the chest and when he was shown fell into a deep swoon. When he recovered he swore vengeance on his wife and sent the body of his mistress to Godstow Nunnery where it might be buried with all honours. The facts are that Rosamund herself decided to go into the nunnery and repent for the life she had led, and there she stayed with the nuns until she died.'

'And that,' said the Queen, 'is the story of another Eleanor and Henry. Remember it, husband. If you take a mistress, be wary of your wife.'

'That could never happen to me. How could I ever look at another woman?'

'I believe you now.' She sighed. 'But perhaps the day will one day come....'

'Never!' he declared. 'But it amuses me. These ancestors of mine are held up as examples and yet are they such heroes?'

'Many men become heroes when they are dead. I should prefer you to stay alive and be a normal man.'

'All my life as King I have heard my grandfather and my great great grandfather spoken of with awe. As for that other ancestor, The Conqueror, they speak his name with a hushed reverence they do not give even to the two Henrys. They imply that I cannot be a great King because I am not like them. Yet my father they hate and abhor and constantly they watch me to see how like him I am growing.'

She laughed at him. 'They are perverse indeed. But what care we, Henry? We are well content with each other. Is that not enough?'

'If I can give you all you want ... yes.'

'I want a son. I fear people will begin to think that I am barren.'

'Nay, you are so young. My mother was several years before she conceived. Then she had five of us.'

'Perhaps here at Woodstock....'

'Let us pray it may be so.'

They walked through the maze and back to the palace. Later they hunted in the forest and when they returned, pleasantly tired from the chase, Eleanor dressed herself in a gown of blue silk edged with miniver and wore her hair in two plaits which hung over either shoulder in a manner which delighted Henry.

In the hall they feasted. The King and Queen seated at the high table with a few of the most exalted of the party and the rest at the great table with the enormous salter in the centre to divide the company into those deserving respect and those who were considered of lesser degree.

The Queen had arranged for some of the minstrels she had kept with her to sing to the company. She liked to do this to show the people who so deplored the foreigners she had brought into the country that their performance was superior to anything the English could do.

It was while the minstrels were singing that the mad priest came into the hall. There was a sudden silence throughout as this man stood there facing them all.

His clerical garments, which were in disarray, proclaimed him as a priest; and his eyes were wild.

In the silence, a voice cried: 'Why 'tis Ribbaud, the priest.'

Henry stood up. 'Who knows this priest?'

The man who had spoken stood up. 'My lord, I know him. He is the mad priest of Woodstock.'

Eleanor had reached for Henry's hand and gripped it tightly for the priest had come to stand before the high table immediately in front of the King.

Henry looked at the tousled hair and the wild eyes of the man and he said gently: 'What would you have of me?'

The priest said in a voice of thunder which echoed about the hall: 'You have my crown. I am the King of England. Give it back to me. Usurper!'

Two of the guards had come forward; they gripped the priest by his arms and held him pinioned.

'Why do you make such statements?' asked Henry still gentle, for he was always sorry for the weak. It was only the strong who made him uneasy; he could feel compassion for those who were afflicted.

'I speak truth,' cried the priest. 'I am the King of England. The true King . . . robbed of his crown.'

'How do you make that out?' asked Henry. 'My father was King, my grandfather was King and I am my father's eldest son.'

'No,' muttered the priest. 'You have stolen my crown. I have come to claim it. You will never prosper until you give me back my crown.'

'My lord,' said one of the guards, 'what is your wish? What shall we do with this man?'

'Hang him,' cried a voice from the hall.

'Cut out his tongue,' said another.

'Nay,' said Henry. 'Hold. This man is not to blame. He is a man with an addled brain. Through no fault of his he has been sent into the world so afflicted. It is only a man who knows himself not to be a true king who would fear such as he. I would be merciful. Take him away and let him go free.'

There was a murmur of amazement as the priest was taken from the hall.

Eleanor pressed his hand. 'You are a good man, Henry,' she said. 'Few Kings would have let him go.'

'My father would have had his eyes put out, his ears or his nose cut off. But then my father was a wicked man. There

was no godliness in him. I want these people to understand
that although I am my father's son there was never one less like
him than I am. My ancestors, what would they have done? The
Lion of Justice would have freed him for he has committed no
crime.'

'He has shown disrespect to your person.'

'What he has done is dictated by madness. It was not Ribbaud who spoke but the demons within him. He has gone. Let
us forget him. Call for the minstrels.'

The minstrels sang and it was said in the hall that Henry
was a good man and it was sad that he could not be as
good a king as he was a man.

* * *

Night at Woodstock was enchanted with the moon high in
the sky, shedding its light on the still trees of the forest.
Through those trees the King and Queen walked together,
arms entwined, down to Rosamund's Bower haunted by the
spirit of the Second Henry whose lust had been at the heart of
Rosamund's tragedy.

Here they had sported together; here they had played out
their secret lives. There was an aura about the place. The
spirits of the past brooded there. In these rooms the King's
bastards had been born—the children who, it was said, the
King loved better than those he had had by his Queen.

'It is almost as though she is here—sweet Rosamund,' said
Henry. 'Do you sense that, my love?'

Eleanor did; poet that she was her fancy was always ready to
soar. They walked through the rooms—small by palace standards—charming rooms, with much of the furniture still
remaining, for this place which had become known as Rosamund's Bower had been kept as it was in Rosamund's day on
the orders of Henry II and the care had continued through
the reigns of Richard and John until now.

Eleanor said: 'Let us stay here a while just ourselves—in
Rosamund's Bower. Here her children were born. I have
a notion. There is magic in the air tonight. Something says to
me "Stay". Perhaps here our son would be conceived. Henry,
there *is* some thing which tells me we must stay. It was so
strange when that crazy priest stood there. I kept thinking
of him. Henry, you were so good to him. You saved him. The
saints will reward you ... tonight here....'

'What odd fancies you have. But there is a magic in the
air tonight.'

'Here that other Henry made love with his mistress. Why should not this Henry make love here with his wife?'

Henry laughed. 'Delightful notion,' he said.

She sat upon Rosamund's bed and held out her hands to him.

He took them, kissed them fervently.

He said: 'There is nothing in the world I would not give you.' She was happy; she was content; she was glad he had been lenient to the mad priest.

*   *   *

It was past midnight when they wandered back into the palace.

In their bedchamber was noise and confusion. A babble of voices, a man bound by robes trussed in a corner.

In the light of the torches the King looked round the room and saw a knife imbedded in the straw of the bed he would have shared with Eleanor.

A guard said: 'We caught him as he was making away, my lord. And when we came here we saw what he had done. God's mercy was with you tonight, my lord, for had you been in your bed the madman's knife would have been buried in your heart.'

The priest began to shout, 'I am the true King. You stole my crown.'

Henry looked at the pale face of Eleanor, the terror in her eyes and he thought of her lying in that bed, covered in blood, dead ... beside him. Two of them victims of the mad-man's knife.

'This is a dangerous madman,' he said.

There was a sigh of relief. It was clear that the guards had feared he might have wished to save Ribbaud's life yet again.

'Take him to the dungeons,' said the King. 'We will decide what to do with him tomorrow.'

When they had gone he turned to Eleanor and took her into his arms.

'He might have harmed you,' he said; and a terrible anger took possession of him.

He had been a fool and seen to be a fool. He had once more shown himself to the world as a weak man. His act of mercy in the great hall might have cost both him and his Queen their lives. It would be whispered of ... remembered.

Eleanor was shivering.

'Have no fear, my love. He shall pay for this. No more mercy for the mad priest.'

Nor was there. The next day the man was tied to four wild horses and when they rode off in different directions he was torn to pieces.

Birth of Edward

THE Queen believed that that night there had been a miracle. In Rosamund's Bower there had come to her the desire to stay there, and so they had while a madman tried to kill them and would certainly have done so if they had been asleep in their own bed. And when she discovered that she was indeed pregnant, she was certain of the miracle.

This was happiness indeed. There was only one irritation and that was the rejection of her Uncle William and the inability of Henry to force his acceptance at Winchester. Moreover Uncle William was not in very good health which was a great concern to her.

But the fact that she was to have a child superseded all minor irritations. Henry was beside himself with delight. He agreed with her that there had been a miracle that night and although they could not be absolutely sure that their child had been conceived in Rosamund's Bower, that mattered little now. It had actually happened.

Henry cosseted her more than ever. He regarded her with a kind of wonder; he admitted that he had feared they might never have a child but so much did he love her that even that had not made him regret the marriage.

She became very friendly with her sister-in-law Eleanor de Montfort. Eleanor was herself the proud mother of a boy—Henry—and was therefore knowledgeable about pregnancies, having just emerged from one.

The Princess was happy in the Queen's company because

she was missing her husband who had gone to Rome to get a dispensation regarding their marriage.

The two found great pleasure in sitting together stitching and embroidering—and it was their joy to make garments for their children. The Queen dismissed her attendants and set them to work in another chamber so that she and the Princess could talk more intimately.

They had a great deal in common—two contented wives. The Queen thought it strange that the Princess had found happiness in marrying beneath her when she, the Queen, had found hers in the grandeur of her marriage. She could never have been content, as the Princess was, with the lowering of her status.

Yet there were compensations she realized. Simon de Montfort was a strong man; a forceful and ambitious man. Could it be that he had married the Princess because she was the King's sister?

Henry was a weak man; she knew that. But he made up for his weakness in the strength of his passion for her.

The Princess talked as they stitched; Simon would be home soon, she believed. It was her fault that he had had to go away. 'I should never have made that foolish vow,' she added.

Then she told the Queen how when she had been very young she had thought she would like to go into a convent and Edmund the saintly Archbishop of Canterbury had made her take a vow to embrace the vestal life.

'And you made this vow?' asked the Queen.

'Well, I did not really take it seriously. I was staying with poor Isabella—Richard's wife—at the time; and I knew how unhappy she was and I thought: So that is married life. I want none of it. And with Edmund almost forcing me, I suppose I did agree.'

'And then you married Simon.'

'Yes, I married Simon. I was determined to. For me no one else would do ... nor any other life. And you see how right I was. I have my little angel Henry now ... and soon Simon will be back with his dispensation and that will silence old Edmund.'

'I doubt anything would silence him. What a trial saints can be.'

The Princess agreed. 'Oh how fortunate we are in our marriages,' she cried. 'I often wonder if you realize it. Henry adores you. In his eyes you are the perfect Queen. He has changed since you came.'

The Queen nodded in agreement.

'You have made him so happy,' went on Eleanor the Princess. 'When I think of Richard's marriage.... Well, that was why I decided I would never marry. Of course I had been married to William Marshal ... if you could call that a marriage. I was a child and only sixteen when he died. Perhaps I should have accepted my life if he had lived, but now that I have met Simon I realize what I would have missed.'

So they stitched and talked and the Queen told the Princess of Richard of Cornwall's arrival in Provence and how the poem she had written had brought her to Henry's notice; and the Princess told of poor sad Isabella who had borne six children to her first husband and had given Richard only one.

'Of course he dotes on young Henry. A fine boy he is too. I think Richard loves him more than anything else in the world. He is fond of women though and has a host of mistresses, I hear. Isabella knows it. It breaks her heart. She always said she was too old for him and she was right.'

So they talked of poor Isabella at length because talking of her brought home to them more clearly their own happy state.

And while they stitched they each looked into the future. The Princess for the return of her husband with the dispensation from the Pope because of the vow she had carelessly made, and the Queen for the birth of her child.

Simon returned with the dispensation and the Princess was happy. The Queen had to wait a little longer for her contentment. On a hot June day her child was born in the Palace of Westminster.

There was great rejoicing throughout the land, for the child was a healthy boy.

*   *   *

Henry could not tear himself away from the nursery. The child must be brought to him, examined, and embraced. He was overcome with anxiety lest it might not have the best of attention. Nothing must be spared in the rearing of this important boy.

The Queen pouted and declared he had transferred his affections from her to their son. Seriously he assured her that this was not so at which she laughed and said she shared his adoration for that wonderful little creature who was so entirely theirs and could quite understand his feelings.

What should they call him?

There was one name above all others which the King preferred. His greatest hero had been Edward the Confessor—that King who had been more of a saint than a King. Henry had always been a deeply religious man; some of his courtiers had likened him to the Confessor with the comment that it was all very well to be a saint when there was not a kingdom to be governed but that it was kings who made the best leaders not saints.

'So,' said the Queen, 'you would have the child named Edward.'

'That is my wish,' replied the King.

So the little Prince was christened Edward, and at his baptism Simon de Montfort, newly returned from Rome, stood as godfather and acted as High Steward.

London went wild with joy, for the citizens had begun to fear that the Queen was barren. Now they had an heir—a boy—and as was sometimes the case, when a Queen started bearing children she often continued.

Many presents were sent to the King for the child, but Henry spoilt the occasion by sending back those which he did not consider grand enough and demanding better of the donors, so that they ceased to be free gifts and were an imposition.

The people grumbled. 'God gave us this infant,' they said, 'and the King would sell him to us.'

But in spite of that England rejoiced in its little Prince.

*   *   *

It could hardly be expected that Richard of Cornwall was as delighted with the birth of the baby as some. He, like others, had begun to believe that the Queen was barren in which case he was next in succession to the throne. Now he had been displaced and if the Queen had more children the farther away would be his hopes of the crown.

He grew more disgruntled with his own marriage, while it was impossible not to admit that this was his own fault. Then he saw his sister and Simon de Montfort revelling in their mésalliance and felt that he was the only one who seemed to be called on to answer for his follies.

Thus the marriage of Simon and Eleanor had angered him considerably. Henry, he told himself and others, had no right to give his consent to it. Henry was a fool—always so firm in the wrong cause; so weak when he should be strong. One would have thought he would be grateful to his brother, but for whom he would never have had his Queen.

If he had a chance to discountenance Henry he would seize it. He liked to prove him wrong and to show how much more wisely he would have acted if he had been in his brother's place.

Richard had always had an ear and an eye alert for what was happening on the Continent and he had been wondering for some time how it was that Simon de Montfort had been able to acquire the dispensation with such speed.

He discovered how it had happened. Those about the Pope were not averse to a little bribery and Simon had bought his way to favour. But Simon was not a rich man, so how had he been able to manage this? The answer soon became clear. He owed debts on the Continent and he had given as his sponsor the name of the King of England.

The month of August had set in hot and sultry. The churching of the Queen was to take place at Westminster on the tenth day of the month and Simon and his wife came riding into London from Kenilworth on the ninth.

Richard called a few days earlier to see the King and after he had paid his respects to the Queen and admired the baby he found himself alone with Henry.

'De Montfort stands in high favour with you, brother,' he said.

'Is he not now our brother?' replied the King.

'Alas, due to this mésalliance.'

'Perhaps not so. Our sister is happy. And Simon now has the earldom of Leicester.'

'And the confidence of his King ... which some might say he does not deserve.'

'Why say you so?'

'I have learned how he so speedily acquired his dispensation. He offered bribes.'

'Well, 'tis done often enough.'

'By those who have the means mayhap. Simon does it in your name.'

'What say you?' cried the King.

'Oh, he is your brother-in-law now. He uses your name. He is royal. Has he not been accepted into our family? His son could be an heir to the throne. He is proud of this.'

'Heir to the throne! How could that be?'

'A few deaths. . . . That is all.'

'That's nonsense. But what is this about using my name?'

'I can prove it to you. You may well find bills presented to you. It may be that you will be asked to pay for the bribes which gave Simon the dispensation.'

Henry's face was crimson with anger. His anger was the greater because Richard had brought him this news and once more proved himself to be more cognizant of what was going on than he was himself.

*   *   *

When the King came face to face with Simon de Montfort his fury overwhelmed him and he was quite unable to control it.

Eleanor, beside him, waiting for the ceremony of churching to begin, laid her hand on his arm but for once he was less aware of her than his anger against this man.

Simon had made him look a fool. It was something he could not forgive.

'You adventurer!' he cried. 'How dare you come back here? How dare you come into this church? Do you think I am not aware of what you are? So you have offered bribes have you? This is how you repay my friendship to you! Where is the money to pay for those bribes? You think I shall pay them, do you?'

'My lord,' stammered Simon, taken completely by surprise, for at the baptism of little Prince Edward the King had shown him the utmost friendliness, 'I understand you not....'

Henry laughed loudly and unpleasantly. The silence in the church was intense but he seemed to be unaware of the place and the unseemliness of conducting this family quarrel at the churching of his wife.

'Nay, you understand not,' he cried, and his voice echoed eerily. 'Take care, Simon de Montfort who call yourself the Earl of Leicester. Yes, take care that that which has been given you may not be taken from you.'

'Pray tell me, my lord,' said Simon recovering a little from his surprise and dismay, 'what tales have you heard? You have been good to me, giving me your sister's hand in marriage ... making a brother of me....'

'You know why I consented to the marriage,' interrupted Henry. 'It was a mésalliance was it not? A Princess, a sister of the King given to a penniless adventurer. Why so? Why so? Many of my barons have asked that question. Now I shall give them the answer. Here in this holy place. You shamed my sister. You seduced her. You made her unfit for marriage to any other man. That is the only reason why I consented to this marriage.'

'It is a lie,' shouted Simon.

'It is no surprise to me that even in a holy place you have little respect for the truth.'

'It is you. . . .' began Simon.

His wife was laying a hand on his arm. 'Let us go,' she said. 'Let us not stay here to be insulted.'

'Yes, go,' cried Henry. 'Go ... go ... and never let me see your face again.'

Henry's own face was scarlet with rage; his drooping eyelid completely covered the pupil. There was a twitch at the side of his face.

Many barons in the hall were remembering when he had drawn his sword on Hubert de Burgh, who had served him faithfully, and how he might have killed him had not the Earl of Chester stepped between them.

Perhaps it was the Queen who delayed him giving full vent to his anger then. She swayed a little and the thought that she might faint turned Henry's thoughts momentarily from Simon. He caught her in his arms.

The Princess meanwhile was pulling at her husband's arm.

'Come away,' she said, 'while there is time.'

Simon turned and strode out of the church, his wife and their few attendants following him.

The ceremony was concluded, but back in the palace the King's anger flared up again against Simon de Montfort. He knew that he had made an unfair accusation. The man might be an adventurer; he had undoubtedly bribed his way to the dispensation with very little to meet his commitments, but there was no evidence whatsoever that he had seduced Eleanor and Henry knew it. Yet ever since he had been reproached for consenting to the marriage, and even being present at it, he had had to have an excuse for his own conduct. He had fabricated this one and because it seemed a sound enough reason for his giving his consent he had stuck to it and even soothed his vanity by believing it now and then.

Simon made him uneasy, so he hated him; he wanted to be rid of him.

He decided to arrest Simon.

Richard, who had been present at the churching, came immediately to his brother's apartments.

'Henry,' he cried, 'that was an unpleasant scene in the church.'

'When we have unpleasant people about us there will be unpleasant scenes,' retorted Henry.

'There are many who are saying that it was no place in which to conduct it.'

'Who says this? Who dares pass judgment on the King?'

'Brother, subjects have always passed judgment on their kings. What of our father ... ?'

'Pray spare me that. I am sick unto death of having my father's mantle thrown about my shoulders.'

'Simon de Montfort could be a dangerous man, Henry.'

'That I know. That is why I shall have him under restraint.'

'What of our sister?'

'She committed the folly of marrying him. She must pay for it.'

'It will not be wise, Henry.'

'And who are you, pray, to tell me what is wise and what not wise? They have repaired to the inn where they were staying, I know. I shall give an order to have de Montfort taken to the Tower and that without delay.'

'Henry, as one who serves you as a subject and a brother, I beg of you do not act rashly.'

Henry turned away impatiently and losing no time Richard made his way to the inn where he knew his sister and brother-in-law were staying.

He found them distraught, discussing the strange conduct of the King.

'You should lose no time,' said Richard. 'Henry is determined to send Simon to the Tower.'

'His temper gets quite out of control,' cried Eleanor. 'I never saw such an unkingly display. He has maligned me. I shall not quickly forgive him for that.'

'My dear sister, it is not a matter of whether you forgive him or not. If you value your freedom get away immediately. There is a boat on the river now which will take you to the coast. Lose no time. At any minute the King's guards may be here.'

'You really think he means what he says....' asked Simon.

'He does. He may well relent in time. Remember Hubert de Burgh. Henry's temper is such that if he feels he has been slighted it breaks into unthinking fury. He has too much power to make it wise to stand in the way of that rage. Come. Be gone. Farewell, sister. I'll warrant it will not be a long exile.'

He went with them to the boat and took an affectionate fare-well of them.

It was just in time. The King's guards had arrived at the inn.

*   *   *

Henry was secretly relieved that his sister and brother-in-law had escaped; but when they reached France he was mildly uneasy. He had many enemies over there and Simon de Mont-fort would not easily forget the insults which had been flung at him.

Richard had hinted that it was unwise to make enemies of men such as Simon de Montfort. What was he doing now? Perhaps making contact with the King of France. Well, Louis should be Henry's friend as his wife was Eleanor's sister; but he would know, of course, that Henry would one day have to conquer all those possessions which his father had lost. His mother had remarried. He had believed that she and her hus-band Hugh de Lusignan would have stood for him; but he had been very disappointed in that, for the Queen Mother of France was a wily woman and she had made contracts and treaties which it had been advantageous for his mother and her husband to accept. So Isabella had forgotten her maternal feelings for the sake of advancement; and as she had a large family now from her second marriage she seemed entirely to have forgotten the children she had had by John.

For the moment he was going to forget the harm de Mont-fort might be doing in France. He was going to revel in his happy home life which now seemed to be dominated by that flaxen-haired wonder in his cradle.

Eleanor came to him in a state of great excitement. With her was a tall handsome stranger.

'My dearest husband,' cried Eleanor, 'my uncle the Count of Flanders has come.'

Henry held out his hands and took those of the newcomer.

'I have written so much of my happiness here in England that the whole of my family yearns to come here,' she said.

The King glowed with pleasure and Thomas of Savoy, Count of Flanders, beamed on his niece and her husband. Eleanor had not exaggerated when she had told them how the King doted on her and how he would be ready to extend his generosity to them also.

They must drink wine together; Eleanor must hear all that

was happening in Provence. She thought of them often. Dearest Sanchia and Beatrice, their parents. Were they missing her?

Indeed they were, her uncle told her, but their sadness was lightening by the glowing accounts of her life in England and they were happy for her sake. And now that she had her darling Edward her contentment was complete.

'How are my sisters?' she asked.

'They are well and happy.'

'They have not yet found a husband for Sanchia then?'

'There is talk of a marriage into France.'

'But whom would she marry there? One of Louis' brothers I dareswear.'

'Nothing has been settled yet. You two elder girls made the two greatest marriages in Europe. Your father never tires of speaking of it.'

'And Marguerite?'

'Happy and well. A little plagued by her mother-in-law, I fancy.'

'And Louis is very solemn, I believe.'

'He is a good king and takes his duties seriously.'

'I confess,' said Eleanor, to Henry's delight, 'that I found him a little too stern. He believes that there is something wrong in fine garments and I daresay that means other pleasures. I am thankful that we do not think that way in England.'

'Oh, it is easy to see who has made the *happier* marriage.'

And indeed it was, for neither Louis nor Blanche would allow Marguerite's relations to come to their court to enjoy the pickings.

Louis might be a good husband but lacked the uxorious qualities of Henry. Marguerite was loved but she was not indulged as Eleanor was.

It was soon clear that Henry, seeing his wife's delight in her newly arrived uncle, was determined to please her more by giving him what pleased him best.

He made a present of five hundred marks and for extra measure gave him a tax on English wool.

Little could have incensed the barons more. In fact at first the necessary seal on the document granting the concession was refused. Henry's reply was to dismiss the men who had protested.

Having seen his conduct towards Simon de Montfort, they who had demurred decided that it would be better to give

way; but although that seemed like an easy victory for the
King, the murmurings of discontent had begun again.

*   *   *

It had been a great grief to Henry that he had not been able
to give the See of Canterbury to Uncle William de Valence.
He had always promised himself that in time he would do so.
He was not going to be dictated to by the people; that much
they must learn.

The City of London was out of love with him. There was
constant mention of Magna Carta. How he hated that document which had curbed the power of the throne and was
always held up as a symbol.

His constant need of money was always worrying him. He
wanted to shower gifts on his Queen and her family. He so
much enjoyed hearing himself compared with Louis IX who
was far less generous to his wife's relations. Louis would rather
give money to some educational or building project than to
his favourites. Whether Louis had any favourites was
debatable. There were times—as Eleanor said—when Louis
appeared to be excessively dull.

'Poor Marguerite,' she would murmur sometimes; and as
he knew she was comparing her sister's fate with hers he would
glow with satisfaction.

Small wonder that he wished to show his generosity to her
family. It had not been easy to find the money for the Count
of Flanders, but he had been determined to do so.

He had raised the five hundred marks from the Jews. Members of this race had made their home in the City of London
which was the natural place for them because it was where
business could prosper more easily than anywhere else. A quiet
people, eager only to be left to develop their remarkable business ability and to practise their own religion, on account of
their industry and talents they had become the richest section
of the community. This had at first irritated and then angered
their neighbours who did not care to work so hard and consequently lacked the ability to prosper as certainly as the Jews,
so Henry felt that in demanding taxes from the Jewish community he was acting wisely.

The Jews had the money; a little gentle persuasion could
extort it; and since the natives of London would not be asked
to contribute they would not be displeased.

Thus he gathered the five hundred marks for the Count

of Flanders by threatening the Jews with expulsion if they did not provide it.

The Jews paid up but the Londoners were alert, wondering where the next demand would be levied; but since it was only the Jews who were penalized, the matter was swiftly settled. Eleanor was delighted; Uncle Thomas declared that it had been a happy day for the house of Savoy when one of their family had married into England; and Henry enjoyed the role of benefactor which pleased him as much as any.

To raise five hundred marks was easier than to procure the See of Canterbury, but he had not given up hope.

Then William de Valence, who had been ailing for some time, fell ill and Eleanor was stricken with grief. She loved her uncles dearly and had been very sad when he had been obliged to leave the country—even though he had taken such quantities of treasure out of it.

At the beginning of the autumn the condition of William de Valence weakened. The King's doctors attended him but there was little they could do. He missed the warmer climate of his native land but he said it had been worth a little discomfort to be with his niece. He had certainly gained more than the discomfort and was richer than he could ever have hoped to be had he stayed in Savoy. Moreover, until this time when he had become so ill, he had never given up hope of the See of Canterbury.

Now Eleanor knelt by his bed and she talked to him of the days in Provence when he had visited her father's castle and there had been feasting in the great hall. He would remember how she was brought forward to read her latest poem to him, and how his praise meant so much to her.

Henry sat with her, suffering with her because of his love for her; and when the last rites had been administered and William de Valence had closed his eyes for ever, he led her from the death chamber and in their own he sought to comfort her.

She wept bitterly, talking of her dear Uncle William, and Henry said that he would always regret his inability to give him what he knew he had craved for: the See of Canterbury.

'Rest assured, my love,' he told her, 'that Canterbury shall one day go to your Uncle Boniface. I swear it. I will not be provoked by my own subjects. But there has always been this conflict between Church and State.

She was not listening. She was thinking of her beloved Uncle William who was no more.

There was nothing he could do to comfort her, until he went to the nursery and took the child from its cradle.

The bright blue eyes regarded him with interest and he put his lips to the flaxen hair.

'Beloved child, my Edward,' he murmured, 'you alone can comfort your mother in her grief.'

So he took the child and put him into her arms.

She smiled, laid her cheek against his face and was comforted.

A Newcomer to Court

Isabella, Countess of Cornwall, knew that the birth she was expecting would be a difficult one. The last years of her life had been sad and lonely; and she was fully aware of her husband's boredom with her society and the regrets he felt for his marriage.

It should never have been. How often had she said that to herself. She had told him from the start that a widow who had already borne her first husband six children was no fit wife for a man such as Richard of Cornwall.

He had refused to listen and perhaps she had not been as insistent as she should have been, because she had been in love with him and believed in miracles. For a year or so it seemed that that miracle had happened, but then reality took over from dreams. His visits were less frequent; and when he did come he was clearly in a hurry to get away.

Desperately he wanted a child—what ambitious man did not?—and during the first four years although she had borne children they had not lived. At last their son had been born. Sometimes she could believe that made everything worth while. Young Henry—named after his uncle the King—was indeed a boy to be proud of. And proud Richard was.

His visits were more frequent, but he came to see the boy, of course.

Young Henry was bright, intelligent and handsome—everything one could wish for. At least she had given Richard his son.

But Richard was young, lusty, fond of female society; he had the glamour of royalty; there had been a time when it had seemed that Henry and Eleanor might not have children, and Richard was looked upon as the heir to the throne. He had but to beckon and most women came readily enough. It was small wonder that his visits were rare and when he did come it was obvious that his main desire was to see the boy.

It was so cold in the castle at Berkhamsted—as cold as the fear in her heart. The draughts seemed to penetrate even the thick walls and Isabella found it difficult to keep warm in spite of the great fire.

Her women said it was her condition. They tried to comfort her by telling her that her child would almost certainly be a boy. But even if it was and Richard was temporarily pleased, what would that do to bolster up their marriage? The existence of young Henry—much as his father loved him— had failed to do that.

No, here she was an ageing woman whose husband was weary of her. He had tried to find an acceptable reason for divorcing her, but having failed must now be praying for her death.

A wretched state for a sensitive woman to come to. Perhaps she had been happier with Gilbert de Clare—a marriage which had been arranged for her by her mighty father. Gilbert had been his prisoner when, immediately after the death of King John, Gilbert had supported the Prince of France and William Marshal, her father, had been determined to set Henry on the throne. Gilbert had been a worthy husband for the Marshal's daughter, so, without consulting that daughter the marriage had been arranged. It had been a not entirely unsatisfactory marriage and when he had died she had mourned him sincerely with her three sons and three daughters. Then she had fallen in love with Richard of Cornwall and had married him romantically half believing in his protestations of undying love because she wanted to while her common sense warned her that such a man was unlikely to remain faithful to any woman let alone one so many years older than he was.

So the unsatisfactory marriage had gone on for nine years and during those years she had produced one son—their now five-year-old Henry. And it was to see Henry that Richard came to Berkhamsted now and then, for the child was the only reason that Richard did not entirely deplore his folly in marrying her.

Now here she was—an ageing woman, about to be delivered of a child, uneasily feeling that all was not going well with the birth and a premonition coming to her that she might be living through her last days on earth.

Through the windows she could see the snow fluttering down, whipped to a blizzard by the bitter north winds. Young Henry, rosy-cheeked, was sitting at her feet playing with a board and dice—a game which was called 'tables'. Two should have played it but because his nurse had said no one must disturb Lady Isabella and she seemed to find comfort from the society of her son, Henry who was a resourceful child was playing the game against himself.

She watched him tenderly. He was indeed a handsome child.

He looked up at her and seeing her eyes on him, he said: 'My lady, will my father come?'

She was so weak that she could not restrain the tears which came to her eyes.

'I am not sure, my dearest.'

'Are you crying?' he asked wonderingly.

'Oh no.'

'You look as if you're crying. Is it because something hurts you?'

'No, no. Nothing hurts. I am happy because you are with me.'

'He,' said Henry, pointing to the other side of the board, 'is losing and I am winning.'

He laughed, forgetting his momentary alarm.

He bent over the board and chuckled as he threw the dice.

The pain seized her suddenly and she said: 'Henry, go now and tell them to come to me at once.'

He stood up, the dice still in his hand. 'I have nearly won,' he said reproachfully.

'Never mind, my love. Go now.'

He hesitated, glanced at her and was suddenly frightened to see her face distorted in pain. Then he ran out of the room shouting to her attendants.

*   *   *

Her child was dead and she was dying. Richard had come but she was only vaguely aware of him. He was sitting at her bedside, and the priest was there too, holding the cross before her eyes.

So it was over—this brief life. Richard would have his freedom and he would have Henry too. Thank God Henry was a boy and Richard had always wanted a boy. No matter whether he married again Henry would always be his first-born. He would remember that and do his best for their son.

She wanted to be buried at Tewkesbury beside Gilbert de Clare. He had been her first husband and he had cherished her. It was fitting that she should lie beside the father of her three sons and three daughters.

She had made her wishes clear. There was nothing left now but to die.

She was aware of Richard at her bedside. He was weeping as were her attendants. Richard in tears? Crocodile tears? He must be inwardly rejoicing. He had tried to divorce her and had been angry and frustrated when the Pope had refused to accept his case. Now Death was giving him what the Pope had denied him.

But perhaps there was a certain regret. Perhaps the tears were genuine. Perhaps he was remembering the early days of their passion. But she was too tired to wonder any more.

Her great concern was their son.

'Henry,' she whispered.

Richard's face was close to hers now.

'Have no fear for Henry. I love him as I love my life. He is my son. Never fear but that I shall do everything for him.'

She nodded. She could believe that.

She closed her eyes and departed from this life in peace.

*   *   *

So his marriage was over and he was free. Only the direst hypocrite could pretend he was not relieved. For years now—in fact after the first two years of marriage—he had known he had made a bad mistake in marrying Isabella. He thought of Henry with his young Queen and how excited he, Richard, had been at the Court of Provence among those young girls and now he envied Henry.

Well, now he was no longer encumbered. Poor Isabella. She had been a beauty in her youth. But youth passed her too quickly and her melancholy brought on by his infidelities did not add to her charm. Had she accepted the inevitability of his dallying with other women, he might have been inclined to visit her more frequently.

But what was the use of going over it? It was over. He was a free man.

She had expressed a wish to be buried at Tewkesbury beside her first husband. That was a reproach to him, being a suggestion to the world that her first marriage had meant more to her than the second, He was not going to have that. She should certainly not be buried at Tewkesbury. He would bury her at Beaulieu, the proper place for a wife of his to lie.

It was unwise however to ignore the wishes of the dead, and Richard was adept at compromise. He knew what he would do. Her heart should be taken from her body, placed in a silver gilt casket and buried before the great altar at Tewkesbury. That should satisfy both the dead and the living.

Having made this decision he dismissed the matter from his mind.

Isabella was dead. He would go on from there.

He had, since the birth of Prince Edward, been preparing for his crusade. Before that he had hesitated, because it had seemed that Henry might not have children, in which case if he were to die suddenly Richard would be King. It would have been extremely unwise to leave the country when such a contingency was possible. But now there was an heir to the throne who showed every sign of growing up into a healthy man. Richard had taken a step back from the throne; therefore he could continue with his plans to leave the country.

He sent for his son and when the boy was brought to him he dismissed his attendants that he might be alone with the child.

He drew the boy to him and taking his chin in his hand turned his face upward. A skin fair and flawless, strong brown hair, bright eyes and well marked brows; and above all an alert intelligence which delighted his heart.

'Henry, my child,' he said soberly, 'you have no mother now.'

'She is dead,' agreed Henry.

'But you still have your father who loves you dearly.'

Henry nodded and waited.

'Never fear, my son, that I shall forget to care for you.'

'But you forgot to come and see my mother.'

How innocent he was. He did not seek to please. He spoke the truth as he saw it naturally as though it were the only thing to do.

'I had much with which to occupy myself. I have been fighting in the King's war.'

'Shall I fight the King's war?'

'When you are old enough. But first, son, you have to grow up, and that can take a long time. You are but five years old but seem older. You have worked well at your lessons and at your sport. Your riding master tells me you took to the saddle as though you had been born to it.'

'I like much to ride, father. I no longer have the leading rein.'

'That is good.'

'Would you like to see my falcon?'

'Later. Now I want to talk to you.'

Henry nodded gravely.

'Where has my mother gone?' he asked.

'Did you not understand, my son? She has gone to Heaven.'

'When will she come back?'

'She has gone to stay with the saints. She will be so happy with them that she will not wish to come back.'

'She will want to come back for me,' said Henry confidently. 'Perhaps she will take me back with her.'

'God forbid,' said his father, suddenly catching him to his chest in a firm grip.

'Yes, she will,' said Henry confidently. 'She never liked me to be away from her too long. I wonder what it is like in Heaven. There would be a lot of horses ... white ones I think.'

'Henry my son, there is something we must talk of. It will be different here ... now that your mother has ... gone away. You will miss her so I am going to take you away for a while.'

'With you?' cried Henry.

'Nay. I am going to fight the Saracens. I have long planned to do this but have been delayed again and again. Now I shall go.'

'I could come with you and fight the Saracens.'

'You have to grow up before you can do that. But perhaps you will one day. But first there is much to be done, and I am going to take you to London and there you will be in the King's palace. You see he is your uncle and there comes a time when we who belong to the Court must be of it.'

'Is that King Henry?'

'It is indeed. Your uncle King Henry, who has heard much of you and would welcome you at his Court.'

'What should I do at his Court, father?'

'Much as you do here. Take lessons, play games, learn to joust and tilt, study the laws of chivalry, become a knight worthy of your birth and standing.'

Henry listened attentively.

'Then I shall come back and by then my mother will be here.'

Richard did not answer. It was as well, as yet, to let the

boy think that his mother's departure was not permanent.

'We shall set out tomorrow for the King's Court,' he said. 'You will like that, little son. You and I will ride together. You are going out into the world.'

Henry thought he would like it. He wished his mother was coming with them; but in time he would come back and tell her all about it. That would be something to which he could look forward.

* * *

The King was something of a disappointment to young Henry. He was a little frightening because one eye was half hidden and the boy could not stop looking at it. The Queen was different. She was beautiful and smiling and he loved her at once.

'This is my son,' said Richard.

The King bent over him and said: 'Welcome, nephew, to the Court.'

The Queen knelt down and put her arms about him. She kissed him and overwhelmed by her beauty, Henry put his arms about her neck and kissed her.

'You are the most beautiful lady I ever saw,' he said.

A diplomat already? thought Richard. There was nothing the boy could have said which would have better pleased the King or the Queen.

Eleanor had taken his hand and sitting down on the ornate chair beside the King's, put her arm about the boy.

'You are going to stay at our Court, Henry. Do you think you will like that?'

'Will you be there?' he asked.

'Oh yes, I ... and the King and our little son. You must meet our little son, Henry. You and he are going to be such friends.'

'What sort of horse does he ride?'

'He is too little as yet to ride at all. You will have to be patient with him, Henry.'

Henry nodded. 'Is he only a baby?'

'Only a baby,' said the Queen. She looked at her husband. 'Let us take Henry to the nursery so that he can meet his cousin.'

Still holding his hand they went, his father and the King following. And there in a cradle lay a baby whom the Queen picked up with great care, indicating to Henry that she thought him very precious indeed.

'Come look, Henry. This is your little cousin, Edward. Is he not a beautiful baby?'

Secretly Henry did not find babies beautiful but he said nothing as he did not want to contradict the Queen.

'Take his hand, Henry,' said the Queen. 'Gently. Remember he is but a baby. There. Now say: Edward I will be your friend.'

'Can I be friends with such a little baby?' asked Henry.

'He won't be a baby always. He'll grow up very quickly, then you won't notice that he is younger than you. Come. Say it. Say you will be his friend.'

'I will be your friend . . . if I like you,' said Henry.

Everyone laughed and the King said fondly: 'Our nephew is too young yet to swear fealty.'

'Kiss his hand,' insisted the Queen.

Henry took the baby's hand and kissed it.

And the Queen seemed satisfied.

He was then given to the nurses who were told that he would stay in the royal household until such time as his father wished him to depart. As there were other boys of noble families living at Court—after the custom—no one was very surprised to see the son of the Earl of Cornwall among them.

Richard went away to make his last preparations for the crusade with the conviction that Isabella's death had really been a happy release not only for herself but for her son and husband.

A Sojourn in Provence

THE King accompanied Richard to Dover where on a hot June day he set sail for the Continent. Among those who left with him was Peter de Mauley who had been his old tutor and governor in the days of his childhood at Corfe Castle. Many distinguished knights, eager to win honours and a remission of their sins in the Holy War, formed his company. So it was an impressive party that left the castle to take ship for France.

The King watched the departure with mixed feelings. He could not in honesty say that he wished he were going with them. The thought of leaving Eleanor and their son filled him with horror. Of course Eleanor might have accompanied him as his grandmother Eleanor of Aquitaine had once gone with her first husband to the Holy Land and created such a scandal there that it had never been forgotten. But little Edward could certainly not have gone and one of the great joys of Henry's life was to slip into the nursery and gaze at that wonderful child with the perfect limbs and the healthful looks—his son, who would one day be King of England.

Moreover he was glad to have Richard out of the country. He knew that Richard disapproved of much that he did and that chiefly he objected to the favour he showed to foreigners —foreigners being Eleanor's relations and retainers.

As if they were foreigners! Dear Uncle William now dead. How Eleanor had loved him! He was glad he had been able to show his appreciation to him before he died. And he was going to do all he could for Uncle Thomas and it was now being suggested that her Uncle Boniface would come over to England too.

She was delighted. The Uncles had been a part of her childhood. Little gave her as much pleasure as to receive them in England and show them how happy she was in her marriage. And since it delighted her, he also was delighted.

But some of the killjoys in his kingdom wanted to spoil that —and he feared Richard was one of them. He had said before he left that the Bishop of Reading was deeply disturbed by the intrusion of the Queen's relations and had urged him not to leave England at this time.

'Why not? Why not?' Henry demanded.

'Because,' Richard had said, 'he fears that the barons are growing more and more displeased by these foreigners coming here.'

'Why should they not come here?' Henry had asked. 'They are my wife's relations.'

'If they merely came that would give little offence. The point is that when they are here they proceed to fill their pockets and take that which by rights belongs to Englishmen. If they leave—as in the case of the Bishop Elect of Valence— they certainly do not go empty-handed.'

'I am surprised,' Henry had said piously, 'that you can speak ill of the dead.'

'I trust I speak the truth of anyone ... dead or alive,' had been Richard's retort.

He had gone on the crusade though and Henry was not going to let himself be disturbed by the vague murmurings of the barons. It was a great pity they had ever been allowed to produce Magna Carta which had given them too high an opinion of their own power.

He returned to London where Eleanor was awaiting him and together they went to the nursery to gloat over Edward.

'I am not sorry he has gone,' said Henry. 'He is full of apprehension about the future. He talks continually of the barons' displeasure. One would think they ruled this country.'

'Perhaps now he will find a suitable wife and settle down. That is what he needs.'

Henry slipped his arm fondly through hers.

'I believe you have a fondness for Richard,' he said.

'Naturally, but for him you and I would never have been brought together.'

'Well, for that I will forgive him a great deal,' said the King.

* * *

Arrived in France Richard began his journey across the country and when he reached Paris he was greeted by the King of France, his wife and mother who gave him a very royal welcome.

He was impressed by the young King—as indeed all must be, for his was a character of great distinction and there was a nobility in his face, bearing and manner of which none could be unaware.

His mother adored him; she had worked for him as tirelessly as she had for his father and although Louis IX had shown himself very capable of governing his kingdom—far more so than his father had ever done—she still seemed to be under the impression that she was needed.

Richard was interested to meet Marguerite, the sister of Henry's Eleanor. A beautiful woman but lacking Eleanor's forceful nature. Richard wondered what would have happened if they had changed roles and Eleanor gone to France and Marguerite to England. Queen Blanche would not have had the easy victories over Eleanor that she clearly had over Marguerite.

Marguerite was eager to talk to him. She wanted to know all the news of England and how Eleanor lived there. She plied him with questions and talked about her own life and how fortunate she was to have such a husband as Louis.

'I doubt not that you could have wished for a mother-in-law who was not ever present.'

Marguerite was silent, not wishing to speak ill of Queen Blanche.

'The King's mother is ever alive to his interests,' she said.

'I doubt it not,' replied Richard. 'I see how often he is in her company.'

'He came to the throne when he was only a boy. She had to be there then to guide him.'

'He would seem to be a King who knows which way he is going and needs no guidance now.'

'He will do as he thinks best, but he loves her dearly and he is always sad when it is necessary to go against her will.'

'And you?' asked Richard. 'Do you not find her sometimes taking him from you?'

Marguerite was silent and Richard thought of what he would say to Eleanor when he returned to England.

There was another matter in which Eleanor had been more blessed than her sister: Eleanor had a son; Marguerite only a daughter—and even then the child had to be called Blanche.

In a way, mused Richard, it seemed that Eleanor had made the more fortunate marriage. But this was not entirely so. Richard was looking into the future. The strong character of Louis IX, the determination to rule well, the clever logical calm mind ... these were the making of a great King. Louis would have the reins of government firmly in his hands.

Richard wondered then if there might come a day when the Barons decided they would rise once more in England as they had under King John, when they would tire of a King on whom they could not rely. How would Henry stand the strain? And Eleanor? Did she realize that the people were murmuring against her, that they could not forgive her for bringing her family and friends to England and keeping their pockets well filled?

There could be no doubt who was the greater King; and if Marguerite had a forceful mother-in-law and so far only a girl child—who could not inherit the throne because of the Salic law which existed in France—perhaps her position was after all more secure than that of her sister Eleanor.

'It has been wonderful to have news of my sister,' said Marguerite. 'I often think of the days when we were all to-gether in the nursery—the four of us. How happy we were! Then I went away and the three of them were left. There will only be Sanchia and Beatrice now.'

'I remember too when I went there and saw the three beautiful princesses. That was after I had read Eleanor's poem.'

'Yes, that was so romantic. But for her poem ... she might not now be Queen of England. She must be ever grateful to you for I know she is very happy.'

'Her uncles have been to England to see her,' said Richard, his mouth tightening a little.

'How contented she must have been!'

He did not say that the people of England had been a good deal less content.

'Eleanor was always devoted to the family,' went on Marguerite, 'as we all were.'

'Do they not visit you in France? They are much nearer to you.'

'They come. But they do not stay long.'

Wise Louis! thought Richard. He has more sense than to

spend his country's revenues on his Queen's impecunious uncles.

'They stay in England,' said Richard.

'I have heard that the King is very generous to them.'

'More generous than he can afford to be, I fear.'

'Oh dear! Still generosity is a fine quality. I think Eleanor must be very happy. And the little boy?'

'Edward flourishes. Yes, I should say that your sister is happy in her marriage. As for the King, he adores her.'

Marguerite clasped her hands together.

'I am so pleased for them.' She laid her hand on his arm. 'You should go and see my parents as you pass through Provence.'

Richard remembered that easy-going Court—the charming Count and his Countess, the beautiful daughters, the songs and the ballads; the balmy climate, the lush woods and gardens and he felt a sudden desire to be there.

He would return to England in due course and talk to the Queen of his meeting with her sister. How amusing it would be to tell her that he had rested awhile at her father's Court.

* * *

It was pleasant to sit in the gardens of Les Baux and listen to the songs of Provence. How beautiful were the daughters of Count Raymond Berenger! Only two of them left now, Sanchia and Beatrice.

Sanchia was just as beautiful as her sister Eleanor and sixteen was such a charming age. She was not as dominating as Eleanor—she was more gentle, rather of Marguerite's temperament, which was an advantage.

Charmingly she sang songs of her own composing.

'Of course,' she said when he complimented her, 'they cannot compete with Eleanor's. None of us is as clever as she is.'

'I find you delightful,' Richard told her.

He kept comparing her with poor sad Isabella. How she had aged in the last few years of her life. In comparison, Sanchia was so adorably young.

He had intended to stay but a few days, but the visit lengthened. He was closely watched by the Count, the Countess and their chief adviser Romeo de Villeneuve.

'What think you of what we see?' asked the Countess.

Romeo replied: 'The Earl of Cornwall is undoubtedly enamoured of the Lady Sanchia.'

'The others married kings,' said the Countess.

'The two greatest marriages in Europe!' Romeo replied complacently, reminding them both of the part he had played in bringing about these desirable alliances. 'But where shall we find a third king for Sanchia ... and a fourth for Beatrice.'

The Count shrugged his shoulders. 'Nowhere,' he said.

'Then I reckon we could not do better than marry Sanchia into England. Eleanor would be delighted. Imagine ... two sisters for two brothers. The influence they would wield! Already Eleanor has seen that much good has come to the house of Savoy.'

The Countess nodded in agreement. 'My brothers are delighted with the match.'

'So should they be, my lady. Think what benefits have come to them through their visits to England.'

'And more will yet, my brothers tell me. William almost gained the See of Canterbury. Alas....'

'Let us hope that it may go to Boniface,' said Romeo.

'Boniface!' cried the Countess. 'That would indeed be a blessing. Eleanor has done her duty by us. I would not be averse to a marriage between Sanchia and the Earl.' She looked earnestly at her husband.

He replied: 'I am in agreement, but I should like Sanchia to want this marriage of her own free will.'

'He is so indulgent,' said the Countess looking fondly at her husband.

'Nay, I merely want to see my children happy.'

'She seems happy enough in the Earl's company,' commented Romeo.

'I know she is,' said the Countess. 'She conceived a romantic feeling for him when he came here after Eleanor had sent him her poem. She has never forgotten him.'

'The King of England's brother! They say he is one of the richest men in England. If anything should happen to Henry....'

'There is Edward,' said the Countess sharply, 'our grandson.'

'Yes, yes,' replied Romeo. 'But it is always wise to be prepared for anything that might happen.'

'I think we are agreed,' said the Count. 'Let us wait for a few days and see if Richard speaks to us of Sanchia. The sun ... the music ... our little girl's beautiful eyes ... all these are having their effect on him. He is falling in love with her ... and she with him. I want to see her happy.'

The Countess exchanged glances with Romeo; then she went to the Count and took his arm.

'I think,' she said, 'that ere long we shall be losing our daughter.'

*   *   *

'Soon,' said Richard, 'I shall have to leave Provence. Already I have delayed too long.'

'My parents will be sad when you go,' replied Sanchia.

'And you, Sanchia, how will you feel?'

'I shall be sad too.'

He reached out and took her hand.

'Will you think of me while I am away fighting the Saracen?

'Every day.'

'I would to God I need not go.'

'I wish it too.'

'I could spend my life here in these beautiful gardens ... with you.'

It was not true of course. He was a man who must be moving forward all the time. He was ambitious and if sometimes he wearied of that ambition before he had time to carry it out, still he would go on making plans for his own advancement.

'I love you, Sanchia,' he said.

'I know,' she answered.

'What shall we do about it?'

'We could ask my parents.'

'I am a free man now. Would you marry a man who has already had a wife?'

'If I loved him.'

'And do you love me, Sanchia?'

'I have loved you ever since you came to thank Eleanor for her poem.'

'You are a dear sweet child. We will marry when I return from the Holy War. You will be older then, sweet Sanchia, and ready for marriage.'

She clasped her hands together. 'You will soon return from the Holy Land.'

'Would I had not vowed to go. I would stay here with you and teach you how to love me.'

'Such lessons would not be necessary since I do already.'

'You are young and innocent. I am much older than you. I had a wife for nine years, and I have a son who is nearly six years old and very dear to me.'

'He shall be dear to me, too.'

'Oh, what a happy day when I came to the Court of

Provence! And there will not be another happy day for me
until I ride back and claim my bride.'

He rose and taking her hands kissed both of them.

'I shall go to your father now and ask him for your hand.'

*   *   *

There was great rejoicing at Les Baux. The Count embraced
· his prospective son-in-law. He was delighted, he said; nothing
could have pleased him more. Though naturally he wanted
great marriages for his daughters, their happiness meant more
to him than anything else, and if the two objects could be
combined he was indeed content. He had noticed the rapture
of Sanchia these last days and he knew that in addition to the
joy she would find in her husband she would have the comfort
of living near her sister Eleanor.

There was a great feast on the night before his departure—
a bitter sweet occasion for Sanchia who was romantically in
love and while she was so happy because of her betrothal she
was sad because he had to leave her.

They sat side by side, he feeding her with the titbits from
his platter which she felt too emotional to eat.

It was very moving when the minstrels sang of lovers.

The next morning Richard and his company left Les Baux
and Sanchia settled down to wait for his return.

*   *   *

When Eleanor heard of her sister's betrothal to Richard
she was overcome with joy. Henry listened indulgently, delighted to see her pleasure.

'You know what this means to me, Henry,' she said. 'I shall
have my sister near me. We were always closer to each other
than any of the others. And now she is to marry Richard! Is
that not wonderful news?'

'If it makes you happy it is indeed good news.'

'I hope he will be a good husband to her.'

'He was scarcely that to his first wife.'

'I shall insist, Henry.'

'Ah, my dearest, even you could not do that. Richard is over
fond of women, I believe. Let us hope that this marriage will
sober him.'

'I could not hope that he will be as good a husband as his
brother,' said Eleanor.

'My dearest, he could not have such a wonderful wife. Even
your sister cannot compare with you.'

'Sanchia is a beautiful girl but. . . .'

'Do not say it. I know. You were the beauty of the family and the clever one. No, I won't ask you to confirm that. No confirmation is needed. I know it.'

'When they are married we must have entertainment worthy of my sister and your brother.'

'We shall.'

'I want her to know what a wonderful country she is coming to. We must give her the greatest welcome we have ever given to anyone.'

'Of course we shall. Is she not your sister?'

'Oh, Henry. You are so good to me.'

'And mean to be more so,' he answered.

Eleanor chafed against the delay. She was longing to show Sanchia how fortunate she was.

There was news from abroad which gave Henry the opportunity to prove to Eleanor how much he wished to please her.

Edmund, the old Archbishop of Canterbury, who had been in conflict with the State for some time, and was a very uncomfortable man since he was recognized as a saint, had left England. He was very old; he was a disappointed man; he deeply deplored the trouble which he saw brewing in England and he thought he would like to end his days in peace. That end he was sure was not far off.

Two of his great predecessors, St Thomas à Becket and Stephen Langton had both sought refuge in Pontigny when they found life in England intolerable and it was to Pontigny that Edmund decided to make his way. He rested there for a while and tried to come to terms with himself and see if there was a solution which would bring peace between the Church and the State.

He was in very poor health and it was not long before it became obvious that his end was near. He was visiting Soisy when it became obvious that he was in such a state that he should have taken to his bed, but being Edmund he refused to go. He had rarely slept in a bed, preferring to sleep fitfully fully dressed usually on his knees, or perhaps occasionally allowing himself the luxury of sitting.

Even now, when his life was ebbing away he sat on his couch with his head resting on his hand.

And so he died. He was taken to Pontigny for burial and immediately miracles were said to take place at his tomb.

When the news reached England Henry felt relieved. He hated to be in conflict with the Church and would have pre-

ferred a more comfortable man than Edmund as his Archbishop. How he had longed to give the See to William de
Valence! Eleanor had said nothing he could have done would
have pleased her more.

And how he wanted to please Eleanor! He wanted to
astound her with his generosity. He wanted to show her how
fortunate she was, how much more beloved than her sister
Marguerite Queen of France!

He had an idea.

He told her of Edmund's death. 'So the old man is gone at
last then,' she said.

'He was said to be a saint. Miracles are taking place at his
tomb.'

'People imagine there are miracles. I shall never forget how
unhappy he made your poor sister simply because he had
forced her into taking a vow of chastity.'

Henry agreed with her. He had almost forgotten his quarrel
with Simon de Montfort, the result of which had been to drive
Simon and his wife from the country.

'The See of Canterbury is vacant,' he said. 'This time I am
going to place it in the right hands. Your Uncle Boniface shall
come here and be our next Archbishop.'

Eleanor threw her arms about him.

'Oh Henry, how good you are to me!'

'I think, do you not, my dear,' he said, 'that he will be a very
good choice.'

*   *   *

It was a great joy to Henry when Eleanor became pregnant
once more. They had the adorable Edward but a royal nursery
should be well stocked, for even the healthiest children could
suddenly take sick and die. There had been one or two alarms
concerning Edward's health. He was at Windsor which his
parents thought would be more healthy for him than London
under the care of Hugh Giffard, a man whom they trusted
completely and there had been several times when messages
had come to them that there was anxiety in the nursery. Then
they would leave everything to go to Windsor; nor could they
be induced to leave until they were assured of their child's
recovery.

Thus it was a great delight to contemplate that there was to
be another child.

Eleanor was absorbed by the prospect which was well

because there was some irritation throughout the country over the election of Boniface.

First, as was to be expected, there was opposition. The monks of Christchurch wanted to resist the King's choice but remembering the recent mulcting of the Jews in London they hesitated, and while they hesitated were lost.

They were not bold enough to resist.

However there was a further delay. There was vacancy at the Vatican for the new Pope had not yet been elected and, until he was, there could be no confirmation of Boniface's election from Rome.

Thus there was a delay and Boniface chafed against it and wrote continually to his niece urging her to use all her influence with the King to end it.

But there was nothing she could do until the Pope gave his sanction and as at the moment there was no Pope, Boniface must needs wait.

She became absorbed in preparations for the birth. Henry and she talked of little else. He fretted about her health and was absent-minded with his ministers.

'There will be no sense from him until the child is born,' they said, and while they applauded his husbandly virtues they deplored his inattention to State matters.

In due course Eleanor gave birth to a child. They were a little disappointed that it should be a girl, but Henry was so delighted that Eleanor came safely through the ordeal and that she had produced another child fairly soon after the birth of Edward, that he declared he could not have been more pleased.

Eleanor said: 'We will call her after my sister, the Queen of France.'

Henry agreed that was an excellent idea, but instead of giving her the French version of Marguerite, she should have the English Margaret.

Several months passed, with the doting parents happy in their nursery. Edward was now two years old. Handsome and bright, the perfect child. As for his baby sister Margaret, they adored her too.

Even those who were highly critical of the King for his weaknesses and the Queen for bringing the foreign harpies in to the land, admitted that it was a pleasant sight to witness the conjugal bliss of the royal family.

*   *   *

Richard was still away from England, and little Margaret was a year old when a situation arose which could not be ignored even though it threatened to take the King from his happy domesticity.

Henry's stepfather, the Count of La Marche, wrote to him telling him that if he would come to his aid now he could promise him the help of not only the Gascons and Poitevins but also the King of Navarre and the Count of Toulouse. If Henry was ever to regain the possessions which his father had lost this was the time to do it.

There was also a letter from Henry's mother in which she told him she thought of him often and longed to see him. She wanted very much for the family to be reunited; and it seemed that they could serve each other by remembering their family ties.

The fact was that the Count of La Marche (through his wife who governed him) had quarrelled with the King of France, because Louis's brother Alphonse, who had been promised to the daughter of the Count, had married Joan of Toulouse; moreover he had been created Count of Poitier and the Count and Countess La Marche were therefore called upon to pay homage to him. This was something they could not stomach. Hence the desire to go to war.

Henry was nonplussed. He was asked to make war on the husband of Eleanor's sister. Yet, here was the opportunity for which he had been waiting ever since he had come to the throne. Always he was overshadowed by the sins of his father; everyone seemed to be waiting for him to display the same follies. What glory it would be if he were to regain all that his father had lost in France.

He went to Eleanor first and showed her the dispatches from his stepfather.

'You see, Eleanor,' he said, 'it is natural for the Kings of France and England to be enemies. Ever since great Rollo with his Norsemen forced his way into France so that the King was obliged to give him Normandy the French wanted to regain what had been given away. When William of Normandy came to England, England and Normandy were under one sovereign and the French want us out of France. My father lost so much that was ours. It has always been my dream to regain it. I would not hesitate but for one factor: the Queen of France is your sister.'

Eleanor was thoughtful. 'Henry,' she said, 'I want you to be the greatest king on earth. You can only do that by regaining what your father lost. I love my sister—but this is not our quarrel. With so many allies it will be easy for you to regain what is lost. You must go.'

'What of us? We shall have to be separated.'

She was thoughtful for a while. Then she said: 'I could not let you go alone. You would need me with you. I will come with you, Henry.'

'My dearest love. Oh how blessed I am!'

'Alas,' she said, 'we shall have to leave the babies in England.'

* * *

Richard had landed at Acre. He was not enthusiastic about this crusade. Crusades were always so exciting to plan when one was exalted by religious fervour and the belief that one was expiating one's sins, but the reality was often less enticing when one had to contend with sand storms, flies—and worse, poisonous insects—dysentery and the realization that the Saracen was not a savage, not a heathen but a man of high principles and deep religious feeling—the only difference being that he followed other doctrines.

Moreover Richard wanted to marry. Had it not been for the crusade he would be married to Sanchia by now. Perhaps she would be pregnant with a son. And here he was at Acre, attempting to drive the Saracen from the Holy Land—a task which mighty warriors, his uncle Coeur de Lion among them, had failed to do. Could he hope to?

Simon de Montfort who had decided to join the crusade, arrived at Acre and Richard was pleased to greet his brother-in-law. Once he had recovered from the shock of his marrying his sister, Richard had decided that Simon would be a good ally, and both of them appeared to have forgotten the antagonism which had existed between them at the time of Simon's marriage.

Richard discussed his plans and how he intended to return home as soon as possible.

'That is what I should like to do,' said Simon, 'but as you know the King was incensed against me.'

'Henry's anger soon passes,' Richard assured him, 'though it can be dangerous when it arises. He would have had you in the Tower and God knows what would have happened to you if we hadn't acted promptly.'

'For which I have to thank you.'

'Well, are we not brothers-in-law?'

It was a comfort to both to know that the other was his friend.

Richard busied himself in Acre, first by offering to take into his ranks all those pilgrims who wished to go home and had not the means to do so. He marched to Ascalon where he reconstructed the fortifications of that city, and made a treaty with the Sultan of Krak which brought about the release of many prisoners. He went on to Gaza where many Christians had been slain and roughly buried. He had their bodies dug up and given Christian burial.

He considered then that he had done his duty, earned the remission of his sins and was now justified in returning home.

He had reached Sicily when he heard from the King that his presence was needed at home without delay as Henry was planning an expedition to France.

*   *   *

Richard arrived in London in time to take part in the arrangements for the expedition. He told Henry that their brother-in-law de Montfort should be ordered to join them in Poitou.

'He will be pleased to do so,' said Richard, 'and it will be a fitting end of your quarrel if he acquits himself well in your service, which I am sure he will.'

Henry agreed to this.

In view of the situation the marriage with Sanchia would have to be delayed for a while, but that was inevitable because of the war. When Henry had regained his possessions he, Richard, would be an even more desirable husband.

It was a warm May day when the fleet sailed from Portsmouth. The King was accompanied by the Queen, Richard and seven other earls, and three hundred knights. The King had also brought with him thirty casks of money. He was in high spirits so sure was he of success. There was only one sorrow. He had had to part from his children.

They were in the best of hands, of course, as was the Kingdom in the hands of the Archbishop of York. There was no Archbishop of Canterbury yet. He was awaiting the election of the Pope for the installation of Boniface.

He held Eleanor's hand as they watched the coast of England fade away.

'When we return,' he told her, 'I shall have shown the French the stuff of which I am made. And the barons at home too. When I have regained that which my father lost they will have to think twice before comparing me with him. This is not only a war against the French, my dearest. It is a war against my own barons.'

She nodded. She was imagining victory. The greatest King in the world. She would be kind and gentle with Marguerite, the wife of the conquered. 'My dear sister,' she would say, 'rest assured no harm shall come to you. Henry would never do anything that would make me unhappy. You are safe.'

And so they came to France.

* * *

What a different story it was from that which they had been led to expect.

The King's mother Isabella de Lusignan greeted him with an affection which was surprisingly warm and emotional considering she had not seen him for more than twenty years and had during that time seemed to have ceased to remember his existence.

Bitter disillusion was to await Henry. The French were by no means unprepared. Louis was ready for him; moreover Henry had been misled by his mother who unknown to her husband had misrepresented the situation.

It was a disillusioned King who retreated before the French, as the realization that he was not the one who was to win the victory was brought home to him. He had been used by his mother whose feud with the Queen Mother of France would take her to great lengths—and which would in time result in her self-destruction.

In the meantime there was nothing for Henry and his army to do but retreat to Bordeaux and there hope to make some truce with the French.

There was one incident to lighten their melancholy.

Since they had left England, the Queen had once more become pregnant, and at Bordeaux she gave birth to another daughter.

'I will call her Beatrice after my mother,' declared Eleanor.

The little girl was beautiful and healthy and the King was able to forget his failure. He ordered that there should be great rejoicing and feasting in the castle of Bordeaux in spite of the fact that much of his treasure had gone in waging this unfortunate war.

When he returned, he said, he would impose a tax on all those who had not accompanied him to France. It was only right that they should pay for the privilege of staying at home.

He would find money somewhere.

And there were always the Jews.

*   *   *

Now that the war was over and a treaty made with Louis it was time for Sanchia to come to England that she might be married to the Earl of Cornwall.

Eleanor was beside herself with delight for Sanchia had sent a message to say that her mother had decided to accompany her.

'That makes you pleased, my love,' said Henry. 'You will have your sister and your mother at the same time.'

'Oh Henry, I am longing to show them our babies. I want them to know how happy I am.'

'I tell you this,' replied Henry. 'There are going to be such celebrations, such rejoicing that never was seen before.'

Eleanor threw her arms about him and told him he was the kindest and best of husbands in the world.

He was complacently happy. With such a wife it was easy to forget recent humiliations in France.

The arrival of Eleanor's mother and sister absorbed him. It must indeed be an occasion which would be remembered for ever. No expense must be spared, but where was the money coming from? Already there was grumbling throughout the land. No more taxes, said the citizens of London. No more poor and needy foreigners to be brought into England to live off the fat of the land provided by Englishmen.

'It will have to come from the Jews,' said Henry.

And from the long-suffering Jews it came.

Groaning under the iniquitous laws of taxation yet they paid, for they feared expulsion and going from bad to worse.

Not very long ago the tallages levied on them were fifteen thousand marks—a sum which would have been expected to cripple them. Yet they had paid, worked harder and continued to amass more money. Two years later the taxation had been raised to eighteen thousand marks.

'What can we do?' they asked each other. It was either pay or expulsion. And they could expect little sympathy from their less industrious neighbours. If they did not want to be exploited they should work less; they should not be so concerned with making money. If they hadn't got it they couldn't pay it.

The next imposition had been a third of their worldly goods

and even after that they were called on to raise twenty thousand marks.

It was heart-breaking for these people who while they loved work, loved even more the rewards it brought and must see this frittered away by the King on the friends and relations of his wife. It would have been intolerable if they had no alternative but to endure it.

Moreover, few had any sympathy for them. 'The Jews!' was the comment accompanied by a shrug of the shoulders. 'They have it. Let them pay it.'

So it was the Jews who must finance the enormous amount needed for the wedding celebrations of the Earl of Cornwall.

The King quickly forgot how the money had been raised, so happy was he in the Queen's pleasure.

'To have my mother and my sister here completes my joy,' she told Henry. 'I must be the happiest woman in the world.'

' 'Tis not more than you deserve,' he told her sólemnly.

Beatrice of Provence was as delighted to be with her daughter as Eleanor was to be with her.

How they discussed the old days! Little Beatrice was the only one left at home now.

'There is talk of one of Louis' brothers for her,' said the Countess.

'Then she will be near Marguerite as Sanchia will be near me.'

'It is a very happy state of affairs. I could not have wished for better,' declared the Countess.

'My only regret is that dear Father is not here.'

'I have something to tell you, Eleanor,' said the Countess. 'I had not done so before for fear of spoiling your happiness. Your father has been ailing for some time.'

'Oh, Mother, is he really ill?'

The Countess hesitated. 'The doctors think they can save him.'

'Oh dear, *dear* Father.'

'He is happy because you girls are so well settled. He talks of you continually, Eleanor ... even more than Marguerite. Of course at one time we thought that Marguerite had made the grandest of all marriages, but now we realize that you were always the clever one.'

'Marguerite is happy with Louis, is she not?'

'Oh yes. But she does not rule with him, as you do with Henry. Having seen you two together I believe that he would never do anything that did not please you.'

'I think that is so.'

'Marguerite is in no such position. Neither the King nor his mother would ask her opinion or listen to it if she gave it. This seems to suit Marguerite. Oh, she is not of your nature, Eleanor!'

'Nor ever was.'

'Nay, you were the leading spirit in the nursery. You always were. You have made yourself indispensable to the King. It is easy to see how he dotes on you. And your first-born a son. Little Edward!'

'He is four years old now, Mother. Is he not the most adorable creature you ever saw?'

'I found you girls as lovely. But Edward is indeed a beautiful child and Margaret and Beatrice are adorable. It made me very happy that you should call the child after me.'

'It was my idea and Henry of course agreed. He only wants to see me happy. And I am ... Mother, oh I am. Of course it was a pity we did not succeed in France....'

Eleanor looked sideways at her mother wondering how she felt about that, for victory for one daughter could have meant defeat for the other.

'Henry should never underestimate Louis,' she said slowly. 'Louis is a great King.'

'He is very serious I know, deeply concerned with state matters.'

'It leaves him less time to indulge his wife,' said Beatrice, 'but it is good for the Kingdom.'

'Oh, his mother insists. I believe she rules him still!'

'From what I hear, Eleanor, Louis rules himself as he rules his Kingdom. Marguerite thinks he is some sort of saint, I believe.'

Eleanor grimaced. 'Saints don't usually make good husbands.'

Beatrice took her daughter's hand. 'You have been fortunate. You have a husband who loves you dearly. You have three wonderful children and the eldest a boy!'

'And Marguerite only has girls—Blanche and Isabella.'

'She will have her boy in due time, I doubt not. But it is always agreeable when the first-born is a boy.'

Eleanor indulged herself by extolling the wonders of her son and Beatrice listened indulgently.

Thus they passed the time happily together and the day came when at Westminster Richard married Sanchia with more pomp and splendour than had been seen in London for many years.

'The King is determined to honour his wife's family,' said the people.

'At whose expense?'

'Oh, it is chiefly the Jews.'

As long as it was chiefly the Jews they could shrug aside the expense and revel in the decorated streets. They could line those streets and shout their greetings to the bride and groom.

So—apart from the Jews—people were happy on the wedding day of Sanchia and Richard of Cornwall.

*   *   *

Now that Sanchia was married the Countess Beatrice was ready to return to Provence.

It had been a wonderful occasion, one she would never forget. 'Such splendid entertainment,' she declared to Eleanor. 'The King did indeed honour us. Now I must return to your father. Poor Provence! We are very poor, Eleanor. Even more so than we were in the days of your childhood. Not that you ever realized that. Your father and I always kept that from you.'

Eleanor embraced her mother and replied that she trusted there was enough money to provide her father with what he wanted.

The Countess shook her head and looked sad. 'But I must not worry you with our problems. We are content because you have so much. So has Marguerite, but the French are parsimonious. They would give little away.'

Eleanor said quickly: 'I am going to speak to Henry. I am sure if I ask him he will not allow you to go back empty-handed.'

Nor did he. When the Countess left she took with her four thousand marks for the use of her husband.

What tears of sadness flowed when they said good-bye. The Countess must leave her two beloved daughters behind, but at least they had each other.

'Your father will weep with joy when he knows how happy you are. It will do him more good than anything else possibly could. Henry, my beloved son, how can I ever thank you for the happiness you have brought my daughter.'

Henry was deeply touched. He had been a little anxious about giving her the four thousand marks from his depleted exchequer, but it was worth it. Everything was worth it to please Eleanor and win the approval of her family.

Queenhithe

THERE was good news from Rome. Innocent IV had become Pope and soon after his installation in the Vatican he confirmed the appointment of Boniface of Savoy as Archbishop of Canterbury.

Henry joyfully took the news to Eleanor who embraced him warmly. This was indeed triumph. The greatest office in the country—outside that of the King—to go to her uncle.

Boniface lost no time in setting out for England where he was warmly welcomed by the King and Queen. He was not so happily received by the people who asked themselves how many more foreigners the Queen would introduce into the country to the detriment of its natives.

Eleanor was in fact becoming very unpopular. She was unhappy about this while pretending to ignore it; but when she rode out there were sullen looks cast in her direction and the King was only cheered when he was not with her.

She refused to be overawed by their dislike. She told herself that if she wanted to bring her friends to England, she would.

It was the city of London which was particularly aroused against her. There had been too many taxes to be paid by them to raise money for the Queen's dependents and they blamed her for the King's extravagance.

They disliked her haughty manners and there was one thing for which they could never forgive her and that was what had come to be called Queenhithe. Her uxorious husband who was always considering ways in which he could win her approval and show his affection had allowed her to insist that all vessels carrying the valuable cargoes of wool or corn must unload at the quay he had given her. She made it an offence for them to land their goods elsewhere, thus making sure of receiving heavy dues.

There was a great deal of murmuring in the streets about Queenhithe as they called this tax and there was many a dispute about it.

'It was a bad day for England,' it was said, 'when the thieving foreigners were brought to our shores.'

The arrival of Boniface did much to aggravate this situation, and although he was received at Canterbury it was with no good grace. He had come attended by a retinue of his own countrymen and naturally places had to be found for them in Canterbury.

Both Henry and Eleanor seemed to be quite unaware of their growing unpopularity which was largely concentrated on Eleanor because of the increasing number of foreigners she brought into the country. Boniface was haughty and appeared to believe that since his niece was the Queen of England that entitled him to behave as though the entire country belonged to her. London had always stood aloof from the rest of the country. It was the capital and centre of trade, and therefore determined to have a say in England's affairs. London had always to be won over if it were to give its support to the Sovereign. It was London that had refused to give Matilda a crown and passed it to Stephen. Wise monarchs remembered that. John had been far from wise and it seemed that his son Henry, out of besotted devotion to his wife, forgot it also. At least neither the King nor the Queen thought to remind Boniface that he must go carefully with the citizens of London.

It was not long after the inauguration of Boniface that the Archbishop visited the Priory of St Bartholomew in London which was in the diocese of the Bishop of London.

This visit should not have been made except in the company of the Bishop or at least on his invitation and when the new Archbishop—so clearly a foreigner—arrived at the Priory there was some consternation.

The monks conferred together and decided that since he held the office of Archbishop of Canterbury—although he was not of their choosing—they should show respect to him and they proceeded from the Priory in solemn procession to pay him homage.

The Archbishop told them in a somewhat haughty way
that this was not merely a formal visit; he wished to see how
the Priory was run and whether it met with his approval. This
was too much for the monks and the Sub Prior stepped forward.

'My Lord Archbishop,' he said, 'you are newly come to this
country and know not our customs. We have our revered
Bishop of London whose place it is—and his alone—to come
in this way.'

Boniface was incensed. He was aware of the sullen looks
which followed him in the streets. He knew that his niece
was resented. In a sudden temper he lifted his hand and struck
the Sub Prior across the face with such strength that the
man fell against a pillar and slipped to the ground.

Seeing him thus the Archbishop strode to him, tore the
cope from his shoulders and stamped on it. He was about to
turn on the Sub Prior who had risen shakily to his feet when
one of the monks shouted: 'Save the Sub Prior.' And in a
body they surrounded Boniface

They realized then that beneath his robes Boniface was in
armour and had clearly come ready for battle. Moreover he
gave a shout to his followers, who threw off their outer garments and stood exposed in sword and armour ready for
battle.

'Go to then,' shouted Boniface. 'Show these English traitors
what happens to those who withstand me.'

Whereupon Boniface's armed men fell upon the defenceless monks, beat them, kicked them, tore off their garments
and trampled on them.

Four of the monks escaped and went in all haste to the
Bishop's Palace. He was horrified to see them and even more
so when he heard what had happened.

'The arrogant foreigner,' he cried. 'Go at once to the King.
Show him your wounds and tattered garments. Tell him what
has happened. Only if he sees you thus can he realize the indignity you have suffered.'

On their way to the palace the monks were stopped by
certain citizens who asked how they came to be in such a sorry
state. They told how Boniface, the foreign Archbishop, had
invaded the Priory and ill-treated them.

'We will show this foreigner what it means to ill-treat our
monks,' cried one man. 'We will get this Boniface. He will
be less bonny of face when we have done with him.'

The monks went on to the palace.

The King was with the Queen in the nursery playing with the children when an attendant arrived to say that some monks who had been ill-treated by the Archbishop of Canterbury were asking for an audience with the King.

'Ill-treated by my uncle!' cried the Queen. 'What nonsense is this?'

'They have clearly been ill-treated, my lady,' was the answer.

Henry turned to the man but Eleanor laid her hand on his arm.

'Don't see these monks,' she whispered. 'You know what this means. They are protesting against your choice of Archbishop. Didn't they try to do that before?'

Henry looked at her. So they did.

'You can depend upon it this it a trick. Tell them to go away.'

'Tell them to go away,' said Henry. 'I shall not see them.'

The attendant bowed and retired.

Henry looked disturbed but Eleanor said: Come and see how Edward throws this dice. I am sure he will be a real little gambler ere long.'

And Henry was glad to push the tiresome monks from his mind.

Meanwhile the people of London were gathering in the streets. Here was a chance to show their detestation of the foreigners. The monks had been ill-treated. Were they going to let this pass?

'Where is the ruffian?' they shouted. 'Where is he who calls himself Archbishop and ill-treats our monks.'

It was a moment of horror for the Archbishop when, from the upper turret of the Priory, he saw the approaching mob.

He was armed and so were his followers but although they could defeat defenceless monks they might not stand such a good chance against an angry crowd bent on destruction.

'Quick. We must get out of here,' he shouted.

'The river, my lord. Let us get down with all speed to the privy stairs.'

The man was right. There were several boats tied at the stairs, and in these there was room for everyone so the alarmed Archbishop accompanied by his servants managed to escape down the river.

At the palace he alighted and went at once to see the King and Queen.

Eleanor ran to him in some alarm.

'All is well,' he told her. 'The monks of St Bartholomew's should be reprimanded. Do you know they attacked me in their Priory.'

'This is monstrous,' cried the King.

'I told them I would have none of their insolence and I taught the Sub Prior a lesson.'

'Let us hope that he learned it well.'

'I think he may do if you give him no pity. I feel sure that he and his fellows will come complaining to you of their ill-treatment. I know your wisdom, nephew. You will give them short shrift.'

'Henry will know how to deal with the rogues,' declared Eleanor. 'He knows they are telling him that they believe they should choose their Archbishop when all know it is the prerogative of the King.'

'They will get no mercy or pity from me,' said Henry firmly.

Eleanor laughed softly and slipped her arm through his.

* * *

Such incidents added to the gathering storm but neither the King nor the Queen seemed aware of this. When money was needed it seemed easy to inflict taxes. Henry indulged the Queen's countrymen and women because it pleased her that he should. His personal extravagance was building. Architecture gave him a singular pleasure and he liked to plan new buildings and change old ones.

One of his favourite residences was Windsor. Here the countryside was particularly beautiful with the Thames winding its way through meadow and woodland. The very name owed itself to this for it was said by some that the Saxon name Windlesofra meant winding course. Others said that the name came from Wynd is Sore because on the high ground the wind in winter was fierce, while some insisted that Windsor meant Wind us Over and referred to the ferry boat with ropes and pole which was used to take people across.

However the name was derived Henry loved the place. Perhaps he had been drawn to it in the first place because his idol Edward the Confessor was reputed to have kept Court here. William the Conqueror had been there too. So, less happily, had Henry's father John who had stayed here during that wretched period of his life when he had been forced to sign Magna Carta.

With his passion for building Henry had made alterations to the Castle. He had enlarged the Lower Ward and added a chapel of which he was very proud. He never tired of telling people that it was seventy feet long and twenty-eight feet wide and the wood roof had been lined and painted like stone and covered with lead.

He regarded Windsor as second in importance only to the Tower of London and it was much more pleasant to live in.

So to Windsor he came whenever he could and he and Eleanor both liked the children to be there because they considered it to be most healthy.

It was while they were riding through the streets of Windsor that they noticed a little girl begging by the roadside. Her clothes were tattered and her hair hung limply about her little white face.

The Queen turned to Henry who understood immediately what she meant and he threw a coin to the child. The Queen's eyes softened as she saw the little creature catch it and the joy which illuminated her face.

In her own nursery while Eleanor gloated over her healthy children the face of the little beggar girl kept rising in her mind.

'What is it?' asked the King. 'You are sad today.'

'I was thinking of that child. She could not be much older than our Edward. To think that she is often hungry ... so dirty and tattered. And there must be many like her.'

The King nodded.

'There have always been beggars,' he said.

'I like not to see little children go hungry,' replied the Queen.

And every now and then she would remember the little beggar girl and a certain melancholy would linger.

Then the King had an idea which he thought would please her. He came to her beaming with satisfaction.

'What do you think I have just done, Eleanor?' he asked, and as she could not guess, he told her.

'I have sent out an order that all the poor children from the streets of Windsor and the surrounding villages shall be collected and brought into the castle. There in the great hall there shall be such a feast as they will remember all their lives.'

'Henry,' she clasped her hands and gazed at him in delight. 'You are doing this for me,' she added soberly.

'What better reason could there be?'

'You are so good, Henry. I never dreamed ... so long ago it seems now ... in Provence....'

He put his arm about her. 'We shall be there,' he said, 'you

and I, to see their pleasure. We shall sit at the high table and
watch them. We'll have the babies there.'

'The girls will be too young to know what it is about.'

'Edward then.'

She was thoughtful visualizing it. 'The people must love you
after this,' she cried. 'There has been so much unkindness ...
we have been so criticized....'

'I was not thinking of it to please the people but to please
you.'

'I cannot tell you how it pleases me. But will anything please
them?'

'For a day, mayhap.'

The arrangements were made and it must have been the
strangest sight the old hall had ever seen when the poor children of Windsor came crowding into it. They looked incon-
gruous there among the grandeur which was the home of
kings.

But Henry and Eleanor were delighted. They wore their
crowns because they thought the children would expect it and
indeed the most inspiring sights in that hall for most of the
children were the two glittering figures at the high table. Eyes
were fixed on them until the good things they were to eat were
set on the trestle tables.

Eleanor had at the last moment been afraid to bring Edward
down.

'Such children might have some disease which could harm
him,' she decided.

No, the little boy was safe with his nurses although she
agreed with Henry that it would have been a good experience
for him to see how a monarch's popularity should be courted.

The feast was a great success; and when the children had
eaten the tables were cleared away and games were played.

Some of the children's parents were allowed into the castle
and to these Henry announced that his own children were to
be weighed and their weight in silver would be distributed
among the poor.

The people cheered and cried: 'God Bless the King.'

And for a week whenever he and the Queen ventured out
in the town of Windsor they were greeted with vociferous
affection.

'It was a very clever thing to do,' said the Queen admiringly, 'as well as a good one.'

*   *   *

Richard was happy in his marriage with Sanchia. The bond between the sisters was firm and because of this Richard found himself more and more with his brother and consequently giving him his support. This was noticed by the barons who had looked to him as their leader in their conflicts with Henry, and they viewed the situation with some dismay because Richard had seemed such a natural leader.

Through Richard's first marriage with Isabella, who had been William Marshal's daughter, he had been often in the company of the barons who were determined to uphold Magna Carta; and now his links with them were weakening; through Sanchia and her constant contact with her sister he was definitely veering towards the Court.

At the same time he was able to take a clearer view of the state of the country than Henry was, and there were often times when he was disturbed by the way in which everything was going.

Sometimes he visualized the barons rising once more against Henry as they had against John. That had been a dangerous precedent. It had been done once and could be done again. Once a king had been brought to his knees it was something which would never be forgotten.

There was a great deal to live down and sometimes he thought that Henry deliberately shut his eyes to this.

Richard knew that there was a great deal of dissatisfaction particularly in the capital. He had his men placed in the taverns and along the water front that they might inform him of what was being said.

The constant cause of complaint was the Queen's family . . . the foreigners. And of course the Queen's family was Sanchia's family.

He talked to Sanchia at times for he wondered if perhaps she might be the one to warn the Queen who would warn the King.

Sanchia was more reasonable than her sister; of a gentler nature than Eleanor she was ready to listen—particularly to Richard.

'It is difficult to tell Eleanor anything she does not want to hear,' she explained.

'I know it well,' replied Richard. 'I am surprised that it should be so in one so intelligent.'

'Eleanor always believed that she was capable of anything, and so much that she tries for she gets.'

'We are dealing with a nation,' he replied. 'People can sud-

denly rise against their rulers. They endure a good deal and
then something happens which may seem trivial ... and that
is the spark which starts the fire.'

'And you are very anxious Richard?'

'I see trouble ahead. Not immediate perhaps ... but on
the horizon. This affair of your Uncle Boniface....'

'Oh, that is over and forgotten.'

'Forgotten. It will never be forgotten. The Londoners will
store it up in their memories and it will be brought out at
some later date. It is not forgotten, I assure you, and it was
most unfortunate. Sanchia, when you get the opportunity try
to make your uncles understand the English. They are not
always what they seem. They accept something—appearing to
be meek. Make no mistake. That is not meekness. It is a kind
of lethargy, a disinclination to arise and do something ...
but depend upon it in due course the urge will come ... and
then when they rise up you see them in their true colours.
They will then go on fighting until they get what they want.'

'I will do what I can.'

He nodded slowly. 'One canker in the heart of the Londoners is Queenhithe. As long as that continues the discontent
will grow. I have tried to explain to Eleanor that the people
do not like it, that every time they pay their dues they curse
her. They blame her more than the King. He is an Englishman. She is a foreigner. I think I will seize the first opportunity
of speaking to her about the Queenhithe for it becomes more
dangerous the longer it goes on.'

Sanchia said: 'I can see that you really are concerned.'

He nodded. 'I was too young to see what happened to my
father, but Heaven knows it was drummed into me enough.
Peter de Mauley and Roger d'Acastre explained it to me
continually when I was at Corfe. I think they believed then
that I might one day be King. The way my father went was
the way not to go.'

'You don't think Henry is going that way, do you?'

'Not so blatantly. Henry is a good man ... a religious man,
a faithful husband and a good father. He is not always wise
in his kingship though and that is what I am afraid of. One
step out of line and you can hear the whisper Magna Carta
in the very air.'

'What shall you do, Richard?'

'Everything I can to keep him on the throne.'

Yes, that was it. A few years ago he would have been less
loyal to his brother. He would have talked of these matters

with Clare, Chester, any of his friends who were determined
that the King should not have too much power. He was the
King's man now and his main object was to keep his brother
on the throne.

He was often at Windsor because that was where the children were and his own son Henry was there. So far Sanchia had
given him no children which was sad, but while he had Henry
he could be grateful. Henry was a fine boy—bright, intelligent and handsome. He was now about ten years old and it
was a joy to see him. What a son did for a man! And he owed
Henry to Isabella.

The young Edward was growing up steadily although
plagued by one or two minor ailments which sent his parents
frantic with anxiety. The two little girls were pleasant and
Henry seemed set fair to have a fine family.

If only he would be a little more discreet in welcoming his
wife's relations and when they came showering them with gifts,
which had to be paid for by his subjects. It was folly. It might
well be madness.

He found Eleanor working at her tapestry with several of
her women. There was an air of smugness about her, he
thought.

My God, he thought, I believe she is pregnant again.

'My dear brother.' Her welcome was genuine. She had
always had a fondness for him since in a way she owed her
presence here to him; and now that he was her sister's husband
he was doubly dear to her.

'Dear lady,' he murmured, kissing her hand.

He raised his eyebrows in a manner to indicate that he
would like to speak to her alone and she immediately waved a
hand to dismiss the women.

'How is my sister?' she asked.

'Very well.'

'It seems long since I saw her though I suppose it is not. I
am so happy that she is in England.'

'She is happy to be here.'

He seated himself on a stool close to her.

'You seem particularly content this day,' he said looking at
her interrogatively.

'Did you guess then?'

'So it is indeed so. Henry is delighted, I know.'

'He is beside himself with joy. It should be a boy this
time.'

'Ha, that will put young Edward's nose out of joint.'

'He said he would like a brother. He is a little contempt-
uous of two sisters. Your Henry is a great friend of Edward's
already.'

'He is a good diplomat, my Henry.'

'Oh Edward has the sweetest nature.'

'Madam, I know from Henry that you are blessed with the
paragon of all children.'

She laughed. 'Come, Richard,' she said, 'you have a very
good opinion of your son Henry.'

'What fortunate people we are to possess such children! I
wish we could go on talking of them all through the day for I
swear we should never get tired of the subject. But there is
something else I have come to say.'

'Say on, Richard,'

'It is easier to talk to you....' A little flattery did no harm
and she was very susceptible to it. 'I am concerned.'

'On what?' she asked sharply.

'There is a lot of dissatisfaction throughout the country ...
and particularly in London.'

'The Londoners are always making trouble.'

'They are a proud people.'

'They think London is England, and that no city in the
country compares with theirs.'

'Nor does it, my lady, for trade, for riches, for importance.
We have to remember that these people who are murmuring
are the merchants ... the traders ... important to the wealth
of the country.'

'The Jews perhaps.'

'Perhaps the Jews.'

'They have no right to be here. They should pay for the
privilege.'

'If we lost them we should lose a great deal besides. But I
have not come to talk to you of the Jews. There is this matter
of the Queenhithe which is causing such dissatisfaction in
London.'

'Oh I know. They grumble every time they pay their dues.
The dues at Queenhithe have always been the perquisite of
the queens of England.'

'With this difference,' insisted Richard, 'that you have induced Henry to command that all the richest cargoes are
landed at Queenhithe and that the price of the dues has been
considerably raised.'

'It is no more than they owe me.'

'They do not see it as such. It is one of those seemingly

unimportant matters which can be the beginning of big trouble.'

'Do you want me to go to the people and say I am sorry. I should never have taken these dues?'

'No. But I will buy Queenhithe from you.'

'You, Richard! It would be very costly.'

'I am not poor. I am very serious on this. I believe that if something is not done about this matter the next we hear will be of rioting.'

'The rioters will be punished.'

'It is not as easy as that, Eleanor. The mob can be terrible. It is never wise to arouse it for once it is there one can never be certain where it will end.'

She was silent. He would have to pay a large sum for the Queenhithe. He could do so, for it was true that he was very rich. One rarely heard of his being short of money, which was Henry's continual complaint. Richard was different from Henry. He lacked his generosity. Uncle Boniface had asked him for money and Richard had said that he could not give it but would lend it, if he wished.

Uncle Boniface had not wished.

Henry would have given the money generously, to please her.

To give up Queenhithe! Well, it would be a test. There was constant complaint. When she rode out into the streets people whispered it. She knew it was a matter which caused great displeasure.

She would sell. Richard should take over Queenhithe. Then he would see that the venom of those grasping merchants was turned on him.

Once it was in Richard's hands he let it to the Mayor of London for a rent of fifty pounds a year. The Mayor could deal with it as he thought fit; and if the London merchants did not like what he did the matter was between them and their mayor.

He had lifted the royal family out of the quarrel.

Ceremony at Beaulieu

WHILE Eleanor was awaiting the birth of her baby there was sad news from Provence.

Her father was very ill.

Sanchia immediately came to Windsor where Eleanor was at this time. The sisters embraced and Eleanor took Sanchia to her private chamber where they might be alone together.

'Our mother said how ill he was when she came for your wedding,' said Eleanor.

'Yes, I know. He wanted to come ... oh how he wanted to come, but he was too feeble.'

'Do you think,' said Eleanor, 'that he is already dead?'

'What makes you say that?'

'Our mother would warn us first. She would think it would lessen the shock.'

They stared blankly at each other. It was a long time since Eleanor had seen her father but her memories of him were still very fresh and in their minds both she and Sanchia could easily slip back into those happy days of their childhood.

'It is so difficult to imagine it without him,' said Eleanor. 'Our poor mother will be desolate. I shall bring her over here.'

Sanchia was silent thinking of what Richard had said about the people of England and their attitude to the Queen's relations.

'There is still Beatrice left,' said Sanchia.

'Our father will not be able to find a husband for her now. Romeo will help.'

'Poor Beatrice, how sad for her.'

While they talked another messenger arrived at the castle.

It was as Eleanor had feared. The Count was dead.

*   *   *

Eleanor was mildly irritated when she heard that her father had left everything to his unmarried daughter Beatrice.

'He had forgotten that he had four daughters,' she said with some asperity.

'Oh no,' replied Sanchia. 'Marguerite and you and I are happily married to rich husbands. Beatrice has yet to find one.'

'There will be no dearth of offers for her now.'

The matter of the inheritance took the edge off Eleanor's mourning, and when she heard suitors were arriving in Provence every day she was cynically amused.

The Countess however did not consider any of them of sufficient merit and Henry came to her one day in great excitement because he had received news that Jaime, the King of Aragon, had besieged the town of Aix which he determined to hold until the Countess of Provence gave her daughter Beatrice in marriage to his son Pedro.

What a romantic situation! It was worthy of one of the poems she used to write. And Beatrice was at the centre of the drama—all because she was the youngest one and unmarried, still at home and had therefore received her father's inheritance.

There was a letter from Marguerite to her sisters.

They must not be alarmed on Beatrice's account. It was true that the King of Aragon was invading Provence in the hope of winning Beatrice. They called him the Conqueror because of his victories, but Louis had decided to step in.

The fact was that Louis' brother Charles of Anjou had a great desire to marry Beatrice and had always believed that he would in due course. Therefore Charles was riding into Provence to send the so-called Conqueror Jaime about his business.

It was very exciting and each day she and Sanchia waited for news of the battle for Beatrice.

In the meantime Eleanor was brought to bed. What rejoicing there was when this time she produced a bonny boy.

They called him Edmund and this addition to their nursery so delighted the King and Queen that Eleanor forgot her resentment at being cut out of her father's will. News came of the victorious campaign waged by Charles of Anjou. It had been an almost foregone conclusion that the King of Aragon —Conqueror though he might call himself—could not win against Charles of Anjou who had the support of his mighty brother.

In due course the wedding of Beatrice and Charles was celebrated in Paris. There was now a new Count of Provence —Beatrice's husband.

*   *   *

One of the greatest joys of Eleanor's life was to be with her children and of all of them she could not help loving her first-born best.

Whenever she could be with him, she was; and Henry shared her feelings. It was not so easy for him, of course. He had other duties to perform, but he never tried to persuade her to accompany him because he knew how she longed to be with their children.

When they were together they talked of Edward continually. Henry wanted to endow him with lands and castles, and even Eleanor laughed at him and said that would come later, the child was too young as yet.

One thing she did promise herself that Edward should accompany her when she made the dedication of a new church in Beaulieu Abbey.

'He cannot start too soon to show himself in public,' she said. 'And everywhere he goes people will love him.'

It was true that when the little boy accompanied his parents the populace showed a more kindly attitude towards them, and Henry thought it an excellent idea that his mother should take Edward to the dedication.

Her heart thrilled with pride as she stepped into the nursery and he bounded forward and threw his arms about her knees.

'My darling, is this the way to greet the Queen?' she asked.

Then she lifted him in her arms and covered his face with kisses.

'How is my Edward this day?'

'I am well,' he answered.

She examined him intently. Were his hands a little feverish, his eyes a little too bright? Or was that due to the excitement of seeing his mother?

Robert Burnell, who was his chaplain and confidential servant, was hovering.

'The Lord Edward has been suffering from slight rheum this last few days, my lady.'

Terror gripped her heart as it always did when any of the children suffered some ailment.

'How has he been, Robert? Are you sure this is nothing serious?'

'My lady, he is subject to these rheums.'

She did not like him to be subject to rheums. They frightened her.

'I rode out with Henry this morning, my lady,' said Edward. 'My horse was faster than his.'

Oh God, were they letting him ride too fast? What if he fell? Should he not have been kept indoors with such a rheum?

She looked anxiously at Robert Burnell. 'Lord Edward *will* vie with everyone and do his best to win,' he told her.

'And always does, my lady,' declared Edward.

'Not always, my lord,' warned his mentor and religious instructor Burnell.

'Well very often,' said Edward stoutly.

His mother ruffled his hair.

'I have messages from your father,' she said. 'The King wants to know whether you have been good in your manners and your lessons. What shall I tell him?'

'That I am very good,' said Edward.

'Sometimes,' added Burnell.

Eleanor wished Burnell would let the dear boy enjoy his triumphs in peace but of course she knew that it was good for him to be curbed and he could not have a better tutor than Robert Burnell.

'My dearest, I am going to take you with me to Beaulieu Abbey.'

'When?'

'In a short while. We are going to be present at the dedication of the Church.'

'It will be a very solemn ceremony, my lord,' said Burnell.

'Oh, must I be solemn then?' Edward coughed slightly, and Eleanor's fears rose again.

'It is a small cough, my lady,' said Burnell. 'It goes and comes.'

'We must see that it goes and does not come,' she answered tersely.

Were they caring for him? Did they realize how precious this child was? Oh, some might say, he had a brother and was not so important now. They were wrong, wrong. No one could ever mean to her what her beloved Edward did ... not even Henry.

*   *   *

How proud she was of him riding by her side on his little white palfrey. His cousin Henry, four years his senior, rode on the other side of him—a handsome boy but in her eyes insignificant compared with the flaxen beauty of her own son.

He coughed a little as they rode and she became more and more uneasy as they approached Beaulieu; she felt almost angry with young Henry for being in such obvious good health.

The Abbey had been founded by Henry's father, King John. It was one of his more laudable acts which he performed from time to time, more, Henry said, from a sense of placating Heaven than for his own virtuous inclinations. Set among beechwoods it was a beautiful sight and the Cistercian monks would be delighted at this sign of royal patronage with their Queen and their future King gracing the dedication of the newly erected church.

The tolling of the bells and the sombre clad monks clearly fascinated Edward, but as his cough persisted his mother grew less and less interested in what was happening about her.

The monks filed into the church chanting as they came. The Queen with her son beside her and Henry and Edward's knights seated behind—among them Robert Burnell—witnessed the ceremony of the dedication.

When it was over the Queen took her son's hand and to her dismay found that it was burning hot.

She turned to Robert Burnell and said: 'The lord Edward has a fever.'

'It is the rheum, Madam,' answered Burnell. 'It would be a good plan to get back to the castle without delay.'

'It is too dangerous,' said the Queen. 'He must not go out. He shall stay here and the doctors shall come to him. Please send for them at once.'

'My lady, he cannot stay here. This is a very strict order.'

'I care not how strict it be!' retorted the Queen. 'My son is to run no risks whatever the order.'

'It will give great offence to the Abbot.'

'Then pray let us give offence to the Abbot. Send for the doctors without delay. Then let a message be delivered to the King.'

Robert Burnell knew that it would be unwise not to obey the Queen when she was in such a mood. It was useless to remind her that the boy often suffered these fevers and that doubtless they were a childhood weakness that he would grow out of as he became older.

The monks who had heard what was going on immediately

went to the Abbot to tell him. He came out without delay.

'Madam,' he said, 'I hear you want to nurse the lord Edward here. The monks will care for him.'

'I have sent for the King's doctors.'

The Abbot bowed his head. 'My lady, you may safely leave him in our care.'

'Leave my son! Oh no, my lord Abbot. When my son is ill, I am the one who cares for him.'

'My lady, women cannot stay in this abbey. The order is very strict.'

'Then the order shall be changed,' declared Eleanor imperiously. 'I am not merely a woman, my lord Abbot, I am your Queen. You would be wise to show me more hospitality. Take me to a bed that my son may be made comfortable. And let me tell you this: *I* shall stay here until he is well enough to travel. *I* shall look after him, so you and your monks had better get accustomed to housing a woman in your abbey.'

The Abbot was nonplussed. He could not allow her to stay. It was unprecedented. The boy could be cared for, yes indeed, but the Queen must go.

He tried to explain but her fear for her son sent her into a raging fury. How dared this fool of an Abbot quibble about his Cistercian laws when the heir to the throne was sick and might die? The thought sent her into a frenzy.

'I will hear no more,' she cried. 'Remember that you owe your existence to the favours of kings. My husband's father founded this place. The Queen can as easily destroy it . . . ay, and she will if aught happens to her son through your negligence. I want every comfort for the lord Edward and that includes having his mother to nurse him.'

The Abbot knew himself beaten. It would go ill with them all if the boy was taken away and died. Everyone would say it was due to his action. So it was wise to waive rules and allow the Queen to stay with her son.

The doctors arrived and were a long time with Edward. The Queen said she insisted on knowing the truth which they assured her they had told her. The boy was suffering from a slight fever—nothing which good nursing could not cure. The Queen was unduly disturbed.

But she was taking no chances. She was at her son's bedside for several days and nights and not until he had lost his fever did she sleep a little.

Then she gave thanks at the altar of the newly dedicated church for her son's recovery and with great joy she rode back to the castle, though she insisted that her son be carried part of the way in a litter. Edward protested loudly at the idea of being carried. He was able to ride, he cried. He was the best rider of all the boys. People would laugh at him for being carried.

Very well, she said, he should ride awhile but if she saw the least hint of fatigue he should go into a litter.

She was so happy to have him beside her, the healthy colour back in his cheeks, his flaxen hair glinting in the sunlight while he chattered about his new horses and falcons.

*   *   *

The effect of Henry's weak rule was beginning to be felt throughout the country. It had always been so. In the days of the Conqueror, England had been made safe for travellers simply because the Conqueror severely punished any man or woman who was caught stealing. No one thought a purse of gold worth the loss of ears, nose or eyes—or a foot or a hand. The punishment instigated by the Conqueror might have been harsh but it was effective. He had determined to make England safe for travellers and he had done so. In the reign of Rufus law and order disappeared but it was brought back by Henry I. Weak Stephen allowed it to lapse again and the robber barons sprang up. Travellers were waylaid, taken to the residences of the robber barons and held to ransom, robbed of everything they had, tortured for the barons' amusement and that of their guests and lawlessness prevailed. Henry II was another such as Henry I and the Conqueror. He wanted a prosperous land which could only flourish within the law. The disaster of John's rule had been felt far and wide but under the wise direction of William the Marshal and Hubert de Burgh the law had once more been enforced. Now it was lagging again and the signs of disruption were beginning to be seen throughout the land.

The country needed a strong King supported by strong men; and since Henry's marriage, his one idea seemed to have been to bring his wife's friends and relations into the country and lavish every favour upon them.

So bad were the roads becoming that when the King and Queen were travelling in Hampshire with a small retinue they were set upon by a band of robbers; much of their baggage was stolen and their lives were in danger. They were saved by the realization of who they were for even robbers must be afraid of what could result if they murdered the King and Queen.

An example of how the authority of the law was fast waning was given by one man who, when summoned to appear before the King's Bench, forced the King's officer, who delivered the royal warrant, to eat it.

There was growing anxiety and it was becoming obvious that many of the barons were meeting to discuss the state of affairs and they were setting themselves against the King and what they called his foreigners. The conflict would have come to a head before but for the marriage of Richard of Cornwall with the Queen's sister, for since that time his wife had subtly brought him round to her way of thinking which was of course to support the Queen and her relations.

But with or without Richard's support the barons were beginning to feel that something would have to be done.

The people of London were the most vociferous and rebellious. They had a personal grudge against the Queen because of memories of the Queenhithe and whenever the royal pair needed money—which seemed to be all the time—it was to rich London that they looked to supply it.

Henry and Eleanor began to dread going to Westminster, for there they were made more aware of their unpopularity than anywhere else.

News came from France of the death of Henry's mother Isabella of Angoulême. Her turbulent life had ended in the Convent of Fontevrault and it was a relief to everyone.

Henry's mind was taken off the troubles in his kingdom when rebellion broke out in Wales. There was no money with which to conduct a campaign and Henry would have attempted to raise it from the Londoners. Richard saw that the citizens of the capital were getting towards the end of their patience and he himself supplied the means for conducting the campaign by pawning his own jewels.

This campaign proved fruitless and after the destruction of Welsh crops which meant privation for the Welsh and by no means increased their friendship with the English, Henry left the field of action with nothing gained and the situation worse than it had been in the beginning.

'The King is another such as his father,' was the grumble throughout the land. Because he was a good father, a loving husband and a religious man did not mean that he was a good King, and every serious-minded man in the country knew that what England needed more than anything was a wise ruler.

In the midst of these troubles Eleanor gave birth to another son. He was called Richard after his uncle the Earl of Cornwall and his great uncle Coeur de Lion. Alas the child was sickly at his birth and he died within a few months.

Eleanor was very melancholy, and Henry gave himself up to comforting her. They spent a good deal of their time in their nurseries. They had four healthy children—two boys and two girls, he kept telling her, but it was difficult to console Eleanor for the loss of her baby. She watched over Edward even more assiduously than before and any minor ailment could throw her into a frenzy of anxiety.

A year after her panic at Beaulieu the same fever attacked Edward again and this time he was really in danger. Eleanor was frantic. So was Henry. They sat by the boy's bed day and night; they neither slept nor ate. They remained on their knees throughout the long hours pleading with Heaven to spare this boy who was the delight of their lives.

In every monastery and church prayers were offered up for his return to health. Promises were made to Heaven. What monasteries should be built, what churches dedicated. God had only to name his price.

And it seemed God answered for one night the fever passed and the doctors declared Edward would live.

Henry and Eleanor clung together in their relief. Their darling lived. There was nothing else at that moment that they wanted in life. They were completely happy.

Moreover in a few weeks Edward emerged as bright and energetic as ever, as though he was some superhuman being who could throw off a fever as others did a common cold.

Every morning for a month the Queen went to his chamber as soon as she arose just to assure herself that her beloved child was really there.

Edward, forceful by nature, a little arrogant in his youth, had naturally come to the conclusion that he was a very important person indeed.

He was clever as well as able to excel at sport. He spoke French and Latin fluently and had a fine command of the English language. For some reason he had developed a slight stammer but even this the Queen found enchanting. He was very fond of the outdoor life—far more so than he was of learning although his tutors said he could have been a scholar with application. But Edward liked better to joust, to outride his companions, to excel at ball sports and in his training for knighthood. He could always be seen among his companions because he was so much taller than they were and his bright flaxen hair was readily recognizable. His parents called him affectionately, Edward Longshanks, and they marvelled at his healthy good looks while they were terrified of that childhood fever which had been the bogy to haunt their lives. When a whole year passed without a return of it they were gleeful. Robert Burnell was right. It was a childhood complaint and he would grow out of it.

*   *   *

The Queen's mother, the widowed Countess of Provence, paid another visit to England.

It was a great joy for Sanchia and Eleanor to be reunited with their mother and to hear from her all the excitement there had been over Beatrice's marriage. They laughed to think how cleverly everything had worked out. Beatrice had married the brother of Marguerite's husband and Sanchia the brother of Eleanor's.

Such a closely knit family could not but rejoice in an arrangement like that.

Eleanor wanted her mother to be fêted as lavishly as she had been when she had come over for Sanchia's wedding and the Countess seemed to take everything that was done for her as her due. And of course Henry must please Eleanor, who had now won Sanchia to her side and Sanchia did her best to persuade Richard that her family were the responsibility of the English crown.

Eleanor had come to England, had given the King great happiness, had provided the people with Edward the heir who, however unpopular his parents might be, was cheered wherever he went. Therefore the House of Provence should be rewarded.

There was a further obligation. On the death of Isabella of Angoulême her children decided to pay a visit to their half-brother. News had come to them that the Queen's family were doing very well in England and they did not see why some of the pickings should not come to their family—after all they shared the King's mother.

Within a year of Isabella's death there arrived Henry's half-brothers Guy de Lusignan, William of Valence—who became known as such after the death of Eleanor's uncle—and Aymer de Valence. Not only did they come but they brought their sister Alicia with them. She needed a rich husband and the young men needed wives who could bring them lands.

Henry was delighted to discover his family and he welcomed them warmly. However not only did they add to his financial burden but in their train they brought their friends and attendants, all hungry for what they could find from what seemed to them the King's inexhaustible coffers.

In desperation he found a husband for Alicia in the Earl of Warrenne who was rich and by no means averse to allying himself with the royal family. The great asset of the Lusignans was that they were the King's half-brothers.

Henry immediately arranged for William to marry Joan de Munchensi the only surviving child of a wealthy baron; the girl's mother had been the fifth daughter of the first William Marshal and had brought to her husband her share of the very rich Marshal inheritance. Henry promised that there should be equally good opportunities for the others and as Aymer was in Holy Orders his advantages could come through the church.

All this which was so gratifying to the recipients was sullenly watched by the natives of England who saw the country's riches being frittered away to foreigners.

The troubles of the country were multiplying. Robbery and violence had increased still more on the high roads. Simon de Montfort, who had undertaken, at the King's request, the government of Gascony, one of the few remaining English possessions in France, was continually asking for help to pay his men and keep order there. His pleas were constantly ignored. It began to dawn on the English that if this state of affairs continued Gascony would be added to the list of lost possessions.

But Henry seemed to be intent only on playing the fairy godfather to his wife's friends and relations, his half-brothers and sisters and their friends.

There were constant demands for money and Henry simply did not know where to look for it. He could only think of the Jews and there began a persecution of the members of this unfortunate race as yet unprecedented in England.

They were the easiest people to mulct as they did not attempt to form mobs and march against the King as the London merchants were inclined to do. They were aware of being aliens and they knew that their plight received little sympathy. Moreover they continued to prosper even though they were so unfairly taxed. The richest of the Jews, a certain Aaron, paid three thousand marks of silver and two hundred marks of gold in the course of a few years. The people were turning more and more against the King. And because of his appearance made unusual by his drooping eyelid he was recognized wherever he went and the Londoners nicknamed him 'The Lynx with eyes that pierced all things.'

Only the barons knew how unpopular the King was becoming—and the Queen was more so. They were biding their time.

Henry in desperate straits sought about for means of getting money in addition to taxation and he hit upon the particularly unpleasant habit of asking for presents from everyone who came for an audience, and this was even more to be deplored when if the gifts were not costly enough he complained and asked for them to be exchanged.

It was a greater act of charity to give money and goods to their King, he told the people, than to beggars who waited for them at church doors with their begging cups.

During this time Eleanor was pregnant again and gave birth to another son, christened John—an unfortunate name and so it proved, because it was not long before little John followed his brother Richard to the tomb.

Two little boys and both dead! The Queen was very depressed and needed costly presents to raise her spirits. These must be provided by any means and as she was inordinately fond of fine garments and rich jewels these were procured for her.

Richard remonstrated with his brother but not as firmly as he had once done. He was to a certain extent under the influence of his wife who herself was persuaded in the way she should think by the Queen. Eleanor and Sanchia were constantly together and as their mother was also at Court with many of her friends there was a Provençal coterie at the head of which was the Queen.

The barons were watchful. Their moment would come as it had in the last reign and when it did they would be ready.

Richard at length did persuade the King that his extravagance to foreigners was becoming an issue of complaint with many of the leading barons and that he should curb his expenditure. Henry decided to cut short the allowances for the royal servants and not to eat in his royal castles and palaces but in the homes of his friends. He would travel from castle to castle with the Queen and often Edward and many of his foreign friends, and there expect to be feasted in royal manner at the expense of others.

The King's attempt at economy was regarded as a joke by

all those who were not obliged to feel the force of it. What was becoming clearer and clearer was that with each day the King and Queen—particularly the Queen—added to their list of enemies.

'It was a bad day for the royal house,' said Henry, 'when father allowed them to force him to sign Magna Carta.'

Magna Carta! It was talked of constantly. People in the streets of London spoke of it without knowing exactly what it set out. All they knew was that it was the Charter to preserve the liberty of the people and curb the power of Kings.

There was great excitement in the royal apartments when news came that a fire had broken out in the Pope's Palace and destroyed the contents of one of the rooms, for in this room was the original of Magna Carta.

'Praise be to God,' said Eleanor, 'that infamous document is destroyed. Now we have done with it.'

The King immediately levied a tax on the Londoners for harbouring, as he said, a man whom he had sent into exile.

Richard came with all haste to Westminster.

'This must be stopped,' he said. 'The people are all quoting Magna Carta.'

'But Magna Carta has been burned,' cried Eleanor. 'It no longer exists. I see the hand of God in this.'

'You are mistaken,' explained Richard. 'The principal document has been destroyed. But there are copies and these are safe in England. Once a King has signed away his rights it is unlikely that they will ever be regained. The fact of the fire has no bearing on this. The Charter remains.'

'It is time the people were taught a lesson,' said Eleanor.

Richard frowned. Once he would have been firmly on the side of the barons. He realized with a sudden horror that there might come a time when it would be necessary to take sides.

'Henry,' begged Richard, 'I pray you explain to the Queen. I have never seen the people in such a mood as they are now. It is unwise ... unhealthy ... and unsafe for us all.'

The Queen listened and shrugged her shoulders. The people of England, she declared, were so ungrateful. They had a King who would be good to them if they would but mend their ways. They had a Queen who had given them the finest family of children ever seen.

'They should rejoice in Edward,' she said. 'He grows every day. He is taller than all his companions, our dear, dear Long-shanks. Do you know Burnell is constantly reminding me of

how he always said Edward would outgrow his childish ailments. He is saying I told you so to me. But I like him for it.
He is a good man. He loves Edward as his son.'

Richard said: 'I pray you go carefully that there may be
a kingdom for Edward to rule when his time comes ... which
I trust will be many years yet.'

'You are in a serious mood today, brother,' said the Queen.

'Some of us must be serious at some time,' replied Richard.

And he began to ask himself whether he would always be
able to stand beside the King.

The Sad Little Bride

THERE were several boys in the royal nursery, but Edward was the leading spirit and always had been. He was eleven years old, very tall for his age and although his hair had darkened a little it was still very fair. His cousin, Henry, although four years older was of a more gentle nature. Henry was also handsome, but less so than Edward as he was less tall. Henry was a good friend and cousin and they shared most things.

In the royal nurseries were also the de Montfort cousins. Their father, Simon de Montfort, and their mother, Edward's Aunt Eleanor, were in Gascony where Simon had undertaken the government at the King's request. After Henry's outburst about Simon's seduction of his sister he had been ashamed of himself for so blatantly lying and in giving him the governorship of Gascony (a turbulent province which he had been unable to manage) he was getting rid of him and at the same time offering him the olive branch. So with their parents away the de Montfort children were the wards of the King.

The de Montfort boys—Henry who was a year older than Edward, Simon who was two years younger and Guy four years younger—were a wild element in the establishment, always urging their cousins on to disobedience. The eldest of the group, Henry, son of Richard of Cornwall, was a restraining influence and as he was the senior by three years

(Henry de Montfort being next in seniority) his influence was great.

Then there were the two girls, Margaret who was a year younger than Edward and Beatrice three years younger than Margaret. Then came Edmund the youngest of all—five years old and only rarely in the company of the others.

Margaret—although at this time she knew nothing of it—had at the age of two been betrothed to the son of King Alexander of Scotland who was a year younger than herself.

There had been and still was an uneasy situation between England and Scotland and at the first sign of disaster the Scots were ready to overrun the border. The suggested marriage had therefore been of great importance to Henry and even after the formal betrothal there had been a further outbreak of trouble and in the settlement of this it had been agreed that the marriage should take place as soon as the children were old enough.

As she played with her little sister Beatrice and her brother Edmund—for it often happened that Edward excluded them from the manly games he played with his companions and even kind cousin Henry of Cornwall could find no place for them—Margaret had no idea that change was so near to her and that the happy life in the royal nurseries was coming to a close for her.

It was one summer's day when the Queen came to the nursery and seeing the young children at the window-seat looking out onto the fields where the boys were performing all manner of equestrian tricks, Eleanor decided to talk to Margaret.

They turned to her and threw themselves into her arms. Eleanor loved all her children dearly and, although Edward was her favourite, they all knew this and accepted it as right, for there was something very special about Edward. That did not mean that she had not unlimited affection to shower on all her children.

'My lady, look at them,' cried Margaret. 'Look at Edward. He has cast aside the reins. See. He holds his hands above his head.'

'I see. What a noble figure he makes. How fortunate you are, my darlings, to have such a brother.'

But while she watched and marvelled at his skill she was filled with apprehension on account of his daring.

'I shall ride like that,' Edmund told her.

She kissed him and said: 'Why, little son, you will ride exactly like Edward. Perhaps Edward will teach you.'

'Cousin Henry might,' admitted Edmund.

'First you must go on with your lessons, my darling. Beatrice, my dear, take Edmund to the schoolroom and bring me your books. I want to see how you progress. Margaret, stay here with me.'

Margaret was delighted. There was nothing the children liked better than to have their mother to themselves.

When they were alone Eleanor drew her daughter closer to her.

'Margaret, you are going to be married, my child.'

Margaret was silent. Her lovely eyes round with wonder regarded her mother.

'Yes, my dearest. You are going to marry the little King of Scotland. Think of that. You will be a queen.'

'Shall I wear a crown?'

'You will wear a beautiful crown. I am sure you will be very happy.'

'Where is he then?'

'He is in Scotland.'

'When will he come here?'

The Queen was silent. 'My dearest, he will not come here. A bride goes to her husband.'

'Shall we all go to Scotland then?'

'We shall all go with you to York where you will be married. Then you will go with your husband to Scotland.'

'I won't go unless you and my father and Edward and Henry ... and Beatrice....'

'My dear, you are the daughter of the King and Queen. That is a very important thing to be. It means that when you marry you can make peace between nations and that is what your father wants. I want it too and so must you.'

'I do, but I want us all to make peace and all be together.'

'You are very young, but daughters of kings and queens must grow up quickly. You will do your duty and be a good wife to the King of Scotland as I was to the King of England. You know what a happy time I had with your dear grandmother of Provence and my dear father whom you have never seen and your Aunt Sanchia....'

'They are all here.'

'They were not at first. I came alone and I had not seen your father before our marriage. Then we met and we loved each other for ever and we had you dear children and ours was the best marriage in the world and there will be one other like it—that of my darling little Margaret and the King of Scotland. Then we shall all meet ... often. I promise you, my darling. I shall insist that we travel north and you will travel south ... and we shall be together. And you will show me your dear children whom you will love as I love you all ... and you will wonder why you were ever afraid.'

'But I don't want to leave you and my father and....'

'No, of course you do not. Little brides never want to and then they find so much more happiness than they ever dreamed of.'

Margaret lay against her mother whose heart was torn with apprehension while she painted a rosy picture of what marriage would bring.

When the younger children returned with their books Margaret was almost convinced that all would be well.

* * *

Preparations were going on apace for the marriage between the King's daughter and the young King of Scotland. The usual questions arose as to how it was to be paid for. The Londoners declared that they had had enough of royal extravagances and would pay no more.

Henry was incensed and in a moment of violent temper, seeking for revenge he hit on the idea of setting up a fair in Tothill Fields for the benefit of the people of Westminster. If while the fair was in progress, which he intended to be for two weeks, the London shops opened they would incur a fine. So they had the choice of losing business for two weeks or facing the King's tax and as the King's insatiable demands were well known it seemed that the easier to bear would be the loss of business.

'How much longer,' asked the merchants of London, 'are we going to endure the arrogance of this King? The country suffered under the rule of his father until the people rose and rid themselves of him. Are we to suffer in the same way from the son?' What was the difference between John and his son Henry? There was a great difference. Even his enemies had to admit that. John was a fiend, a mad man without respect for his fellow human beings or even for God. Henry was a weak King. His rule was ineffectual. But he was a deeply religious man, a faithful husband and a doting father. If the people despised him, his family loved him dearly. His son Edward, the heir, was growing up into a strong man and there could be no doubt on whose side he would place himself.

All the same, said the people of London, the King should take care.

The Queen devoted herself to poor bewildered little Margaret. When one of her children was unhappy or in danger all her thoughts were directed on that one. Even her darling Longshanks took second place at this time. Eleanor was with her daughter every day, advising her, discussing her wardrobe, trying to make light of what was happening to her. And so happy was Margaret in her mother's company that she forgot her coming ordeal.

Eleanor, who greatly relished fine clothes and jewels, was in her element choosing garments for the wedding. She aroused such enthusiasm for the clothes which would be worn that the little girl could forget her apprehension in contemplating them.

One day when at Windsor Eleanor and Margaret were with the seamstresses examining the cloth which would be used for the gowns when the sky suddenly became so overcast that the seamstresses could no longer see to work. It had been a hot sultry day and during the last week the weather had been oppressive.

Margaret was a little frightened. The darkening sky added to her general apprehension.

'It is nothing,' said the Queen. 'We were bound to have a storm after the heat. What do you think of this quintise, Margaret? You are to wear it the day after the ceremony, for I think we should all be as grand then as we were on the day itself.'

Margaret said she liked the quintise which was so called because this type of garment was considered quaint. It took any shape; it could be long and trailing the ground or end merely at the ankles. It could be allowed to hang loose or be held up and the edges of the sleeves were often bordered by scallops. The Queen had taken a great fancy to these garments and enjoyed introducing new ways of wearing them which were immediately followed by the ladies of the Court.

But as the storm gathered overhead even the Queen lost interest in the quintises.

A violent crash of thunder seemed to set the castle rocking. The Queen went to the window. Lightning was streaking across the sky. The rain fell in torrents and then suddenly it was as though the foundations of the castle itself trembled. From the chimney came a shower of bricks and dirt. The

Queen seized her daughter just as the two of them were thrown to the floor.

They lay together, Margaret's heart beating fast, but she was comforted by the proximity of her mother. All her life she had believed that while her mother was near no harm could come to her; and in that moment of terror she realized that what frightened her was not the thought of marriage and a husband but that she would be separated from her parents.

There were shouts from without. The King came running into the room.

'My dearest....' He was on his knees. He had the Queen in his arms and was reaching for Margaret. The three of them clung together.

'Where are the children ... Edward....' began the Queen.

'They are safe. This is where the damage is. And you two here.... My dearest Eleanor.'

'All is well. We are not harmed.'

'Let us get out of here,' said the King. 'We don't know what damage may yet be done.'

He had his arms about them both. Knights, attendants men and women were everywhere. They all expressed their joy at the sight of the Queen. In the great hall they assembled. All the children were safe. The Queen uttered up prayers of thanks. Henry was gazing at his family, his eyes ranging over them as though to assure himself that not one of the precious band was missing.

It turned out that the thunderstorm had done a great deal of damage. Not only had the Queen's apartment been struck by lightning but many sheep had been destroyed in the fields and even some of the great oaks in Windsor Park had been uprooted.

Contemplating the damage, Margaret shivered.

'Is it an omen?' she wondered.

* * *

The cavalcade made its way to York. Margaret rode between her father and mother and every now and then she would throw a poignant glance in their direction as though she wanted to remember exactly what they looked like so that they would live vividly in her mind when she was no longer with them.

Both King and Queen made a great effort to be merry but they could not hide their sadness from their daughter, who shared it; and even Eleanor, who would have been prepared to oppose any law of the Kingdom for the sake of her children, realized the necessity for this marriage and tried to console herself that the bridegroom was even younger than the bride and Margaret was of a strong enough nature to be able to look after herself.

Eleanor could not but find some glory in the grandeur of the occasion. On the surface there was no hint of the King's pecuniary difficulties. All along the route people had gasped at the splendour of the royal entourage for accompanying the King were a thousand knights and each of them appeared to have attempted to outdo the others by the magnificence of his garments. Gold and silver ornaments adorned their persons and everywhere was the glitter of jewels.

None looked more splendid than the Queen, her beautiful hair gathered into a golden net, the trailing skirts of her quintise gown held lightly in her hand so that the skirt might not impede her progress.

The young King of Scots and his attendants were less elegant, but his six hundred knights, though slightly less grand than the English, made a fine spectacle.

People crowded the streets of York and there was talk of nothing but the coming wedding. Everywhere there was excitement; the only two who did not seem to share in the excitement were the two little principals.

Henry and Eleanor though were very much aware of their daughter's ordeal and what worried them most was the fact that she must leave them.

Henry said: 'If they make her unhappy I will wage war on them. I will make them regret it if they hurt our daughter in the smallest way!'

Eleanor put her arm through that of her husband and for a moment he was afraid that she was going to ask him to call off the marriage. It would be impossible now ... even to please Eleanor.

He said suddenly: 'The marriage must take place early in the morning, before the people realize it. Otherwise the press will be disastrous.'

Eleanor thought this a good plan. She had a feeling that once Margaret was married she would begin to accept her fate as inevitable and feel better about it.

So early in the morning of that grey December day, Alexander and Margaret were married by Archbishop Walter Grey of York and as she walked through the southern transept, which was the pride of Archbishop Grey's heart because it had been built by him over twenty years before, she felt as though there was a dead weight where her heart should have been and she prayed for another thunderstorm to shatter the Archbishop's transept so that the ceremony would not be able to take place.

Alas, if it did not now, it would at another time.

There was no escape.

She had to say good-bye to home—to her beloved parents, to Edward, Edmund, Beatrice and all the cousins. She had to go to a strange bleak land with this boy who had become her husband.

The ceremony over, the feasting began.

The King of England must show the Scots how powerful he was and what a happy day it was for them when their King made an alliance with his daughter.

The wedding celebrations had coincided with those of Christmas so the feasting was doubly lavish. They would pay for it afterwards, Henry promised himself. Were there not all those rich Jews? And the merchants of London could always find money for what they wanted and why not for their King?

Royalty should not be bothered with such mundane matters as paying for its fancies. This, however, was a matter of state. Was not the daughter of England marrying the son of Scotland? Were not the two countries being united and did this not mean peace between them which was to the benefit of all?

He crowned the occasion by knighting Alexander. A fine boy. He would make Margaret a good husband in a few years time.

At the ages of ten and eleven they were scarcely ready yet; but it was an understood thing in royal marriages that the ceremony should take place and after that the young pair wait for a suitable time for the consummation.

When he had knighted Alexander, a ceremony which was loudly applauded by the Scots, he said: 'My dear son, this is indeed a happy occasion. I know you will make my daughter happy. To complete this momentous occasion you should pay me homage for your kingdom.'

Alexander was young but he had been brought up to regard himself as a future King and his advisers had warned him to be very careful in his dealings with the King of England.

He hesitated, but only for a few seconds. Then he said:

'I have come here peacefully and for the honour of the King of England, that by means of the marriage tie I might ally myself with him. But I could not deal with such a solemn matter until I had held deliberation on this matter with my nobles, or taken proper counsel as to so difficult a question.'

Henry realized that the boy had wisdom beyond his years and it would be no use trying to take advantage of his youth, so he waved aside his request.

At length the time came for farewells.

Margaret clung to her parents and the Queen wept with her daughter.

'All will be well, my love,' whispered Eleanor. 'Alexander will be kind to you and anyone who is not will have to answer to your father.'

* * *

How bleak the country seemed as they rode north! The wind was keener and wrapped up as she was in her cape lined with vair she still felt the cold. Beside her rode her husband —a boy of ten, his face stern and set and she knew that he, like herself, was trying to make the best of this thing which had happened to them.

In the company were a few of her attendants but she knew they would not be allowed to stay with her. The Scots were different from the English. They were dour, hardly ever smiled, and were far more serious.

She thought of home—and the games they used to play and how Edward lorded it over them all and how he was constantly quarrelling with the de Montfort cousins who were always telling everyone they were as royal as the King's children. They had the Conqueror's blood in their veins too, they maintained. King John was their grandfather just as he was Longshanks' and Margaret's and the rest. And the elder Henry, son of Uncle Richard, had always tried to make the peace. He used to say that there were so many of them with royal blood that they shouldn't boast of it to each other. How she longed to be with them!

She tried to talk to Alexander as they rode along but he was as suspicious of her as she was of him.

We at least ought to be friends, thought Margaret.

She spoke of the English Court, her mother and father and the brothers and sisters. He listened attentively and politely but he said little of himself.

Onward they rode through the bleak countryside.

'It is so cold,' said Margaret. 'Is it always like this?'

'Only in winter.'

She shivered and thought longingly of Windsor with the

glowing fires and the children all playing games and their parents coming to watch them and sometimes join in.

Then she remembered the thunderstorm at Windsor and that moment when she lay on the floor clasped in her mother's arms.

'An omen.... An omen....' she whispered. And she was sure of it then.

The castle stood high on a hill, granite walls grey and forbidding.

Slowly they rode up the incline and through the gateway.

Her limbs were numb with the cold but her spirits were lifted a little when she entered the hall and saw the blazing fire.

'We're home,' said Alexander.

They were surrounded by dour-looking men and women. One of them in flowing black robes of mourning came to Margaret and said she would take her to her chamber. There she could rest awhile and food would be brought to her, for she had had a long and irksome journey and would be weary.

It was a cheerless room with thick stone walls, stone floor and the barest necessities of furniture.

'I am Lady Matilda de Cantelupe,' the woman told her, 'and I am to act as your governess ... until such a time as you are ready to join the King.'

It was what her mother had said. 'You will not be a wife immediately. They will wait until you are of an age ... and Alexander too, for he is but a boy. They will give you a governess whom you will love and who will help and advise you.'

But there was something forbidding about Matilda de Cantalupe.

Margaret said she would rest awhile, for she was tired, and Matilda covered her with a fur rug to help her get warm. Afterwards she ate a little and in due course went down to the great hall where Alexander, similarly fed and rested, awaited her.

He had come to say farewell. He was leaving her with her guardians Robert le Norrey and Stephen Bausan. They, with Matilda, would be in charge of her household until such a time as she was ready to be a wife.

She wanted to cling to Alexander. At least he was young and if not exactly frightened, apprehensive. There was a fellow feeling between them. If he could have stayed she would have felt better. But he was going away. He was going to leave her with these solemn people.

She was frightened. She wanted her family ... and desperately she wanted her mother.

Alexander gave her a cold kiss on the cheek.

'I will come back for you,' he said.

She nodded dumbly and she stood in the courtyard wrapped in her fur-lined coat with Matilda de Cantalupe and the two formidable men who were to be her guardians standing behind her. She watched Alexander ride away with his attendants.

Then, in the company of those whom she was beginning to think of as her jailers, she went back into the castle.

The King and Simon de Montfort

SIMON DE MONTFORT had returned to England.

He was weary and disillusioned. He had constantly asked Henry for help to govern but Henry seemed to think that funds for this were not necessary. He himself was in constant need of money to govern his kingdom; that Simon de Montfort should ask for it in Gascony seemed an affront.

It was Henry's nature that if he had wronged someone he could not like them again. He had a conscience of a kind which reproached him and while he tried to pretend it did not exist it continued to worry him. He would not admit the real cause of his grievance against a man or woman which was of course that he had wronged them and this made him uneasy so he always tried to find fault with their actions so that he could give himself another reason for disliking them.

Thus he began to criticize Simon's governorship in Gascony and although Richard pointed out that no one could govern any place without the necessary finance, still he found fault with Simon.

Simon at length found the position impossible. The Gascons were rebellious and he had no means of quelling them. Dispirited, realizing that he could not carry on unless he was able to get support from England, he came home to plead in person with the King.

He found Henry in a melancholy mood. He had just said good-bye to his young daughter and he knew that the Queen was grieving. Eleanor felt that before she went to Scotland, Margaret should have waited until she was old enough to consummate the marriage, and she was reproaching herself ... and Henry ... for allowing the child to be taken from them, and Henry could not bear to do anything that seemed wrong in her eyes.

So when Simon de Montfort arrived Henry was in an ill temper and Simon received a bleak reception.

'I find it impossible to keep order in Gascony, my lord, without the financial help I need,' he attempted to explain.

'I have heard,' retorted Henry, 'that much of the trouble is of your own making.'

'That is false!' cried Simon angrily.

Henry replied: 'I will dispatch commissioners to Gascony that they may report on what is going on there.'

'My lord,' he said vehemently, 'these Gascons are trouble-makers. They know the King of France is ready to woo them. Give me arms, give me money and I will subdue them.'

'Our expenses here in England are great,' said Henry.

Yes, thought Simon, jewels for the Queen, fine garments and feasting for the Scottish wedding. Pensions for the Queen's friends and relations, for your half brothers, for all those foreigners who are here for pickings.

There was, thought Henry, something formidable about Simon. When he was in his presence he was aware of a certain power in the man. He vaguely sensed that Simon was a man of whom he must wary.

'I will give you three thousand marks,' said the King.

'It is not enough, my lord.'

'It is all I can give. Can you raise more?'

'From my own estates I could find a little. I need men too.'

'Then return with this money and the men you need. I shall then hope to hear better news from Gascony.'

Simon left the King. He had heard much talk of the dissatisfaction among the barons and he was wondering whether in time the King would be facing trouble not unlike that which had beset his father.

Simon returned to Gascony where the people led by rebels were in revolt. They had gathered together at Castillon, where Simon besieged them and achieved a victory. Temporarily he brought peace to Gascony—though an uneasy one. He returned to England and told the King that he had made peace, subdued the rebels and now had decided to ask leave to remain in England.

Meanwhile the Gascons had set out their complaints against Simon and these were presented to the King, and because of his attitude to Simon, Henry preferred to believe his accusers rather than to believe Simon.

This seemed such gross ingratitude that Simon's disgust with Henry filled him with anger. He declared that the accusations should be brought to light and he would be judged by his peers as to who was making trouble in Gascony.

Henry agreed and made it clear on whose side he was. He was cool to Simon whenever they met and made much of his Gascon enemies.

Simon's wife, the King's sister Eleanor, was furious with her brother.

'Henry has never forgiven himself for that accusation he made against you,' she told her husband. 'He knew it was untrue and is ashamed. Therefore he seeks to lay the blame for everything on you as he tries to convince himself that he was in the right.'

'Sometimes I wonder what will happen to our land under your brother,' said Simon.

'I wonder too. The trouble with Henry is that he is so weak. What of this trial? Do you think that they will prove a case against you.'

'Not if they adhere to the truth.' Simon turned to her. She had been a good and faithful wife to him, and neither of them had ever regretted their rash marriage. 'My dear Eleanor,' he went on, 'the barons are powerful ... as powerful as they were when they forced King John to sign the Magna Carta. They are with me ... you may depend on that ... and are determined not to allow the country to slip back into tyranny ... and so am I. I have a feeling that I have but to offer myself as their leader and they will be with me ... to a man.'

'You mean rebellion against the King?'

'I mean the preservation of liberty in this land. The barons would soon be ready to do with Henry what they did with his father. They deplore the increasing numbers of foreigners on whom the King dotes. His extravagance, and mostly that of the Queen, offends him. They hate the Queen as few Queens have been hated because they see the trouble stemming from her. It is her relations who are sucking the exchequer dry. She is a proud and arrogant woman. But have no fear, Eleanor, I can tell you this: The barons are with me. I will serve the King your brother while it is possible to do so ... but if it should become impossible ... then I ... and the barons ... would consult together and I doubt not some action will be taken.'

'Should not Henry be warned?'

'He is constantly warned. Richard at one time was well aware of what was happening. The barons believed that he was ready to place himself at their head. But since his marriage with the Queen's sister he has become the King's man. The sisters are so close. The Queen is a forceful woman. She guides her sister and she in turn influences her husband. The barons would no longer look to your brother Richard, Eleanor.'

'I know,' she answered. 'They would look to you. You are the strong man of the country now, Simon.'

'It may be so. But rest assured I shall do my best to placate the King and bring about a peaceful settlement of our differences. Civil war is a disaster for any country, no matter who is the victor.'

'These Gascons are foolish. They have no case against you.'

' 'Tis true. But the King *wants* there to be a case and he will do all he can to hold one up.'

'How ungrateful he is! When I think of those years in Gascony ... when we would rather have been at home in England....'

'I know. Kings are by their very office ungrateful. Rest assured, Eleanor, I shall not accept the King's injustice.'

'Henry is a fool.'

'Hush. Remember he is the King. Remember how we were forced to fly by river when he was threatening us with the Tower.'

'I shall never forget it. I shall never feel the same about my brother again.'

'I know that you will be a firm supporter of your husband always ... and that could mean one day that you may be in opposition to the King.'

He gripped her hands and looked into her eyes.

'There are no regrets then?' he went on. 'The daughter of a king is happy in her marriage with the foreign adventurer?'

'She has no regrets and will stand by him in whatever campaign he finds himself compelled to make.'

'God bless you, Eleanor,' said Simon de Montfort.

*   *   *

The trial was over and Simon acquitted. It had to be so because there was no case against him. It was clear that he had done all that was humanly possible to keep order in Gascony and everyone knew that without arms, men and money he could do very little. What he had done was little short of a miracle.

Henry was furious with the result of the trial. Desperately he had wanted to see Simon brought low, and when Simon was before the Council Henry could not contain his anger. He glared at his brother-in-law and with that lid over one eye —it always seemed more in evidence when he was angry— he looked really formidable, to all who did not know his weak nature.

He said: 'So you will go back to Gascony I doubt not?'

Simon replied: 'I would go if all the promises you made to me were kept this time. You know full well, my lord, that the terms of my vice-royalty were not adhered to.'

Henry's temper burst out. 'I keep no covenant with a traitor.'

Simon, usually calm, decided that was something he could not accept. He was deeply conscious of those about the council table watching while they almost held their breath.

'When you use that word of me, you lie,' he said coldly. 'And were you not my sovereign, an ill hour would it be for you that you dared utter it.'

The blood rushed into Henry's face. He tried to speak but he could only splutter. This upstart ... to insult him at his own council table with so many looking on!

At last the words came. 'Arrest him! Arrest this man!'

Several of the barons had risen and put themselves between the King and Simon.

'My lord,' they said, 'the Earl has done nothing but defend himself which he has a right to do. He cannot be arrested for this.'

Henry lowered his eyes. He was uncertain. In moments such as this he always wondered what his great ancestors would have done.

The moment passed. Simon had turned and left the chamber.

*   *   *

Simon prepared to return to Gascony and before he left he went to see the King.

Henry received him with the utmost coldness. The heat of anger had passed and he felt only a burning resentment against this man who had behaved with greater dignity than he had in the council chamber. There was a cool determination in Simon which disconcerted the King.

'Well, so you will go back to Gascony then,' said Henry 'I

have ordered that the truce shall remain so you will be able to work peacefully.'

'I doubt it, my lord,' was Simon's rejoinder. 'The Gascons are determined on trouble.'

'*They* are determined on trouble? I think not. Your father did very well in his war with the Albigensians, I have heard. Much treasure fell into his hands. Go back to Gascony then, thou lover and maker of strife, and reap the reward as your father did before you.'

Simon looked steadily at the King, and although hot words of protest at this slight on his father and contempt for the man who had made it rose to his lips he said calmly: 'Gladly will I go. Nor do I think to return till I have made your enemies your footstool—ungrateful though you are.'

Henry glared at him. He felt very uneasy.

On reaching Gascony Simon found that it was impossible to serve the King, for it seemed as though Henry was fighting with Simon's enemies, who were in truth his own also.

Far from respecting the truce they had made with the King, the Gascons were besieging towns and taking castles and there was nothing to do but defend these.

But it was not long before messengers arrived accusing Simon of breaking the truce.

'The King is impossible!' cried Simon. 'He allows his personal enmity to come between himself and reason.'

Next came dispatches from the King telling him he was removed from office. Simon replied that his appointment had been for seven years, a fact which the King appeared to have forgotten. Henry then sent to say he would buy him out and this offer Simon accepted.

He went to France where he was warmly received by the French. Louis had watched events in Gascony with great interest and was amazed at Henry's treatment of a man like Simon de Montfort.

If Simon would care to remain in France some high office should be found for him, he was assured.

Simon shook his head. 'I am the servant of the King of England,' he replied, 'and if he is an ungrateful King, still I am his servant.'

But he remained at the Court of France.

Eleanor was not with him. As she had been pregnant she had remained in England and while he was in France Simon had news that she had given birth to a daughter whom she had named Eleanor after herself.

It seemed that he would in due course go home to England. The King would never be his friend, and if he continued to act in this irresponsible way who knew what would happen.

The barons would endure only a certain amount before they rose as they had during the reign of John; and when they did they would look to a leader.

It could well be that, if the King would have none of Simon de Montfort, the barons might.

*   *   *

The King decided that since Simon de Montfort had, as he said 'deserted' he would give young Edward Gascony. Edward was thirteen, a fine healthy boy grown out of his childish ailments completely, full of life and energy, the delight of his parents and the people, who were already saying that in Edward they would have a strong King, which England had discovered through bitter experience, it needed.

So in Westminster Edward was declared ruler of Gascony and received the homage of the Gascons in London. And just as the Court was in the midst of rejoicing over this dispatches came from Rome to the effect that there was some doubt as to the validity of Henry's marriage to Eleanor.

Henry read the dispatches through and trembled.

This was direct from the Pope. It had been brought to the the notice of His Holiness that the King had been betrothed to Joanna of Ponthieu and it might well be that that betrothal was binding, in which case the marriage with Eleanor of Provence was no marriage.

Eleanor found him with the documents in his hands. She snatched them from him and read them.

'How dare they suggest such a thing! Our marriage not legal! Our children then would be bastards! Edward would not be the true heir to the throne!'

'Don't worry,' said Henry. 'I shall set this matter right. I shall make this malicious person eat his words ... no matter who he may be.'

But Henry was shaken. Horrible ideas crept into his mind. What if they were going to prove he was not truly married? He thought of Philip Augustus of France who was excommunicated for living with a woman whom he had declared was his wife and whom the Church maintained was not.

Couriers went back and fourth. If Eleanor and Henry were not truly married, neither were the King and Queen of

Castile, for Joanna who had been jilted by Henry had married the King of Castile.

Eleanor was frantic. Her babies, she cried, what of them? She would not allow them to be proclaimed illegitimate. Anything must be done to stop that.

Henry said that he believed it was a trick of Innocent's to make him pay for expensive bulls and dispensations.

'So it is only money,' cried Eleanor immensely relieved.

'I'll swear it is.'

'We shall settle that then.'

Of course they would settle. There were always the people to be taxed; there were always the Jews.

In due course the matter was settled, but most expensively and as usual it was the people of England who paid for the bulls and dispensation.

Each month they grew more restive. It could not go on. Why should it? Experience and that not so long ago had taught them that kings rule by will of the people.

*   *   *

There was bad news from Gascony. Simon de Montfort was no longer there and the Gascons were taking advantage of the situation. Their thirteen-year-old governor was in England and they would not in any case have been much in awe of him. The Gascons were making overtures to the King of Castile and the fact was the King's presence was urgently needed there.

Henry was disconsolate. He was beginning to see how foolishly he had acted with Simon. He had dismissed the very man who, with support, would have held Gascony for him. Now there was nothing he could do but take out an army led by himself.

What was so upsetting was the fact that Eleanor was pregnant and could not accompany him.

When he told her what had happened she shared his dismay. To be separated was what they most dreaded.

'I must come with you, Henry,' she said.

'Nay,' he replied, 'I could not permit it. Think of the crossing alone, which could be rough. I should not have a moment's peace if I thought you were over there in danger. No, you must stay at home with the children. I shall have to be content with that. It will be better than the continual anxiety.'

'Henry, when the child is born I shall come out to you.'

He embraced her. 'That is the answer. Have the child and when it is safe for you to travel you must come. The hardest thing I have to face in my life is doing without you and the children.'

He delayed as long as he could but finally was forced to leave. The Queen with her sister Sanchia and Richard of Cornwall and all the royal children accompanied the King to Portsmouth.

Henry took a tender farewell of them all and it was most touching when it came to Edward's turn to embrace his father, for the boy broke down into bitter weeping.

'Edward my dear son,' cried the King, 'you must not. You unnerve me.'

'My place is with you, father,' said Edward. 'I want to fight beside you ... to protect you ... I want to make sure that you are safe.'

'Oh my son,' said the King, 'this is the happiest and saddest moment of my life. Beloved boy, take care of your mother. I leave her in your hands. Soon we shall be together. Rest assured that at the earliest moment I shall send for you.'

They stood there watching the ship sail.

The King was on the deck, his eyes fixed on his family. He told himself that he would carry the memory of Edward's tears to his grave.

*   *   *

The Queen was compensated for the loss of her husband by the Regency. Power was hers. She had often secretly thought that Henry was too lenient with his subjects and did not exert his royal power enough. It was true the people groaned under taxation but as she said to Sanchia, they must have had the money otherwise they would not have been able to pay it.

Sanchia agreed. She was happy to be in England and to settle under the domination of her elder sister just as she had as a child. She now had a little boy, Edmund. Her first born had died a few months after his birth but Edmund was a sturdy child. Richard was devoted to him but she suspected none could compare with his son by his first wife, Isabella. Henry was indeed a noble boy and a great friend of the heir to the throne. He and Edward went everywhere together.

Sanchia worried a little about the Queen's unpopularity which was manifested every time they rode out into the streets. They were accustomed to sullen looks but now and

then there would be a hostile cry and when the guards looked
for the offenders they could never find them. Sometimes
Sanchia wondered if they tried very hard. She had an uneasy
feeling that they did not like the Queen very much either.

Richard had said once or twice that much of the unpopularity directed against the King was due to the Queen.

'One of these days....' he began.

But Sanchia laughed. 'Eleanor always had her own way
when we were children. She will continue to get it all her
life.'

Richard was uneasy. He had been annoyed when Henry
had bestowed Gascony on young Edward. That seemed a
stupid thing to do. Edward was after all only thirteen. How
much more sensible it would have been to bestow it on him,
Richard. The quarrel with de Montfort was stupid also.
There was a man Henry should have kept on his side.

Now Richard was co-Regent with the Queen and his main
task was to keep Henry supplied with arms and money which
he needed for the campaign—not an enviable task for it
meant imposing taxes and that was about the most unpopular
thing a ruler could do.

Richard had momentary bouts of an undefined illness. He
had no idea what it was—nor had the doctors, but every now
and then he would be overcome by such lethargy that he did
not care to bestir himself. It would pass and his old energy
would be back with him.

At this time he did not feel inclined to support Simon de
Montfort although his common sense told him he should be
on the side of his brother-in-law. Now he should take a firm
hand with the Queen and explain to her the mood of the
country. Sanchia could not see it any more than the Queen
could. They seemed to have the idea that anything that their
family did must be right. Eleanor was supreme—the one they
all bowed to. They appeared to think that any injustice
Eleanor cared to impose would pass simply because Eleanor
had imposed it.

There will be trouble, thought Richard. People will be
taking sides.

And which shall I be on? Before his marriage there could
have been no doubt. The barons had looked to him then but
he believed that now they had their eyes on Simon de Montfort.

The King was writing from Gascony. He was finding the
task of subduing the Gascons almost impossible. Gaston de

Bearn was a traitor. He was trying to get Alfonso of Castile as his ally. 'If he does,' wrote the King, 'that could be disaster. I have sent to Simon de Montfort, who knows the country and the people, and commanded him to come to my aid.'

Richard shook his head.

Henry would never be a great soldier. He would never be a great King.

But if Simon de Montfort was ready to forget his grievances and help the King, there was a hope of victory.

* * *

The hatred between the Queen and the citizens of London was mutual She must raise money. The King needed money for his campaign. *She* needed money for her wardrobe and household expenses. There was never enough money, but the merchants of London knew how to make it.

First of all she revived the *aurum reginae*—the Queengold which was a percentage of the fines which had been paid to the kings for their good will. This had been reasonable enough in small sums, but as the King had inflicted heavy fines to pay for his campaign abroad, the citizens were furious when Eleanor demanded a payment on these.

The citizens stood firm. They would not pay. Eleanor imperiously ordered that the sheriffs should be sent to the Marshalsea Prison.

A deputation presented itself to Richard of Cornwall. The Queen must be told that the City of London was separate from the rest of the Kingdom. It had its own laws and dignities and it would not submit to the Queen's orders. The sheriffs should be released at once or the entire city would rise up and free them. It would not see its ancient privileges swept away by foreigners.

Richard talked to the Queen.

'You must understand,' he said, 'that the City stands apart. If you offend the City you have a strong enemy at your throat. Queen Matilda was never crowned Queen of England but she might well have been if she had not offended the City of London.'

'So I must release these men?'

'You must indeed and without delay. If you do not the City will be on the march. Heaven knows where that would end. Henry would be overcome with anxiety, for the country would be in danger and so would you.'

'It angers me to give way to them.'

'There are times, Eleanor, when we all have to give way.'

She saw his point and trouble was averted.

But the Londoners' hatred of the Queen was intensified, and even when she gave birth to her child at Westminster it did not abate. The baby was a little girl and because she was born on St Katharine's Day the Queen called her Katharine.

*   *   *

There was a letter from Henry.

Simon de Montfort had come to his aid and he had subdued Gascony. One of the reasons for this was that he had formed a new ally in Alfonso of Castile.

It had been necessary to cultivate this friendship, for if he had not done so Gaston de Bearn would have made Alfonso his friend. Gaston had promised Alfonso lands and castles but Henry had been able to offer more.

'It is time our son had a wife,' he wrote, 'Oh, he is young yet but this was necessary if I was going to hold Gascony. I know you will agree with me, my dearest wife, when I tell you that there was nothing to be done but to agree to a betrothal between him and the half-sister of Alfonso of Castile. She is a beautiful girl. Her father was Ferdinand III and her mother that Joanna of Pontheiu whom I thought I would marry until I knew of the existence of the only Queen for me. She is very young and docile. I think she will suit Edward very well. I hope you will be pleased but remember it was this betrothal or the loss of Gascony. Alfonso insists that Edward comes out here and marries her. He will not hear of her coming to England until after the ceremony. I have agreed to his request. Now, my dearest, it is for you to tell Edward what I have arranged for him and to bring him out here. How I long to see you.'

Eleanor was excited. Katharine was old enough to be safely left. She would take the other children with her. How she wished Margaret was with them. She was a little uneasy about Margaret and yearned for news of her. Scotland was so far away and by all accounts a cold and desolate country. Sanchia should come too. How wonderful it would be if they could travel to Provence and see her mother, or to the Court of France.

It was exciting. She needed new gowns ... beautiful gowns. Henry would expect her to look magnificent and she must not fail him. Foreigners must never say the Queen of England lacked the money to buy herself fine clothes.

To be with Henry again. How delighted the family would be! But she was selfish, keeping the news to herself. She would go and tell them all that they were going to join their father.

There was of course a little more to tell Edward.

He was to have a wife as well.

The Bride from Castile

EDWARD was now fifteen years old. Lusty, healthy, he was a natural leader. That had been obvious from the time he was five years old. He it was who had taken on the role among his playmates. His cousin Henry, son of Richard of Cornwall, was a brave boy who excelled at all sport, but he was more thoughtful than Edward, more fond of his books. Edward could have been a scholar; he had the ability to learn and did to a certain extent, but there was so much out of doors to tempt him. *He* wanted to ride the fastest, to shoot an arrow farther than anyone else; his falcons must be the best. He must devise the games they played and take the principal part.

That he was the King's eldest son and heir to the throne was a fact which must weigh with everyone. Already men were subservient to him and women eager to please. He knew that the Queen could scarcely bear him out of her sight; he knew that his father loved him better than his other children and he was a devoted father to them all. He was the centre of the Court and he could not help but be constantly aware of it.

His de Montfort cousins were constantly urging him on to daring. They were very conscious of the quarrel between their father and the King and the fact that the King disliked him. They were always trying to show how much bolder they were than other boys. It was as though the more unpopular their father became with the King the more eager they were to prove their royalty.

Sober Henry of Cornwall was constantly keeping them in order, a fact which they resented and consequently there was always a certain amount of tension between the boys.

The elder Henry noticed that Edward was often led into acts of folly through his de Montfort cousins. They would urge him to do something which Edward really had no desire to do and indeed left to himself might have been ashamed of doing, but the de Montforts somehow made it appear that to forgo the deed would be weakness.

Thus during this period Edward was often led into mischief of some sort and the more Henry tried to remonstrate the more daring the de Montfort boys became and they were determined that Edward should share their adventure, for if he did not, they implied, he was lacking in daring.

Since he had been given his own establishment Edward had taken to riding through the countryside with some two hundred followers and when they passed through villages they would make sport with the people, overturning waggons, stealing horses, taking off the girls; and what had begun as high-spirited games often became cruel despoliation; and when it was discovered that the young heir to the throne was at the head of the band, people shook their heads with dismay and asked themselves what sort of a King would he make. They remembered King John who had behaved in a similar fashion. They would not have another such as he was. The King was weak; he was extravagant; he favoured foreigners, but at least he was a deeply religious man, a good husband and father and not given to violence.

With the King out of the country and the Queen and Richard of Cornwall co-regents, Edward seemed to give himself up more and more to this wanton and foolish behaviour.

When his cousin Henry tried to remonstrate with him he told him to be silent. 'If you do not wish to accompany us, pray stay behind,' was his comment.

Henry took advantage of this and often stayed behind.

It began to be said that after Edward had passed through a village it was as though a horde of invading soldiers had come to it or the place had been struck by the plague and deserted by all its inhabitants.

On one occasion the disorderly band broke into a priory where the monks were sitting at their frugal meal; they drove them out, ate their food and beat their servants.

At the time it seemed a great joke, but when he told his

cousin Henry about it, Edward was angered to see that Henry despised such conduct.

'It was good sport,' Edward murmured.

'What? For the monks?'

'Monks! They have such dull lives. That was excitement they will remember for the rest of their days.'

'With the utmost ill feeling I'll warrant. Edward, you are the heir to the throne. You should remember that. You should take your position seriously.'

'And you should remember who I am and not tell me what I should do.'

'I tell you because I fear for you. Do you want the people to hate you before you are their King?'

Edward laughed. 'What matters it to me? It is not for them to pass judgment on me.'

'All men pass judgment on each other but never so severely as they do on kings.'

'You always wanted to spoil the sport,' cried Edward angrily and slunk away.

A few days later his cousin was one of the party and rode beside him. His criticism was still festering. Edward had tried to forget his words but had found it impossible. They kept coming back to him and worrying him. This made him irritated with Henry. Henry had no right to set himself up in judgment. Henry was self-righteous. Henry was a spoil-sport. Henry pretended to be so wise simply because he was four years older than Edward.

As they came along the road a young boy appeared. He could only have been a year or so older than Edward himself. He saw the party of riders; hesitated and recognized them for who they were. He stood still in the middle of the road unable to move, so frightened was he. Edward and his followers were the terror of the countryside and this boy had been walking along deep in his own thoughts when suddenly he was in the middle of them.

'What do you here, boy?' shouted Edward.

The boy was too frightened to answer.

'Does he not have a tongue then?' cried Guy de Montfort. 'If he does not know how to use it he deserves to lose it.'

'Do you hear, boy?' shouted Edward.

But the boy still could not speak or did not know how to answer.

'Seize him!' said Edward.

Two of his men had leaped from their horses.

'See how he stares at me,' cried Edward. 'Insolent boy.'

'He should lose his eyes for his insolence,' said a voice.

Henry cried: 'No. Let the boy go. He does no harm.'

'He displeases me,' retorted Edward, irritated and determined to ignore Henry's advice.

One of the men had lifted the boy's hair. 'He has two ears, my lord,' he said.

Then he took out his sword and held it aloft.

'Shall I remove one of them, my lord, since they appear to be of little use to him?'

'Oh cruel. . . .' murmured Henry.

Edward was angry suddenly. 'Shall I be told by Henry what I am to do?' he asked himself. 'Henry is a weak man . . . afraid of losing the goodwill of the people. I'll show him.'

'I'll have his ear,' he shouted.

The sword came down. The boy fell fainting to the ground. The man with the sword was bowing before Edward, holding a piece of bloodstained flesh in his hands.

'By God,' cried Henry, 'I'll be no part of this.' Then he leaped from his horse and picked up the boy.

He murmured to him: 'Fear not. I will take you to your home. No more harm shall come to you.'

There was silence in the group as Henry walked away carrying the boy in his arms.

'Ride on!' shouted Edward.

When they had gone one horse remained patiently awaiting for the return of his master.

Sickened by what had happened and the lighter by his purse which he had left with the boy's family, Henry rode slowly back to the palace.

* * *

Henry scarcely looked at his cousin. He could not bear to. He felt nauseated when he did.

He would never forget holding the quivering body in his arms and contemplating the wanton cruelty of what had happened.

He would ask his father to let him go abroad. He no longer wished to be of Edward's company. He believed he would never be able to look at him again without seeing that boy's mutilated head.

When Edward returned to the castle, he wanted to be alone. When he was he sat on his bed and buried his head in his hands.

Why should he feel thus? He asked himself. Why could he not shut out of his mind the memory of that boy's bleeding head and the look of contempt in Henry's eyes?

Then he thought of the boy. He would carry his mutilation with him throughout his life and when people asked about it he would say: Edward did that.

Henry was right. It was a stupid, senseless act of cruelty. It brought no good to him and terrible suffering to that boy and his family. And all because he had seen the look in the eyes of his de Montfort cousins—ready to sneer at him, as far as they dared, ready to call him a coward.

They hated Henry because in a way they were jealous of him. Henry's father was the great Richard of Cornwall, brother to the King, one of the most powerful men in the country. They would do anything to discountenance him, but that was difficult. Henry, because of his high principles, was aloof from them—as he was from them all.

Edward had always looked up to Henry. He wanted Henry's good opinion. Ever since they were babies in the same nursery Henry had been as the elder brother.

Now Henry despised him.

He had to talk to Henry. He wanted to explain. He would find out where the boy lived and send some compensation. It seemed as though he had suddenly grown up and saw how silly he had been. His behaviour had not been that of a man who was learning to be a great ruler.

He decided to go to his cousin's chamber without delay. He must talk to him.

Henry was not in his chamber.

'Where is my cousin?' he asked one of the servants.

'My lord, he left this morning early.'

'Left? He did not tell me.'

Edward stared ahead of him.

He knew that he would have no peace of mind until he had seen Henry.

*   *   *

Henry found his father at Westminster where he had been since the departure of the King for Gascony. As Regent it was necessary for Richard to be at the centre of affairs.

When he saw his son his eyes lit up. More than anything on earth he loved this boy—more than power, wealth, or Sanchia. He was a son to be proud of. Tall and strong, Richard could never look on him without being reminded of the boy's mother for he was very like her. She had been one of the great beauties of her day, poor Isabella. He did not really want to be reminded of her, for he was a little ashamed of his treatment of her. That marriage had been doomed from the first. Still it had brought him Henry and no man could ask for a finer son.

Henry was not only brave and manly, he was good. He was a man whom others would follow because of that essential honesty and integrity which was obvious to all who knew him. He was grandson on his mother's side of great William Marshal, one of the finest men who had ever lived. William Marshal was a man who had never once stepped aside from the paths of honour and duty. Henry was such another. Yes, he must be grateful to Isabella. On his father's side he had King John, Henry II and back to the Conqueror. And that produced this son of his.

He clasped him in his arms.

'Welcome my son. It does me good to see you.'

'How fare you, Father?'

'Oh well enough. There is much to occupy me as co-Regent with the Queen. It is never easy to work with another. It would be so much simpler to stand alone. You are troubled I can see.'

'I have come for your advice.'

Richard glowed with pleasure. There was nothing more gratifying than to know this beloved son came first to him when he was in difficulties.

'What is it, my son?'

'I would like to leave Edward's service.'

'Oh. What is it? A quarrel?'

'I find I can no longer stomach his behaviour.'

'Rough riding through the country. That boy is growing into a fool.'

Henry gave his father an account of the boy who had lost his ear.

'My God,' said Richard. 'What a fool he is! He is like his mother. He does not realize that the people in the end decide on whether he shall keep his throne. And you were there.'

'I tried to remonstrate, but I knew that advice from me makes him act more violently. It has happened in the past. I took the boy to his home and gave the family a purse.'

Richard nodded. He knew that Henry would take the right action.

'I feel that I can no longer serve him. I want to go abroad.'

'To go abroad. That means to Gascony to serve with the King.' Richard frowned. 'I would not have that. And to leave Edward! One day he will be King, you know.'

'If he is going to be like our grandfather I would have no wish to serve him.'

'I understand that well. If he is going to be like his grandfather he will not long be King. Henry, you could stay with me. Nothing would delight me more. Edward will want to know why you have left him.'

'He would know. He is fully aware of my disgust. Father, I can no longer ride out with him when cruel senseless disgusting acts are likely to take place at any moment. I *will* not, Father.'

'Nor shall you. By God, you are as royal as he. But for the fact that his father was older than I by a few months you would be the heir to the throne. What a happy thing for England that would be! So, as my son, you need not serve your cousin if you do not wish to. But I could not agree to your going abroad, Henry.' Richard hesitated. 'You are no longer very young. You must know what is happening. The Queen grows more and more unpopular and the King is not loved by his people. This matter of Simon de Montfort's quarrel with the King has been watched by the barons. There could come a day when they will take sides as they did in the days of your grandfather. Henry, you should be here. You should learn what is happening.'

'I have learned a little,' Henry answered. 'I have seen the people's sullen looks when the Queen rides by. I have heard the whispers and now and then the shouts.'

'It is not a healthful state of affairs. I do not see enough of you. Stay here for I see no reason why you should remain in Edward's household if you have no wish to do so.'

It was not long before Edward arrived at Westminster. He had come he said in search of his cousin Henry and would speak with him.

When they were alone together Edward grasped his hands.

'Henry, you left me,' he cried reproachfully.

'Yes,' said Henry.

'It was on account of that wretched boy.'

'Wretched boy indeed ... now and all his life. Think what you have done.'

'I have thought of little else since it happened. I shall never forget the sight of you picking him up in your arms.'

Henry said: 'I shall stay with my father.'

'I want you to come back with me.'

'I prefer to stay here.'

'You forget your place, Henry. I am your lord.'

'Oh, what will you do if I refuse to come back? Cut off my ears?'

'Henry, we have always been good friends. It was always the two of us. We were the ones. I want it always to be like that. We used to make plans together, talk of what we would do when we grew up. It was always good fun.'

'We were children then. Perhaps you have still to grow up since you find pleasure in roaming the countryside tormenting people.'

'I want to stop all that.'

'What? Give up your games! Give up your sport!'

'It was no real sport. This is why I want you to come back. I want to go to that boy's home. I want to show him my remorse. I want to give him money....'

'I doubt money could compensate for the loss of an ear.'

'I will do something for him. I am going to take a vow, Henry. If you will come back with me I will change. Yes, I will. I am not a boy any more. I suddenly saw how silly it all was. One day I shall be King. I want to be a good King. I want to be like the great Conqueror. He would not have gone around the country making cruel sport with the people.'

'He would never have become the great ruler he was if he had.'

'You are right, Henry. You have always been right. Oh, I listened to Henry, Simon and Guy de Montfort. I think they wanted to lessen me in people's eyes. I was foolish. I listened to them. No more, Henry. You will see. So come back with me and our first task shall be to recompense that poor boy.'

Henry hesitated. 'Do you mean this, Edward?'

Edward held up his hand as though making a vow.

'I swear it. From now on I change my ways. From now on I shall begin my training. I am going to be a great King, Henry, when my time comes. My name shall be spoken with those of the greatest of my ancestors.'

Henry took his cousin's hand.

'I will come back with you,' he said.

Two days later the Queen came to her son in a state of great excitement.

'I have heard from the King,' she cried. 'We are to prepare to join him. Edward, he has a bride for you.'

*　　*　　*

The royal party set out from Portsmouth on a warm May day, and the Queen was in a state of high excitement at the prospect of being reunited with her husband. Edward's feelings were mixed. The prospect of marriage did not displease him and the reports of his bride were promising. Henry was staying behind with his father who, with the departure of the Queen assumed the entire Regency.

Sanchia was with them. She was sorry to leave her husband but she had the compensation of her sister's company and she could not forgo the opportunity of seeing her family once more.

Henry was impatiently waiting at Bordeaux for their arrival, in a fever of anxiety lest disaster should befall them; and when he saw his Queen he was wild with joy.

It was his happiest moment since he had left her, he told her. They embraced fervently; then he turned to the rest of the company.

In the castle a great feast had been prepared. Never had he felt more like celebrating anything, said the King. He wanted to hear what the family had been doing and how baby Katharine fared. Poor darling, what a pity it was that she was too young to join them!

Later he explained the position to the Queen and Edward.

This marriage was necessary if they were to keep Gascony. King Alfonso who had come to the throne on the death of his father Ferdinand III, was being very firm in laying down his conditions.

The little Eleanora of Castile, the bride-to-be, was very young. She was the daughter of Ferdinand by Joanna Countess of Ponthieu—that lady whom Henry had churlishly treated in order to marry Queen Eleanor. Joanna, after being jilted by Henry, had married Ferdinand who had already had Alfonso by a previous marriage. Thus the young Eleanora was the new King's half-sister and he was in control of her destiny.

He had offered her to young Edward and Henry had seized on it as the only way out of the predicament he found himself in after his quarrel with Simon de Montfort, which could have lost him Gascony.

Once the marriage ceremony was performed, Gascony would be safe for Henry.

It had to be admitted that Alfonso was a little cynical regarding the intentions of the King of England.

This was not to be wondered at. Young Eleanora's mother

had been badly treated by Henry who after being betrothed
to her had abruptly broken off his contract. Moreover the
young girl's grandmother had been that Princess Alice who
had been sent to England as the bride-to-be of Richard Coeur
de Lion, and had been seduced by Richard's father when she
was a child and kept by him as his mistress so that the marriage she had come to England to make had never taken place.

Nothing of this nature was going to happen to his half
sister, Alfonso determined; therefore she should not go to
Edward but Edward should come to her; he should travel to
Burgos and if he did not arrive by a day which Alfonso would
appoint, the contract would be broken and he would invade
Gascony.

Henry said: 'You see what a position we are in.'

'What an arrogant fellow!' cried the Queen.

'He is indeed, my dearest. But we are in his hands. If we are
to keep Gascony, Edward must be in Burgos before the date
expires.'

'He shall be there,' said the Queen.

No time was lost, as soon as the contracts were signed and
agreed on, Eleanor and Edward set out for Burgos. Henry's
presence was needed in Bordeaux so he could not accompany
them.

Travelling across the Pyrenees was hazardous, but at least
it was summer, and the Queen's determination was well
known.

Michaelmas day marked the end of the period allowed
them.

They arrived on the fifth day of August, thanks to the indefatigable efforts of the Queen; and there was great rejoicing
in Burgos.

*　　*　　*

The young Infanta Eleanora saw the arrival of the cavalcade with the Queen riding at the head of it, her son beside
her.

This was Edward—who was to be her husband.

Her heart leapt with excitement for he was very handsome.
She knew at once who he was because of his bright flaxen
hair. There was a distinction about him. He was very young—
not much older than herself; and she thought that since she
had to marry and leave her home she would rather it was with
this Edward than any other.

Her home had never been the paradise enjoyed by the

Queen of England and her sisters. In the first place her
mother had not been her father's first wife. Ferdinand had
never been very interested in her; his favourite child had
naturally been Alfonso, son of a previous marriage, and
Alfonso had shown very clearly, since he had become King,
that he ruled them all.

Alfonso had little time for his half-sister and regarded her
merely as a pawn in his political game. But she was very useful
at this time, he admitted; and he would be glad to see her a
potential Queen of England.

His interests were divided between politics and astronomy,
and he was reckoned to be very clever. In fact he had invented
tables concerning the heavens which were known as the
Alfonsine Tables of Astronomy. He was known as The Wise,
and his knowledge of the stars had brought him great prestige.

So he had little time for his stepmother Joanna and his
half-sister Eleanora, except when they could be of use to him.

Joanna, who had herself been buffeted from one bridegroom to another, had told her daughter that this was what
an Infanta must expect; but the King of England was notori-
ously devoted to his wife and it seemed likely that his son
would be the same with his.

Therefore the little Infanta having lacked the happiness
in childhood that some had had, at least had the compensation
that it was no great wrench to leave her home.

Down to the courtyard. Her mother held her by the hand.
And there he was, the flaxen-haired boy, his eyes eagerly
scanning those assembled until they came to rest on her.

Then he smiled and she blushed a little.

Her heart leaped with pleasure for she read in his looks
that he was not ill pleased.

*   *   *

They were married. She did not have much time to speak
to him before the ceremony but he did let her know that he
was happy to be her husband. He spoke a little of her language
and she had been taught his so it was not hard to communi-
cate.

She thought he was the most handsome young man she had
ever seen—and not only handsome, but different from any
other.

She was a little in awe of her mother-in-law, who was very
beautiful and clearly determined to have her own .way. They
had the same name—or almost. The Queen's had been made

Eleanor instead of her native Eléanore; and Eleanora, which
the Infanta was called now, would, the Queen told her, doubtless be changed to Eleanor when she was in England, for the
English thought their way of doing everything—even spelling
names—was better than anyone else's.

The Infanta told the Queen that she did not mind how
they changed her name as long as they liked her.

At which the Queen grunted and said they were a difficult
people and in particular the Londoners.

However Edward was more reassuring. The people would
love her, he told her, because she was pretty and moreover
gentle. He liked her gentleness too. In fact he was very pleased
with his marriage.

Alfonso was eager to show the English Queen that he could
give her as good entertainment in Burgos as she had in
England and there was a rich feast and a festival which was
more stately than those held in England. Edward was most
impressed but most of all he liked to sit beside his little wife
and let her explain her country's customs to him.

Alfonso knighted Edward and the little Infanta was moved
to see handsome Edward kneel before her half-brother.

As the bride was so young—she was only just ten years old
—there was to be no consummation of marriage. That, said
Alfonso, could wait.

The Queen replied that the best way was to allow these
things to settle themselves naturally; and in any case the
little girl must finish her education first and this should
have the Queen's personal supervision, which she had given
to her own children.

This was all arranged to the satisfaction of Alfonso and in
due course the party set out for Bordeaux and this time the
little bride rode with them.

*   *   *

How delighted was the King to see them. He embraced the
Queen, his son, and the little bride.

'My dear little daughter,' he said, 'how glad I am to welcome
you into this family!'

Eleanora was delighted. It was such a pleasant family. The
King loved them all so dearly and her mother had told her
how important he was. He ruled a big country. The Queen
was kind provided one did exactly what she wanted. And
Edward was so gallant and rode with such skill and was so
distinguished that she glowed with pride to watch him. Then

there was the Queen's sister, the Lady Sanchia, and Edmund who was her own age and Beatrice who was a little older. It was a wonderful family and what she had missed most— although she had not realized this until now—was a family life.

The King was determined to welcome her warmly and his way of doing this was to give a grand banquet in her honour. There was a good deal of grumbling about the cost of this and the Infanta heard it said that it had cost three hundred thousand marks which was a very large sum of money.

'We'll find means of raising it,' said Henry, cheerful as he always was when the spending of money was concerned; it was only when the need to find it arose that he lost his temper and became irritable.

They stayed at Bordeaux until the end of the summer and as more brilliant festivals were devised to celebrate the marriage, the King's friends grew more and more restive when contemplating the cost.

Henry continued to shrug all that aside and finally decided that they would leave Bordeaux and start their journey home. First though he and the Queen would make a pilgrimage to the shrine of St. Edmund, who had been his Archbishop of Canterbury until he died and been buried in Pontigny. Edmund had always been an uncomfortable man, being such a saint who, while he did continual penance for his own sins, had a habit of magnifying those of others.

Having paid their homage to the dead St. Edmund they felt considerably better about all the money they had been spending and travelled on to Fontevrault where Henry commanded that the body of his mother be removed from the grave in the cemetery there and put in the church. He ordered a tomb to be placed over it.

By this time he was feeling very virtuous.

The Queen was overcome with joy when messages arrived from the King of France to the effect that he would take it amiss if the party did not come to Paris and give him the pleasure of entertaining them.

*　　*　　*

Now the Queen was to experience the greatest pleasure because at the Court of France she would be with her three sisters.

There was great rejoicing when the party arrived in Paris

and, to please his wife, Louis insisted on giving the English party the finest lodging at his disposal. This happened to be the Temple which was the headquarters of the Knights Templars in France and was a magnificent palace.

It was a wonderful moment when Eleanor was greeted by her sister Marguerite, recently returned from the Holy Land where she had accompanied her husband; and with her was Beatrice, now the Countess of Anjou, having married Louis' brother Charles.

To add to their joy the Countess of Provence, hearing that Eleanor and Sanchia were to be in Paris had decided to join them. So that the four sisters and their mother were together.

'There is only one missing,' said Marguerite. 'Our dear father.'

'We must not grieve,' said the Countess of Provence. 'He would rejoice to see us thus, and perhaps he can. Let us, while remembering him, be happy in each other.'

Henry determined to court popularity—and also to let the French know that he was a rich King—spent his first morning in Paris distributing alms to the poor. This insured his popularity and meant he was cheered wherever he went.

'I know how happy you are, my dearest,' he said to Eleanor, 'and I am going to give a grand banquet to which I shall invite all the nobility of France. It will show the world how I honour your family.'

'You are the best husband in the world,' cried Eleanor. 'The more I see of the men my sisters have married the more blessed I know myself to be.'

This was the sort of remark which delighted Henry and Eleanor was adept at making such. She was implying criticism of Louis and Charles of Anjou and of Richard of Cornwall, her sisters' husbands. Of course he and Louis were the Kings and therefore desirable and he was a little piqued by hearing the compliments which seemed to be showered on Louis and to witness how his people seemed to revere him when he rode out.

'His people are more demonstrative than they are at home,' he said. 'My people are not so affectionate towards me.'

'Louis has just returned from a crusade,' replied Eleanor. 'That makes the people regard him as a saint.'

But it was not only that. There was a humility about Louis IX which coupled with a dignity set him apart. There was compassion in him. This was a King who cared for his people. He would never harry them with taxes for his own needs. Louis set little store by the splendour of his rank; he did not greatly care for festivals. He cared about the people, what they were thinking, how he could better their lot.

It was rather trying, Eleanor thought, when her sister Marguerite talked to her of him. Marguerite was completely devoted to her saint and continually singing his praises, when it was clear to Eleanor that Louis did not dote on her in the same way that Henry did on his Queen.

The four sisters sat together, they walked together, they shared the tapestry which Marguerite was making and they talked and were transported back in their thoughts to Les Baux.

It was like being young again and it was amazing how they slipped back into their roles of subservience to Eleanor.

'Do you remember ...' The phrase was constantly occurring and they would talk of the old days, laughing, being young again.

Then they talked of the present, and the change in their lives since the days in Provence. Marguerite had adventured most for she had been with Louis to the Holy Land.

'I would not let him go alone,' she said. 'I insisted. His mother did not want him to go. No one wanted him to go. They thought he should stay at home and govern his kingdom. I remember the day he was so ill that we thought he was dead. I remember how he lay on his bed and one of the women wanted to draw the sheet over his face because she thought he was dead. But I would not let them. I would not believe that he was dead. I forbade them to cover up his face. I cried: 'There is life in him yet,' and then he spoke ... in a strange hollow voice as though he were far away. He said: 'He, by God's grace, hath visited me. He who comes from on High hath recalled me from the dead.' Then he sent for the bishop of Paris and said to him: 'Place upon my shoulder the cross of the voyage over the sea.' We knew what this meant. His mother and I looked at each other and although she tried to shut me out and I did not like her, for I feared that she resented his love for me and wanted him all for herself, we were at one in this for we knew what Louis meant. He was going on a Crusade. We begged him to make no vows until he was well, but he would take no food until he had received the cross. I remember how his mother mourned. Her face was blank and she was as one who has the sentence of death on her. He took the cross and kissed it and when she had drawn me from the chamber, she said to me: 'I must mourn him now as though he were dead for soon I shall lose him'. She meant of course that if he went on a crusade she would die before he returned.'

'You did not like her overmuch,' said Eleanor. 'She was always determined to shut you out.'

'At first I resented her. But later I understood. She loved him so much ... could not bear that anyone should come before her with him. He was her life. It had no meaning for her if she lost him.'

'And then he went away,' said Sanchia, 'and you went with him.'

'It was not until three years after that, but I knew it was in his mind. He used to talk to me about it. He had had a vision when he was lying close to death and he believed he had been sent back to Earth to fulfil a purpose. He had to go to the Holy Land, because it was ordained by God.'

'They say he is a saint,' said Sanchia.

'They are right,' replied Marguerite.

'I would prefer to be married to a man,' retorted Eleanor.

'Louis is a man,' replied Marguerite. 'Doubt it not. He can fly into a rage but it is mostly over injustice. He does not want to hurt anyone. He wants to make people good and happy. . . .'

Eleanor yawned slightly. She began to tell them about the wonderful feasts Henry had given at Bordeaux to celebrate the marriage of Edward and the little Infanta.

Beatrice whose husband had gone on the crusade with Louis brought the subject back to the great Crusade and said how happy they had all been when it was over.

'It was a frightening time,' Marguerite told them. 'Often I thought we should all be killed. Louis was torn between his need to take part in the crusade and to govern his country. He said that his grandfather had felt the same when he went to the Holy Land with his Queen.'

'She had some gay adventures, I believe,' said Eleanor. 'I was always interested in her because we shared the same name.'

'Eleanor of Aquitaine,' murmured Beatrice.

'My husband's grandmother,' added Eleanor. 'I think I should enjoy going on a crusade.'

'It is so exciting when you plan to go,' said Marguerite. 'Less so when you arrive.' She shivered. 'I hope Louis never decides to go again, I shall never forget his mother's anguish when he left. She knew she would never see him again. It was a premonition. I can hear her voice now and see her blue eyes, usually as cold as ice, misty then soft with love for him. She said: 'Most fair son, my tender boy, I shall never see you more. Full well my heart assures me of this.' Nor did she. Four years later she died and we were still there. It was because of her death that we came home. Louis knew that that was where his duty lay. He thought it was a sign from God that he should return home.

'And all the time you were there, poor Marguerite, Sanchia and I were living comfortably in England.'

'It is wonderful that the two of you are together,' said Marguerite.

'Is it not like some fateful pattern?' demanded Beatrice. 'Two sisters for two brothers, and two more sisters for two more brothers. I wonder if it has ever happened before in families?'

'We elder ones had the Kings,' said Eleanor.

'Romeo used to say that he would have kings for all of us,' Beatrice reminded them.

'Romeo was boastful,' said Sanchia.

'Well, we can all congratulate ourselves,' put in Eleanor, 'for after all we were very poor were we not and had little to recommend us but our beauty and our brains.'

'Not only,' said Beatrice, 'did you two marry Kings but those Kings loved you and have been faithful husbands. That is what seems strange to me. One does not expect a King to love his wife and be faithful to her.'

'Louis is a saint,' said Marguerite.

'And Henry will tell you that I am the perfect woman,' added Eleanor lightly.

Then they started to talk of their men; Marguerite of Louis's piety; Eleanor of Henry's devotion to her and his family; Sanchia of Richard's lethargy which would suddenly beset him and as suddenly depart leaving him eager for some action which would probably be defeated by a return of the lethargy; Beatrice of her husband's temper which was sudden and violent. Marguerite nodded. It was clear that she did not greatly like Beatrice's husband. Eleanor suspected that Sanchia's husband was not always faithful and she marvelled that the two who had made the most brilliant marriages should also have made the most happy ones.

But she could not help feeling a sense of rivalry with Marguerite. She wanted the King of England to shine more brilliantly than the King of France. She wanted his feasts and banquets to be the more extravagant. She knew that they would be because she would convey this to Henry and he would do everything to please her. Moreover Louis had no great regard for splendour.

Oh, it was wonderful to be with her sisters, to talk and talk over the old days, the present and the future.

And as ever it seemed that Eleanor was the brilliant one, the one who had her way.

In spite of their marriages and all their experiences, they still looked up to Eleanor, the most beautiful and the cleverest member of the family.

*   *   *

Edward was happy. He had ceased to think of the mutilated boy. If he did it was to regard him as a burning beacon in his life. Through him he had seen the folly of his ways. He was going to begin a new life, learn to be a great King. He had a little wife who was beginning to adore him. She was only a child and he was glad of that because her youth made him seem mature and splendid in her eyes. He was kind and gentle to her; he was chivalrous, courteous, all that a knight should be to his lady. He rode beside her, ready to defend her, make sure that she was treated with the utmost courtesy; he talked to her of England and how he would care for her and told her how she would never have anything to fear with him to look after her.

The little Infanta had never been so cherished. It was small wonder that she was in love with her handsome bridegroom.

Henry and Eleanor were delighted and Henry told the child that she was now a member of their family which was the finest family in the world because everyone in that magic circle was loved by everyone else.

The Queen was less effusive but she showed quite clearly that she doted on Edward and that if Edward was fond of his little wife and was happy with her, then the Queen would be fond of her too.

It was a wonderful revelation for the little girl.

As for Edward he wanted to talk incessantly of the crusade. He admired the King of France, not because of the stories he heard of his goodness to his people, but because he had taken up the Cross and been to the Holy Land.

He begged the King to tell him of the crusade and Louis would sit with him or walk with him in the gardens of the palace and talk.

He told Edward how, after having received the oriflamme, the scrip and the staff at St. Denis, he took leave of his mother and went to Aigues Mortes where his fleet was assembled and how he set sail arriving first at Cyprus which was the meeting place for the forces of the expedition. His ship was the *Mount-joy* and on this flew that banner of red silk split into points and born on a gilt staff which was the oriflamme—the royal standard of France. They set sail and the gales were so violent that many of the ships were dispersed. It was June—one year after he had left France—when they arrived before Damietta. 'All the leaders came aboard the *Mountjoy*,' said Louis, 'and there I spoke to them. They looked to me as a leader because I was the King of France and I told them I was but a man, as vulnerable as they were. It might be that God would choose to take me in this struggle. It could as easily be me as any man. "If we are conquered," I said, "we shall win our way to Heaven as martyrs and, if we are conquerors, men will celebrate the glory of God. We fight for Christ. It is Christ who will triumph in us, not for our sake but for the blessedness of His Holy name."'

'And you made war on the Saracens and you won the battle. You brought great glory to France.'

'I came back,' said Louis. 'But it was no great victory. Men leave for the Holy Land full of good intentions. Often they are surprised by what they find. Great suffering has to be endured. Victory is elusive. I have heard disappointed men say that it seems God fights on the side of the Saracens not on that of the Christians.'

'Pray, my lord, tell me more.'

'I see you have adventure in your eyes, my lord Edward. Ours was no glorious victory for Christianity. We took Damietta with the utmost ease. We should have moved on. We had tarried too long in Cyprus and now we waited at Damietta. I believed more crusaders would join us. There was a great deal of revelry. Those who had helped to take Damietta wanted to rest there. They feasted, they lived on the booty they had taken. They took the women and the riches of the city. I protested but they would not heed me. Soldiers who have fought and won a victory demand their rewards. That is what the soldiers did at Damietta. By the time we were ready to march the Musselmans were ready for us. There was a battle at Mansourah—some twenty leagues from Damietta. My brother Robert, Count of Artois, led the advance forces.'

Louis put his hands over his eyes and turned away.

'Pray go on, my lord,' urged Edward.

'But you do not want to hear these sorry tales, I am sure. They are not valiant hearing.'

'I do want to know,' said Edward. 'I long to hear of your crusade.'

'At first my brother had an easy victory. Alas, he was over confident. I ordered him to wait for me with the rest of my forces, but he was impatient. He went on in pursuit of the enemy, but the Saracens had re-formed and rallied and they had been joined by others. My brother was surrounded. He fell pierced with wounds. He had ever been impetuous. And so I lost a brother.'

'But you beat the Saracens.'

Louis shook his head. 'We managed to defend ourselves ... nothing more. We had to retreat and give up Damietta. It was no glorious victory. My men were sick and dying. There was news from France. My kingdom was in danger from the English. If I left the Holy Land many Christians who were living there would be in danger. So I asked those who were with me what decision they thought I should make.'

'You are the King. You make the decisions,' said Edward.

'I have always felt that those who shared my defeats and victories should have their say. But their opinion was divided as was my own and in the end I made up my mind to stay a little longer. It was my great dream to win back Jerusalem to Christianity. So I stayed, and for four years I passed along the coasts of Palestine and Syria and I made it my task to succour the sick and make life possible for the population there. All I was doing was keeping the Christian stronghold. My dream of capturing Jerusalem passed me by as it did your great uncle Richard Coeur de Lion who came very near to bringing it to Christianity and just failed. Then news came to me that my mother had died and I knew then that I must return to France.'

'My lord,' said Edward, 'I am going on a crusade.'

'It is the dream of many a young man.'

'For me it will be a dream fulfilled,' said Edward fervently; and it was as though he had taken a vow.

The Unhappy Queen of Scotland

WHILE the English party was in Paris Pope Innocent IV sent a message to Henry which gave him immense satisfaction. Innocent who was in conflict with Manfred, the King of Sicily, the illegitimate son of the Emperor Frederick II, needed money to carry on his war and was determined to depose Manfred. Henry seemed to have a way of raising money when he needed it and Innocent thought that he could be of help in the Sicilian conflict. Of course Henry must be rewarded for his help; and it was this reward which caused Henry such pleasure.

He took the news to Eleanor without delay.

'My dear, look at this ring which the Pope has sent.'

Eleanor took it and held it in the palm of her hand. 'Why does he send it?' she asked.

'Ah, my dear, it has a special significance. It is for the King of Sicily. You look puzzled, as indeed you may. The Pope is at war with Sicily. He will dethrone Manfred. In return for help he sends me this ring which will be put on the finger of the newly appointed King of Sicily.'

'And who ...?'

'One of my sons, he says.'

Eleanor smiled. 'Edward....' she began.

'My dearest, Edward has England. He will regain much of France. I thought Sicily for Edmund. You will have two Kings for sons then, my dear.'

Eleanor laughed.

'You are right,' she said. 'It must be Sicily for Edmund.'

Henry immediately gave a special banquet to celebrate his son's elevation to the throne of Sicily. There was a certain murmuring among members of his entourage as to how the crown of Sicily was going to be paid for. More taxes. Would the people endure it? That was the question. The King did not seem to realize that they were growing dangerously restive.

Meanwhile there was a splendid celebration. Eleanor insisted on her younger son's wearing the Sicilian costume and everyone declared how well it became him.

* * *

At last it was time to return to England. The King and Queen of France with their Court accompanied them for a day and the English party then continued its way to the coast. On a cold January day they crossed to Dover and prepared to make the journey to London.

There was a ceremonial entry into the capital where the traditional present of one hundred pounds was made to the King. It seemed, complained Henry to the Mayor, a very small appreciation when it was considered that he had been absent so long on the country's business. The Mayor consulted with the merchants and a fine piece of plate was produced. The beauty of this pleased him but he was still disgruntled.

'Trust the people of London to spoil my welcome,' he grumbled to Eleanor.

Both Henry and Eleanor, much as they had enjoyed the homage paid to them by the Court of France, were delighted to be home.

The first thing Eleanor did was rush to the nursery to see her little daughter Katharine. The child was very pretty and healthy and she wondered why the nurses had a somewhat, apprehensive air.

'What is wrong?' demanded the Queen. 'Is the child ill?'

'Not exactly, my lady, but....'

A fearful anxiety came to the Queen. While she had been enjoying life in France all was not well with her baby.

'Come,' she cried sharply, 'tell me. Don't dare hold anything back.'

'My lady, the child does not speak.'

'You mean ... she cannot....'

'It would seem, my lady, that she is dumb.'

Eleanor took the child and held her tightly in her arms.

She crooned over her. 'My baby Katharine.... This to be ... and I not to know.'

She kissed the child fervently. Katharine smiled back at her, gently loving but dumb.

The Queen shed many tears. She reproached herself.

'My dearest,' said Henry, 'there was nothing you could have done had you been here.'

Eleanor could not be comforted. That her child should be less than perfect shocked her; and while she mourned over Katharine she began to feel uneasy about her eldest daughter Margaret.

'It is long since we heard of her. She was so young to go away. Alexander is only a boy. Henry, I must see Margaret. Coming home and finding Katharine thus has frightened me.'

Henry was ready to soothe her.

'I will send to Scotland without delay and tell them that Margaret is to visit us. Perhaps we could travel up to York and be together there.'

'Let us do that without delay. I shall not know a moment's peace until I have seen our daughter.'

'You have allowed yourself to be fearful because of this. . . .'

'Perhaps. But I have a feeling for the children. I believe that if any of them is in danger I should be aware of it. And I am very uneasy about Margaret.'

'The messengers shall leave without delay.'

The Queen could settle to nothing while she awaited news from Scotland. When it came it was disconcerting. There was nothing from Margaret herself but the guardians of the King and Queen, Robert de Ros and John Baliol, sent word that it was quite impossible at this time for Queen Margaret to leave Scotland.

This threw the Queen into a panic.

'Something is wrong. I know it. Oh Henry, why did we ever let her go to that bleak land?'

'The marriage was necessary if we were going to keep peace on the border. But I begin to share your anxiety.'

'What can we do?'

'If they refuse to allow her to come to England there is nothing we can do. We would have to go to war and. . . .'

'Then we would go to war,' said the Queen fiercely.

Henry put a soothing arm about her shoulders. 'It may well be, my dear, that you are worried unduly. We must discover why Margaret does not write and why it is impossible for her to come to see us. But we must do it with care.'

'I have it,' said Eleanor. 'I shall send one of our doctors up to see her. They cannot deny him entrance to the castle. If he brings me back a good report of her health and word from her that she is happy I shall be reassured.'

The King agreed that this was a good idea and they sent for Reginald of Bath who was the finest physician they knew.

'You are to leave at once for Edinburgh,' said Eleanor. 'There you will go to the Castle. You will see the Queen of Scotland and tell her that you come on behalf of the King and Queen of England and you want to hear from her own lips that all is well. And I shall want a report on her health.'

Reginald left immediately.

*   *   *

How long and dreary were the days, and how Margaret yearned for the happy times of her childhood. She hated Scotland. As for her husband Alexander, who was younger than she was, he might have been a good companion but she was only rarely allowed to see him.

Edinburgh Castle was as dour and grim as those who had set themselves up as her guardians. She longed for Windsor and her dearest mother and father always at hand, always ready to listen. She wanted the hectoring company of the boys—even though they had spurned her as a girl and rarely let her join in their games—she wanted Beatrice and young Edmund. She wanted to look out of the windows and watch Edward lording it over the others with his flaxen hair waving in the wind and his long legs putting him above everyone else.

She wanted to go home.

From the moment she had seen this castle it had seemed like a prison. Built high on a rock; grey and forbidding it was grimmer than the Tower of London. It was a sad and solitary place; there were no green fields and gardens around it; it was unhealthy, she was sure, because she had felt ill ever since she came here. But perhaps that was homesickness.

She hated the long lessons with Matilda de Cantelupe, the governess who rarely smiled and who never complimented her however hard she worked. And sometimes she did work hard to make the days pass more quickly. Alexander was in another part of the castle, and their guardians, those two dour men, Robert de Ros and John Baliol, visited them from time to time. They asked her questions about England and wanted to know whether any communication had been smuggled in to her.

Yes, indeed she was a prisoner.

Each day she walked along the ramparts of the castle with Matilda de Cantelupe, who kept close to her almost as though she feared she would run away.

Alexander was allowed to walk with her sometimes, but never so that they could exchange confidences. They were never allowed to say one word to each other out of the hearing of one of their jailers.

She wrote to her parents but the letters were taken away from her and as there were no replies she wondered if they ever reached them. She knew that her parents would write to her, but she never had letters from them either.

Sometimes she would feel very angry and demand of Matilda why she was treated thus. Matilda's reply was: 'You are well treated. You are fed and looked after. Your education is attended to. What more do you ask?'

'I ask to be free. I am the Queen of Scotland.'

'Then I must ask you to behave as the Queen of Scotland.'

'How should she behave? Should she allow herself to be treated as a prisoner?'

'This is nonsense. Is this room a dungeon?'

'No, but it is a prison nevertheless. Why do they treat me thus?'

'You are being brought up to be the Queen of Scotland.'

'Then I would rather be a humble serving wench for I am sure she would be happier than I.'

'You talk foolishly, my lady.'

Margaret kicked a footstool and sent it sliding across the room. Matilda gripped her arm so firmly that Margaret cried out in pain.

'Take your hands from me,' she shouted. 'Forget not that I am the daughter of the King of England.'

'We forget it not. Pray be calm. Methinks you have madness in you.'

Oh God help me, prayed Margaret, are they going to pretend that I am mad? What will they do to me then?

She fell silent.

It was so hard to know what to do when one was only fifteen.

She thought a great deal of her parents and all the love that had been showered on her when she was a child. If they but knew, how angry they would be. They would come and take her away. She knew that by marrying her to Alexander they had made peace with the Scots but they would make war if they knew this was how the Scots were treating her.

What could she do? She would not be fifteen forever. Alexander was young. He would help if he could but they treated him in the same way as they treated her.

Homesickness obsessed her. A deep feeling of melancholy came to her. If she heard England mentioned she was ready to weep helplessly so much did she long for her home and family.

She began to feel ill and listless. She ate very little and grew pale and thin.

Matilda was angry with her and so were those fearsome men who came more frequently to see her. But they could not make her eat if she would not.

'You are ungrateful,' scolded Matilda. 'We do our best for you and how do you repay us?'

'If this is your best I cannot imagine your worst,' answered Margaret.

'What do you want then?'

'To leave this prison. To go home.'

'This is your home. You have a husband now.'

'He is no husband to me. He is your prisoner ... as I am. I hate you all. I want to go back to England. I want my mother and my father.'

'Thus do babies cry,' said Matilda sternly.

* * *

Seated at the window, she looked out over the countryside. There was no escape from the castle. Sometimes she dreamed that her brother Edward came or her cousin Henry. They were such perfect knights and in the old days they would have enjoyed playing at rescuing imprisoned ladies.

It would be wonderful to see her brother riding up to the castle with his standard flying in the wind. She pictured the scene. 'I have come to take my sister home.' He would thrust aside de Ros and Baliol. He would laugh at Matilda de Cantalupe. He would seize his sister in his arms and place her on his horse. She could almost feel herself flying along in the wind with Edward, laughing as they went, and singing some song about rescue and adventure.

A few months ago Matilda had told her that her parents were in France and Edward was with them. He had married the half-sister of the King of Castile. There had been rejoicing and feasting and much extravagance.

Why did she tell her? It could only be to make her prisoner long for them the more.

They have forgotten me, she thought. They are rejoicing in Edward's marriage. Lucky Edward, who will not have to leave his home because he has married. What manner of girl was his bride? She would be coming to a happy home. The King and Queen of England would never be unkind to young people. They would welcome Edward's bride. Happy girl to marry into such a family.

When she had walked with Alexander he had tried to comfort her.

'It will not always be thus,' he had assured her. 'It is only because I am not old enough yet to be a proper king and this is a regency.'

Perhaps it would end then. But he had a long time to wait before he would be considered old enough to be a real king.

While she sat disconsolately at the window she saw a party of riders coming towards the castle. She was alert immediately.

She watched them come up the slope and enter through the gateway. She could hear the horses' hoofs clattering on the cobbles.

She was aware of the tension in the castle, and she knew that something extraordinary was afoot. Any excitement was welcome in this dull life and there was always the hope that the visitors had come from England.

Footsteps on the stone stairs! They were coming up this way.

She stood up as the door opened.

A man came into the room. Matilda de Cantalupe hovered behind him uncertainly.

'I come on the command of the Queen of England,' said the man, and Margaret felt as though she were fainting with relief.

'You are welcome,' she stammered. 'How ... how fares my mother?'

'Your mother fares well and is anxious for news of you.'

Oh God, thought Margaret, You have answered my prayers. I knew she would send someone. She would never forget me.

Her melancholy dropped from her. 'Leave us,' she said to Matilda.

Matilda replied: 'I think, my lady....'

The man looked amazed. 'Madam, did you not hear the command of the Queen of Scotland?'

'My orders are....'

'You have just heard your orders from the Queen herself. What I have to say to the Queen I wish to say to her alone.'

There was an air of such authority about the man that Matilda hesitated. Her orders would have been not to allow a messenger from England to be alone with the Queen. She knew that. On the other hand if that was obvious it would create an even worse impression than if the Queen complained of their treatment. She decided to leave them alone together and send a message at once to her masters de Ros and Baliol.

When they were alone Margaret ran to the visitor and gave him her hand.

'How glad I am to see you. You come from my mother. What messages do you bring? Tell me quickly before we are disturbed.'

'Your mother has suffered great anxiety about you. She feared all might not be well.'

'Oh I knew she would. My dearest, dearest mother. She would never desert any of us. My dear father too.'

'He too is concerned. They have heard nothing from you.'

'But I have written often. *I* have heard nothing from them.'

'This is indeed a conspiracy. They have sent letters to you and received none from you. They must have been intercepted. Your mother wants a report on your health. I am a doctor. You may have heard of me. Reginald of Bath.'

'But yes,' cried Margaret excitedly.

'I have to take back a report on your health and I fear it has been impaired by this place.'

'I am so tired. I have no appetite. It is so cold and cheerless. I am ill in the winter. Sometimes I feel I want only to lie down and weep. I long to be home again.'

'I shall report this to your mother. How do you live here?'

'Like a prisoner. I am only allowed to walk in the castle grounds. I rarely see Alexander, who is treated as I am. My jailers de Ros and Baliol come to see me now and then and ask me many questions about England. It is easy to see that they hate our country. Tell my mother that I am sick with longing for home. If only I could see her and the others and the green fields and forests of Windsor I should be as well as I ever was. I am ill ... and my complaint is Scotland. Oh, Doctor Reginald, I want to come home.'

'I will tell your mother all you have said. I shall stay here but briefly for the Queen is impatient for my report. You may rest assured that when she has it she will take some action. I shall tell her how your health is suffering and I know that she will not allow that to continue.'

They talked awhile and she remembered indignities she had suffered and told him of them and that she was treated like a prisoner.

Matilda had given orders that an apartment be prepared for Reginald and he told her that he would need it only for one night. The next day he intended to return to England where the Queen was eagerly awaiting news of her daughter.

'It would seem strange,' he added, 'that correspondence intended for the Queen of Scotland has never reached her and that which she sent to the King and Queen of England has not come to them.'

'The roads are treacherous,' replied Matilda. 'Messengers are often waylaid and robbed.'

'Aye,' was the answer, 'particularly in Scotland.'

Supper that day was taken in the great hall and Alexander was present, and although her melancholy was lifted, Margaret could eat little through excitement.

Alexander was clearly amazed at this change in their fortunes and Reginald listened intently to the young King's corroboration of Margaret's story.

He would certainly have something to report to Queen Eleanor and King Henry.

The next morning he left and shortly after his departure Robert de Ros and John Baliol arrived at the castle. They had come with all speed on receiving Matilda's communication and were furious because the doctor had already left.

They made Matilda tell them everything that had happened. They realized that she could not have kept him away from Margaret but they deplored the fact that she had not remained with them to hear what was said.

How long had he gone? They must be after him. He must not be allowed to take his report to England.

* * *

Reginald, with his small party, was riding south, well pleased with his work. The mission was successful. He had found out what he had come to seek and he would have the royal approval for what he had done.

He had confirmed their suspicions. All was not well in Edinburgh. Some action would have to be taken for it was clear that the treatment Margaret was receiving in Scotland was, as Queen Eleanor had feared, affecting her health.

A day after he had left the castle his party fell in with some travellers on the road who were making their way south. They were pleasant companions and explained that they were frequent travellers along this road and would be delighted to give their English friends the benefit of their experience.

They could guide them in the making of short cuts for they could see that their friends were intent on speed.

They came to an alehouse and were received warmly by the landlord. He could as it happened provide them with some good meat and drink and his wife had just baked fresh bread. His home made ale was renowned throughout the neighbourhood and he would be proud if the distinguished travellers would sample it.

They talked together and during the conversation Reginald somehow revealed that he was a doctor and that he came from Bath. He was a well known doctor in England, he could not help hinting, and served the great.

The ale was good and after he had drunk well of it he began to feel very sleepy. His bed was a pallet on the floor in the gallery above the alehouse parlour. He slept heavily but awakened in the night feeling rather strange. He was beset by violent pains which his medical knowledge suggested had been brought about by something he had drunk or eaten.

By the morning his friends were alarmed for he could not get up from his pallet. Their new friends who had brought them to the inn departed as they said they must and wished them good speed on their journey.

Before that morning was out Reginald of Bath was dead.

*   *   *

Eleanor, impatiently awaiting news from Scotland, was filled with foreboding. She had come to accept Katharine's dumbness. The child was so pretty and appealing and she could forget her affliction in her charm.

Now her thoughts were all for Margaret. She knew that something was amiss. She could not imagine what was keeping Reginald. But perhaps she expected too much. Henry kept reminding her that he had not been gone very long and as he had impressed on him her deep anxiety he was sure the good doctor would make all possible speed.

When the party returned without the doctor and she heard that he was dead, she was in great dismay.

She fired questions at his attendants and wanted to know what he had found in Edinburgh Castle. They had not seen the Queen of Scotland, but they did know that Reginald had been horrified by the condition of the young Queen and he had said that she was more or less a prisoner of the Scots.

'It is because he was bringing this news to us that he has

been poisoned! Oh Henry, what are we going to do? We must bring our little girl home.'

Henry was horrified but talking the matter over with his brother Richard he realized that he could not make war on the Scots. Money would be needed for such an operation and he was already committed to helping the Pope in Sicily—a matter which was causing considerable complaint from his subjects who were being taxed to find the money needed.

Henry decided that he would send the Earl of Gloucester to Scotland with a suitable retinue and there arrangements must be made to give Margaret an establishment in keeping with her position, the regency disbanded, and Alexander and Margaret to rule as King and Queen.

This should be done, said the Queen, but it was not enough. She must see her daughter. Nothing would satisfy her until she had.

Since Eleanor was so determined that they must go to Scotland, go they must.

The Earl of Gloucester reported that the King and Queen of Scotland were now living together in their own establishment which was very different from their quarters in Edinburgh Castle. They would be travelling to Wark and Roxburgh and there they would meet Eleanor and Henry.

How delighted Margaret was! There was no ceremony. She must fling herself into her mother's arms while they wept together.

'I knew you would come. I knew you would never forget me,' sobbed Margaret.

Eleanor laughed. 'Forget one of my children! My darling, that I never would.'

'Oh I knew everything would be all right if only I could reach you.'

'It must never happen again,' said Eleanor sternly, looking at her husband; and he assured her that it never would.

The mother and daughter would not be separated. Eleanor must hear everything that had happened since her daughter had parted from her. She told Margaret of their adventures in France, how she had met her sisters and her mother and how pleasant that had been—marred only because her darling daughter was not with her.

She told about Edward's little bride.

'A charming creature. Very young and she adores him already.'

'Anyone would adore Edward,' said Margaret; and Eleanor

agreed with her. 'You would like her. We must all be together before long. She has brought with her some tapestry which it seems in Castile they hang on walls and use on furniture. It is very pleasant and we are already using it in England.'

'Oh, my dearest mother, how happy it makes me to be with you,' cried Margaret.

They were going to make sure that there was no return of this monstrous behaviour, Eleanor assured her daughter. Those villains de Ros and Baliol had already been dismissed. They would regret the day they had made the Queen of Scotland a prisoner. Young Alexander was acknowledged as King and no petty little lords were going to prevent that.

'Edward is coming to see you soon,' said Eleanor, 'and my love, we shall expect you at Woodstock before long. I tell you this: if you do not come, your father and I will come and fetch you.'

Margaret gazed at her parents with loving wonder. Hadn't she always known they could put everything right?

My Son! My Son!

RICHARD had been watching events with a certain bitterness. He was angry with his brother for having bestowed the crown of Sicily on young Edmund without consulting him. He could have told Henry that that crown would have to be won and that it would be a costly matter winning it. Henry seemed to have no financial sense at all. He thought his coffers were magical and refilled as a matter of course as he emptied them. Heaven knew he had been in enough difficulties and should have learned that one of the reasons for his increasing unpopularity was his continual demand for money. Richard was different; he was rich ... very rich. He respected money; he rarely gave it away though sometimes he lent it if it was profitable to do so. The foreigner-hangers-on had quickly learned that they could get nothing from Richard.

Since he had been on his crusade he had had some reputation in Europe. He was looked up to as a man of courage and importance, and the Pope had already offered him the crown of Germany. He declined this offer which he knew would have offended his brother-in-law Frederick II; but now Frederick was dead and so was the son Henry he had had by Richard's sister Isabella.

The situation had changed and Richard did not greatly care for the way events were drifting in England. He could see trouble ahead, if Henry could not. Richard would not take sides in the conflict between Henry and the barons. His loyalty prevented him from siding with the barons and his common sense would not let him agree with Henry. Henry was a fool and his doting fondness for his wife made him eager to give her relations anything they asked; he seemed to have a fondness for foreigners for he showered gifts on them and showed this absurd generosity to his half-brothers and sisters.

He now let it be known that if the office of King of the Romans was offered to him he would stand for election.

There was another candidate for this honour. This was Alfonso of Castile, half-brother of the Infanta who was now Edward's wife, and Alfonso had the support of the French who did not care to contemplate more English influence in Europe.

Richard's reputation however carried him through. His valour in the crusade; the wealth he had amassed; his skill in keeping clear of the troubles which beset his brother, won the day for him.

He was elected King of the Romans.

He was exultant. This was his great opportunity. He had always wanted a crown and had resented the fact that he had been born too late to have attained that of England. Now he was a King in his own right.

Sanchia was delighted to be a Queen, of equal rank with her two elder sisters. Romeo had not been far wrong when he had said he would make them all queens.

Richard talked long and earnestly to her of their future. There would be certain trouble with the German Princes. It was fortunate that Alfonso's half-sister was married to Edward; that would make it difficult for him to show hostility. They must prepare now to leave England.

'And,' he confided in her, 'it could not be at a better time. Trouble is coming very near. The murmurings through the country are growing to a rumble. You should remonstrate with your sister. She could do a great deal to show the King the folly of his ways.'

'It is impossible to advise Eleanor. She has always believed she knows best.'

'This I fear is one of those occasions when she does not,' said Richard.

He sent for his son Henry and when he came he told him to make his preparations for he wanted him to be present at his coronation at Aachen.

Henry could see how elated his father was and rejoiced with him. It would be a great pleasure to witness his triumph. He was a little sad at the prospect of leaving Edward, for their friendship had deepened since the mutilation of the youth and Edward's genuine repentance had touched him.

'This has come at the best of moments,' Richard said. 'Any man of sense must see the way things are going. There will be trouble in England sooner or later, Henry. That much is clear.'

'The King has a way of avoiding it simply by pretending it does not exist,' said Henry.

'It is a method which can work for a while, but sooner or later the truth has to be faced.' Richard shrugged his shoulders. 'Well now, we must make ready for our departure.' He laid his hands on his son's shoulders. 'This will further our fortunes, my son, and nothing gives me greater pleasure than to contemplate what I can do for you.'

On a warm May day Richard with wife and son set sail for Dordrecht in a splendid company of fifty ships.

At Aachen he and Sanchia were crowned King and Queen of the Romans.

*   *   *

There was sorrow at Windsor. Little Katharine was dangerously ill.

Nothing could upset the Queen as much as threats to her children. Their health and well-being had been a constant cause of anxiety to her; and even when there had been no cause to worry she had been uneasy.

But there was no doubt that little Katharine was very ill. She had always been a strange child—aloof from the rest because she was dumb. The Queen had loved her the more for her affliction and had taken great pains to insure that she felt no lack because of it.

Katharine had been exceptionally pretty and Henry used to say that more than any of the girls she had inherited her mother's beauty.

And now they were going to lose her.

The Queen would not leave the child's bedside and the King hovered over the Queen.

'You will make yourself ill, my darling,' he admonished her, but she only shook her head. It was as though she had some belief that while she was there death would not dare to take her child.

The little girl's eyes pleaded with her to stay; the hot little hand clung to hers.

But it was no use. Not even the Queen's fierce determination could save her daughter's life.

On a bleak May day Katharine slipped away from life as quietly as she had lived it.

*   *   *

Soon after Katharine's death it became clear that the patience of the barons was becoming exhausted.

Simon de Montfort—the King's brother-in-law—who never failed to arouse uneasy thoughts in his mind—was back in England and it seemed that the discontented barons were looking to him as a leader.

There had been an outcry when Aymer of Valence, the King's half-brother, had been given the see of Winchester. This meant that Boniface of Savoy, the Queen's uncle, had Canterbury, the King's half-brother Winchester and the most powerful member of the foreign party was William of Valence, another half-brother of the King.

Conferring together the barons decreed that soon not a single position of authority would be left to the English and the King's penchant for foreigners must be blunted.

There was no doubt that the foreigners were a greedy company of men. The more the King bestowed on them the more they tried to get. Trouble began when William de Valence tried to extend his lands and in so doing encroached on those of Simon de Montfort.

Simon was determined not to let this pass; knowing that he had the backing of most powerful English barons he took the matter up with the council.

William de Valence, arrogant in the belief that he had his half-brother the King behind him, declared before the assembly that he had no desire to parley with a traitor.

Simon cried out: 'I am no traitor ... nor traitor's son.' This was a reference to the father of William de Valence, Hugh de Lusignan who had taken up arms against his King. 'My father,' added Simon, 'was not like yours.'

William rushed at Simon; his hand on his sword.

They had to be parted.

The quarrel in itself might have been insignificant. Such quarrels did arise now and then between barons. But this was the leader of the foreign party against the man to whom the barons were looking more and more to lead them.

As Simon left the council chamber he was joined by Roger Bigod, the Earl of Norfolk.

'My lord,' said Roger, 'a halt must soon be called to the arrogance of these foreigners.'

'I am in complete agreement,' replied Simon.

'Praise God. There are thousands like us. What shall be done in the matter?'

'We must call a meeting of those who share our anxieties. We must make up our minds then what action to take.'

There was no lack of men to join them.

* * *

The next meeting of the King and the parliament was a stormy one.

The King began by telling the assembly of his financial difficulties. They knew that there had been a famine due to the poor harvest; the Welsh were giving trouble and he was none too sure of the Scots. He had incurred great expense in the service of the country and he now needed further grants.

He was answered that had he not bestowed great gifts on the Queen's family, his half-brothers and sisters and their foreign friends, he would have had ample funds for dealing with the country's needs.

The King's friends immediately rose in his defence while those barons led by de Montfort insisted on putting their point of view, which was that it was impossible to impose further taxation on the people and that economy might start by sending some of the parasites back to their own countries.

The squabble between the opposing parties might have grown into a fight if the King had not called a halt to the proceedings.

A few days later at Westminster Hall the King was confronted by several barons all in armour. He was startled. He knew now that they were serious in their intentions to curb him.

He noticed that none of them carried a sword. Each man had left his weapon at the door of Westminster Hall to show that this was not an attack, merely a threat.

'What means this?' cried the King. 'Are you trying to make me your prisoner?'

'Not so, my lord,' answered Roger Bigod. 'We but come to tell you that the aliens must be sent away. They are draining the country's resources. The people will not endure it. If something's not done the whole country will be in revolt as it was in your father's day.'

Henry was very serious. The people were becoming restive. He was aware of it. It shocked him when they regarded him sullenly. Worst of all was when they shouted after Eleanor.

She pretended to despise them, but he knew she was upset.

'What we ask of you,' said Simon, 'is that you promise to be guided by twenty-four elected magnates. There must be reforms.'

Henry looked at the stern faces of the barons. It was as though he saw the ghost of his father at Runnymede lurking behind them.

He agreed.

*   *   *

Simon moved into action supported by men such as Roger Bigod. Twenty-four men were selected—half by the King, half by the barons. This community was to meet three times a year to bring about reforms in State and Church.

Then the Parliament selected another twenty-four members. Thus it consisted of forty-eight men. From these was chosen a Justiciar, a Chancellor and a Treasurer. It was made clear that the assembly was to be of temporary duration. At the end of one year they would answer to the King and the Council for their actions.

The first act passed by the Parliament was that the aliens should surrender to the King those castles which he had bestowed on them. This brought a protest from William de Valence who refused to give up anything. 'Your castle or your head,' was the retort of Simon de Montfort. The answer of William de Valence was to take shelter in the castle of Wolvesey which had been bestowed on his brother Aymer.

Henry was in a quandary. He was now expected by his barons to besiege the castle and fight against his own half-brothers. He wanted to refuse but he dared not. He was forced to obey and in due course the castle surrendered to his army.

He felt completely robbed of his power. He discussed the state of affairs with Eleanor who wanted him to stand out against the barons. He was the King, she pointed out, and should make this fact known.

Gently he explained to her the power of these men and that he must be cautious. There was one man he feared more than any other and that was Simon de Montfort.

'I should never have allowed him to marry my sister,' he mourned. Yet he knew in his heart that there was nothing else he could have done. Simon had made up his mind to marry Eleanor, just as he had made up his mind to reform England, to bring rule through a parliment which meant of course curbing the power of the King.

His thoughts were heavy as one July day his barge carried him down the Thames. They matched the sky which had suddenly become overcast. In the distance he heard a rumble of thunder. It seemed prophetic.

'There's a storm about to break, my lord,' said his boatman.

'Aye,' said the King, 'I know it well.'

At that moment the clouds opened and there was such a deluge of rain that the boat seemed likely to sink and that moment the sky was illumined by a flash of lightning overhead and the roar of the thunder was deafening.

There had been some violent thunderstorms lately. A few years ago the Queen's apartments at Windsor had been struck while she was in them. There had been another great storm when Eleanor had been visiting St. Albans with the children and lightning had struck the Abbey. The laundry had been burned to the ground and it was said that the monks there had seen an angel with a flaming sword and a torch. It was believed by some that the angel was there to protect the Abbey but others were sure it was a warning against the Queen's extravagance. Had she not come near to being killed at Windsor? And it seemed God's vengeance had followed her to St. Albans.

So between the barons and God Henry felt he was indeed being persecuted.

He could laugh at these superstitions when he was with the Queen, but the thought of her being in danger always sobered him; now looking up at that sky and knowing that the lightning was right overhead he was afraid, and when the boatman said they must take shelter he agreed.

By some ill chance they were closest to Durham House which was the home of Simon de Montfort and as the King's barge drew up at the stairs, the Earl himself came down to greet him.

'My lord,' said Simon, 'have no fear, the storm is already moving from overhead.'

Henry looked at him steadily.

'I fear thunder and lightning exceedingly,' he said, 'but by God's head I fear you more than all the thunder and lightning in the world.'

And as he followed Simon into Durham House where he might remove his sodden cloak and partake of some refreshment, he knew that in that moment he had spoken the truth and in doing so had betrayed himself to Simon de Montfort.

*　　*　　*

Edward was now twenty years of age. He had spent a great deal of time at the Court of France where he had distinguished himself in equestrian arts and because of his height, good looks and interesting personality he had become very popular.

He thought often of his wife but he had been unable to live with her as such on account of her youth and he had left her to continue her education while he perfected himself in the art of chivalry and knighthood.

Alarming reports were coming to France of the trouble which was brewing between the King and the barons, and Edward consulted the King of France, whose judgment was greatly respected throughout the world, and he gained very little reassurance by what Louis had to say. That trouble was coming to England seemed obvious, and as heir to the throne Edward must be there.

He hastened back to England and found his father at Winchester. Henry embraced him warmly, his eyes filling with tears to contemplate his handsome son. He must first be assured of his health and well-being. 'Your mother will be beside herself with joy to see you,' he said.

Edward thought his father looked far from well and he put this down to all the trouble of which he had heard.

'I have heard reports of what is happening here,' he said.

'We have some tiresome men in this realm, Edward. They give me little peace.'

'It is true that the barons have formed a parliament which dictates to you?'

'It is not exactly so. I have some say in choosing the men. Of course it is all a question of money. They think of nothing else.'

'A kingdom cannot run without it, my lord.'

'Nay, that's what I tell them. They think I can conjure it up out of nothing.'

'Louis does not believe in harsh taxation, Father.'

'So you have become one of Louis' worshippers then?'

'He is very wise and greatly admired. I have always believed he spoke good sense.'

Henry nodded. 'A very serious man and dedicated King. I think he is less plagued by unruly subjects than I.'

Edward started to say that Louis had won the love and respect of his subjects, but realizing that this seemed a criticism of his father, he desisted.

But he did feel this criticism and it shocked him a little. The family had always stood together. But what happened when one felt the head of it was leading it to disaster?

Henry then explained what had been happening during his son's absence: the quarrels between William de Valence and Simon de Montfort, the sharp words which had been spoken in the council chamber.

Edward was very disturbed.

'I am glad to say that there is a difference of opinion among the barons,' went on Henry. 'Gloucester seems to be falling out with de Montfort. If they quarrel among themselves perhaps they will disperse and we shall get back to normal. That would be a happy state of affairs.'

'Father, are you prepared should there be trouble?'

'Trouble! What do you mean, son?'

'What if the barons should rise against you as they did against your father?'

'That is a thought which is constantly in everyone's mind. I have never been allowed to forget my father's misdeeds. Am I responsible for them?'

'I think it is feared that you might repeat them.'

Henry looked at his son with amazement. Was there just the hint of reproach there? Could it really be that one member of this family was not exactly behind another?

His son's homecoming had given the King some uneasy qualms.

*　　*　　*

Simon de Montfort came to see Edward. He had heard of his arrival in England and believed that the young man was sensible.

It might be easier to convey the danger to him than to Henry, and surely he would want to do something about it, for the crown his father wore would one day be his.

'My great desire,' said Simon earnestly, 'is to avoid an outright war.'

'You think there is a real danger of that!'

'I think there is an imminent danger.'

'But now that you have this parliament....'

'In which there is not agreement, I fear. Your father must abandon the Sicilian project. The title for your younger brother would be an empty one and very costly to this nation to acquire. It seems that the King and Queen are dazzled by this crown.'

'Then if that is so there must be no more thought of Sicily.'

'My lord, I knew you would see reason. There is much I have

to tell you. You must join us and then you will understand what all this trouble is about and, pray God, help us to avoid it.'

'I will with all my heart,' Edward assured him.

It began to be noticed that the heir to the throne and Simon de Montfort were often in each other's company and an understanding seemed to have arisen between them.

* * *

It was sad, said Eleanor, that all the children were growing up. Particularly so with daughters who must leave their home and family.

John de Dreux, the Duke of Brittany, had offered for Beatrice and as it was a good match and one which would be advantageous to England and it was time Beatrice was married, there could be no excuse for not accepting it.

What had happened to Margaret had made the Queen very apprehensive. She said she wished she had had all boys and then there would not have been the same need for them to leave the country.

However, the alliance was accepted and Beatrice prepared to leave for Brittany.

The King, who had business in France, was to accompany her but in view of the state of the country it seemed unwise that the Queen should go also.

'You will have Edward to help you, my dearest,' said Henry, 'and rest assured that I shall return as soon as possible.'

The Queen was in a way not sorry to remain. By accompanying the party she would have had a little longer with her daughter but at least she was spared that harrowing moment when Beatrice was formally handed over to a stranger. That seemed to her most distressing and she would never forget seeing little Margaret married to Alexander of Scotland.

She said good-bye to the King and her daughter and went back to Windsor where she was finding pleasure in the company of Edward's young wife, a docile, pleasant creature who adored Edward; and therefore they had something in common.

* * *

Soon after Beatrice's wedding had taken place the Duke of Gloucester joined the King in Brittany. Gloucester was an ambitious man who had shown himself to be jealous of Simon de Montfort's power in the barons' party and had therefore set himself up in opposition to him.

He had come to the King with a special purpose and he lost little time in making Henry aware of the reason for his visit.

'My lord,' he began, 'what I have to tell you fills me with distress for I know what pain it will cause you. I ask in advance your forgiveness for bringing this to your notice but I believe it to be something you should know.'

'Pray tell me without more delay,' commanded Henry.

'It is that your son Edward has allied himself with Simon de Montfort.'

'That is impossible,' cried Henry.

'I fear, my lord, it is so.'

'I will not believe it.'

'Others will confirm it.'

Henry shook his head. 'There is some mistake' he insisted.

'No, Sire. The lord Edward is constantly in de Montfort's company listening to what de Montfort tells about what are, in his opinion, the wrongs committed against the people.'

Henry covered his face with his hands.

This was more cruel than anything. He could endure the loss of his crown but not that of the love and loyalty of his family.

He would listen to no more. He dismissed Gloucester and sat alone.

There must be some mistake. Edward ... his son, Eleanor's son ... to stand against him! It was not possible.

Oh God, he thought, is history repeating itself? His grandfather Henry II had likened himself to an eagle who, when he was old and weary, was attacked by the eaglets whom he had fathered. He, Henry III, had gloried in his own children, had thanked God for them and greatly pitied his grandfather. Now could it be that his son had turned against him?

It could not be true. It was a malicious lie. He would never believe it. Eleanor would never allow it. He would trust Edward with his life.

There was only one thing to do and that was to return to England.

*   *   *

How cruel it was. It was true. Edward *was* seeing de Montfort and had declared that he understood the reason for his grievances.

The King could not bear to see anyone. He went to the

Tower of London and remained there. His grief was making him ill.

Richard, the King of the Romans, hearing rumours of England's trouble, had come to see his brother.

He went to the Tower and when he saw Richard Henry broke down. He wept silently for a few moments and then he said sadly: 'At least you have come to me, brother.'

'Henry,' said Richard, 'I understand full well your feelings. Have I not a son of my own? I should be desolate if my Henry ever seemed to turn against me. But why don't you see Edward? I hear you have refused so far.'

'I could not see him. You know my love for him. If he stood before me now I should not be able to stop myself kissing him.'

'Which would perhaps be good.'

'What of the Queen?'

'The Queen is torn between the two of us. She will hear no ill of Edward.'

'Henry, Edward is no longer a boy. He is going to be a great King one day ... though that will be far distant I hope. He has, it is true, listened to Simon de Montfort and, make no mistake, that man has a certain greatness in him. It is true that the people are in revolt against the immense taxation which has been levied upon them. You must agree to this. I am sure that is all Edward has done and he will be most distressed if you allow him to go on believing you think he is against *you*. It is the last thing he is. He is loyal to you, but there are certain matters which he wishes to reform. After all de Montfort is our brother-in-law.'

'Would to God I had never allowed it.'

'Our sister was determined on it and you would not have been able to stop her.'

'I only gave way because he had seduced her.'

'Both he and she have given the lie to that ... and it is a matter of which they would have all the evidence. Nay, brother, they are married. You consented to the marriage. Let us forget that. It is not the issue. What I want is an end to this difference between you and your son. See him. Listen to him. He will tell you his feelings in the matter.'

'It may well be that you are right, Richard, but when I see my son I know all feeling will desert me except the joy it will give me to look on his face.'

'Then relish that joy ... and talk afterwards. I am sure you will see that you have been mistaken.'

'Oh, Richard, if I could believe that you are right in this.'

'Give yourself the opportunity of finding out.'

Richard lost no time in sending a message to Edward.

* * *

Edward came to the Tower accompanied by his mother. Eleanor had been with her son trying to understand what this matter was which had come between them.

Edward swore that he had no intention of working against his father. He had listened to Simon de Montfort, certainly. There was much wisdom in what he had to say. He firmly believed that his Uncle Simon was the King's loyal subject and was genuinely concerned at the growing discontent in the country.

He went in alone to see his father and when he saw him he rushed into his arms.

Henry embraced him, kissing him on both cheeks and their tears mingled.

'My dear, dear father, how could you ever have thought I would be against you?'

'Forgive me, Edward. Forgive me. I listened to evil tales.'

'I had seen de Montfort it is true. Father, he is a man of honour. He means you no harm.'

'He has seduced you with fair words, my son. He and I have had our differences. I do not believe he will be a friend of mine until I do as he says. But no matter, you are here. You have come to me. You assured me of your love. That is enough for me.'

'Never believe I would stand against you.'

'I do not believe it. I never did ... in my heart.'

'It is merely that I felt there was sense in what Simon de Montfort told me. But if he were to be against you then I would bring whatever strength I had to stand against him. Never think, Father, that whatever the cause I would stand against you.'

'This is a happy day for me, Edward. I could almost be glad of my wretchedness because it has made me so joyous now.'

'Let us tell my mother that all is well between us. It has been a most anxious time for her. She came with me. She was so happy that you had sent for me. I will bring her to you.'

So she came and the three of them were together.

'This must never happen again,' said Eleanor. 'Nothing on earth will ever mar our unity. We are as one. Oh please, my son ... my husband ... remember it.'

There were tears in Henry's eyes and Edward said: 'Who was it who brought these tales to you, Father? Methinks he is no friend to you nor to me.'

'It was Gloucester,' said Henry.

'I shall regard him as my enemy until one of us dies,' declared Edward.

So there was reconciliation and Edward was constantly in the company of his parents until he left for France, for there was to be a great tournament at the French Court and he was anxious to play a part in it.

Conspiracy in the Bedchamber

EDWARD was in France; Beatrice had gone; there was frustration over Edmund's accession to the crown of Sicily which the people of England were so much against; and Henry longed to raise the Queen's spirits.

He had an idea and without telling Eleanor, for if it failed he did not want disappointment to make her more melancholy than ever, he sent a messenger to Scotland with the suggestion that the Scottish King and Queen should come to England.

He knew that if it were possible Margaret would agree immediately; and he was right. His messenger brought back a letter from Margaret in which she said that they were preparing to set out at once.

Gleefully he went to Eleanor.

'News from Scotland,' he said carelessly.

'Margaret is well?' she asked quickly.

'It seems she is very well.'

'Thank God.'

'And very eager to see her mother ... and I believe she takes some pleasure in her father's company.'

'What do you mean, Henry?'

'I mean, my love, that our Margaret is coming to see us. At this very moment she is on her way.'

'Oh, Henry!'

'I knew that would please you. That is why I arranged it.'

'And said nothing to me.'

'Because I feared it might not be possible. I could not bear that you should be disappointed.'

'Henry, you are so good to me.'

'No more than I should be, my love.'

* * *

To go home! Margaret's spirits leaped at the thought. To leave grim old Edinburgh for beloved Windsor, Westminster or even York. What mattered it as long as it was England. The South was better though because it was farther away from Scotland.

To go home again! To be with those beloved parents. To talk over everything with her mother....

To talk over everything! Oh, what good luck that she had not told anyone, for if she had they would have done everything they could to have stopped her going.

She had almost told Alexander, but she had wanted to be sure. She had not wanted him to be disappointed. Now she *was* sure and had been on the point of telling but mercy of mercies she had not.

She could imagine those grim old lairds. 'The bairn must be born in Scotland. In view of her condition the Queen must not travel.' They would enjoy stopping her pleasure. She knew them well. So thank God, she had told no one.

There was a lot of dour shaking of heads over the proposed visit. They would like to shut her and Alexander up as they had when she had first come here. But they were taught a lesson then. Her dear parents would not allow her to be treated like a prisoner. The Scots knew it and it was important that they did not offend the English.

What joy to turn the head of her horse southwards. How she laughed to herself when they crossed the border. Soon she would be home.

They passed through York where she had half expected her parents would be waiting to greet her. No matter. State affairs kept them in the South. Only a short while and she would be with them.

As they came near to Windsor, Alexander sent messengers ahead of them to herald their approach and so it happened that both the King and the Queen with a royal party came to meet them.

What joy there was in the reunion! The Queen must study her daughter, to see if she was plump enough, well enough, happy enough.

Margaret laughed. 'Dearest lady,' she cried, 'how could I
fail to be happy when we are together!'

So they rode through the forest to the castle. Oh beautiful,
noble castle, beloved of the family because the King had had
it refurnished when he had married the Queen.

Into the great chamber they went.

'Nothing is changed,' cried Margaret. 'It is as it always was.
Dear Father, how is your grassplat?' She ran to the window
and looked out. There was the grassy rectangle which he had
designed and of which he had always been so proud. Margaret
turned and threw her arms about him. 'Oh let everything stay
the same.'

Alexander was looking at her in some surprise. She did not
care. The Scots rarely showed their feelings, but Alexander
knew something of the perfections of her parents and the
happy childhood she had spent with them so that nothing that
ever happened afterwards could compare with it.

'Oh, it is so wonderful to be home!' she cried.

Henry could not hide his delight, even though he felt it
must be rather disconcerting for Alexander. But then he must
not expect to give Margaret the happiness she had found with
her incomparable parents.

Margaret was longing to be alone with her mother so that
she could tell the secret. How they would laugh together. But
first of course there must be certain formalities. After all she
was a Queen and Scotland was by no means unimportant if
only because it could cause so much trouble on the border.

There were the usual festivals which Henry so loved to give
in honour of his family and which the people so hated to pay
for. This was just another instance of the extravagance incurred by the royal family.

Already the people were grumbling.

'They grudge us a little happiness,' said the Queen.

*   *   *

'How wonderful it is to be alone together, dear lady,' said
Margaret.

'I am so happy that you are here, my dearest.'

'I have thought of nothing since I left England but the joy
I should find in coming back.'

'Alexander is kind to you?'

'Yes, he is kind.'

'A good husband.'

'I suppose you would say so, but you see I compare him with

my dear father and no one could compare with him, could they?'

The Queen agreed that this was so.

'See what you do,' said Margaret. 'You make us all love you so much that we have not much room for anyone else.'

It was not in Eleanor's nature not to be delighted by such a revelation though she told her daughter that she had prayed that she would find the greatest happiness of her life in her marriage.

'It will be different, my darling, when you have children.'

'Dear mother, I have something to tell you.'

Eleanor took her daughter's face in her hands and looked into her eyes. Margaret nodded, laughter in her eyes and her upturned lips.

'You have just learned....'

'I knew before. You are the first I have told.'

'Margaret! Alexander....'

'He will know all in good time.'

'But why this secrecy?'

'You do not know what they are like up there. I should never have been allowed to travel if they had known I was with child.

Eleanor began to laugh, but she was quickly serious.

'We shall have to take good care. My dear, how soon?'

'It should be in February....'

'A long time yet. They are right, you know, about your travelling. We shall have to see that you leave in good time. We must take great care.'

'I am going to take great care, dear Mother, that when the time comes for us to go it will be too late for me to travel. You will help me, won't you? This is our secret ... as yet. Tell no one ... but my father. He may know. Let it be our secret. Then when it is too late ... we shall tell.'

'My dear child, what a schemer you are!'

'If you knew how I longed to be with you. I will not have my visit cut short. I am going to make it as long as I can. Please, dearest Mother, help me.'

Eleanor took her daughter into her arms and laughed.

They clung together until Margaret was almost hysterical with laughter.

Then Eleanor said: 'We will tell the King. It will amuse him. He has had much of late to frustrate him. Let us tell him something to make him laugh.'

Together they went to the King's chamber. The Queen

signed to him that she wished to speak to him alone and he
dismissed everyone. When the three of them were alone together Eleanor said: 'Shall you tell him or shall I?'

They began to laugh and Henry looked from one to the
other in a state of happy bewilderment.

'Please, my darlings, may I share the joke?'

'Go along, Margaret, you tell him.'

'Please, my lady, I had rather you did.'

'Margaret is with child. It is a secret between us three. The
Scots do not know. Nor does she wish them to. She feared they
would stop her coming and that she could not endure. She is
going to keep the secret and only when it would be unsafe for
her to travel back shall it be known.'

The King smiled slowly. Then he too was laughing.

How happy he was. While he had this dear family he could
not be seriously disturbed by the troublemakers in his realm.

All would come right. In the meantime there was this deli-
cious secret—shared by the three of them.

*   *   *

It was such a joy to be in England. Wherever the Court was
there were Margaret and Alexander.

'How good it is for the relationship between our two countries,' said Margaret.

Alexander agreed on this and he had to admit that they
could not have been made more welcome.

'We shall have to think of returning soon,' he said.

'We must not leave too soon. That would offend my father,'
Margaret pointed out.

'Perhaps then we should stay a little longer.'

When she sensed that he was about to broach the matter
again she told him that she was feeling a little unwell and her
mother wished her to see the royal physician.

When she had done this her parents summoned Alexander
to her bedchamber and there they played out the little farce
which they had arranged between them.

The Queen said: 'Margaret is with child, Alexander. It is
one of those unusual pregnancies. It is only just apparent. It
seems that the child is due in February and in view of this the
doctors feel that it would be unwise for her to travel.'

Alexander was taken aback.

'Naturally,' said the King, 'this has been a great surprise to
you, but an agreeable one, I am sure. The doctors have told
us that Margaret will be perfectly all right if great care is taken.

I would wish my physicians to care for her. Her mother will not hear that she leaves.'

Alexander, still bewildered, said: 'It is the custom for the heir to the throne to be born in Scotland.'

'Of course, of course ... but better for the heir to be born in England than no heir at all ... and perhaps danger to the mother, who is my daughter.'

Alexander must agree with this. He embraced Margaret and told her how happy he was that at last they were to have a child. He was uncertain about staying in England, though.

Henry laid a hand on his shoulder. 'Do not fret, my son,' he said. 'Leave this to the Queen and myself.'

Alexander realized at length that there was nothing else he could do; and in due course he returned to Scotland leaving his wife in her mother's care.

*   *   *

They were very happy months. There was Christmas at Windsor. What fun they had, for Eleanor said this must be a very special Christmas, since they had the Queen of Scotland with them.

They were together all the time and Eleanor constantly congratulated Margaret on her clever manoeuvre. She certainly had showed herself to be a true daughter of her mother.

Messages came from Alexander. There was great anger and resentment in Edinburgh, he said. It was even hinted that the Queen must have known of her condition before she left and it was suggested that she had deliberately concealed it.

Margaret showed her mother this letter and they laughed together. 'They are not entirely foolish then,' said Eleanor. 'But what matters it? Let them think what they will. All that matters is that your child will be born here and I shall be at hand to make sure all is well.'

'There could not be a greater comfort in the world,' said Margaret.

On a snowy February day in Windsor Castle Margaret gave birth to her first child. It was a girl and she was called Margaret after her mother.

There was great satisfaction and rejoicing through the castle.

'You cannot make the journey back until the late spring or summer,' said the Queen. 'Your father would never allow it.'

And Margaret settled down to make the most of the time.

The Passing of a Dream

MARGARET had returned to Scotland. It had been heart-rending to say farewell to her and the Queen was plunged into deeper melancholy when messengers came to her from Berkhamstead to tell her that her sister Sanchia was ill and asking for her.

Eleanor left with all speed and when, arriving at the castle she was taken immediately to her sister, she was shocked by the sight of her. Sanchia had not been in good health for some time but she had not expected to see her so obviously ill.

'Thank God you sent for me,' she said. 'You should have done so before.'

'I would have done so, but I knew you had much to occupy you. I would not have asked you to come now but I feared if I did not I might never see you again.'

'What nonsense. You are soon going to get well. I shall see that you do.'

'The Queen commands,' said Sanchia with a smile.

' 'Tis so. What ails you?'

Sanchia touched her chest. 'It is difficult to breathe . . . often.'

'How long has this been going on?'

'Oh some time . . . but it is worse now.'

'Does Richard know?'

'Oh Richard has much with which to occupy him.'

'His wife's health should be the first of his concerns.'

'We are not all as fortunate as you, Eleanor. Ah, how lucky

you have always been. You had the perfect marriage, the perfect husband, the perfect children....'

'Oh come. You were happy with Richard.'

'Richard is not Henry, Eleanor. I don't think he was meant to be a husband. Henry was, of course. That is why he is the perfect one.'

'You sound bitter. Tell me, has Richard been unkind to you?'

'No ... not that. Neglectful, yes. He has had so much to occupy him. He is a King now.'

'And has made you a Queen.'

'Perhaps the title does not mean so much to me. I should have liked a husband who loved me as Henry loves you. You found that—and a crown as well.'

'Oh Henry is a good husband and I have the children. But you have your son, Sanchia.'

'Yes, I have my son. He is a good boy ... ten years old. But no one means as much to Richard as his son Henry. Edmund knows this. Richard is rarely with us you know.'

'I'm sorry, Sanchia.'

'How I dreamed ... after you left. It was so romantic was it not? The poem and the way Richard came to Les Baux and what grew out of it! I used to imagine his coming back ... and when he did it seemed like a dream come true. I expected too much.'

'No one expects too much, for it is expecting and believing first that makes good things happen. Providing one does everything in one's power to make them.'

'You speak for yourself, Eleanor. You were always sure of yourself. You knew what you wanted; you determined to get it ... and you did.'

'Things do not always go smoothly, Sanchia.'

'No, but you are always in command. And you made your husband love you and your children adore you. It is your right. I admit it. But the less successful of us should be forgiven for being a little envious now and then.'

'You are talking nonsense, Sanchia. You have been very happy with Richard. You know you have.'

'When we have been together sometimes ... but I always knew that there were others. It wasn't quite what I had dreamed at Les Baux. But never mind. It is the end now.'

'The end! I won't have you talk such nonsense. I shall stay here until you have recovered.'

In spite of her assurance the Queen was worried. Sanchia

had grown very thin and there were violet shadows under the eyes. She was listless and when the paroxysms of coughing seized her, Eleanor was afraid.

She sat by her bed, and as the days passed she scarcely left her for it was clear that Sanchia was growing weaker.

They talked of Les Baux and their childhood; Eleanor sang some of the poems she had set to music and she knew that as Sanchia lay with her eyes closed she was back in the hall of the old castle and that the old days were more real to her than this bedchamber.

If only the weather were better, thought Eleanor. If only it was spring or summer, then I could take her into the gardens and it would indeed be like Les Baux. But it was dismal November; the days were short and dark, the mist penetrated the castle and hung about in patches. As the days grew darker, Sanchia became weaker and at length Eleanor was forced to admit that her sister was dying.

It was a terrible blow to her. Greatly she loved her family, and that this sister, younger than herself, would shortly leave the world filled her with melancholy.

She sat in the window-seat looking out across a landscape which reflected her mood. The branches of the trees denuded of their leaves stretched up to the greying sky. Across the field to the marshy land the reeds looked like red parchment and the woolly seed heads of the thistles were everywhere. There was no sign of spring and there was a deep sadness in Eleanor's heart.

Each day Sanchia's condition weakened. Eleanor stayed with her.

She was at her bedside when she died which she knew gave her sister great comfort.

She was buried with the usual ceremony at which her Uncle Boniface presided. Richard did not attend, although he was in England. He had business in London.

Eleanor was very anxious that all honour should be paid to her sister and that no expense should be spared in giving her a funeral worthy of a sister of the Queen of England.

When she intimated this to Henry he agreed with her. No expense must be spared and as it seemed unlikely that Richard would agree to such extravagance, Henry would pay for it.

London's Revenge

THE state of affairs between the King and the barons had
deteriorated and the King had found it necessary to fortify
the Tower and Windsor Castle against attack which he feared
might take place at any moment.

He was accused of having violated the Provisions of Oxford
which was the reform laid down by that Parliament which had
been called the Mad and which had been held in Oxford in
1258. The members of that parliament had drawn up reforms
for the Church and the royal household, which meant that
the King's extravagant spending must be curbed. Later
another clause had been added which was designed to exclude
foreigners from entering the country and to drive out those
who were already there and who were considered responsible
for the King's continual need to tax his people in order to
replenish his exchequer.

The fact that the King ignored these rules and was indeed
spending more and more, and often on the foreigners, had
given rise to such discontent that the leading barons, under
Simon de Montfort, were determined that the position should
not be allowed to endure.

Henry was depressed. He could not ride out without an
armed guard. The barons were turning his subjects against
him, he said.

He remembered how his grandfather had, in the depth of
his melancholy, caused a picture to be painted of an eagle in
a nest with the young eaglets attacking him. Henry repre-

sented the eagle, the eaglets his sons. His was not quite such a sorry case. He could imagine nothing as bad as having a man's own family turn against him. Thank God, that had not happened and that unfortunate matter with Edward had been resolved and had been proved to be due to malicious Gloucester's envy of Simon de Montfort. Edward was his very good son and if he wanted proof of his family's affection he only had to think of how Margaret had deceived her husband and his ministers because of her great desire to come to England and be with her family.

Now it was the people who were traitors to their King—the barons led by that man who had menaced his peace of mind for so long—Simon de Montfort.

He went to pray in the Abbey of Westminster and when he was returning to the palace he passed one of the monks who was painting a picture of the Abbey. He paused to admire it. It was exceedingly clever how the monk had caught the gleam of the stone.

'A fine picture, William,' he said.

The man bowed his head in pleasure.

'You are indeed an artist.'

'God has been good to me,' said William. 'All that I have comes from Him.'

'That's true. But that He has chosen you as His instrument redounds to your credit.'

The King stood for a few moments studying the picture.

'You shall paint one for me, my good monk,' he said. His eyes narrowed. 'You shall depict me with my subjects who are endeavouring to tear me to pieces; but I shall be rescued ... rescued by my own dogs. Would you do that then, good William?'

'My lord, I could paint a picture no matter what the subject.'

'Then here is a subject for you. It will show future generations what I had to endure from those who should have served me best. Rest assured, you will be paid well.'

The monk bowed his head and the King passed on. As he continued to paint the picture of the Abbey William was thinking that the King was overwrought and small wonder if rumours he heard were true. There was trouble brewing, and when a King's subjects were restive and ready to rise against him it needed only one little spark to set the conflagration going.

The King would forget he did not doubt and he was surprised when the following day he was summoned to appear before him. That very day the picture was begun.

When it was finished, the King declared himself well pleased. There was no mistaking the meaning there.

Henry said: 'It shall be placed in my wardrobe here in Westminster. I come here when I wash my head and I shall never fail to look at it and marvel at the ingratitude of those men whose duty it is to obey me. I have commanded my treasurer Philip Lovel to pay you for your work. You have done well.'

So the picture was hung and for several weeks the King would look at it every morning when he came into his wardrobe. After a while he forgot, for Simon de Montfort, realizing that the country was as yet unripe for rebellion, left for France.

* * *

There was trouble in Gascony and the King's presence was needed there.

He told the Queen that he would have to go and he could not bear to be parted from her.

'Then I will come with you,' she said.

Henry frowned. 'I could not contemplate going without you but I am afraid to leave the country.'

'That wretched de Montfort is no longer here. The people seem to be coming to their senses.'

Henry shook his head. 'It is not quite the case. People do seem to hate us less, but we have enemies all about us. We cannot afford trouble in Gascony now. I want at the same time to see Louis ... to sound him ... perhaps to get his help.'

'You think he would give it?'

'No king cares to see another deposed.'

'Deposed! You don't think they would dare?'

'They tried to do it to my father. That was the worst thing that ever happened to the monarchy. It lives for ever in their minds. I think Louis would not wish to see me toppled from my throne. It sets a precedent. He might help.'

'He should help,' said Eleanor. 'After all he is Marguerite's husband.'

'Alas, my love, all have not such strong family feeling as you are blessed with.'

'I must come with you, Henry. I insist. You have not been well of late.'

'The thought of going without you makes me desolate indeed.'

'We have a son. Let Edward return to England. He is of an age now to take the reins in your absence. Oh, my dear Henry, you hesitate. No child of mine would ever stand against his father.'

Henry took her hand and kissed it. 'I see you are right as you so often are. I should let myself be guided by you. Edward shall return. Our son will take charge of matters here in our absence; and you and I will not be parted.'

The Queen was to be grateful that she had accompanied the King for it seemed that luck was against him. When in France he was smitten with a fever which rendered him very feeble and even endangered his life, and but for the untiring nursing of the Queen he might have died. Without her, he admitted, he would have felt listless and in no mood to fight for his life. But she was here to make sure that he had doctors and attention and everything possible to sustain him. Most of all she assured him that he must live for the sake of her and the family.

She reminded him how Edward had sobbed when he had sailed for France years ago when Edward was but a boy; she recalled Margaret's recent visit. Did it not show how loved he was?

Was it so important that his subjects were ungrateful and easily led astray when he would always have his beloved family beside him? He must think of them, for if he did not fight for his life and keep his hold on it he was condemning them to such misery as he could well understand, for what misery would *he* know if she, his wife and Queen, were taken from him.

He began to recover under the Queen's ministrations but he had not achieved the purpose of his visit. He had been several months in France; the trouble in Gascony had resolved itself but Louis was not inclined to offer material help. All he could give was advice which was something Henry thought he could well do without. Henry returned to England.

*   *   *

Simon de Montfort was back and his absence had endeared the rebels to him. They had feared that he had wearied of the struggle and had left them to fight the battle with the King, and on his return he was welcomed with such enthusiasm that it seemed the moment was ripe to start bargaining with the King.

They agreed to meet the King and Simon arrived with a

party of barons led by himself and Roger Bigod of Norfolk.

The Provisions of Oxford must be adhered to, said the barons. These have been laid down by the Parliament and even the King must accept the wishes of his people.

Roger Bigod said: 'My lord, since your return from France you have brought even more foreigners into the country. This is against the wishes of your people.'

'My lord Norfolk,' answered the King, 'you are bold indeed. You forget whose vassal you are. You should go back to Norfolk and concern yourself with threshing your corn. Remember, I could issue a royal warrant for threshing out all your corn.'

'That is so,' retorted Bigod. 'And could I not reply by sending you the heads of your threshers?'

This was defiance, and Henry was never quite sure how to act in such situations. He looked angrily at the barons who were watching him closely. One false move and that could be the spark to start the fire.

A curse on Bigod and a greater one on de Montfort!

Henry knew they were poised for action.

He shrugged his shoulders and dismissed the meeting. But he had betrayed his weakness.

'The time is near for us to strike,' said Roger Bigod.

* * *

There was tension throughout the land. Neither the King nor the Queen dared ride out unless they were protected by armed bands. Henry was fast fortifying his castles and those which were of the most importance, the Tower of London and Windsor Castle, were equipped as for a siege.

London was ready to rise. The citizens had had enough taxation. There was no possibility of getting rich, for as soon as their trade increased the King or the Queen would invent a new tax as a means of taking their profits from them.

Those who suffered most were the Jews, but this did not endear them to the other citizens who were irritated by the Jewish ability to rise above persecution, to pay the exorbitant taxes and then in a short time become rich again. It was not natural, said the London merchants.

Punitive measures had been introduced against the Jews. There should be no schools for them; in their synagogues they should pray in low voices so that they did not offend Christians. No Christian should work for a Jew. No Jew should associate with a Christian woman or Christian man with a Jewess. Jews should wear a badge on their breasts to denote their race. They must never enter a Christian church. They must have a licence to dwell in any place. If any of these rules were disobeyed there should be an immediate confiscation of their goods.

All these rules the Jews could overcome; what made life impossible for them was the excessive taxation. Yet even so they would make the most of the periods when they were left alone and always seemed to prosper quickly.

This gave rise to great envy and there were constant skirmishes when Christians would attack the Jews always in such a way as to enable them to rob them of their possessions.

The Queen was at the Tower and the King at Windsor with Edward. She was aware of unrest in the streets and did not venture out because she was told that the mood of the people was uncertain and as always it would be against her.

She told her women that she would be easier in her mind if she were with the King and she thought it might be an excellent idea the next day to take barge to Windsor. This suggestion met with the immediate approval of all whose duty it was to protect her.

Unfortunately that very night there were plans afoot to attack the Jews. The mob had arranged that at the sound of St. Paul's bell at midnight they would assemble and march against them surprising them in their beds so that they would not have time to hide their possessions.

The Queen in her chamber heard the bell strike and almost immediately there was shouting and screaming in the streets. The attack on the Jews had started.

Into the houses occupied by Jews streamed the mob, shouting and screaming vengeance. Throats were cut, bodies mutilated, but the main purpose was to appease envy and greed by robbery.

The Queen dressed hurriedly and sent for guards.

'What goes on?' she demanded.

'My lady, the people are running wild in the streets. They are robbing and murdering the Jews. There will not be many left in the city of London this night.'

'We should not be here. Who knows where such violence will end.'

The guards agreed that the people, knowing she was at the Tower of London, might, when their evil work was done with the Jews, turn to her. They were in a violent mood and the lust for blood was on them. It could be said that the people's hatred of the Queen was as great as that they bore towards the Jews.

'Let us go then,' said the Queen. 'Let us lose no time.'

She had begun to tremble, remembering the venomous looks which had often been turned towards her; she had always known that the people of London would do her injury if they dared. They would never forget the Queenhithe she had demanded from them; they blamed her for the heavy taxes they had been forced to pay to reward her relations.

'Have the barge made ready,' she cried. 'We will slip down the river to Windsor.'

Her women wrapped her cloak about her. She was eager to be gone without delay.

At the stairs the royal barge was ready. With great haste she boarded it.

'Let us go without delay,' she cried.

They moved along the river and then suddenly there was a shout from the bridge.

'Look you there. It is the Queen. It is the old harpy herself.'

Faces appeared looking down from the bridge. Some spat.

'Oh God save me from the mob,' prayed the Queen.

Now came a deluge of rotting food and filth. It spattered the Queen's garments.

'Drown her!' came the cry. 'Drown the witch.'

'They will kill us,' said the Queen. 'Oh my God, is this the end then?'

'My lady, if we go on they will sink us,' said the bargeman.

It was true. The mob was tearing up wood from the bridge. It was rough justice. The bridge was in a state of decay and had been declared to be a danger. The reason was that the King had given the bridge tolls to the Queen who had collected the money but had not attended to the repairs. One large boulder splashed into the river just missing the barge. It sent the water high all over the occupants.

They could not go on. 'We might reach St. Paul's and stay at the Bishop's palace there,' said the Queen desperately. 'He must offer us sanctuary. We shall be safe there. The King will hear of this and there will be some who will suffer for it.'

It was a good suggestion. In fact it was their only possible hope. The bargeman brought the vessel to the steps and they scrambled out.

In terror, filthy and dishevelled the royal party arrived at the Bishop's Palace.

There they were admitted. It was sanctuary.

The next day the Queen left very quietly for Windsor. When the King and Edward heard what had happened their fury was great.

'This is an insult I shall never forgive,' cried Edward. 'The Londoners shall pay for what they have done to you. I shall remember it.'

The King also vowed vengeance on his capital, and the Queen felt a little mollified. It had been the most frightening ordeal of her life.

* * *

'I can never have a moment's peace after what has happened,' said Henry. 'I cannot always be with you. You realize, do you not, my love, that we are fast moving towards war?'

'Can nothing be done to avert it?'

'The barons are determined on it. They are rallying to de Montfort. I am going to ask you, my dear, to go to France. Go to your sister. I could not do what I have to do if I thought you were here in danger. You must go. I beg of you.'

'If you are in danger, Henry, my place is with you.'

'You could not follow me into battle, my love, and I should be able to fight the better if I knew that you were in safety. Go to France, I beg of you. Perhaps you can plead your cause with Louis. Marguerite might help you. We may well need his assistance.'

She was thoughtful, but the memory of the mob on London Bridge remained vividly with her. She had nightmares when she dreamed that those murderous people were about to close in on her.

Henry was right. She should leave England. She would be of greater use to the cause in France. There she could raise money for Henry. She would not cease to work for him simply because she was not beside him.

So finally she agreed to go. Henry insisted on accompanying her to the French Court and there he left her as he said in the best possible hands.

He then returned to England and war.

* * *

Henry had taken up his headquarters in the Castle of Lewes. He knew that conflict was imminent, but he was hopeful. He had a good army. His son Edward was beside him and his brother Richard, King of the Romans, who had hastened to England when he knew that war threatened his brother, was there to fight with him. The Queen was safe in France, and he was certain that his chances were good.

The two brothers conferred together in one of the rooms of the castle with Edward and Richard's son Henry. They knew that the barons' army was encamped close by, and that only a miracle could prevent a conflict.

Richard was saying that they had the superior men, better trained, better equipped. Only the greatest ill fortune could bring them defeat.

'Defeat,' cried Edward. 'I am surprised, my lord uncle, that you can use such a word. Let us talk rather of victory.'

'I believe,' replied Richard, 'that it is better to consider every contingency.'

'Save that of defeat,' cried Edward.

He smiled at his cousin Henry, somewhat conspiratorially. They were the young ones with a belief in themselves which their elders lacked. Edward had no doubt of victory.

The King spread a map on the table and they studied it. Edward was to take up the right flank while Henry would be serving with the main forces under his father's command.

'The Londoners have sent a force to serve under Hastings for de Montfort,' said the King.

'They'll have little quarter from me,' cried Edward, his eyes flashing. 'When I contemplate that they might have killed the Queen I promise myself revenge. They did not succeed in that evil design, praise be to God, but they insulted her. Think of that. The Queen. Our beautiful Queen to be treated so! I am glad they are here today. It gives me even greater heart for the battle.'

'What we have to think of,' said Richard, 'is making the barons see that because once they rose against a king they cannot make a habit of it.'

'They were powerful then,' said the King.

'They are powerful now,' answered Richard.

He went to the window and looked out. 'Something is happening,' he said. 'It looks like a messenger from the enemy.'

There were footsteps on the stairs. Edward flung open the door and one of the guards entered.

'A messenger, my lord, from Simon de Montfort, Earl of Leicester.'

'Bring him in,' said the King.

The messenger bowed. He was one of the minor barons.

'My lord,' he said, 'I have come on behalf of the Earl of Leicester.'

'Anyone who comes from our enemy is not welcome here,' said Edward sharply.

'My lord Leicester would put a proposition to you, my lord. He deplores that the country should stand divided. He believes that a settlement of differences should be discussed around a table and that this would be a more satisfactory way of dealing with them than through war.'

Henry said: 'In that I am in agreement with him but it seems our conferences have come to naught.'

'My lord,' cried Edward hotly, 'we know what this means. De Montfort is afraid of defeat. It is the only reason why he would wish to talk.'

'The barons, my lord, would give thirty thousand marks to the treasury if an agreement were reached.'

'Thirty thousand marks,' mused the King, his eyes glistening. It would be a victory, for all would believe that de Montfort was eager to avoid the fight. And thirty thousand marks!

Edward was hotly indignant.

'I would avenge the insult to my mother,' he cried.

'It did not come from de Montfort and the barons.'

'Out there the men of London have come to support de Montfort's army,' cried Edward. 'They have been our enemies these many years. Have they not shown their antagonism to you? And their insults to our lady Queen will never be forgiven. I would hold myself in contempt this day if I did not stand and fight.'

How noble he looked with his tall figure and his flaxen hair. A god come to earth, thought the King. My son! My son Edward!

Yet thirty thousand marks and peace....

Edward was beside him. 'It would be an uneasy peace,' he said. 'They would plague us as before. Nay, Father, let us settle this matter. We are set for victory. It is only because they fear us that they would make these terms. Do not let us be deluded.'

Young Henry of Cornwall was looking to his father. He believed that it would be wise for the King to parley with de Montfort for he knew the Earl was a man of courage and integrity who genuinely desired to make England a well governed country. If the King had not been his uncle, Henry might have seen fit to support de Montfort, but he could not, of course, go against his own family. He looked to his father now. Richard was wise. He would know.

But the King of the Romans was undecided. He felt ill and

the familiar lethargy had come to him. It was after all not
really his battle. He had come to Henry's aid because he was
his brother and it was necessary to keep him on the throne.
Perhaps it might be wise to make terms with de Montfort, to
avoid slaughter. But he was not sure and he lacked the vitality
to interfere.

Young Henry understood. He had been worried about his
father's health for some time; but periodically there would be
those bursts of action when Richard showed himself as the
able leader he might have been.

He was not going to act now, Henry realized; and Edward
was talking in his fiery fashion to his father. Nothing must stop
them. Victory would be theirs. People would remember the
battle of Lewes while history lasted.

The King, of course, was carried away by his admiration for
his son.

'You have heard my lord Edward,' he said to the messenger.
'Go to your masters and tell them we will have none of their
offer.'

*   *   *

The battle had gone well for the King's forces which were
so much more numerous than those of the barons. They had
been right not to parley, thought the King. Richard was a
good soldier; his young son Henry was with him. And best
of all there was Edward. What a leader he made—the sort of
King men would follow to the death!

This was going to be victory. He was certain of it.

So was Edward. The day was all but won. He led the cavalry
and his men could make no mistake that he was there. His
height set him above others. 'Edward Longshanks,' they cried
as they went into battle.

This was what he wanted. To lead men. To show his father
that he would serve him well. He wanted to wipe out for ever
the memories of that time when the King had doubted him.

In the thick of the fight he suddenly found his cousin Henry
of Cornwall beside him for in the mêlée of battle he had been
separated from his father.

Edward gave him a nod of welcome. He was glad to have
his cousin close, for of all the boys who had shared their early
days they had been the two who were closest together.

Then Edward noticed a body of men riding forward to
attack them. They were led by Hastings shouting the battle cry
of London.

Edward's heart leaped. These were his greatest enemies. These were the men he had determined to destroy.

He dashed into the attack with such fury that in a short while the Londoners, in disorder, turned to retreat.

'Follow them!' cried Edward.

Henry wanted to protest. They had driven off the Londoners, who were retreating from the field. There was nothing to be gained by following them. Nothing but revenge.

'Forward!' shouted Edward.

Henry rode beside him ... at full gallop, Edward's faithful followers with them shouting their battle cry.

On and on rode the remnants of the scattered London force but Edward would not give up the pursuit. He was determined that they should be punished for what they had done to his mother.

'In the name of Queen Eleanor ... vengeance!' he cried. 'Death to the Londoners. In the name of the Queen.'

The road was littered with fallen bodies but Edward was determined that none should escape if he could help it. Shouting the Queen's name he was killing men all about him; but still there were some to ride on.

They had come as far as Croydon before the band of Londoners was exhausted and could go no further. Many of their horses had fallen. They begged for mercy but Edward would show them none. The slaughter was merciless.

'This is for the Queen!' he cried. 'The noble lady whom you dared insult.'

* * *

There was quiet all about them. On the bloodstained grass lay the victims of his revenge. His men were tired; their horses were showing signs of fatigue.

Edward then remembered the battle.

They had come far from Lewes but must return without delay. They must be there to rejoice in the victory. How he would enjoy telling his father of the vengeance he had wreaked on those who had dared insult the Queen.

The cousins rode side by side back to Lewes.

'We should never have left the field,' said Henry.

'Not left the field! What mean you, cousin? There at my mercy were my mother's enemies. They will know now what happens to any who insult my family.'

'The King would expect us to be there.'

'Nay ... the battle was won. Now we go back and claim the spoils.'

But Edward was wrong.

The battle of Lewes had not been won when he left and the loss of Edward and his cavalry had proved disastrous for the King's side.

Henry had been taken prisoner with his brother Richard and when Edward and Henry returned they were surrounded, captured and told they would be held as hostages.

Oh yes, the battle of Lewes had been almost won but because the heir to the throne had withdrawn on his own private war of vengeance he had left his father's flank exposed—and the victory had gone to Simon de Montfort.

* * *

Five thousand men had been slain at the battle of Lewes; and the King was no longer a free man.

Simon de Montfort received him with great respect and assured him that he meant him no harm.

'I shall never forget that you are the King,' he told him.

'Yet you make me your prisoner,' cried Henry.

'You shall be treated with respect. But you will understand that the country must be governed with more justice than we have hitherto seen. The taxation which is crippling our industries must cease. The aliens must not be allowed to suck our prosperity. This is what we have fought for and it is what we intend to have.'

'You tell me I am your King and then you continue to rule me.'

'I am determined to bring law and order to this country and that it shall be ruled by its Parliament.'

'So you would depose the King?'

'By no means, but I would have him work with his Parliament not against it.'

Simon then said that he proposed to call a parliament in the King's name. Two knights from each county, two citizens from each city and two burgesses from each borough should be summoned, and they should represent the people from the districts whence they came.

'I never heard the like of this,' said Henry.

'Nay and it may be that it would have been better if you had. This form of parliament makes sure that the country is represented. It means we must make laws which do not offend the people.'

'And you are asking me to agree to this?' demanded Henry.

'I am asking you to, my lord,' replied Simon, 'while at the same time I must point out that, as the barons' prisoner, you have no alternative.'

Thus Simon de Montfort brought into existence a form of parliament which had never been known before this time.

Evesham

At the Court of France, Eleanor heard news of the disaster
The King, Richard, Edward ... all the prisoners of Simon de
Montfort! A new form of government being imposed on the
land! Representatives from the various parts of the country
to help in its government! It was monstrous.

'What can I do?' she demanded of Marguerite.

'You can pray,' said Marguerite.

'Pray! My dear sister, I must do more than that. I must
raise money. I must raise an army. I will never allow that
traitor de Montfort to hold Henry prisoner.'

'You are clever I know, Eleanor, and although you long
to do everything for your husband and son, you must be
cautious. It is a very dangerous situation.'

Eleanor shook herself impatiently. Did Marguerite think
she could tell her!

'Louis is of the opinion that you should await the outcome
of events,' went on Marguerite.

'Louis!' retorted Eleanor almost contemptuously. What had
Louis done to help Henry? He had known that the barons
were massing to make war and he had offered no help. He had
implied that it was Henry's own behaviour which had brought
about the calamity.

But, of course, she could say very little about her sister's
husband since she was enjoying their hospitality. And where
would she go if they would not receive her?

Marguerite was docile enough except when any criticism was levelled at Louis. Then she could become very fierce.

In spite of Marguerite, Eleanor busied herself with raising money. She was constantly sending messengers to England to those whom she believed to be her friends. She was confident that in due course she would raise an army and she would place herself at the head of it. She smiled at the thought of the admiration in Henry's eyes when he realized what she had done.

He would be pleased, however, that she was safe in France. For her to be humiliated as a captive would have hurt him far more than suffering that fate himself.

She brought all her energies to her campaign and she began to get some responses in France and from England.

She was going to build up her army. But how long it took! She was sustained though by the knowledge that she would in time free her family and she comforted herself by imagining the indignities she would heap on Simon de Montfort and their enemies.

How frustrating it was. Marguerite tried to help. She knew how she would feel if Louis were a captive in the hands of his enemies.

'You must be patient, Eleanor,' she said. 'When we love we must suffer.'

'What have you ever known of suffering?' demanded Eleanor almost contemptuously.

'A great deal,' replied Marguerite.

'Oh you are so meek ... so pliable ... ready to go this way or that. You never had much will of your own.'

'The meek often suffer as much as the strong.'

'Then if they do nothing about it it is their own fault.'

'You rarely saw any point of view but your own,' said Marguerite. 'You have had your own way too much in life.'

'Only because I have fought for it.'

'Sometimes it takes more strength to endure. Can you imagine how I felt living under the shadow of my clever mother-in-law Queen Blanche? She did everything so well. She was so respected, so admired. She came before me ... right until the time she died.'

'You were a fool to allow it. I should have made Louis understand. ...'

'Louis did understand how I felt. He once told me he loved me so much because of the way in which I did not make strife between him and his mother. It would have been so easy to.

Often it was my inclination, but I knew that could only bring
pain to him ... and to me. So I stood aside for her. And I
think she came to be fond of me, too.'

'Of course, since you let her have her way! Oh you were
always so mild, Marguerite. You don't know what it is to have
deep feelings.'

'I have had great adventures in my life, Eleanor,' Marguerite defended herself, 'and I think I have lived more
dangerously than you ever did.'

'I was near death in London. I shall never forget the evil
faces of the mob as they looked down on me from the bridge.
I knew they intended to sink my barge. It was awful.
Sometimes I dream of them now ... I hear their voices
shouting "Drown the Witch." You could not understand,
Marguerite.'

Marguerite laughed.

'I will tell you something, sister. You have forgotten that
when Louis went on his crusade to the Holy Land, I accompanied him. The fear you experienced during one night in
London, was with me constantly for months. I was a woman
in that strange land. We were in perpetual danger from the
Saracens. Do you know what they did to women if they captured them? They might torture them; they might merely
cut off their heads; but what was most likely was that they took
them off to serve in some harem. You dream of London Bridge.
My dear sister, I dream of the Christian camp where I, heavy
with child, waited night after night for some fearful fate to
overtake me. Often the King left me. I was in the camp with
only one knight to protect me. He was so aged that he could
not join the others. I made him swear that if ever the Saracens
came to my tent he would cut off my head with his sword rather
than let me be taken.'

Eleanor was subdued. It was borne home to her that her
own joys and sorrows had always seemed so much greater than
those of others, that she had rarely thought theirs worth considering.

Now to think of Marguerite, pregnant, lying in a desert
camp, was sobering.

'But that is all in the past,' she said. 'My trouble is here
right before me.'

'All troubles pass,' Marguerite assured her. 'Yours will no
less than mine did.'

'Does that mean I should not do everything I can to disperse
them?'

'Nay, you would always work for your family. But be patient, dear sister. All will be well.'

But it was not in Eleanor's nature to sit down and wait for miracles. She redoubled her efforts.

One day Edward de Carol, the Dean of Wells, arrived in Paris. He had letters from the King, he said, and joyfully Eleanor seized on them.

When she read what the King had written she was filled with a dull anger. He begged her to desist in her efforts to interfere with the course of events. What she was doing was known in England. It could do no good.

The Dean did not have to tell her that the letter had been dictated by her enemy Simon de Montfort, because she knew as soon as she read it.

She remembered Marguerite's admonition to be patient. She wrote back to the King assuring him that she would respect his wishes.

When the Dean had left she went on with her work. She was certain that in time she would raise an army.

Messengers continued to come to the Court of France and they brought news of the royal captives. It was thus that she learned that they had been taken to Dover. The nearest port to France. Wild ideas filled her mind. Would it be so very difficult to get a party to land, to storm the castle, to rescue the captives and bring them to France? There they could place themselves at the head of the army she was sure she would raise. They would be free to win back the crown.

While she was turning this over in her mind and making plans to bring it about, more messengers came.

The barons felt that Dover might be a dangerous spot in view of its proximity to the Continent. They were therefore being moved to Wallingford.

She could have wept with rage, but very soon she was making fresh plans.

Her indefatigable efforts had won the admiration of a number of people and her devotion to her family was touching. Even those who found her overbearing were ready to work for her and thus there were plenty to bring her news of what was happening in England. The royal prisoners, she learned, were not so well guarded at Wallingford as they had been at Dover. One of Edward's favourite knights had sent word to her that he would do anything to help the royal cause and she immediately decided to keep him to his word.

Sir Warren de Basingbourne was a young and daring fellow

who had often jousted with Edward and whom she knew was
devoted to her son.

'Gather together as many men as you can,' she wrote to
him. 'Go to Wallingford, lay siege to the castle—which I
know to be ill defended. Rescue the lord Edward. He can then
come to me here and place himself at the head of the army I
am preparing.'

Eleanor excitedly settled down to await the arrival of her
son.

*   *   *

Edward had never ceased to reproach himself. This disaster was due to his folly. It was no use his father's trying to
comfort him. It was clear that if he had not pursued the
Londoners the victory would have gone to the King.

What folly! What harm inexperience could do!

Edward was a young man who quickly learned his lessons.

He thought often of his young wife with whom he was in
love. It had been a marriage after his own heart. She had been
so young at the time of the ceremony and he had seemed so
much older to her that she had begun by looking up to him.
They had been separated, it was true, while she completed her
education and grew old enough to be his wife in truth. And
then he had not been disappointed in her.

He believed she was now pregnant.

Poor little Eleanora—or Eleanor as they insisted on calling
her, for their future Queen must have an English name—she
would be fretting now, as he knew his mother was.

He was glad his cousin Henry was with him, although it
would have been more satisfactory if he could have been free
to work for the King. They played chess together; they were
even allowed to ride out although only in the castle surrounds
and in the company of guards. Simon de Montfort treated
them with respect. He was always anxious for them to know
that he had no intention of harming them, and that he merely
wanted to see just rule returned to the country.

While they sat at the chess table one of their servants came
running in. He was clearly very excited.

'My lord,' he said, 'there is a troop of men marching on the
castle!'

'By God,' cried Edward. 'The country is rising against de
Montfort.'

They rushed to the windows. In the distance they could see
the horsemen making straight for the castle.

Someone said: 'They are Sir Warren of Basingbourne's men, I'll swear.'

'Then they come to save us,' said Edward. 'Warren would never place himself against me. He is my great friend.'

There was activity throughout the castle. At the turrets and machicolations soldiers were stationed. The alert ran through the castle. 'We are besieged! Stand by for defence.'

It was frustrating for the prisoners to be unable to take part in the fighting as they were forced to listen to the shouts and the cries and the groaning of the battle engines as they went into action.

Edward heard his own name called.

'Edward. Edward. Bring us Edward.'

His eyes were shining. 'Our friends have risen at last,' he said. 'I knew it was only a matter of time. Our captivity is over.'

'First they have to break the siege,' Henry reminded him.

'By God they will. We are poorly defended here.'

Half a dozen guards had come into the room.

They approached Edward.

'What would you have of me?' he demanded.

'We but obey orders, my lord.'

'And they are?'

'Your friends out there are demanding that we bring you out to them.'

'And you, knowing yourself beaten, are meeting their wishes?'

'We are not beaten, my lord. But we are giving you to them. We shall bind you hand and foot, as we shall tell them, and we shall shoot you to them from the mangonel.'

Edward cried out in horror at the thought of being shot through this terrifying engine which was used for throwing down stones on the enemy. It would be certain death.

'You do not mean this.'

'It will be done, my lord, if your friends do not go away.'

'Let me speak to them.'

The men looked at each other and one of them nodded and retired.

When he returned he said: 'Orders are that your hands should be bound behind your back, my lord. Then we will take you to the parapet. From there you will speak to your friends. If you tell them to go away, your life will be saved.'

'I will do it,' he said, for indeed there was no alternative but terrible death. So they tied his hands and he stood on the parapet and told them that unless they wanted his death they must disperse and go away, for his captors meant that if he came to them it would be by way of the mangonel.

Sir Warren hastily retired; and when news of what had happened was sent to Eleanor she wept with anger.

* * *

Simon de Montfort came in all haste to Wallingford. The news of Basingbourne's attempt had shocked him. It could so easily have succeeded. It had been a brilliant idea to threaten to shoot Edward out to them. However, an ill defended castle was no place for such prisoners.

In the hall of the castle all the prisoners were brought to him.

'My lords,' he said, 'I am grieved that you have been treated with less than respect. I assure you that it was no intention of mine.'

'You do not make that intention very clear,' retorted Edward.

'I am sorry if you have not perceived it,' replied Simon calmly. 'It is true that your movements are restricted but I trust you lack no comfort here in the castle.'

'You traitor,' cried Edward. The others were silent. Simon shrugged his shoulders and turned to the King.

'My lord, it was no wish of mine that this should have happened. The laws of the country must be justly administered. Our Parliament will do that and if we can come to some agreement....'

'We shall make no agreements with you, my lord,' said the King firmly.

'Then I will continue with the matter of which I came to speak. You must prepare to leave Wallingford.'

'Where is our next prison to be?' asked Edward.

'You are to go to Kenilworth.'

'Kenilworth!' cried Edward.

'It is my own castle. Your aunt will receive you there. I think you will be happier with a member of your own family.'

The prisoners were silent. This was interesting. The King's own sister was the châtelaine of Kenilworth. Surely she would be sympathetic to the members of her own family. But they had to remember that she was also Simon de Montfort's wife.

They left that day for Kenilworth, where the King's sister Eleanor de Montfort, Countess of Leicester, received them with affection.

'At least,' said Edward, 'it will not seem as though we are prisoners here.'

'Eleanor!' Henry's eyes filled with tears at the sight of his sister.

She embraced him and said, 'Oh Henry, this is a sorry business. Richard, Edward, I would you had come here in different circumstances.'

'Do not blame *us* for the circumstances,' said Edward.

The King put up a hand to silence him. Simon de Montfort was Eleanor's husband and they must not take it amiss because she was loyal to him.

They sat down in the great hall. They might have been paying a family visit, but of course they knew that the castle was surrounded by de Montfort's guards and that they were in a stronger prison than they had been in at Wallingford.

The long days slowly passed. Eleanor did all she could to make them comfortable. She would now allow them to criticize Simon, and she made it clear that although she wished to treat her family as her family while they were under her roof she clearly believed in the righteousness of her husband's actions.

'Eleanor was always a woman of strong beliefs,' said Henry to the King of the Romans. 'And once she had made up her mind on a course of action it would take strong men to move her ... and then she would outwit them.' He could not help but admire her. Her character was not unlike that of his own Eleanor. His sister had determined to marry Simon de Montfort when he had seemed to be nothing more than an adventurer; but she had sensed greatness in him, for Henry had to admit that a man who could take a country from its rightful King and set himself up as ruler, however misguided he might be, had an unusual power.

Now, in a dignified manner, of which Henry could not but admire, she played the role of hostess to her imprisoned relations while never for a moment did she forget her loyalty to her husband.

Christmas came and Eleanor endeavoured to make the celebrations as gay as was possible in the circumstances, but always the guards remained stationed at certain points of the castle and encamped outside the walls.

Edward was frustrated.

There seemed no hope of escape. Meanwhile Simon de Montfort with his new Parliament was controlling the country.

* * *

There was trouble for Simon from an unexpected direction.

One of his firmest supporters had been Gilbert de Clare, Earl of Gloucester—the grandson of that Isabella who had been the first wife of Richard, King of the Romans. Gilbert, in his early twenties—called the Red because of the colour of his hair—was, on account of his inheritance on the death of his father but a few years before, one of the most influential barons in the country. He had formed a friendship with Simon, whom he greatly admired, and because of his wealth and energy he had become second-in-command of the baronial party. Gilbert had had the honour of taking the King's sword from him when Henry was taken prisoner at Lewes. He had had a hand in drawing up the truce between the King and the barons which was known as the Mise of Lewes in which the Provisions of Oxford were confirmed. In this, there was a special clause exempting Simon de Montfort and Gloucester from any punishment for their conduct.

Gloucester was young and impressionable, and with him the friends of one day could become the despised enemy of the next. He was fickle, a fact of which Simon in the early days of their relationship, had not been aware.

Many of the royal supporters who had escaped after Lewes had taken refuge in that part of the country on the Welsh border known as the Marches of Wales. The lords who owned castles there were the Marcher Lords and they had always been a source of irritation to the English. It seemed to Simon that Gloucester, far from attempting to force the Marcher Lords to give up those whom they were sheltering, was protecting them.

This was disconcerting.

Gloucester began to bring charges against de Montfort. He declared that Simon had taken the larger share of the castles which had been confiscated after the royal defeat at Lewes, and discussing the matter with his wife Simon showed himself to be growing uneasy.

If the King ever regained his crown what would happen to Simon and their sons? Simon reminded her of the clause in the Mise of Lewes but Eleanor shook her head.

'Do you think that would be considered. We should have to fly the country, I suppose. It would be necessary for us to get out in time. Vengeance would be terrible. Edward would show no mercy even if Henry did.'

'My dear, we must not contemplate defeat.'

'No, but I believe we should consider it. It is well to be prepared for anything that may happen.'

'I have to see Gloucester without delay. I have to find out what all this is about.'

'You can safely leave me in charge of your prisoners.'

'I know. Henry and his brother will be safe. It is Edward I fear. I believe at this moment he is planning escape. He is different from his father. I can see a great King there, but at this time he is young and rash. I think he will attempt to escape. No, I must go to Gloucester, but I shall take Edward with me.'

'And leave the others here?'

'I believe that to be the wise thing to do.'

When Edward heard that he was to leave Kenilworth he was excited. Any movement was better than this lack of action.

*   *   *

The journey proved to be more exciting than even he had dared hope. It was not long before he realized that there were traitors in Simon's camp. A man such as de Montfort who had achieved so much and was admired by some almost to adoration was certain to attract a great deal of envy and although there were many who would have died for him there were others who were ready to risk their lives to harm him.

The latter were those who could be of use to Edward.

One of these was Thomas Clare, the Earl of Gloucester's younger brother. Thomas managed to exchange a few words with him as they rode along.

'My lord,' he whispered, 'you have friends among us.'

'That makes good hearing,' replied Edward.

'The Queen your mother is amassing an army which is almost ready to march.'

'I have heard that is so,' answered Edward.

'If you could join it ... with some of your loyal friends who are waiting to serve you. ...'

The conversation was interrupted but Edward's spirits were soaring. This undignified state of affairs was coming to an end. He felt it in his bones. He was not meant to remain a prisoner.

On another occasion Thomas de Clare said to him, 'There is a plan, my lord. Roger Mortimer is prepared to help.'

'Mortimer!' cried Edward. 'He is a traitor.'

'No longer so, my lord. It is true that he gave his support to de Montfort, but he is withdrawing it at the best moment to be of use to you.'

'Can I trust a man who was once a traitor?'

'Mortimer does not regard himself as a traitor. He says he serves England and he thought best to do so under Leicester. Now he has changed his mind ... as my brother has. De Montfort is an ambitious man. He has taken the King's castles for himself. Men are turning against him. You can rely on Mortimer now. Besides his wife has always been a supporter of the Queen and your father. She has at last prevailed on her husband to change sides and this he has done.'

'I like not men who change sides.'

'My lord, suffice that they come to serve you. You need men who will leave Leicester and come to you.'

'You are right, Thomas. What will Mortimer do?'

'It is a simple plan, my lord. When we reach Gloucester you will be allowed certain freedom. The Earl of Leicester is most anxious that your royalty shall not be debased. You will take exercise in the grounds inside the castle walls. All know your interest in horses. You will challenge your attendant guards about their horses and ask to test their endurance. There should be four of them. You will challenge them to races and you will see that every horse including your own will be exhausted. You will continue until then. Then you will mount your own tired horse and ride out. You will not be followed because they will know that you cannot go far. But there hidden by the trees Lord Mortimer will be waiting with a fresh horse. You will mount it and ride away with him. Your own tired mount will return to the castle ... without you.'

'A simple plan,' said Edward. 'Will it work?'

'It is for you, my lord, to make it.'

'I will,' cried Edward. 'By God I will.'

* * *

It was working. They believed him. He had always been interested in horses.

He would test them, he said. They would have a wager as to which of the five—their four and his—were the best. He insisted that they race with him. Round and round the castle they went. He contrived to finish neck and neck with one or two of them and insisted that they race again ... all five of them.

To the guards it seemed as good a way of passing the time as any. Their horses would be tired out but the day was almost over and they could go straight to their stables.

Edward won the race. The horses were sweating and fit for little.

'Poor old fellow,' said Edward, patting his. 'You have had enough, I'll warrant. Never mind. You have done well and shall rest.'

The guards were leading their horses towards the stables; Edward was with them.

He lagged behind and then turning his horse suddenly made his way towards the thicket a short distance from where they had run their races.

His heart beat wildly with hope for there was Roger Mortimer as had been arranged. He was seated on a horse and holding another—strong, fresh, ready for fast riding.

Edward said: 'Thank God.' And leaped into the saddle.

'Which way?' he said.

'Follow me, my lord.'

In a few seconds he was galloping away to safety.

*   *   *

In Ludlow the Earl of Gloucester was waiting for him.

The Earl received him with great respect and congratulated him on his escape.

'My lord,' he said, 'there are many barons in the country who would be ready to serve with you. They are still against the King but if you would give certain promises I am sure that they would be ready to follow you.'

'You do not think I would go against my father?'

'You mistake me, my lord. They would merely wish you to give certain assurances and would ask you to persuade your father to stop acting in a manner which has brought about this rebellion. The people want the good and ancient laws brought back and obeyed. They want an abolition of those evil customs which recently have overtaken the kingdom. Aliens must be removed from the realm and from the council. They must not be allowed to retain the castles which have been bestowed on them, nor take part in the government. All we ask, my lord, is that England be governed once more by Englishmen. If you are victorious, if you defeat de Montfort, would you bring this about? If you will give your solemn word, I can promise you the help of powerful lords.'

'I swear it,' said Edward.

'Then I will summon a council of those who would be prepared to work with you.'

'Pray do this,' cried Edward.

It was gratifying to be joined by Hugh Bigod and Earl Warrene.

Edward was in fine spirits. He was free. He was bent on victory. He was determined to learn from his earlier mistakes that nothing of that nature would happen again.

With a good army—for more and more barons were coming to his aid—he took possession of the country along by the Severn and destroyed the bridges so that de Montfort's army was cut off. He knew that de Montfort's son, the younger Simon, was raising an army in London where there would be plenty of volunteers to come against the King and his en- deavour was to stand between the de Montfort armies and to prevent their joining up.

News came that young Simon was on the march and had reached Kenilworth. Now the position seemed to have changed and instead of Edward's splitting the two de Montfort armies, he was caught between them which was not an enviable position to be in.

But there was some good news. The Queen, as indefatig- able in her efforts as ever, had succeeded in raising an army and was waiting at the French coast for the weather to allow it to cross the Channel. The gales at this time made the journey impossible, but it was a comfort to know that it was there.

While he was in his tent with Thomas de Clare, Mortimer and Warrenne going over the possibilities of attacking the de Montfort armies and carefully considering the position in which they found themselves between Simon de Montfort the elder and the younger, and Edward was saying that they must not act rashly, remembering how the loss of the battle of Lewes was due to him, a woman was brought into the camp.

A camp follower! Edward wondered why she should beg to be taken to him!

The woman was tall, and her face was hidden by a hood so that it was not easy to see whether she was handsome or not. Edward had no desire to dally with women. He had given up his amorous adventurings when he had settled down with his wife; moreover thoughts of military matters now occupied his mind.

'Who is this woman,' he demanded, 'and why do you bring her to me?'

'She calls herself Margot, my lord,' said the guard who had brought her in, 'and she begs to have word with you.'

'For what purpose?' cried Edward and was about to order her to be removed when he remembered afresh his rashness at Lewes.

'Leave her with us,' he said, and the guard retired.

'Pray state your business,' said Edward.

Margot removed the cloak. It was immediately obvious that this was no woman.

'My lord,' said 'Margot', 'I pray you hear me. I would serve the King and your noble self. I come from Kenilworth.'

'Ah,' said Edward. 'Say on.'

'The traitor de Montfort has commanded his son to attack you. He intends to squeeze you between the two armies.'

'That we know well.'

'My lord, the army at Kenilworth is not as disciplined as that of the elder de Montfort. They are not expecting attack. They are waiting for the signal from the elder de Montfort, then they will advance and begin the battle. At night they are not well guarded. They leave their horses and their weapons unattended. It would be a simple matter to creep up on them after dark and destroy them.'

Edward looked at his friends.

'There seems sense in this.'

'Do we trust this man?' asked Edward.

'My lord, I came here ... risking my life for the King. If you do not believe me then do not act on my advice. Let me stay here your prisoner until you have proved my loyalty.'

Edward was on the point of rewarding the man and sending him on his way but again he remembered his rashness at Lewes.

'Let us do this,' he said. 'If we find you are indeed our friend, you shall be rewarded.'

* * *

A dark night. The castle was silent. Only here and there on the battlements a torch flickered. Slowly, silently, Edward and a picked force crept forward. A little way behind was the bulk of the army ready for attack.

'Margot' had not lied. The de Montfort troops were taken completely by surprise. All those on guard in the castle were taken within half an hour, including their weapons. Those in their beds in the castle were caught without their clothes let alone their armour.

Many were slaughtered. A few escaped and one who did, to Edward's regret, was Simon de Montfort the younger.

Saddened, disillusioned, beaten by his own carelessness he, with a few of his followers, was able to reach the stables and ride off to safety.

For Edward and his friends this was a triumph which almost effaced the disgrace of Lewes. Moreover there was now only one army to be faced.

He sent for 'Margot' and told him that he could name his reward to which he was answered simply that all that was asked was the chance to serve under the lord Edward.

Edward clasped his hands.

'You are my friend,' he said, 'for as long as you care for that friendship.'

That there must be no delay was obvious. They must attack the elder Simon before he realized what had happened to his son's army.

Their great chance was in the element of surprise.

'To Evesham,' was the cry.

* * *

Simon de Montfort in the castle of Evesham believed that victory was near. Young Simon must be almost on Edward's army now. Simon was a good general. He would choose the right moment to attack.

The anxieties of the last weeks had been great. Ever since he had heard of Edward's escape he had been uneasy. The King he feared little. He saw him as an ineffectual man caught up in the great affection he bore to his family. He had allowed this to govern his life in as much as through it, determined to please the Queen, he had acted against the good of his subjects. Simon could understand that; but Henry had carried his fondness beyond the bounds of good sense.

The country to be governed by a king *and* his parliament. That was what Simon had worked for and was achieving. A parliament representing the cities, boroughs and counties of the nation. It was the only fair method as he saw it. And he had achieved it. He could be proud of that. All had gone well, until those fools had allowed Edward to escape.

In the far distance that which could be an army was detected marching on Evesham castle.

Simon went with his barber Nicolas to the top of the abbey tower for Nicolas not only had exceptionally keen eyesight but was an expert on the cognizance of arms.

'What see you, Nicolas?' asked Simon.

'My lord, I can make out the de Montfort ensigns. They are holding your standards high.'

'God be praised. It is my son. I knew that he would be with us ere long.'

Simon was elated. Young Simon had either evaded Edward's army or destroyed it and he could only believe that it was the latter. This would be the end of Edward's revolt. This would be triumph for him and justice.

His company would be delighted. They need not prepare for war but for the happy reunion. The two armies together would be invincible and young Simon would have his tale to tell of victory.

Nicolas came to him white-faced and trembling.

'My lord, I see other banners. It is only in the van of the army that they carry the de Montfort ensigns.'

'What do you see? Tell me quickly.'

'My lord I can make out the triple lions of Edward and Roger Mortimer's ensigns.'

'God help us,' cried Simon. 'We have been deceived. What does this mean? How have they come by my son's banners?'

There was no time to speculate. They must go into action without delay. But precious time had been lost and the enemy was almost upon them.

Simon was a man of great military ability but he realized that the advantage had been lost. With as much speed as he could muster he gathered his troops together. Many of them still believed that the advancing army was their ally and it took some time to get them to realize that they must prepare for battle.

Indeed the advantage was lost and full well did Simon know the importance of that.

We have been deceived, he kept thinking. What has happened to my son? This Edward has become a man, and I have been thinking of him as a reckless boy.

They had tricked him, and they should be tricked. Thank God he had the King in his possession here. The King should be placed in the forefront of the battle. He should stand against his own son who had come to rescue him.

Simon had time to marshal his troops and took up his stance at the top of a hill where he could watch the advancing enemy.

'By the arm of St. James,' he cried, 'they come on skilfully. Edward has learned his methods from me. He will never commit the folly of Lewes again. In conflict with me he has become a great general.'

It was two hours after noon and the hot August sun was almost overhead. The battle had begun.

*   *   *

The shame of it! To be there in the front of the enemy
troops. He, the King, to be so treated! How dared Simon de
Montfort, his own brother-in-law, inflict this indignity on him.
Was this to be the end? Killed in battle ... by his own son who
mistook him for the enemy!

He thought of his adored Eleanor working so hard for him
across the water. He thought of his beloved son. What anguish
would be his when he knew that his men had killed his own
father.

A curse on you, de Montfort! he thought. Would to God I
had never shown you favour.

There was the pride of seeing the superiority of Edward's
forces; the advantage that initial surprise had given him.
Edward would be the victor this day. He knew it. He would
rejoice but how he would mourn when he came upon his
father's dead body on the battle field.

The fight grew more fierce; Edward's men were closing in.
A spear pierced the King's shoulder blade and he turned and
saw the murderous eyes of his assailant, his arm raised ready
to finish what he had begun.

'Hold!' cried the King. 'I am Henry of Winchester. Placed
here by the traitor de Montfort. Kill me and you answer to the
lord Edward.'

The man hesitated. For a second or two it seemed as though
he was going to treat the King's outburst with contempt. But
one of the barons was nearby and Henry recognized him as
Roger of Leyburne.

He shouted to him.

'By God,' said Roger. 'It is indeed the King. Hold man!
Take care not to harm the King. Come ... my lord....'

When Edward saw his father he was overcome with joy.

He took the King's arm and drew him to a place of safety.

There were tears in Henry's eyes.

'My son,' he said, 'I was never more proud than I am on this
day.'

*   *   *

It was dark before the battle was over—a complete victory
for Edward and the royalists. The slaughter had been terrible.
Both Simon de Montfort and his son Henry had been killed.
No quarter was given. The carnage was frightful; one
hundred and sixty of de Montfort's knights were slain on that
battlefield and countless numbers of ordinary soldiers.

That was not enough. As night fell the rabble of Edward's

army roamed the battle field and coming upon the bodies of Simon de Montfort and his son Henry they set up a cry of delight; they fell upon them, stripped them of their armour and with hideous cries of glee that sounded like no human noise, they proceeded to mutilate them in every obscene manner they could devise. And this was the end of the great earl Simon de Montfort.

* * *

The young Simon de Montfort who had escaped from Kenilworth had gathered together the remnants of his army and was marching on Evesham.

He saw in the distance a band of drunken revellers who held something high above their heads and sang ribald songs as they came along.

As young Simon came near he saw what they held. It was a sight which he would never forget while he lived.

His own father's head being carried on a pike!

'Would I had died,' he cried, 'ere I had seen such a sight.'

He turned his horse and with his followers rode back to Kenilworth.

There he mourned for the loss of his father and his cause; and in time his sorrow was replaced by a great yearning for vengeance on those who had so debased a great man.

Meanwhile the soldiers with their gruesome burden marched on.

Their trophy was a gift from Hugh Mortimer to his countess who had ever been a faithful supporter of the King's cause.

She was at prayers in her chapel when they arrived, and when she saw what they had brought her she cried out in great joy and gave thanks to God for His goodness.

Murder at the Altar

EDWARD now had a little son whom they had named John and his wife was pregnant again. There was great rejoicing throughout the family for now the Queen was back and their delight in being together again was boundless. Henry was beside himself with joy and pride in his family. Eleanor had worked devotedly all through their separation and it was the brilliant tactics of his son Edward which had saved him from his enemies.

The battle of Evesham, though decisive and resulting in the death of Simon de Montfort, did not completely end the war.

Simon and Guy de Montfort, determined to avenge their father, kept bands of rebels together in various parts of the country. There were battles for the castles whose castellans had declared themselves against the King; but Edward was now a seasoned warrior and he was beginning to emerge as a general of great ability, a rival to his great uncle Richard Coeur de Lion.

Richard, King of the Romans, had married again, although the general opinion was that he might have been thinking of making his peace with God rather than starting a new life. Richard had suffered a great deal during his captivity and those periods when he had been listless and unable to work had increased. But his marriage to the beautiful young Beatrice of Falkenberg revived him and it was with great pride that he brought her to England to introduce her to his brother.

Edward meanwhile was clearing up the rebel patches

throughout the country. He was fast becoming a hero to his fellow countryman. His height and good looks made him immediately recognizable; he was clearly a man of great strength and while he could be affable there was no sign of his father's weakness in him.

The fact that they had such an heir to the throne was one of the main factors in giving the country a feeling of security. They despised Henry who had brought so much trouble to the country through his folly; but they were inclined to forgive him and his arrogant avaricious queen because whatever they had taken, they had given them Edward.

In due course Edward had freed the country of the rebels. Young Simon and Guy de Montfort were in exile in France. Edward had added further to his aura of heroism my meeting in single combat the last of the rebels. This was Adam Gurdon, a man of almost superhuman strength whom no one had ever been able to overcome. Edward achieved what had seemed impossible; and when he had Adam at his mercy he continued in his noble role and gave him his life out of respect for his valour. Rounding off this romantic episode in the perfect manner, Adam asked to be able to serve Edward and as long as he lived acted as one of his closest servants and bodyguards.

It was incidents like this that were circulated about the heir to the throne which delighted the people. They forgot Simon de Montfort and his cries for justice and his introduction of a parliament of which the like had never been seen before.

The country was settling down.

Edward now had a daughter, Eleanor after his wife and that obliging lady was once more pregnant. In due course she gave birth to a son who was named Henry after his grandfather.

Henry was delighted. He imposed a fine of 25,000 marks on the Londoners, who surprisingly paid it, and the whole of it was put to the Queen's use.

'This is for you, my love, and only now can I begin to forgive those wicked people for their treatment of you.'

Eleanor was ready to be placated as the sum was so large. The people would always hate her—and in particular the Londoners—but she could shrug that aside in the pleasure she took in her family.

News came from France that Louis was contemplating going on a crusade. People were beginning to regard him as a saint and it seemed to the whole world that he was the most fitted to lead such a venture.

Edward reminded his father that they both had at times declared their intention of taking up the cross and now that the country was at peace and Henry was in good health, might be the time for Edward to keep their vow.

The more he talked of it the more the idea appealed to him. He had developed a great skill—and taste—for battle. How better could he use it than in the service of Christ?

The King and the Queen, while they would regret his absence, understood his desires and they believed that it would be good for him and the country if he were to strike a blow for Christendom.

Only his wife, Eleanor, was so stricken with grief and so insistent in her pleas to accompany him that he pointed out in great detail the dangers she would have to face.

'I would rather face any danger than be without you,' she said.

He was deeply touched and she went on to point out that other wives had accompanied their husbands. Louis' own wife Marguerite, many years ago had been with him on his crusade.

It was true, agreed Edward, but she had suffered great hardships. He would not wish to see his gentle Eleanor in such circumstances.

But his gentle Eleanor showed a sudden hitherto unsuspected strength.

'If you will not take me as your wife I will disguise myself as one of your soldiers and you will not know I am in your company until we arrive. Then you will have to recognize me.'

He embraced her with fervour. 'My dear good wife,' he said, 'plead no more. You shall come with me. In God's truth, why did I ever think that I could go without you?'

So it was settled and Edward left for France with his cousin Henry, the son of Richard, for Henry had also taken the cross.

They would go to the Court of France and there make their plans.

It was good to be together. They had always been the closest friends from the days of their childhood when they had been brought up in a household of royal children.

Henry had many fine qualities and Edward would never forget that it was Henry who had shown him the folly of his ruthless cruelty to the boy who at his command had lost an ear. Henry had despised that act and taught Edward to do the same.

There was something quite noble about Henry.

'God's truth, cousin,' said Edward, 'I am glad you will be with me.'

Henry had recently married the daughter of the Viscount of Bearn—a beautiful girl named Constance. So there they were two happily married men, about to set out on an adventure together—one of which they had often talked in their boyhood when they had vied with each other in describing the valiant deeds they would perform.

They were received with honour at the Court of France but Edward had to plead poverty, for the recent civil war had had such an effect on the English exchequer that there was no money with which to support a crusade. It was agreed that Edward should travel as the Duke of Aquitaine which meant that he would be a vassal of the King of France. As such Louis would offer him financial aid.

This was agreed upon and the two young men returned to England to make their final preparations.

Then Edward and his wife said a farewell to their children and set sail for France.

A shock awaited him when he arrived at Tunis. Louis had died of a fever and sickness raged through the French camp. The new king Philip under the influence of his uncle Charles of Anjou had made a truce with the Saracens.

This changed their plans considerably. Edward was indignant.

'By God's blood,' he swore, 'though all my fellow soldiers and countrymen desert me, I will go to Acre with my groom only and keep my words and my oath to the death.'

But he was uneasy.

He talked long with Henry.

'Who would have believed this could have happened? You look sad, Henry. Do you think I am wrong to go on?'

'Nay. I think you are right. I was but thinking of my father. He lies sick. I have a feeling that I shall never see him again.'

Edward was thoughtful.

'There is trouble in Gascony. My father will need help. Henry, I am going to ask you something. Will you go home. Tend to your father. I know he loves you as he loves no other. I have seen his eyes light up at the sight of you. We have a capability for loving our families, we Plantagenets. Perhaps it is because my grandfather was so ill treated by his sons and there is much to make up for. Henry, I have a feeling that you should go back.'

'Perhaps you too, Edward. This is an unexpected set-back.'

'Nay. I am determined to stay. I shall go on. I have made my vow and I shall keep it. You are young. You will have time yet. At this moment I feel that you must go back, Henry.'

Henry was thoughtful. He was greatly concerned about his father. He had known for some time that he had been ill; but of late his weakness had grown.

'I will go,' he decided, and the cousins took an affectionate farewell of each other. Edward went on to Palestine while Henry sailed away to the Mediterranean coast.

*　　*　　*

Henry had been sad to leave Edward but, as he travelled through Italy in the entourage of the King of France, he felt a great need to see his father.

He feared that Richard might die before he could reach him. Because of the strong bond between them he could not now stop thinking of his father. It seemed to him that his father was trying to reach him, that death was hovering and he wanted to see him while there was yet time.

As he rode Henry was going over memories of the times they had spent together. Richard had loved him, he knew, more than anyone else. He had had a certain passion for his wives—Sanchia had greatly attracted him for a while and it was the same with Beatrice. It must at one time have been so with his mother. But that was before he could remember. He fancied, looking back, that as a child he knew how his mother longed for his father to come to them, and how when he did come, although he showed the utmost affection for his son, he wanted to get away. And then later they had become great friends. They had fought together at Lewes; they had been the prisoners of Simon de Montfort.

Henry often thought of Simon. There was a great man who had dreamed of bringing justice to England. It was a pity that men like Simon de Montfort must die on the battle field.

He knew that his two sons—Simon the younger and Guy— were now in Italy. They were exiled from England but Guy had married the only child of Count Aldobrandino Rosso dell' Anguillara and had been made governor of Tuscany by Charles of Anjou. His brother Simon had joined him in Italy, so they could not now be far away.

He wondered whether he could see them, in which case he might bring about some reconciliation between them and the King and Edward.

He was sure that Edward would be ready to forget the

trouble between them. After all they were his cousins. The King and Queen, whatever their faults, were not vindictive. King Henry was a man who liked to live in peace.

The thought excited Henry. As the party came into the town of Viterbo he decided that he would do all he could to find his cousins and, when he had, he would try to persuade them that they must bear no more resentment for the brutal murder of their father.

All enmity must be forgotten.

He was sure that the King and his son Edward would be prepared to let bygones be bygones.

It was Lent. The time for repentance and forgiveness.

Tomorrow he would go to church and pray for success.

*　　*　　*

As the party rode into the town of Viterbo two men were watching from a window of an ale house.

They had come to this place in disguise for they wished to discover whether a certain man—whom they had reason to believe was a member of that party—was in fact of it.

They talked in low tones.

'He is bound to be there. I know he left Edward and he would naturally return through Italy with the King's party. The time is at hand, brother.'

Guy de Montfort nodded. 'Never fear, Simon, his time is at hand.'

Simon de Montfort said: 'I can see it still ... that ribald crowd. And aloft they held his head. They jeered ... they shouted obscenities ... and when I think of him ... that great man....'

Guy said: 'Rest assured he shall not escape.' His eyes glinted with an almost demoniac light. He had always been more bloodthirsty than his brother. He was thinking of those days in the royal courtyards when Henry of Cornwall had, with Edward, been a leader of them all. He had had a great influence on Edward and among all the boys was his greatest friend.

'He was so virtuous,' said Guy. 'He was always right. Noble Henry! Ere long it will be a different story.'

'I have heard that our father was murdered after Henry of Cornwall and his father were taken prisoner.'

'It matters not. It was his men who did this foul deed and he must answer for it. Look. Who is that coming into the street?'

'By God. Truth, it is he.'

Guy caught his brother's arm. 'So he is here then. Now all we have to do is wait for our moment.'

* * *

There was so much Henry wished to ask of God. His father's health was uppermost; the success of Edward in the Holy Land; the continued peace at home; his future happiness with his beautiful bride.

In the early morning of that Friday which was to be fatal for him, Henry made his way to the church of San Silvestro. He had dismissed his attendants for he wished to be completely alone. He was in a strange mood that morning.

He knelt at the high altar. There was a deep silence about him and he felt suddenly at peace.

And as he knelt there the church door was thrown open. He did not turn even when the clatter of boots on the flagged floor broke the silence.

Suddenly he heard his name and turning he saw Guy de Montfort with his brother Simon at the head of a group of armed men.

'This is the end for you!' shouted Guy. 'You shall not escape now.'

Henry saw murder in his cousin's eyes. He began: 'Guy....'

Guy de Montfort laughed harshly. 'This is for what was done to my father.'

He lifted his sword. Henry clung to the altar and the sword all but cut off his fingers. Henry staggered to his feet.

'Cousin ...' he cried. 'Cousins... Have mercy... I did not harm your father....'

'Nay. Nay,' cried Guy, his eyes alight with demoniac glee. 'He died did he not? Come. What are we waiting for?'

He lifted his sword. Simon was beside him. Henry fell fainting to the floor, his blood spattering the altar.

The de Montfort brothers looked at the dying man.

'We have avenged our father,' said Guy.

'Nay, sir,' spoke up one of his band. 'Your father was not so respectfully dispatched."

'You speak the truth,' cried Guy. 'Come, what was done to my great father shall be done to this man.'

It was the signal. They dragged him from the church; they stripped him of his clothes. Then the gruesome work of mutilation was begun.

* * *

Richard of Cornwall, King of the Romans, was sick and weary. The lethargy which had dogged him all his life had increased. Looking back over his life he could not feel very pleased with it. He had rarely succeeded in what he undertook. The task of ruling the Roman Empire had proved beyond his strength and ability. He was married now to a beautiful woman but somehow she only served to call attention to the fact that he had grown old and feeble.

His brother Henry had been more fortunate. Henry could face disaster, pass through it, and behave as though it had never happened. He had always known this trait in his brother and despised it. Now he began to think that it was a virtue. He himself had had three wives. Isabella, Sanchia and Beatrice ... all exceptionally beautiful women, yet none of them had really satisfied him.

The great achievement of his life had been the begetting of his sons. Henry and Edmund. He lived for them; and the one closest to him was Henry. Often he had marvelled that with his many imperfections he could have sired a son like Henry. Of course Henry had inherited his mother's good qualities and Isabella had been a good woman. He often remembered now that he was ailing how badly he had treated her, and he regretted it.

Henry was coming home. He was glad of that. He had not liked the idea of his going to the Holy Land and had been haunted by the fear of his falling into the hands of the Saracens or dying of some fearful disease as so many of them did. It had been a relief to know he was on the way home.

Soon he would be in England. God speed the day.

There were arrivals at the castle. Letters perhaps from Henry and Edmund who was also on the continent. He lived for news of his sons.

'My lord, there is a man here who would speak with you.'

'Who is it?'

'He comes from Italy.'

'He will be from my son. Bring him in without delay.'

The man entered. He did not speak but stood before Richard as though seeking for words.

'You have brought me letters?'

'Nay, my lord.'

'Come you from my son?'

The man did not answer.

'What ails you?' cried Richard. 'What has happened? Something is wrong.'

He had risen and as he did so he felt a sharp pain in his side.
'Well, well, well?' he shouted.

'There has been a disaster, my lord.'

'My son....'

The man nodded.

'My son ... Henry. He ... he lives?'

The man shook his head.

'Oh my God. Not Henry. What.... How....'

'My lord it was in a church at Viterbo. He was slain by cruel murderers.'

'Henry! Slain! What harm has Henry ever done?'

'His cousins, my lord, Simon and Guy de Montfort, have murdered him. They were heard to say that they did it to avenge their father.'

Richard tottered and the man dashed to him to prevent his falling.

'My son,' he whispered. 'My beloved son.'

* * *

He lay in his chamber for a week and would take no food. He did not sleep. He lay staring before him, murmuring Henry's name.

At the end of the week he bestirred himself and sent for certain of his squires. They must go to France at once and bring Edmund back. Who knew the murderers might try to do the same to him. He would not rest until Edmund was with him.

In due course Edmund arrived and when he embraced his son the tears fell from his eyes but he was a little better after that. But it was noticed how enfeebled he had grown.

He rarely ventured out; he was never seen to smile again. He could be heard talking to Henry although he was alone.

Henry's body was brought to England and buried at Hayles; and one cold December day Richard's servants discovered that he had not risen from his bed and when they went to him they found that he was unable to move or to speak.

It was the end—although he lingered for a few months in this sad state. In April of the following year he died. It was said that he had never recovered from the death of his son.

His body was buried at Hayles, that Cistercian Abbey which he had founded and which stood near Winchcombe in Gloucestershire. He lay beside his beloved son and his second wife Sanchia. His heart though was buried in the Franciscan church in Oxford.

The Poisoned Dagger

AFTER having bidden farewell to his cousin Henry, Edward with his young wife Eleanor sailed for the Holy Land as soon as the weather permitted them to. Although Eleanor had determined to accompany her husband, she was very sad at having to leave her three young children, John, Eleanor and Henry; but she realized it had to be a choice and she believed that she had made the right one.

Eleanor, though outwardly meek, was possessed of a rare strength of character of which Edward was becoming increasingly aware. He had believed when she had first begged to come with him that her presence might well be an encumbrance, instead of which it had proved to be a comfort. She could be self-effacing when the need arose and always seemed to be on the spot when he needed her. He was beginning to thank God for Eleanor.

In due course they arrived at Acre—the great trading city which although at this time was in decline still retained marks of past greatness. It was one of the centres of Christendom in that area; many times the Saracens had attempted to take it but never succeeded; they knew that before they could effectively do so they must immobilize the outposts of eastern Christendom.

Into the bustling city came Edward and his troops to the great rejoicing of the inhabitants who were in continual need of defenders.

Through the streets they rode—those streets which were alive with traders from all parts of the world. In the market halls their merchandise was set up on stalls; men and women of all nationalities assembled there; and the bargaining went on with only now and then a furtive cocking of the ear at some sound which might herald the approach of the enemy.

The grand churches and palaces still remained, models of Latin architecture. In the narrow streets the pilgrims mingled with the rest, usually discernible by their fanatical expressions. The Knights of St. John—those military religious men who had played a large role in the crusades—mixed with the people who lived in the town, enjoying the comfortable existence which could end at any moment. The alert traders watched this medley, coaxing and wheedling them to try their wares.

Edward the heir to England had come. The word spread through the town and beyond. He had an air of his great uncle, Richard Coeur de Lion, who would be remembered as long as the conflict between Christian and Saracen lasted. A new optimism sprang up. Those who had felt the restoration of the Holy Land would never be completed, were filled with new hope.

Edward talked to them, inspiring their enthusiasm. They knew that it was due to him that the Barons' War had ended with victory for the royalists. They had but to contemplate him to know that he was a conqueror.

The Sultan Bibars who had planned a conquest of Acre and had been preparing to lay siege to the town, suddenly abandoned the project as there was trouble in Cyprus, an island which was of the utmost strategic importance to their cause. He therefore was forced to turn from Acre leaving Edward to make forays into Saracen country and wreak a certain damage there.

These were small successes and the heat had become intense. The English could not endure it and were attacked by dysentry and other diseases. The flies and insects pestered them and worse still, many of them were poisonous. There were quantities of grapes which the men ate voraciously. Some of them died through this. Edward began to feel the frustration which had come to many a crusader before him, who had learned that the reality was different from the actuality. All those dreams of riding into victory, routing the Saracen army, bringing Jerusalem back to Christendom, were so much fancy. The fact was heat, disease, quarrels within and a ferocious enemy which was as brave and ready to fight for its beliefs as the Christians were.

During all this Eleanor sustained him.

He was anxious about her for she had become pregnant.

Messengers arrived from France. They came from Charles of Anjou who offered to bring about a truce.

'I refuse to agree to this,' cried Edward.

But the citizens of Acre were not with him in this. The suggested truce would be for ten years and ten years peaceful trading and the opportunity of going on as they were was greatly appealing. The alternative was war—their town destroyed, the soldiers looting, raping and burning. 'No, let it be a truce,' said the people of Acre.

But to Edward it seemed that he might never have come, so futile had the entire operation proved to be.

The truce was signed.

Edmund, his brother, was only too glad to return to England. Edward however stayed on. Though he was anxious about Eleanor's condition, yet he explained to her that he could not leave.

She understood perfectly. He had come here to win glory for Christianity. He could not go back now having achieved so little. She had understood this when she came, and although she found the climate trying in her state, at least she had the satisfaction of being with her husband. She reminded him that Marguerite of France had stayed with Louis in similar circumstances and had given birth to a child in the Holy Land.

This was what she had chosen and she had no regrets.

Edward shortly was to be grateful that she was with him, for if she had not been this might have been the end of him.

There was a mysterious sect in the East at the head of which was one called The Old Man of the Mountain. The legend was that likely assassins were chosen by the satellites of the Old Man and taken to a wonderful garden, the location of which was known only to the inner members of the sect. The captive was heavily drugged and when he was awoken found himself in a beautiful garden which was the embodiment of Paradise. Here everything that a man needed was provided for him. He lived in a rich palace; he was waited on by beautiful girls who were eager to grant his every whim. After he had spent some months in this idyllic setting, he was sent for by one of the agents of the Old Man of the Mountain and given a task to do. It was generally an assassination. When he had done the deed he would earn another spell in paradise until called upon for his next task. If he refused he disappeared from the world.

Thus the legendary Society of the Old Man had built up a band of assassins.

Edward was feeling ill. It was June the seventeenth, and his thirty-third birthday. The heat was intense and he wore only a light tunic, and his head was without covering.

A messenger from the Emir of Jaffa with letters from him had arrived and was asking to present them to the lord Edward, he having been warned not to put them into other hands.

Edward said the man should be brought in.

The Mohammedan entered and gave Edward a letter. He bowed low and moved his hand as though to take another letter from his belt. Instead of this he drew out a dagger and aimed at Edward's heart.

In less than a second Edward's suspicions had been aroused by the man's movements and as he lifted his arm to strike, Edward thrust the dagger aside. It missed his heart so saving his life but penetrated his arm.

Edward was strong. In a moment he had taken the dagger from his would-be assailant and killed him with it.

The man sank to the floor as Edward's attendants, hearing the scuffle, rushed in to find their master covered in blood and the messenger dead on the floor.

One of Edward's attendants picked up a stool and dashed out the assassin's brains.

'That's folly,' said Edward. 'And shame on you for striking a dead man.'

With those words he fell back fainting on his bed. It was not long before it was discovered that the dagger was poisoned and Edward's life in danger.

*   *   *

He was in agony. They did not think that he would live. The flesh around the wound was mortifying.

'If we cannot remove the poison,' said the doctors, 'it will spread throughout his body.'

'He will die,' said Eleanor.

'I fear so, my lady.'

She cried out: 'It shall not be. I shall not allow it to be.'

They shook their heads.

'Perhaps if we cut the flesh....' They conferred together.

But Eleanor said: 'First I will try.' She sent for a bowl and placing her lips over the wound she sucked the poison from it, spitting the noisesome matter into the bowl.

The doctors looked at her, shaking their heads. Edward through mists of pain was aware of her and comforted.

She was with child, he thought. He must not leave her in this alien place.

She lifted her head and smiled at him. The wound seemed cleaner now.

The doctors conferred together. It did indeed seem that the poison was removed, but an operation would be needed to remove the mortifying flesh. It would mean inflicting excruciating agony but there was hope now that it would be successful.

Eleanor wept bitterly contemplating the pain Edward would have to suffer.

'It is necessary,' she was told, and better that she should weep than that all England should do so.

The operation was successful and Edward recovered. Eleanor nursed him and he declared that if she had not been at hand and risked her life by sucking the poison from his wound, he would not be alive that day.

They needed comfort—and they found it in each other—for news reached them of the death of their son John. It was a great blow to Eleanor who was torn with regrets at having left him. Yet she knew that Edward needed her and the fact that she had saved his life—as they both believed she had—pointed to the fact that choosing between her husband and her children she had chosen wisely.

Shortly after Edward's recovery, she gave birth to a daughter. She was named Joanna and because of her birthplace was ever after known as Joanna of Acre.

* * *

It was the month of November. Edward knew as soon as the messenger arrived. He had feared for some time for he had been warned of his father's weakness. But when the news came he was struck with desolation. Dearly they had loved each other and it seemed the greatest tragedy of his life that his beloved father was no more.

Eleanor came to him. He took her hand and kissed it.

'We must go home,' he said. 'I am needed there.'

She looked at him searchingly and he answered: 'You see before you the King of England.'

And they both wept for Henry.

BIBLIOGRAPHY

Aubrey, William Hickman Smith	*National and Domestic History of England*
Barlow, F.	*The Feudal Kingdom of England*
Bémont, Charles Translated by E. F. Jacob	*Simon de Montfort, Earl of Leicester*
Brooke, F. W.	*From Alfred to Henry III*
Bryant, Arthur	*The Medieval Foundation*
Davis, H. W. C.	*England Under the Angevins*
Funck-Bretano, Fr. Translated by Elizabeth O'Neill	*The National History of France— The Middle Ages*
Guizot, M. Translated by Robert Black	*History of France*
Hume, David	*History of England from the Invasion of Julius Caesar to the Revolution*
Jenks, Edward	*Edward Plantagenet*
Labarge, Margaret Wade	*Simon de Montfort*
Norgate, Kate	*England under the Angevin Kings*
Powicke, Sir Maurice	*The Thirteenth Century, 1216–1307*
Prothero, George Walter	*The Life of Simon de Montfort*
Seely, R. B.	*The Life and Reign of Edward I*
Stenton, D. M.	*English Society in the Middle Ages*
Stevens, Sir Leslie and Lee, Sir Sidney	*The Dictionary of National Biography*
Stones, E. L. G.	*Edward I*
Strickland, Agnes	*Lives of the Queens of England*
Tout, Professor T. F.	*Edward the First*

Bibliography

Wade, John   *British History*

Young, Denholm N.   *Richard of Cornwall*